Slowly, Slowly, Perigee Moon

Marcia E. Kellam

Oneiroi Press—Sante Fe, NM
Paperback ISBN: 979-8-9871741-0-4
Library of Congress Control Number: 2022920441
Title: Slowly, Slowly, Perigee Moon
Author: Marcia E. Kellam
Digital distribution | 2022
Paperback | 2022

This is a work of fiction. The characters, names, incidents, places, and dialogue are products of the author's imagination, and are not to be construed as real.

For my mother, Nancy, for her tough love, without which I would not have gotten to this point.

For my father, Jack, for instilling in me a jones for adventure.

"What you seek is seeking you."

– Mevlana (aka Rumi)

Acknowledgements

Many people, places, animals and books helped coax *Slowly, Slowly, Perigee Moon* to fruition. To mention just a few...

I am indebted to the members of the Southside Writers' Group in Santa Fe, New Mexico, for their encouragement and input, most namely: Jodi D., Nathan G. and Brigette R. But also Steve Boga in Santa Rosa, California, for his insight into spinning yarns out of memories.

I cannot leave out my brother, Richard, the first writer I wanted to emulate, or my sister, Barbara, who cajoled me to just jump into scary situations.

Special thanks to Colette F. for talking me into that carpet-weaving workshop. I learned much more than weaving from the wonderful Turkish women who knotted, threaded, tapped and banged alongside me. And to Maryam B. for her expertise, patience, kindness and sense of humor.

I can never forget the residents of Yeşil Üzümlü, Fethiye and Çalış Beach, Turkey for an unforgettable journey.

For Rumi quotes I treasure Coleman Barks' *The Essential Rumi*.

And, lastly, Ron. Thank you for the crucial insights, and for staying on the roller coaster with me.

Pronunciation of Some Turkish Names, Places and Words in this Book

Letters:

C *pronounced "Jeh" as in "jet"*
Ç *pronounced "Ch" as in "cheese"*
Ş *pronounced "Sh" as in "shine"*

Words:

Acemi *pronounced "Ah-jeh-meh"*
Arkadaşım *pronounced "Ar-keh-desh-eem"*
Ayşegül *pronuounced "Aye-shuh-guhl"*
Barış *pronounced "Bar-eesh"*
Çalış *pronounced "Chah-lish"*
Canavar *pronounced "Jahn-eh-vahr"*
Canım *pronounced "Jehn-im"*
Çay *pronounced "Chye"*
Cennet *pronounced "Jehn-net"*
Cezve *pronounced "Jehz-veh"*
Çok *pronounced "Choke"*
Çözgü *pronounced "Chuhz-geh"*
Dolmabahçe *pronounced "Dohl-mah-bah-cheh"*
Dolmuş *pronounced "Dohl-moosh"*
Fethiye *pronounced "Feh-tee-yeh"*
Görüşürüz *pronunced "Guh-ruh-shuh-ruhz"*
Halı *pronounced "Hal-eh"*
Hoşgeldiniz *pronounced "Hoesh-gel-deh-niz"*
İncesaz *pronounced "Een-jeh-saz"*
İnşallah *pronounced "Een-shah-lah"*
Lahmacun *pronounced "Lah-mah-joon"*

Lavaş *pronounced "Leh-vash"*
Ömer *pronounced "Oo-mehr"*
Paşmina *pronounced "Pash-meen-ah"*
Patlıcan *pronounced "Pad-leh-jahn"*
Pide *pronounced "Pee-deh"*
Rakı *pronounced "reh-keh"*
Şahbaba *pronounced "Shah-bah-bah"*
Şalvar *pronounced "Shul-vahr"*
Şerbet *pronounced "Shehr-bet"*
Şerefe *pronounced "Sheh-reh-feh"*
Teşekkürler *pronounced "Teh-shek-oor-lehr"*
Uşak *pronounced "Oo-shak"*
Vişne *pronounced "Veesh-nah"*
Yabancı *pronounced "Yah-bahn-jeh"*
Yeşil Beşik Pansiyon *pronounced "Yeh-sheel Beh-sheek Pan-see-yone"*

Prologue

Autumn 1922

*T*here. It was done.

> Let them come for her now. There was nothing more they could do to her. Ayşegül had made her choice and she had stuck with it. İnşallah, Allah in his mercy would understand why.

She folded the edges of thick wool fabric over her bundle, taking particular care the corners were completely in place, that nothing underneath showed. When she was finished, she looked at her package. It would do.

It would have to do.

~ ~ ~

Tides
(Part I)

Chapter 1

"You cannot get into Paradise without a guide." – Turkish proverb

Wednesday, August 14, 2013, Afternoon - Istanbul

The jumbled call of muezzins drifted through the amorphous yellow mists of the city.

"Allahu Akbar! Allahu Akbar! Fawwwwww..."

Dissonant and distinctly male, the droning tones inscribed the air like an ancient parchment of song notes. I stood at my open pension window listening, and gazed at the many pointed mosque towers beyond. The minarets.

The age-old refrain of the Islamic call to prayer that floated from myriad towers hung suspended for a few moments more in the sky. Was I imagining things, or was exhaustion distorting my vision? For I could almost see the sounds swirling between the distant minarets and skyscrapers, painting the skyline in soft ocher and sienna. The call was an echo of the past, mesmerizing. It haunted me like a memory, cracked and faded, yet it was also filled with pathos, bittersweet and longing. The words are religious, of course, calling the devoted to Allah, the one and only true god. But to my Western ear they held no meaning. Only a sense. Like a musty scent. Saffron maybe. Or a sticky taste—Anatolian honey.

These days the chanting emanated from loudspeakers perched in tiny windows atop the cylindrical towers. In times past there were no such modern enhancements. Only pure voice. Voice that cried and soared throughout the cities and villages to reach the ears and hearts of the faithful. And even sometimes the unfaithful.

The slender, sky-bound grace of the minarets before me held majesty over the tangled streets of incessant movement and cacophony below. I watched as outdated trams lurched and clanked along narrow steel tracks, as twisting pavements swarmed with brown-suited men shouting terse or hearty greetings across the narrow alleyways to other brown-suited men.

1

As delicate white headscarves, some long, some longer, waved in the slight breeze from female forms rushing between outdoor stalls in their long, beige coats. A Bosphorus ferry blasted a warning honk, staccato and harsh. The stink of dead fish, most likely sea bass or mullet, wafted upwards. The minaret roofs themselves pointed like arrows toward the promise of salvation. And throughout all this confusion of sounds and sights and smells, the muezzins continued their summons. Continued that sensuous, lilting sound and claimed its domain over all. What a dichotomy of impressions, the heaven-bound and the earthly. Just as I remembered.

I smiled.

It was good to be back.

Slowly, slowly, like smoke curling into oblivion, the mystical notes faded into the hazy distance, inexplicably penetrating the barriers of time to mingle with the nerve-jangling reality of the present. Awakening from their spell, I jerked back to the now.

∾ ∾ ∾

God, what a trip. My neck and shoulders throbbed with tension from the long, transatlantic flight. My left leg tingled. Even my head pounded. And yet I felt alert. I thought...

At last.

Istanbul.

City of spires and ambition, desires and deceit.

Istanbul.

Architect of my dreams. And my nightmares.

Here, in this faded, bustling metropolis, was where it all began. Fifteen years back. Now I had returned, and this time I felt filled, not with the anticipation of adventure as that first time, nor with dread as later on, but with certainty of purpose and even, surprisingly, hope. Instinctively, I inhaled the fusty air of the walls surrounding me. I exhaled deeply.

Tomorrow I would finish it.

∾ ∾ ∾

"Nothing is at it seems," the scruffy *djinn* squawked. *"Evet. Yes, by now you must this know!"*

His name was Naji and he had traveled forward from the turbulent times

2

of the Ottoman Empire before it disintegrated into history. 1922, I recalled. This was the time when the formidable Mustafa Kemal Atatürk stormed through the empire and launched his attacks on the ruling sultan and pashas, shipping them off into oblivion and reforming Anatolia into the republic now known as Turkey.

Naji informed me he had been haggling with a client from that bygone era when he received my summons, and wanted me to know that I had interrupted an important transaction. He was vague on the details, and for that I was grateful. Nevertheless, part of me wondered if this client was a minor pasha or some influential street merchant from the Grand Bazaar. Whomever it was, I realized, was no concern of mine. I had my own agenda, but for some reason, I could no longer remember it. Still, I was gratified to realize my summons took precedence over whomever Naji had been bamboozling. And bamboozling, it most certainly was. *Sarıkız djinns* were notorious mischief-makers. And Naji was one.

Wait. Perhaps my summons had gotten mixed up with someone else's. Surely, I could not have consciously called such a being to my bedside. I was not, after all, desperate. Was I? But if I myself had not brought him, why *was* he here?

"Very quickly to help you I am traveling," he went on, his breathing heavy and aspirant. *"Almost as quickly as you! What for you I can do?"* He grinned.

Uff, what is that? I asked myself, as a malodorous waft of nastiness careened toward me. I turned my head away and squinched my eyes, but the stench of putrid food continued to assault my nostrils.

The horror that was Naji's black and rotting teeth did not give me much faith either in his character or in the dentists of the time from which he originated, whenever that was. Fifteen years ago, that first time I was here, a hostel clerk warned me to be wary of crooked, toothy smiles. I was sure she was being glib. I had laughed then. But this was offensiveness even that clerk could not have reckoned on. I shivered slightly. Fortunately, Naji did not seem to notice. But time was running short and in this country of ephemeral encounters one could not afford to be too choosy. That is because there was often no choice even if you could afford it. And I could not. So Naji would have to do. But, for what?

"What is this? Why you must ask for me?" Naji's already high-pitched voice now took a strident upturn.

Uh, oh, I thought. *He's getting impatient. Why can't I remember why I wanted him?*

Before I could respond, his thick hands started to drip with moisture and I saw that the black hairs on the backs of his fingers began to grow longer. I blinked. Was that possible? When I dared to look again, I could see the coarse hairs had grown longer still, slowly writhing and twisting around each other like angry vipers.

I felt my stomach grow greasy, queasy. *Uck. What am I doing? Why* had *I summoned this loathsome creature? Or had I? It's all confusing.*

I watched, horrified, as Naji's hands continued their grotesque dance and the thick, dark beard he sported began to split equally into two parts, entwining his threadbare yellow robe and blousy purple trousers upwards from both sides. If that trick was not disturbing enough, the beard now began to gleam from deep within its ever-lengthening tresses and the glow itself spread slowly outward in a pink-orange light. It began to blink. Then swirl. Then blink and swirl. Pink and orange hues alternated and switched, faster and faster.

Swirl, blink.

Blink, swirl.

The viper hands crept out from behind the beard now and I gazed, incredulous, as it grew and twisted upwards like a Hermes caduceus, without the redeeming quality of wings on top. Instead of wings, the creature's head was crowned by a bright red fez, its silky, black tassel dancing from the center. Was it dancing, or was it writing a message for me in the fluorescent vapor that enveloped it? I could not tell. I felt I had somehow lost the whole point of my rendezvous with the repulsive *djinn*. Somewhere in my confused state came the idea that the unsettling vision before me was an out of control aura, a whole body halo gone berserk. But it did not feel holy the way halos should.

It felt quite the opposite.

Now the tips of Naji's purple satin slippers merged to become one, pointing toward the floor as if poised for take-off. What was happening to Naji? What was this transformation all about? Transformation. Something about that word echoed in my befuddled mind. Something important, if I could only think what.

I needed to distract myself from the hideous scene before me. If I could. Instead, my stomach tightened and my eyes blurred. The features of the male genie I had first encountered, the pock-marked skin and bulbous nose that had previously appeared human, albeit an unattractive one, were no longer. Naji was morphing into someone, no some*thing*, else.

Meanwhile, the room, the bed I was lying on, my luggage, disappeared

4

into a smoggy distance. I no longer knew where I was. All I could see was this creature of weirdness.

What had he—or was it "it"—blurted out a moment ago? Somehow, I sensed my time was almost up.

I tried to think. A daunting task with the strange apparition ever-shifting and contorting before me. *What was it Naji said?* It suddenly seemed vital that I know. Absolutely the most vital aspect of this whole obscene encounter. My stomach threatened to heave, so I turned away from the vile thing before me and...

                               ≈   ≈   ≈

God, my brain! What was that all about, anyway? Who was this Naji character and what was he doing in my room?

I could not seem to put together the pieces of our meeting. Was it a dream? It seemed so real and, after all my previous experiences in Turkey, I was not altogether convinced *djinns* did not exist. Here, anything could happen. The more crazy and unlikely, the more probable. My head pulsed and throbbed. I had yet to unearth my ibuprofen bottle from the depths of my travel gear.

What had that unsavory character told me?

"Stop spinning, head," I moaned. "Help me come up with something useful, would you?" Carefully, I pushed myself up from the bed.

I had not journeyed so far to end up in a fug of confusion. I had a purpose. My mobile phone told me I had lost consciousness nearly three hours ago. It was now late afternoon. Soon the next call to prayers would sound. My temples continued to pound like a Ramazan drum and the volume of my stomach's growls rivaled the clamor of traffic outside the pension window. But I had to get functioning for tomorrow's rendezvous with revenge.

Where was that ibuprofen? My daypack was frayed in places—why did I still use this thing?—but I grabbed it and rummaged through the assortment of in-cabin airplane detritus. Crumpled tissues, retractable toothbrush, tiny toothpaste tube smashed, ballpoint pen with no lid, almost empty reusable water bottle, dogeared paperback version of *The House on the Strand* by Daphne du Maurier and five wrinkled twenty-dollar bills paper-clipped together. But no pills. Bother. I threw the pack back onto the bed.

"Food. That's what you need right now." Talking out loud often helped me organize my thoughts. "You'll feel better after some *mezes* or hummus. Appetizers'r better than nothing."

No one was listening, of course. No one was there. Not even the hideous Naji. It occurred to me then that Naji spoke to me in English rather than Turkish. *Hmm.* Well, dreams could be odd in many different ways. Perhaps an English-speaking person cannot dream in Turkish. Who's to say? Be that as it may, it worked in my favor if I got the salient point of it.

If only I could remember what that was.

Standing now, I saw in the grimy mirror over the dilapidated dresser that my travel clothes were, as usual, wrinkled. Plastic Gezer boat shoes, imitation Crocs that I had purchased here on my previous visit eight years ago, hovered precariously near the edge of the rumpled bed behind me. Before Naji's appearance I must have fallen onto the double mattress, which covered most of the available floor space. Thankfully, I had not hit the ceramic tile floor, a mishap that most certainly would have required a stronger antidote than a mere over-the-counter cure. An acrid odor assailed my nostrils. Yes, a shower was definitely in my immediate future. Not a deodorant existed which could cancel the effects of a Turkish August on the armpits.

I glanced around. Some things never change. The rooms at the Yeşil Beşik Pansiyon were just as fetid and cramped as that first time fifteen years ago. So much for the latest website photos promising "muchly space" and old-style "Ottoman delights" in the Sultanahmet section of touristic Istanbul, the so-called "European" side. The west. Back then there had been no Internet, only a late night need to sleep and an accidental stumbling onto this faded, but disarmingly inviting remnant from the bygone days of Constantinopolitan glory.

Back then there had also been Adrian.

"In Turkey a hotel is just a place to put your backpack," he used to say. The four of us spent most of our time exploring the ancient city.

We were students on a budget, Mallie and Paz and Adrian. And, well, me. We coined sayings at random to suit any occasion in which the lack of funds was ridiculously evident. And those were many, beyond just the cheap digs we were forced to rent. Nevertheless, we managed to get into a few tourist sites. At Topkapı Palace, Mallie even insisted we pay the extra lira to see the harem, the *seraglio*, famous for being the home of the reigning sultan's bevy of wives and concubines. Not to mention, the eunuchs. We were all intrigued, of course, as so many tourists are, by the concept of young girls living in luxury and wantonness at the palace solely to serve the sultan. The ornate halls had been converted into a museum. Mallie came away indignant.

"Pfff. Not sad the Ottoman Empire ended, those frickin' misogynists," she had huffed.

There was also the time we headed off to a Turkish bath, the "hamam" our Frommer's guidebook recommended and, short sixteen of the forty-eight Turkish lira needed to enter, smuggled in Mallie and Paz when the attendant had hurried off to help another patron. Another time I sliced a plastic water bottle in half with my ever-present Swiss army knife and triumphantly held up the top end with its fluted spout and blue cap. I turned it upside down and poured in some cheap wine. "Hey, can't drink without a stemmed glass, right?" I announced, grinning.

Humor was our device to stave off disappointment and hunger, rampant during our travels. Laughter was essential to keep our adventure spirits from lagging. We laughed about everything.

And Adrian's eyes glinted with mischief.

The past. Ah, well. It was a habit of mine to reminisce. An escape from my own thoughts? In this case, I suspected it helped distract me from the claustrophobia of my current cramped surroundings.

Besides the bed, my rolling bag and daypack took up all other available floor space. What of it? Nothing less than expected, really. Now, as before, I did not plan to be in Room 7 for longer than a shower and a sleep. The circa 1954 tacky décor was as I remembered, too, with just a bit less shine. The mattress was perhaps slightly flatter than before, the woven brown curtains a bit more faded. Well, I had learned the hard way, best to go with what you know unless you enjoy aggravating surprises. This time, I wanted as few of those as possible. There were plenty to come, no question. I knew the Beşik. The room, including *kahvalte*, the often hearty Turkish breakfast, cost only twenty-eight lira a night, which my foggy brain calculated to be fifteen dollars. Give or take. Double what it had been before Turkey instituted the New Turkish Lira in 2005, the last time I was here. No matter. I did not plan to write lyrical poetry about it on Tripadvisor. It suited me fine.

My journey into the minuscule bathroom took two steps. Typical. Would the shower work, I wondered? I might only get a splash bath. Could I afford another night without a full cleansing? No. Not if I did not want to offend other travelers. Or the street cats who loitered in door and alleyway. No hope for my clothes, though. Save my clean ones for tomorrow's escapade.

7

I turned the plastic faucet to the red-designated "hot" side and cold water spurted out of the mildewed shower head above.

"Figures."

I cranked the faucet to the blue "cold" side and, after a pause, warm water trickled out. I had to stoop to fit my body under the runnel. Can showers be boring? As ridiculous as it sounds, I found myself clicking my fingernails on the tile wall while the tepid water dripped down. At last, I felt my joints begin to reawaken.

The scruffy white towel I had grabbed off my bed had no doubt been whiter once, and fluffier, but it did its job with only minor scratching of skin. Anyway, the Turks were big on exfoliation. I had learned that in my past trips to the hamams. There, the towel-clad attendants scraped your limbs until just before the bleeding point. One of life's quirky pleasures.

"Nothing but the best for our patrons," I said to my towel. "What do you want for twenty-eight lira?"

Scrubbed and slightly less fragrant, I made a mental note to head for the Çemberlitaş Turkish Hamam tomorrow evening. It would be my treat to myself when all was done. I would deserve it for my troubles. At the venerable bathhouse, an attendant would invite me to lie on the heated marble slab in the center of the main bathroom, exfoliate me to a gleaming shine then, in traditional hamam style, follow with a massage of bubbling suds from a *köpük torbası*, really nothing more than a puffed-up pillowcase. When I was dripping in both sweat and water, the same attendant would lead me to a marble seat by a water basin on the wall, brusquely shampoo my hair, douse me with hot water from the spigot on the wall using one of the dented tin bowls kept by, and wrap me tightly like a babushka in thin red and white *peshtemal* towels. Afterwards, he would lead me to a divan and serve me hot *elma çayi*, surprisingly refreshing apple tea. The promise of such reward fueled my resolve.

I had much to accomplish before that indulgence, though.

No one could accuse me of being chic, a trait which proved convenient on many occasions. And no one who knew me expected me to "dress" for dinner. Least of all myself. So far, so good. I managed to dig my brush out from a zippered pocket of my daypack, dragging it through the tangles of my hair. Hurriedly, I brushed on a smidgen of mascara and wrestled into my wrinkled khaki cargo pants and faded pink Hawaiian shirt, which stuck to my damp skin.

Ready.

I side-stepped the puddles in my closet bathroom. Water was

everywhere. For often, in Turkey a shower was not enclosed, and sprayed everything. Including the toilet paper. I pretended to throw water over my shoulder and muttered the Turkish saying:

"*Su gibi git, gel.*"

Go and return, like water.

Silently I prayed my supplication would work. As a flutter of moths tapped at my abdominal walls, I thought of Adrian.

Adrian.

"Get a grip, you," and I shook myself out of my reverie.

Then, squeezing past my luggage, I edged toward the outer door of my room. Onward to Advil and adventure. But first, a meal. I grabbed my hundred dollars.

"*Hadi görüşürüz,*" I called out. "See ya later."

And Naji's puzzling words were lost to the misty cosmos.

1912

"Grab her," said the man with the long, shiny mustache.

His high-pitched voice pierced the country air, knife-sharp. As if slashing an enemy.

"Now!"

The young girl stood, feet apart, like a sentinel. Her small, white hands lay one each on her narrow hips. Akimbo, some call it. Elibelinde.

Another man, horse-mounted, panting, kicked his polished boots into the side of his restless beast, which began to gallop over the grass knoll toward the girl.

Her steel-blue eyes flashed and, fast as any whip, she turned away from the two men coming toward her. It can be said she was lithe and agile and full of spirit. And it can also be said she would do anything to get away from her pursuers.

She ran.

Autumn 1998 – Istanbul

"Adrian, look!"

Mallie leaned over the short parapet, holding in her right hand that goofy, floppy hat she insisted was her good luck charm (the rest of us were not convinced). Her left hand pointed straight in front of her. At what, I could not tell.

Adrian quietly shut his Frommer's travel guide, clenching it to his side, adjusted his own Fedora, and sauntered toward Mallie.

"What you got, Mal?" he asked. His voice was soft and comforting. I never tired of it.

"I mean, look out there," Mallie continued. "Isn't it amazing we're in Istanbul? The minarets. The Bosphorus. It's like being in our own play."

Though Mallie was slightly older than Paz and me, her childlike enthusiasm belied a stoic toughness that even Paz admired. I always felt this dual nature was what drew Paz to Mallie in the first place—that, and her chocolate-hued, saucer eyes.

While Adrian and Mal waxed poetic over the scenery from the Topkapı Palace terrace I thought back to the day I first met Paz and Mal.

It was before Adrian.

An outdoor art exhibition had taken over the quad of the university campus in the spring of 1997. Many times I had passed the makeshift stages and half-built performance spaces en route to my classes. I had even caught a small group of dancers rehearsing, I had supposed it was rehearsing, as they climbed about in odd positions on one of the ad hoc structures. As a liberal arts major I was mildly curious about what art would transpire there on opening night, but I was an indifferent student and spent most of my mental time wondering why I was even at university. Going to the exhibition changed that. It changed me.

To say opening day brought a throng of attendees would be like saying the ice cream truck was swarmed by hungry children. In short, the place was heaving. I was alone, as usual. But the day before I had received a thumbs up from my Western Civ professor on my latest paper and I felt myself smile as I entered the scene.

"Hey. Dude. Watch it. I've got a beer here," a lanky student in a lopsided top hat blurted at me as I nudged my way through the crowd.

He was not the only one already laughing and swaying to the different sounds that pervaded the air space. Was it music? Hard to tell from my point of view. But it was loud and crazy, and it was obvious the performance spectacles were only a prelude to one big party that was well on its way.

The transformation of the quad from the last day I had walked by during the art site's construction until this first day of actual performances surprised me. Sure, I had seen structures and people slowly converting the area. But a lot had changed since those earlier days. What was normally an open space with well-tended grass and four, neat intersecting walkways had devolved into a madhouse. Wooden shapes of all kinds had sprouted haphazardly around the grounds. One, like a rocket, was besieged by loosely clad figures crawling all over its skeletal frame. Another was an open, tilted cube in which a female student dashed around, throwing globs of bright paint onto large pieces of white cloth. A few raised stages of different sizes were abuzz with activity, either small acting groups doing who-knows-what play or quasi-dancers gyrating in unusual movements that did not look like dancing to me. The music and voices from all the different activity collided in aural chaos.

It was fantastic.

I did not have a plan on where to head or which performance to watch, but continued bumping and sidling through party-happy students as I headed deeper into the horde. I hardly noticed at first when a thick voice barked, "Are you ready to be amazed, my friend?"

Was it talking to me?

"You think you can handle it?" the voice shouted.

I stopped for a second now, but shaking my head in confusion, continued on my way.

"No, YOU! Don't go! You'll want to see this. I mean it. It's gonna change your life. YOU! With the moccasins and the purple shirt."

That made me turn around. I was fairly sure I was the only one in the vicinity wearing moccasins and a purple shirt. The guy was talking to me, after all.

"Yeah, what?" I called back. My verbal assailant was dark-tanned, sporting a chartreuse green suit jacket and faded Levis, and gesturing my way. I figured he was about my age. A junior maybe?

"What do you have that's so incredible you had to rip my ear drums off?" I shouted.

"Well, that's what you're gonna find out if you get your ass back here." His front teeth sparkled and I found myself warming to him despite his crassness.

"Really? I guess I better follow you then, huh? 'Cuz I'm here to be amazed."

"What's your major, by the way?" he yelled, as I joined his side. Students often asked this question, as if knowing your major was a vital statistic and led to some greater understanding about you. Maybe it did, maybe it did not. I shrugged.

"What? Oh, nothing really. Liberal arts. Yours?" I yelled back. The noise around us continued, deafening.

"Right now, it's history, but not with a capital H. I don't know. Kinda thinking I might change at some point."

"What's your name?" I asked.

"Paz. Not a nickname. Just Paz. Yours?" We had moved a few paces during our brief introductory conversation and as I was about to answer, he stopped.

"Here we are. Enter, my friend!"

The person called Paz gestured to a triangular cloth flap that led into a beige tent-like structure. I had not seen it earlier. I had not seen any tents. A jitter surged up my legs and charged into my chest. I nodded at Paz, ducked my head and entered.

And dark it was. My eyes felt as if stuffed with the same felt as the tent's fabric.

After a second or two, I began to sense rather than see other bodies near me. Their heat added to my discomfiture. I decided not to move until my visual purple kicked in and I could figure out the lay of the room. I call it a room, but it was more like a dream place. A space without edges or borders. I was floating, disoriented, almost beyond thought when a distant ringing sound echoed through the dimness.

"What the...?" I muttered quietly. And felt glued to my spot.

The ringing came again, slightly louder now, its tone a cross between a Tibetan bowl and a small bell. Deep and resonant, rather than sharp and piercing. I felt, rather than heard, feet shifting on the grass floor. I guessed my fellow attendees wondered, as I did, what was happening, and the anticipation made them uncomfortable.

As my sight began to focus, I saw that the small stage up front, if you could call it the front, was infused with lush red tones, which must have come from lighting instruments hidden somewhere. The effect was like being inside a womb, comforting and close yet with an expectation of possible expulsion. I did not want to be expelled, I realized. That alone was unusual for me, the person who was always uncomfortable, always wanting to move on to something else. And here I was rooted, fixated. Here I was, finally wanting to stay, to see what was coming.

A handful or two of other bodies lingered near what was likely the back wall of the tent space. If wall you could even call it. There were no visible edges. All was seamless and blurry. No seats. Unusual in a theater space, tent or no, I thought.

"What's happening?" I heard someone whisper. Her voice quavered. I sympathized.

"I don't know," her companion said. "I guess we'll find out. Christ, it's spooky as hell in here."

The short, sparse ringing now picked up pace and a few bongs later settled into a rhythmic pattern, hypnotic and soothing. The human mutterings stopped as the audience hovered, waiting to find out what would happen next.

"Whoa, what's that?" someone muttered.

A golden glow began to infiltrate the tent.

"Cool," mumbled another.

Behind me, I heard a swish of fabric and turned to see Paz slip through the flap through which, moments before, I had slipped myself. I watched as he took a spot near the entrance, folded his hands behind his back, and stopped still. His lone figure commandeered the chamber. Guarding. Though from what, I could not guess. What was his part in this ethereal drama? Was he an actor, a musician—a juggler—waiting for his cue? Or was he merely the hawker who brought unsuspecting wanderers like myself out from the hubbub and into this sanctum? His demeanor was inscrutable. And that increased my curiosity. What was he doing here?

I was about to find out.

                      ತಿ   ತಿ   ತಿ

What was that?

A tiny movement? I was sure of it. Or was I? Almost imperceptible at first but, no, there was definitely action at the front of the tent. Not Bruce Willis action, but something. Though there was no stage, as I would have expected, the faint beams of light from somewhere above directed my eyes toward a three-dimensional mass I had not noticed before up front. Or what was passing for up front. I could dimly make out the faces of my fellow audience focused in the same direction.

No one spoke.

Now the rhythmic bong, bong, bong began to wane. As it faded, the mass started to wiggle. It was somehow attached to the tent wall and yet it seemed like a separate being. A thing alive. I found myself entranced. What *was* it?

The bonging bell quietly segued into a haunting sound I found out later was Balinese gamelan music played backwards at half speed. Disturbing and fascinating. I had never heard such a sound before.

As the music quickened its pace, so did the blob on the wall quicken its gyrations. The wiggling motions became more frenetic and, jerk by jerk, it began to form a shape emerging from a kind of cocoon. A shape almost human, but covered with moss-like fibers that seemed to squelch as they separated from their enclosure. Maybe I was imagining it. The creature, as I could now see it was, looked at first bent and deformed. But as its journey from confinement continued and as its audience looked on, transfixed, it began to unfold. Whether a clever trick of lighting design or something else, the creature began to glow with a pink-gold light. My mind flashed to those paintings by Maxfield Parrish I used to love, but this was even more entrancing. Because it was here, in 3-D, not on a two-dimensional canvas. I lost track of time, as I had already lost track of space, and I found myself hardly thinking at all anymore. My being became absorbed in the almost painful transition of this organism from an amorphous, red lump to a light-infused thing of beauty.

Flash!

A sudden burst of light, like a large firecracker that flicked into being and just as quickly vanished, made me recoil in surprise.

Then,

chaos.

Another bigger, blinding light lit up the darkness momentarily and I felt an explosion of slimy stuff land on my face and arms. What was it? What had happened?

The chamber again plunged into gloom and I could hear the other attendees shriek and bustle about in confusion. Someone bumped into me, screaming,

"Fuckin' A, what was that?"

"Oh, my Gawd, that was awesome! I almost had a cardiac!" another squealed. I wiped some of the glop from my arm and shook it to the floor.

Suddenly, up front again, a red light appeared and as the audience settled back into place, I spotted Paz. His sturdy torso jutted out of the just-emptied cocoon as if shot there by some Methuselah-esque magic. How he really got there, I had no idea, as I had never seen him move from his position by the tent flap.

He was changed, though. For one thing, he no longer sported the chartreuse jacket. Instead, his chest was bare. Well, almost bare. For his smooth, tanned skin was drenched in what looked like thick blood and, at first, I thought it was. But as my eyes—and my head—adjusted from the confusion that had just erupted in the middle of our collective euphoric experience, I reasoned that the oozing fluid on Paz's chest was some kind of stage paint. Or I hoped it was. More hideous, however, than the gruesome sight of his transformation from hawker to victim, was the sound.

Gra-err-arrr-ggg! Fre-gah-fa-arrr!

He bellowed and moaned in wordless tones that must have been amplified to echo throughout the chamber and, as it seemed, into my soul. It was a pitiful cry, like that of a captured animal unable to escape. Tortuous, unrelenting. As I watched and listened, the moans went on and on and I saw others look at each other in horror. I could see on their faces that they, like me, wanted to release this pitiful creature from its bondage and pain. But that we did not know what to do. It had emerged from one form of bondage only to become enmeshed in another.

Then the house lights came on and Paz was gone.

It was some time before I learned that the cocoon creature was Mallie.

Now, as I watched Adrian and Mallie from my wooden bench on the Topkapı lawn, I thought about her penchant for drama. And Paz's. That day, that event, was undoubtedly an unorthodox beginning for a friendship, but its effect was powerful. Years later, I had come to learn that it held an almost prophetic power over me. Over all of us. And what was to come.

Chapter 2

"**M**iss, miss! Please. Come. *Gel*."

Mustafa had checked me in earlier, but I was relieved to realize he did not recognize me from fifteen years before, when I had first been a guest here. Well, I used a different name now. And I had changed my look—a lot. But still, this forgetfulness was unusual for the Turks I knew in the tourism business. Normally their memory of names, faces, even preferred drinks was uncanny. Of course, he was getting older, that might explain it. But neither was I quite the same person I used to be. Did it show? I suppose it must. In any case, whatever the reason for Mustafa's lack of recall, it served my purpose, and I was glad I had taken the chance to come back to the Beşik, after all.

But why did Mustafa want me to follow him? I had already paid in full for my three nights and I had not asked for anything to be brought to me. I was not sure if my patience, or my stomach's rumblings, would hold out for any protracted conversation about my plans, or whatever he might try to pry out of me.

"What? Is something wrong, Mustafa?" I asked, feeling my skin tingle. *Please, don't let something be wrong already*, I silently begged the universe.

"No, *hayır*, nothing wrong, but please to come. It is—hmm, how must I say—most important. For you!" His thick voice was redolent with emphases on the ends of words: hard Gs, growling Rs, something I always liked about Turks speaking English. For that reason, and my natural inclination to want to explore a mystery, I could not resist his entreaty.

Curious, I followed, rolling my eyes when his back was turned. I had learned it was prudent in Turkey to be on red alert whenever one was approached by a stranger. You could never predict what the outcome might be. It could be to your benefit. Or it could lead to something quite the opposite. Which was why I was back here in the first place.

Best to be polite, but stay on my toes.

I had emerged from the dark, narrow stairwell into the sunlit foyer of the pension when Mustafa summoned me. Now we headed left into the breakfast room-cum-bar, rather cheerfully painted lemon and draped in yellow and white tablecloths and curtains.

Well, they've modernized some rooms, anyway, I mused. *Maybe they'll get around to mine in the next ten years.*

As we rounded the corner, we passed the aged-wood bar holding fort a few feet from the left wall. They had not changed that; I remembered it from before. Pressed into the wall was the carved-oak counter and long shelving that featured disordered troops of half-filled alcohol bottles and assorted china and glasses. Empty bar stools fringed the counter. Their varnish worn, their frames battered, they seemed to slump like disenchanted soldiers hoping for drinks to be divvied out. Small, square tables set with four mismatched chairs each dotted the room. I remembered this bar well despite the few upgrades.

The four of us had spent several evenings here, trying to learn how to like *rakı*, the favored Turkish brandy that, when mixed with water looked like diluted milk. Its taste, however, was nothing so benign. I had never gotten accustomed to the strong aniseed flavor. Not to mention the effects of the alcohol itself. I guess I was a lightweight in that department.

Still following Mustafa, I surveyed the room in its current incarnation. The anomaly of the old wood juxtaposed with fresh linens was disconcerting and that set off an alarm bell in my memory. That day when everything changed. I should keep alert, I realized, not be taken in by smiles or friendly gestures.

Despite my wariness, I was surprised to see only one other person sitting at the far corner table. It was evening now, and I had expected the room to be full of customers drinking and eating. That was one reason I had planned to dine elsewhere. For the incognito effect. I figured that the more I was away from this place, the less chance that Mustafa's memory of me would return.

Faint echoes of the evening prayer filtered into the atmosphere, though the door to the hotel lobby was closed. I felt suddenly slightly nostalgic for the times I had been here with my friends. But the moment passed as I eyed the lone customer. He sat quietly in the chair against the farthest wall. His face was lean, lined, leathery. His large, oval eyes looked blank and his expression inscrutable. The black zippered jacket he wore was open and I remembered that even on the warmest nights, Turkish men were inclined to wear an over garment, as if in some twist of logic, the extra coating

17

would protect them from the onslaught of the heat. I never understood such reasoning myself. My loose Hawaiian shirt billowed under the welcome air con blasts. No jacket for me.

Mustafa stopped a few feet from where the jacketed man was sitting. I watched, perplexed, as Mustafa's shoulders suddenly slumped forward, his chest sank inwards and the gaze of his eyes lowered to the floor. Even his fingers, where they now encircled each other at his abdomen, curled inwards. This sudden change of demeanor from brisk and business-like to sycophantic and shrinking was unsettling. *What is going on?* I concluded it must have to do with the man in front of us. Something about him was creepy, I had to admit. Maybe it was the way he narrowed his eyes as he stared at us. The hairs on my arms bristled.

Mustafa dipped his head briskly in the direction of the leather-faced man, backed up a few steps, then turned quickly and scurried off through the door we had entered from. He did not look back. I stared at his retreating figure for a moment, feeling abandoned, like a child being dropped off at the school gate for the first time. *What am I doing here?*

"Don't leave me!" I wanted to shout. But I did not. Instead, I turned my head back toward the figure in the chair.

His hands, lying flat on the table, tapered into long fingers and these sported a couple of gold-beveled rings. One encircled a large carnelian, like the ones I had seen long ago in second-hand shops. Its wine-red depths, mysterious and somber, triggered something in my memory and reminded me why I had come back here. Why I had made the day-long trek from the States after all these years. It hit me suddenly—the task that lay before me was probably not going to be as easy as I envisioned. Unnerving at best, potentially dangerous. While back at home in Santa Cruz, California, planning and plotting my revenge, my resolve had been so clear.

But now, if I had not already felt off-guard in the presence of the silent brooding brute, the carnelian he sported on his ring finger brought me almost to panic. It was large to the point of being vulgar, such that the fingers on either side of it were barely visible. I was sure it was actually leering at me. And that color, like coagulated blood, seemed to spill onto the table in front of the man. If a piece of jewelry could ever be said to harbor ill intent, this one was it.

I shuddered.

Still not speaking, the man and I continued to watch each other and I realized that I might well be out of my depth on this journey, all my

18

preparations pointless and ridiculous. I was aware of the incongruity of my feelings, but I did not know how to quell the superstition that now suffused my being. Those hands! The rings! Inexplicably, I started to imagine the horrible crimes they may have committed.

Stop it! You're tired. Pull yourself together. It's just a ring, for God's sake.

I swallowed.

His hands still spread flat on the edge of the small table, the man pushed back his chair, his face expressionless, and slowly stood. I stared, rooted, while my heart knocked at my throat. *Breathe, kid, nothing's going to happen.*

His eyes were now trained toward the door behind me, as if gazing into another dimension. Certainly, he was not looking at me. It was as if I did not exist and he was alone in the room, or at least alone in some corner of time in which I did not figure.

NOT liking this, said my inner voice.

Shut up, I told it. *I can't run, can I? I've got to find out what this is about. Be quiet.*

The silence in the room was thick, like pomegranate syrup. I waited.

"You are here for reason, Molo," a deep voice whispered.

"Excuse me? What?" I bluttered. *Did he just call me Molo? How does he know that name? Only Paz, Mallie and Adrian ever called me that. This is too bizarre. Okay, okay, he knows your nickname, but don't let that unnerve you. Keep calm. Whatever else, do not let him see you're nervous.*

The voice continued, "You come here. Istanbul. You come for reason. I am correct, *evet*?"

I heard the words, spoken in a densely accented English, but somehow I was not connecting their meaning to anything.

"Yes?" it asked again. There was more urgency in the question now.

"Oh, God," I heard my own whimper and hoped the man had not. "*Yes,*" I said louder. "I come—*came*—here for a reason. What do you know about that? *How* do you know? *Nasıl*?"

"You must to follow me. I show you." And he tipped his head, very slightly, toward me. There was no smile either in his mouth or his eyes. His face remained as expressionless—and menacing—as that on the statue of the evil vizier at the Topkapı Palace Museum. And that guy had stabbed people for smiling at him.

I did not smile.

Remembering the fate of the vizier's subjects, I swallowed again, shoved my hands into my khaki pockets, and nodded back. "*Tamam*," I agreed. "Okay."

Resignation was sometimes the only possible response.

You're in for it now, that other voice in me warned.

It's out of my hands, I replied. *Anyway, if nothing else, I need to know how he knows that name.*

He turned away from me and, with no one to witness my predicament except the mute furniture, I stepped in behind him.

We left by the door on the far side of the bar room. I trailed carefully behind, hesitating to hover too close to this cryptic character. It was not just that he reeked of unfiltered tobacco. Many Turkish men did. That, I was accustomed to. But I did not know what to think of him, his weighty silence, his brusque manner, that gravelly voice. He made me nervous.

We entered the small, cobbled street behind the pension. Two- and three-storied buildings, some with the traditional enclosed wood Ottoman balconies so common in these parts, some with false-terraced Juliet balconies, teetered out of the dusk-dyed rectangle of sky. Like old peasant women, they bowed with age and seemed to sway in the evening breeze. Could they possibly topple over? I felt dizzy looking up at them, so I shifted my attention away from the structural anomalies of buildings and focused on human ones.

It was not yet dark, yet few people were about. Just the odd cat lurking in an alcove or tiptoeing to its next haunt. Where was everybody? Normally twilight was a busy time for home-goers or for tourists straggling back to their hotels or searching for an evening eatery. The emptiness exacerbated my dis-ease.

Get a grip! It's an alley, that's why it's so quiet, you moron.

I hoped my taciturn companion could not read my thoughts or hear my inner dialogue, though I felt he had that ability. Too unnerving even to contemplate. I knew I could not show any vulnerability. To do so would only underscore my seemingly servile relationship to him and that would not be to my advantage, as I knew all too well from the past.

I considered vulnerability, and its attendant setbacks, and then I had a sudden flash. A flash of memory. It was about carnelians, something I had read back in my pawn shop days. This remembering gave me a surge of confidence. Because...the thing about carnelians, their metaphysical property, that is, is that they bestow courage, promote trust in yourself and your perceptions.

Well, what do you know, that's something positive, anyway.

And it came to me then that perhaps this man too, for all his fear-inducing attitude, might not be what he seems. *Where had I heard that idea before? Ach.* Anyway, perhaps he was something else. Perhaps he was *not* this intense being who made my arm hairs stand up. Perhaps he was a searcher like me, someone who sometimes put himself in potentially difficult circumstances and needed a talisman, a talisman like a courage-encouraging carnelian, to get him through the troubles in which he found himself. Well, maybe I was fishing, but I felt better for it. I pulled my shoulders back and, buoyed by this partial epiphany about carnelians, this dip into uncertain existential waters, I sucked in my breath, crossed my fingers, and let out a sigh.

I would be okay. I would.

꙳   ꙳   ꙳

Wednesday, August 14, 2013, Later Afternoon - Istanbul

And what is *my* talisman? I wondered. Could it be Adrian still, after all this time?

The question distracted me momentarily. But I did not really want it in my head now. So, I quickened my pace to catch up with Leather-face instead of continuing to skulk behind him like a chastised Labrador puppy. He made no comment, nor registered any change in his demeanor at my sudden appearance by his side.

Well, that's not surprising, is it? I told myself. *Once a curmudgeon, always a curmudgeon.* Even if he was hiding (and doing a stellar job of it) a vulnerable side.

My "abductor," as I now chose to think of him, continued walking. He was lanky like a lot of Turks in these parts, and took longer strides, but I increased my pace to keep up. I wanted to ask him his name now in case the sharing might tear down his stony facade, but I figured he would stonewall me. So, I mimicked his silence. We were like, I don't know, Saint Paul and his detainer heading for the Ephesian cell, not far from here, in fact, where the celebrated saint was imprisoned, back when the ADs were in their genesis. The thought made me shudder. Perhaps it was not a fair comparison as I, at least, was not shackled, as I imagined poor Paul was. My mind temporarily engaged in the distant past, I tripped on the uneven paving stones of the street. Leather-face did not. His unwavering purposefulness was unnerving.

Where are we going? Surely, we're not going to traipse around the Sultanahmet all night.

The Sultanahmet certainly had its ambient charms, such as Hagia Sophia and The Blue Mosque, iconic monuments where travelers worldwide flocked to admire their beauty. I had myself, back in 1998, with my three buddies. Come to think of it, during the daytime the hordes of visitors did resemble flocks of pigeons, strutting this way and that, absurdly trying to figure out which direction to investigate. Charming as the idea was, I did not relish exploring its backstreets at night with a monosyllabic mobster type.

Fortunately, movement always had a way of quieting some of whatever qualms I might have, and this time was no different. Food, too. In fact, it seemed an age since I had been on my way out to eat. All this interruption and plan-changing, though momentarily banishing hunger from my attention, now reasserted itself.

I hope wherever we're headed has lavaş *puffy bread, at least, or some* mezes. *Don't know how much longer I can go. And you, head, stop throbbing, would you?*

We continued our way along the narrow street, never pausing, never slowing. My impressions of the neighborhood were blurred at best: narrow, multi-colored houses with wrought-iron railings crammed side by side, the odd bit of food wrapper balled up in a damp sewer trough, a *kebap* spool dripping with fat while its pungent odor of roasted lamb flesh wafted into my nostrils, a one-eyed ginger cat yowling at a window.

Yep, definitely Istanbul. You wouldn't find this scene back home, that's for sure.

My thoughts wandered and I almost lost track of time. But when I glanced at my mobile phone in my hand, a nervous habit of mine, I saw we had walked for only ten minutes.

At last, my silent steward swerved in front of me and stopped. I nearly smacked into him.

"Here," he said, his voice sharp, and gestured with his hand toward a recessed timbered door.

I did not move. But my stomach somersaulted.

The door was surrounded by exterior walls of stucco work the Brits I knew called "rendering," which filled in the cracks between large slabs of odd-shaped stone. The receding light of the evening made it difficult to see much detail. What kind of place was this? I tried not to let my imagination wander too far toward possibilities such as a meth lab or a smuggling den.

Leather-face reached across me and with no word of explanation—or comfort—thumped four times on the door with his fist. I watched, my heart now performing jumping jacks. Guess I was not as calm as I had tried to pretend.

Thanks, guys, for betraying me. I'm trying to be cool here, okay? Damn! What is this all about? Let's get it over with, for God's sake.

This up and down procession of nerves was not part of my plan tonight. Really. I rocked back and forth on my feet, waiting with some trepidation to see what would happen next. My waiting was short-lived.

The door creaked slowly open, as if by magic. Instinctively, I recalled the old "open sesame" fairy tale invocation overheard by Ali Baba when the forty thieves entered their secret cave. As a kid, I had read the tale with great fascination. Its promises of treasure and adventure still permeated my inner consciousness. It might not even be far-fetched to conclude that the memory trails of those early readings still inspired my decisions. The seeming haphazardness of many of these still rankled my parents. They could never understand my often sudden and offbeat life choices.

I braced myself to enter the cave.

Leather-face brusquely pushed the door further and disappeared inside a forbidding gloom. From inside I heard his gruff voice.

"*Gel,*" it said. Come.

Gulping, I slowly stepped across the gray stone threshold. I wondered if I should cross my heart or perform some similar salvation-like gesture. As I was not particularly religious, it would have been out of character. But in certain circumstances, one could not be too cautious. As a compromise, I merely crossed my fingers and hoped for a miracle.

I found myself, and my newfound "friend," in a narrow hallway. I could barely make out anything except his imposing silhouette. But he gestured to me to continue to follow him, and I did, though I no longer felt the brisk confidence I had feigned on the street outside.

Neither of us spoke.

A few steps on and we arrived at an interior door. This one was also wood, but of a more modern, store-bought smoothness, not the rough-hewn version we had crossed through moments before. Strangely, this impression of modernity brought me a slight reprieve from my anxiety. Perhaps there were no brigands beyond its portal. Perhaps civility of some kind awaited me. But of what variety I still could not conceive. The reprieve did not last long.

Leather-face turned the metal knob and this door also opened inwards.

This time I did not think about Ali Baba. I hardly thought anything. Rather, whatever I had last eaten bashed around the walls of my stomach and threatened to make an embarrassing exit.

Then I heard...

"Molo!"

It was a low, deep voice that called out, a voice I had not heard in years, but that I knew like my own. How could I not? A waterfall of relief gushed through me.

Could it...? Was it possible...? After all this time?

I peered deeper into the darkened room. But the person behind the voice was in shadow. He was sitting atop a small wooden table. Nothing else was on it but a plain Turkish tulip glass half-filled with, what I assumed would be, amber-colored çay. In the dim light I could not see the man's features. But as he called out, his head did two things simultaneously: shook gently side to side and snort chuckled. Gestures I recognized. The kind of reaction from someone who is surprised and amused at the same time. And amused at being surprised and amused. It could only be...

"*Paz?*" I said, my own head shaking sideways in disbelief. "Wha— *you're* here?"

"In. The. Flesh!" my old friend bellowed, with a sing-song emphasis on each word. "Not that long, though." He grinned. "I *tried* to be here before you."

"Before me? You knew I was coming? How? Why? I mean, what's going on?"

I saw him shrug in the dim light.

And then I continued, baffled. "I haven't seen you in, what, five, six years and now you show up in Istanbul? Without..." my turn to shrug, "any warning or anything. I don't get it." I could hear my voice rising.

"Molo..." he said again, quietly this time.

"Don't call me that!" I interrupted. Now I was on the verge of shrieking.

"Why not? Molo. I mean, it's what we all called you. Mallie and me and..."

"Okay, stop. You don't need to say his name. And you don't need to placate me with, you know."

Hearing my old nickname after all this time threw me off guard—it was certainly not what I had expected. I stood silently for a moment, trying to take in this unexpected encounter. Then it occurred to me that there was more oddity to it all than just the fact of Paz being in Istanbul the same time as I was.

"So..." I continued, more than a little shaken, "if you knew I was here, *and* you obviously knew I was at the Beşik..."

"Actually, I didn't know you were there, just figured it was possible."

Paz's explanation rang true, even though it pissed me off. He had always had a talent for subterfuge. Our whole relationship had started with it when he mysteriously appeared up front totally transformed at the tent performance way back when.

"Well, you sent your henchman, or whatever he is..."

"Barış," Paz interjected.

The person in question, the object of my recent discomfiture, bowed slightly in my direction. His be-ringed right hand was pressed lightly over his heart, a gesture of respect much used in this country. As my eyes had by now adjusted somewhat, I saw Paz wink at Leather-face.

"Who?" I asked, looking around the room.

"He's called Barış. Funny, hey? He and I have the same name—Barış, Paz. Peace. Right? Believe me, that was a total accident, but it kinda works, doesn't it?"

I figured Paz's question was rhetorical, so I did not answer. Anyway, what was there to say? It did work in a poetic kind of way. I just hoped that whatever this was all about, the partnership or whatever they called it, of these two and my almost-kidnapping, had something to do with the meaning of their two names and not the opposite. At least, where I was concerned.

"Anyway," Paz continued, his voice more serious now, "look, I asked Barış as a favor if he would see if you were there. He knows Mustafa, so it seemed easier than me going and freaking anybody out." He looked somewhat contrite now.

"Well, you kind of freaked me out, actually. Barış here is pretty intimidating. Not to mention, very short on explanation. You could have just had him tell me where I was going. I mean, who I was going to meet. Would have saved me a bit of anxiety, you know?" I could feel indignation surging within me.

"Yeah, I know. Sorry about that," Paz smirked. "I just..." he squinted and looked up toward the low ceiling with those expressive eyes and I could see he was thinking of what to say next. I had spent so much time with this guy, had had so many adventures and misadventures over a few years, that most of his quirks and moods were completely familiar to me. Now I could tell he was in a quandary. But I could not tell what the quandary was.

"I just..." he continued, "figured this would go better if I got you away from your digs and in a neutral place where we could talk freely." Both his meaty hands gestured, palms up, and he shrugged. "It's not as cool here as good ol' Beşik, I know, but it's more private." He smiled. "And private is what we want. Believe me."

All this mystery! Could Paz just not be straightforward about why he, or rather, *we* were hiding out together in this dingy room in the backwaters of the Sultanahmet on a hot August night? The long flight, the weird Naji dream, the headache, the lack of food, the scare mongering and now this cloak and daggering. It no longer mattered that this person in front of me had been one of my best friends for all my young adulthood. My patience crashed.

"What the fuck are you *on* about, Paz? It's good to see you, yeah, but..." I paused. I could see Paz shrink back at my hostile tone. I did not really want to get into a scene with him so quickly into our reunion, especially as it was obvious he was trying so hard to appease me. So, I took a deep breath and changed my approach.

"...you're being hella mysterious, dude."

Using the slang "hella" with Paz was akin to saying "y'all" to a fellow Texan. Except I had never heard anyone from outside California's Bay Area use "hella." It was like code. A cultural verbal bonding for NorCal cool folk. I guess saying it now, I was indicating to Paz that I was willing to reconsider our differences from the past, our beef, and revisit our friendship. For old times' sake, if nothing else. We had been like siblings back in the day. Closer even than most siblings.

His smile broadened as he nodded. I had hit my mark and he knew it. I decided to put the subject of his scheming aside for the moment.

"By the way," I continued, "where's Mallie? You guys still together?"

"Oh, yeah, you know. Same as always." His head waved side to side. "She's home with the kid."

"The kid?" Another surprise. This evening was full of them.

"Yeah. Our daughter. Caria. She's five now. But she's in school and stuff and you and I have a lot to do, so Mal decided she would stay home and be Mom." He shrugged again. "Mal's actually a pretty good mom." His gaze wandered to the far corner of the room, and the left corner of his wide mouth turned up slightly, musing about his family, I assumed.

A cartoon-like thought bubble hovered over my shoulder. It showed a thirty-something Mal with her cropped black hair and dimpled smile, sitting cross-legged on wild grass with a feisty little girl on her lap--a tanned, dark-haired mite with some funky dress and a mischievous grin. The picture placated me somewhat. It made sense for Mal and Paz to have created a wholesome family after all their years together.

"Wow," I shook my head again. "Sounds great, Paz. I'm happy for you guys. But wait." I blinked. "Go back. What do you mean, 'you and I have a lot to do?'"

                                                    ৵   ৵   ৵

Chapter 3

"The way the night knows itself with the moon, be that with me." –
Mevlana (aka Rumi)

October 25, 1922 - Constantinople

Ayşegül sat alone in front of her loom. Hunched on her low *halı* stool, her knees parallel to her chest, the top of the loom's rough wooden frame was twice her head height. Woven across the lower part of the *çözgü*, or skeleton, of coarse, off-white vertical strands of warp was the barely begun carpet. In this stage, the top edge was unruly and uneven, a painting of wool and dye begun at the bottom and evolving upwards.

But she was not facing her latest creation; in fact, her back was to it and the entrance door to her chamber beyond. After two hours of knotting and slicing strands of wool onto her stringed canvas, she had stopped. Her mind could no longer focus on the new paper pattern lying on the floor off to her left or the design itself. The threading and the pulling. The endless chopping. *Tanrım—my God—so exhausting today!*

The spirals of hand-dyed wool, their variegated tufts of color like lights in the waning sun that streamed through the slats of her window, swung from the top bar of the loom's frame. Woad blue, madder red, bast hemp for bright yellow accents, these were three of her favorites. The sight reminded her of glass lanterns hanging in a bazaar seller's stall and the illuminated rays scattering across the floor. The subtlety of the motion made her suddenly dizzy. She had already laid her *kirkit* tamping tool down on the stool beside her and now, turned around away from the loom, drew her feet and her knees even closer to her embroidered bodice.

Things were changing here. After ten years, she could feel it. Zeliha was right. But what was the change? And, more importantly, how would it affect her? What might happen to her? One of the drawbacks of being here was that it was difficult to get news of the outside world. Sometimes she bribed Estreya, the Jewess who came weekly to sell goods and gossip, with some sweet *revani* cake from the kitchen, or even a few lira if she had sold a carpet, to tell her the latest whispers from the streets of the city. Estreya usually obliged. And usually with a hint of impishness in her eyes. But where was she? She had not come to the *saray* in over a week. Why?

Ayşegül stared at the vertical slats of the one window in her chamber, high enough that she would have to stand on her toes in order to look out its open spaces into the courtyard below. But perched as she was now on her short stool, she was too close to the floor to see the courtyard. It was the sky that held her attention.

Sectioned off in three rectangles because of the window's slats, the view before her was an astronomical triptych of the heavens: sun, sky and...moon, or rather the pale, ghost-like impression of the moon. But Ayşegül knew, from years of contemplating its many moods and shapes, that its full majesty would be revealed once the cerulean blue of the daytime darkened into the Prussian blue of dusk. This evening, the moon looked larger than usual. The contrast between it and the tiny stars that surrounded it was acute.

She thought of an old Turkish proverb:

Ay görmüşün yıldıza itibarı yoktur. He who has seen the moon has no regard for the stars.

Where had she learned this saying? It must have been back in her early days here when Saskar Kadın, Tanju the eunuch, and the others plied her with their crazy language and forced their culture on her. Despite her stubbornness and resistance, despite Tanju's beatings and Saskar Kadın's scoldings, much of what they had wanted her to learn had eventually stuck. As she herself had become stuck. And, although she had survived the many challenges of life at this place, she often felt like one of the knots in her carpets—tight and wedged in place.

They had renamed her, too. Ripped her from her home and her identity. She had become so accustomed to being called Ayşegül that she had nearly forgotten its meaning. But now gazing at the deepening sky beyond, she wondered if it were an omen that she had been given this name. For though Ayşegül meant "happy living one" in Turkish, the first part of her name, "*ay,*" was "moon." Suddenly, the association struck her as fitting. For, as the moon progressed through her varying stages each month, so did Ayşegül herself progress with her own changes and survive each day. And now she had new changes to consider.

The moon must look down on her and recognize her namesake, her younger sister. And surely, as such, the moon would intervene on Ayşegül's behalf. Give her guidance. She was the queen of the night. She had the power, didn't she?

If only Ayşegül had been named Mihrimah, "Light of the Moon," like Suleiman the Magnificent and Hürrem Sultan's famous daughter back in the golden years of the empire. Back in 945 or so, according to the Islamic calendar. Would that give her more prestige in the moon's eyes? Did the moon have eyes? Of course, she did. Otherwise, how could she rule over her night-time realm?

Oh, moon...Why am I here? Why did you let them take me away from Mama and Papa? I don't wish to be ungrateful, for I am safe and fed. I've learned to weave beautiful carpets. But I feel like a prisoner. Help me!

Her supplication fresh in her mind, and still gazing at the ever-brightening orb beyond, she wondered for the first time what the Turkish proverb meant. "He who has seen the moon..." *I have, of course*, she reasoned. "...has no regard for the stars." Her steel-blue eyes squinted while she contemplated the phrase. Obviously, the saying was a metaphor to impart some deeper message about life. But she simply had never thought about this one before. And yet, at this moment it loomed in her mind as something important. For her. Something she should consider to help her with her *ikilem,* her dilemma.

As yet, she had told no one about it. Not even Zeliha, her closest ally.

Meanwhile, the night queen seemed to stare back at her from her airy domain, as if willing her to understand. Ayşegül tilted her head upwards toward the dark brown ceiling, her eyes arcing slowly in thought. Even back when she was ten years old and was only an *acemi,* a novice concubine, she had been clever, had always understood that her mind was sharp and inquisitive. She knew if she concentrated long enough now, the meaning she sought would come to her. And then at last her head nodded in understanding.

"Yes, I see," she whispered.

Her heart quickened slightly as a wave of hope coursed through her. Yes, she had finally settled into her life at the palace, but she had never felt right. Had always felt like a stranger, a *yabancı,* no matter how many carpets she wove or jokes she could utter in the Ottoman language. No matter how much about the Muslim world she had been taught or the *mezes* she had learned to enjoy eating. She would even give up the mouthwatering *patlıcan salatası,* her favorite eggplant salad, to be somewhere else.

30

Now, this evening, the moon had delivered a message, from God or from Allah, she did not know which. But she felt that was a trifling distinction. To her it was all the same. Something out there was telling her enough was enough. She *had* seen the moon and its power and beauty, and beside its brilliance the little stars, though infinitely more numerous, were like the *atkı ipi* in her carpet designs. They were merely the weft, or horizontal background, of the canvas. Stars and *atkı ipi*, in other words, were minute details that existed in order to augment the overall intent and focus of the moon—or a carpet. In stories, the moon would be the main character and the stars, supporting roles.

All Ayşegül's carpets told stories. Stories about herself and her dreams and accomplishments, her character, her history, as was the tradition of rug-making from time immemorial. Or so Maryam, the carpet master, had taught her. And this current carpet would be no different. She would weave something new into it and that something new would transform her. Transform her life. As it was already transforming. She could feel it.

Ayşegül sighed. And then she smiled for the first time in days.

"Whatever is happening, I will find out. And I swear, by tonight's moonlight, I will find a way to make it work for me," she said out loud.

At that moment, Ayşegül's oath was interrupted by a loud knock on her door.

Bang, bang, bang, bang!

Ayşegül stood up abruptly, scattering her *kirkit* and scissors across the floor. She turned to face the sound.

"Who's that?" she called out. Despite her surge of confidence seconds before, her heart thumped. She waited.

Nothing.

"*Merhaba*? Hello? Who is it?"

Though she raised her voice to penetrate the thick door, whoever was in the hallway outside did not answer.

           ॐ   ॐ   ॐ

Wednesday, August 14, 2013, Evening - Istanbul

Barış, I suddenly realized, had slipped out of the room. He must have slipped through the door opposite the one he and I had originally entered through. Doors seemed to be everywhere this evening. Could he have gone

31

into some other chamber? A kitchen perhaps?

"Are you hungry?" Paz asked. "It's gone 7:00 now and I'm famished. Haven't eaten since lunchtime."

"Jesus, I thought you'd never ask," I said. "My stomach has been rumbling so much I thought an avalanche was coming. Before your man Barış accosted me, I was actually on my way to find supper. Can hardly remember the last time I ate. A Turkish sandwich on the plane, I think."

"Good. Let's go out. And then I'll fill you in more."

Paz picked up something from the table and shoved it in his pants pocket. He was so quick, I did not catch what it was. I was sure there had been nothing on the table except the *çay* glass when I had first come in. Perhaps I had not noticed because it was dark, and my eyes had not adjusted to details.

"So, what do you wanna eat?" he asked. "There are a few cheap and cheerful *lokantas* near here. But I haven't had a chance to check any of them out yet."

"Cheap and cheerful" was one of the British-isms we had picked up down south at the Mediterranean in 2005. We knew a few and used them often. American jargon lacked the vibrant flavor of British.

"I don't know, something Turkish, I guess." I laughed. It felt good. Paz joined in. We both knew from before that no matter what we might crave, most establishments served the same cuisine. This reminded me of a phrase some Turk had told me once. I could only remember the English translation—something like "the guest eats what he finds, not what he hopes for."

Around here, that meant...

"Turkish it is!" Paz blurted. "C'mon. *Hadi gel.*"

He emerged gingerly from behind his table desk, the wooden chair legs screeching against the floor, and careened into me with a bear hug.

"It's really great to see you again, Molo. Even the new you," he mouthed into my neck.

I cringed at his use of my nickname again, but decided for old time's sake not to chastise him about it anymore. In a way, it felt good to be reminded of the me that used to be. I hoped being Molo again, at least in Paz's eyes, would not distract me from the me that had to be now.

"Yeah, it's great to see you again, too, Paz. Been a long time." I nodded my head as we pulled apart. Then he grasped my hand with one of his, placed his other on top, and I told myself, *it's all good.*

We emerged from the narrow building through the same thick door that

Barış and I had entered recently. Dusk had faded into early night. The narrow alley no longer seemed menacing, though there were still no humans about.

Curious how things change, I thought. *An hour ago on this very spot I was practically shitting myself and now I'm off with my old pal for a comradely repast. I don't get it, but it sure beats being mugged in a deserted back street of Istanbul.*

I had not yet told Paz why I was in Istanbul. I was not even sure I would. It was my business and my business alone. Or did he know? After all, he knew I was coming. And that was disconcerting to say the least. *What* did he know? And how? Hopefully he would tell me over our meal. I was counting on it.

෪ ෪ ෪

I show up at the double door of a large plank-wood house that emerges out of an open field like a giant canker. It's a mansion, really. Imposing only because of its size, not its glamor. Up close, the square, colonial style building is dilapidated and older than it looks from a distance. Its siding is warped, and faded paint is peeling from the door jamb and exterior boards. Somehow I know that the owners are a wealthy couple in their 50s. I have not met them. It occurs to me how odd that a rich family would allow their home to deteriorate, but I do not question it. I am here to start my new job.

I have not been told what the job is.

The housekeeper lets me in. She's older than I, and her attire reminds me of photographs of my dead female ancestors, crones that died of old age before I was born. Ankle-length dress of calico print, white cotton apron, sensible flat shoes and hair pulled back in a severe bun, this was their uniform. And hers. She never tells me her name, but it is not important.

She leads me down a long, narrow hall with bare floors into a back room. En route there are several doors off each side of the hallway, but the doors are closed. I find this unnerving.

The housekeeper opens a plain door at the far end of the hall and I follow her in.

"Back room," she says. And stands there.

This back room is large and open. It makes me think of a one-room schoolhouse from the 1800s. Except there are no desks or teaching

33

implements. Instead, it is almost bare. But long, thick drapes cover four equally large windows, two on the wall opposite the door we came in and one each on the walls to either side of me. The faded green color runs down the fabric like woodland waterfalls and pools onto the concrete slab floor. I am dimly aware of a large crate on my right. On my left are a couple of black folding metal chairs. They are opened, ready for someone to sit in them. I turn slightly and see that there is a built-in cupboard to the right of the door we just entered through. It juts two feet out from the dim, shadowy wall and is waist height. The pale green cupboard is plain and crudely constructed. Its top is mostly bare, just a small pile of rags and other things I cannot identify on top, and there are several doors with cheap metal handles, like those I have seen in garage shelving, on its front.

The housekeeper stands silently near me.

I walk slowly toward the cupboard. I feel compelled. When I arrive in front of the second cupboard from the left, I lean forward and pull on the thin handle. It is dark inside the compartment, but I reach in with both hands and pull out a large, white, plastic bucket. It feels full of something and is heavy, so I almost drop it onto the floor in front of the still open cupboard.

As I stand up, I spot a rectangular yellow sponge on top of the cupboard. It is the type of sponge used for washing cars. I did not notice it before, and it looks clean, which surprises me because everything else in this room so far looks dingy and old except for the bucket I have just taken out. I pick up the sponge in my right hand.

The lid of the bucket has come off and I see the inside of the container is full of red paint. Red, deep and shiny, the color of some jewels.

While the housekeeper watches, I bend down and untie my shoe laces. Then I remove my shoes and socks. I right myself and slowly unbutton my shirt front. I slide the sleeves down my arms and toss my shirt on the floor. Then I slowly undo the zipper of my trousers and let them fall to my ankles. I step out of the rumpled pant legs like an automaton. I hardly realize what I am doing. Then I hook my thumbs around the elastic band of my undershorts and ease them down my bare legs, bending forward to push them toward my feet. Again, I step out of the cloth and, with my right foot, push both pants and underwear toward the open cupboard. The shed items lie crumpled together like small, sleeping animals.

I have not said a word.

Now I pick up the sponge and dip it into the red paint. At first, I only dip the sponge in a quarter of its length. When I pull it out of the bucket, it is

34

dripping with thick color. I draw the sponge toward my chest while small globs of paint drip on the floor below.

I place the sponge on the left side of my chest and rub it up and down. The sponge and the paint are cold, but it feels refreshing. For the first time since being at this place I feel almost relaxed. The paint oozes off the sponge and some of it dribbles down toward my waist and my navel. It tickles and I feel goosebumps stand up on my arms and my nipples harden. I continue to run the sponge now in circles toward the right side of my chest, but the paint is running thin. So I dip the sponge once again into the bucket and then bring it back to my torso, slowly covering my naked epidermis with another layer of red. The more I work, the more I enjoy the sensation of applying this cold new skin to replace my normally pale whiteness.

As I dunk the now darkened sponge once again into the bucket, I am no longer timid. I plunge my hand in up to my wrist, so that the sponge emerges saturated with the thick paint when I draw it out again. Larger glops of it drool onto the floor as I bring the sponge back toward me and, this time, I coat my shoulders and my arms. I can feel the hairs on my arms rising in protest, but I do not stop.

As I am painting my upper limbs, I become aware of another body entering the room. I barely look up, so concentrated am I on my task, but even so I can see that the newcomer is an older woman, dressed in the same uniform as the housekeeper, and she stands by the open door with her hands on her hips, watching me. Is she in charge of the housekeeper, or just another person who works at this place? I note her presence, but I am not embarrassed, even though I am virtually naked in front of these two women, and engaged in provocative behavior. When I glance up again, both are sitting, straight-backed and silent, in the metal chairs. They are watching me, but now they have no expression at all. Their faces have become smooth and featureless, only raised bumps where their noses had been before.

Nonchalant, I continue to immerse the saturated sponge into the bucket. I start coating my waist area and my hips and then continue down toward my lower stomach, rubbing the sponge into the crease between my legs and around my crotch. I take particular care coating my genitals, and I almost gasp. The paint is still freezing as it merges with my skin and the momentary shock of each initial touch is thrilling.

The edges of my lips lift up in a slight smile.

I keep smiling. Not at the women in the chairs, but to myself, at the strangeness of this ritual. I have never done such a thing before and I realize that it feels natural and wonderful. In fact, my body feels more alive where the paint has not yet dried, where it is still wet and fluid.

I dip and rub. Now my left leg, now my right. Down to my feet and in between my toes. The paint squishes out from those digits and squelches under my feet as I shift my weight from foot to foot. I am standing in a puddle of blood-like muck, and yet it does not disgust me. Rather, I am entranced.

I have some difficulty reaching my backside and I wonder briefly whether I should ask one of the silent watchers to assist me. But in my peripheral vision, I can see that they are like mannequins, expressionless and still. So I reach over each shoulder and around my sides with my dunked sponge and do the best I can.

Now, my face.

This time I do not need to douse the sponge. There is enough paint seeping out of its large pores to cover the skin around my forehead, my eyes, my nose, mouth and chin. I tilt my head back, as if shaving, so that I can complete the process on my neck.

With most of the paint on the sponge used up, it looks orange-colored and spent. Calmly, I place it on the bucket's upturned lid and rub my palms together to coat them with color, as well.

I am done.

The women, sitting hands in laps, stare at me with disinterested eyes. Strange creatures they are. But I do not care.

I am not me anymore.

Not exactly.

Neither nervous nor concerned about how others might perceive me, I move slowly toward the door of the back room, my feet slap-slapping with wetness on the hard, gray floor. I re-enter the hallway, but it no longer looks narrow and dark. Instead, it fills with white-yellow light as I cross the threshold.

Once inside, on the left wall, I notice a mirror. A full-length mirror, thickly gilded around the edges and emblazoned with carvings of birds and vines. I nod. I realize, yes, I have known all along that the mirror would be there.

I close my eyes and pad over toward the mirror, wanting to suspend this moment. Wanting to savor the contrast between my memory of what I once was and the unveiling of what I am about to see. My heartbeat quickens. Once I know I am facing my soon-to-be revealed reflection, I take a deep breath.

And another.

Silently, I urge my eyelids to part. And they obey. Slowly, slowly, like cocoons, they split and eek open. Slowly, slowly, they come apart and my eyes, lying patiently in waiting, begin to focus on the image reflected back from the mirror. What emerges are not some new-hatched insects or infantile reptiles. Or a strange alien being that is unfamiliar to me. What I see in that clear moment of revealing is...me. But not me. Not exactly. It is something like me, but reformed, re-invented, renewed.

My eyes are fully open now and I watch them glinting in the reflection. Shining and wide, they scan the being in the glass. The thing before me, that gazes back at me, is splendid and, there is no other word for it—luminescent. For, instead of a washed out, feeble human covered in dark, dried paint, I find myself staring in disbelief at a being that radiates a shimmering, translucent light. A light that beams outwards from my body in remarkable brilliance and with such an array of tones and hues, I watch my mouth open in a kind of awe at the transformation. The most impressive change is in my face. It is pure light—a living halo. The paint around my eyes sparkles like otherworldly gems and glitters so blazingly that the gleam flashes into my eyes and I feel myself floating away.

I am no longer me.

            ↝   ↝   ↝

Chapter 4

"If a hair on my beard knew my schemes, I would pluck it out." –
Mehmet II, when asked where his army was headed

Wednesday, August 14, 2013, Evening - Istanbul

“**O**kay, out with it, Paz,” I said, before stuffing a black olive in my mouth. While I waited for his reply, I chewed around the olive pit and picked it out of my mouth with my thumb and index finger. I was still holding it when he looked up from his plate of *köfte*.

“Not so fast, Molo,” Paz replied. He was hunched forward, his elbows perched beside his plate on the blue oilcloth that covered our small window-side table. Then his fork started waving in his right hand like a miniature medieval battle spear. “This *köfte* is fuckin' tasty.”

I chucked my olive pit onto the small mountain of denuded pits that had accrued in a bowl to the right of my almost empty platter of *İskender* chicken.

“Knock it off, Paz. I'm going to wop *you* into a meatball pretty soon if you don't start talking. I want to know what this is about. What are you here for, man?”

“Okay, Mole, just give me a few secs. I gotta have some more *börek* to fortify myself after all that traveling and shit.” I noticed I had gone from being the formal “Molo” to the lesser “Mole,” which meant either Paz had had one too many Efes beers or the meal had relaxed him, not a far stretch for Paz even in the most stressful situations. Food was his drug of choice. I decided on the latter explanation.

I sighed and took a large gulp of *ayran*. It was fresh-made on the premises and not from a commercial plastic cup.

“All right, eat up, Paz. I've gotta admit, I've missed this food. And a*yran*. Damn. I know it's not everyone's cup of tea—or yogurt—” I chuckled, “but I love this stuff.”

“Yep,” said Paz, chewing, “you're right about that one. I never could

38

handle the salty, frothy, yogurt drink sensation. Don't know how you do."

"Guess it's an acquired taste," I responded. "But, equally, I don't get how you can plow through a pile of *kokoreç*, either. Grilled lamb intestines. Yuuuuck. Can I have a piece of your *börek*, though? I always liked Turkish pastries. I might have to order some."

Paz sat up straight, looked toward the young waiter who was hovering near the back counter of the nearly empty *lokanta*, and summoned him over with a wave of his left arm. *"Bakar mısınız!"*

The kid rushed to our table, placed his left arm behind his back, and bowed very slightly in Paz's direction. I noticed the light fuzz on his upper lip. Learning the trade early, as so many boys here did.

"Yes, please, I may help, sir?" he chirped in clipped English. They also were quick to pick up any language that would help them make an even quicker buck. Or lira. I admired their cleverness.

"Evet. Bir ıspanak ve peynir böreği daha, lütfen," Paz said, stabbing his fork in the air toward me. "For my *arkadaş* here."

Our waiter looked confused. I figured it took him a second to realize Paz was speaking Turkish to him. Well, a kind of bastardized Turkish. He probably had not expected that. We had ordered our first round in English.

Then he smiled.

"Tamam. Okay. One more spinach cheese *börek.* No problem," and he bowed again before heading to the kitchen.

"Wow, you've remembered some of the lingo, I see." I grinned at Paz. He always had tricks up his sleeve and knew how to charm. Was he working on me, too? No doubt. But it *was* part of his charm, and one of his traits I always liked.

I leaned back in my white plastic chair, crossing my legs at my ankles as I used to do in the old days, and watched him take another bite of his *börek.* While he chewed, staring at his plate, I pulled my mobile phone out of my pocket, flipped it open and checked the time. Damn. Getting late. I stuffed the phone away again and looked at Paz. I had yet to hear why he was here *and* I still had to get back to my room, such as it was, and prepare for tomorrow. Thankfully, my headache had started to dissipate. The food and drink must have taken the edge off the stress of the trip. All without the aid of a pain reliever, thank the stars. That was a positive sign. Hopefully, I would get back to the Beşik soon and get a good sleep. I would need it. But somehow, what with thoughts of tomorrow looming, the transcontinental travel, Paz's surprise attack, and then the revelation of whatever it was he might be about to spring on me, I doubted sleep was going to come easily. It could be a long night.

"*Buyrun,*" said a young voice at my side. I almost jerked out of my chair.

"What?" I said, looking around.

"Your *börek,*" said our waiter. Paz was still absorbed in eating, and I had been so lost in my musings, I had not seen or heard the kid come up to the table.

"Oh, yes, great, thanks. I mean, *teşekkürler,*" I managed to mutter, shaking my head. God, what a goof. I was already losing the plot. I could not allow that to happen if I was going to succeed with my plan. Really, I needed Paz to get on with it, so I could get on with it!

"*Bir şey değil,*" the waiter responded, picking up my empty platter in his left hand, and replacing it on the table in front of me with a smaller plate. On it, squared on top of a paper doily, lay my pastry. I nodded, smiled, and the kid turned and strolled back toward the kitchen.

Paz had lifted his head at this exchange, a crumb hanging on to his lower lip, and I could see him holding back a guffaw. He never liked to miss a chance at making a joke out of a situation. So I opened my eyes wide and glared at him.

"Don't do it..." I warned. "Let's just finish eating and not make a scene, okay?" Then I smirked and sat up. "I'm going to scarf this thing and then *you're* going to talk."

"Alrighty," Paz agreed, wiping his mouth with his hand. "But I'm just telling you, there's only so much I can say right now. Here, I mean. Remember, I told you back in the room with Barış that we want to be somewhere private."

In spite of myself, I rolled my eyes toward the dusty ceiling. "Paaaaz, I'm trashed, dude. And you're playing games with me. Where do you suggest we go, anyway, if the Beşik is also not to your privacy standards? Just...out with it already. I'm eating and you're talking. Go."

He dusted his hands and rubbed them together. Stalling, I was sure. Then he leaned back with his palms on the table. He took a deep breath, blowing it out slowly.

"It's about, you know..." he started, hesitantly. We had stopped saying his name since the incident eight years ago. Our silence was a kind of code. Protecting the past, protecting his memory.

I stopped mid-bite.

"Yeah. Okay, I'll say it. 'Adrian.' I figured." I lowered my gaze toward my lap for a second, then looked back up at Paz and saw his eyes. Instead of being sad, as I thought they would be at the mention of our old friend,

40

they gleamed.

Confused, I continued.

"What about him?" I tilted my head in question. "There's nothing to say anymore, really, is there?" And I stared at Paz, searching his face, wondering what it was he could possibly divulge, knowing full well he understood how difficult this subject was for me. Wondering why he seemed almost excited, instead of circumspect and downcast as I was. Wondering how he could bring up the subject that had changed everything. For all of us.

And yet, I acknowledged to myself, it was why I was here. It was the very reason I had embarked on this trip, planned my plan, brushed my doubts and recriminations aside and forced myself back to this cramped, crowded, filthy, exhilarating, exasperating, confounding, bewitching den of iniquity called Istanbul.

Adrian.

We both sat, not saying a word. Paz at least had the sensitivity, I assumed, to realize my short outburst merited some explanation. Then he squirmed in his plastic seat and quietly said,

"Molo. My friend. I know a lot of things have changed, you've changed, for sure," and he looked deeply at me, his eyes no longer gleaming, but dark and full of empathy, I thought. That was something, at least. Because all these years I had not really known what he thought of me and what I had done. Maybe he was more understanding than I had given him credit for. So, I would try to be patient in return and listen to what he had to say, even though the lion's share of me wanted to dart out the *lokanta's* glass door and not look back.

"And I wouldn't even be here, believe me, if I didn't have to be," he continued. "I've got a kid, Mallie, a life, stuff. You know. But, geez," he paused, "how do I say...?"

I cut him off. "What? What *is* it, for fuck's sake, Paz? Just say it. I'm on edge here. I can't handle any more stalling. Say it!" And I leaned forward, feeling my muscles tense and my hands clench.

"Okay. Here it is." He looked left, then right, then straight at me. And, lowering his voice, said, "Something's happened. Something's come up."

I sat back again, folding my arms across my chest. "Come up? What do you mean, Paz?"

What was he talking about? What could have come up?

"So, you know I work at the McHenry Library at the school, right?" Paz coughed. "Been there a pretty long time now, strange as it seems that I'd

41

still be hanging out in Santa Cruz. Especially at the U.C. Well, anyway, this guy came in one day a couple weeks ago. He was filling out a form at the front and something about him, I don't know, just, he seemed familiar. So, I went near the counter to get a closer look. I stayed behind a column so he wouldn't see me. And, I couldn't believe it, but..."

He stopped.

"But, what?" I asked, squinting at him. "Who was he?"

A split-second flash of hope surged through my mind. I quickly dashed it as being impossible.

Paz bent over the table and whispered, as if someone nearby might be listening. As if uttering a curse. I had a sudden recall of Naji the *djinn*, and my arms tingled.

"It was Ömer."

My heart started to pound. "Ömer?" I asked, hardly daring to utter the name. That was the last person I had expected, or hoped, Paz to name. "Ömer?" I shook my head back and forth. "No way. How could that be?"

Ömer. That word, that name. I had not heard it spoken in so long. Just the sound of it summoned up a panoply of emotions inside me. And none of them were pleasant. While I was dimly aware of Paz fiddling with his fork, my brain was bombarded with images of another kind.

Ömer. My nemesis. The bastard asshole. The sycophantic little fuckwad creep. He made Uriah Heep look like a Teletubby. I hated him. Hated him with everything I had in me to hate with. His short, thick, weaselly visage flashed into my thoughts, unbidden, and I felt like puking.

"Mole, are you all right?" I heard Paz ask. He must have stood up because I could feel him standing off to my left, touching my shoulder. Then he exhaled sharply. "God, I'm sorry. Let's get outta here. I'll pay."

As though through a miasma, I watched him head to the back counter where we had earlier placed our dinner order, and pantomime writing a check to the owner. The owner nodded, pulled a small pad out of his apron, and presented it to my friend. Without a word, Paz nodded back, reached in his front pocket, pulled out a wallet, and presented some paper bills to the patient Turk. I saw the smile beneath his mustache. Paz must have left a generous tip, though no tip was necessary at a place like this; it was usually included in the total.

Paz, I thought. Always a good heart.

But at that moment, my own heart did not feel good. It felt like murder.

ॐ   ॐ   ॐ

Wednesday, August 14, 2013, Night - Istanbul

A memory can be either a feather or a stone. The one floats across your mind with a vague, dreamy quality landing nowhere. The other is heavy and hangs on your heart like an iron weight. For years mine had been the stone version. It is how I would have described my own impression of the disaster that changed everything.

But now visions of past events infiltrated my brain, neither like a feather nor a stone, but with a fierce burning that was more hellfire than anything else. Paz's revelation of seeing Ömer in California had fueled this flare-up. What was he doing there? In Santa Cruz, no less? The very place one would least have expected him ever to go? It did not make sense. It did not fit in with anything I knew about Ömer.

What I also needed to find out was...was he still in Santa Cruz?

Because if he was, my trip to Turkey was futile. For though I had tried to block any images of Ömer if I could avoid it, he *was* my primary target. It was Ömer I had come here for. But I had hoped to destroy him without even setting eyes on him myself. Now it seemed that I would have to. But how?

As I pondered this new state of affairs, I followed Paz out into the sticky night. Neither of us spoke. Both of us stared ahead into the dimly illuminated *sokak*, what light there was diffused through large glass windows of the few street-front businesses still open. The faint odor of burnt *pide* and still grilling *döner kebap* machines enveloped us. Some of the casual eateries would be open for hours longer. I knew that because the four of us had been regulars at these establishments during our two previous trips. And we had often stayed out late, laughing, drinking, stuffing our faces with the local street food. Back in 1998 and again in 2005.

Until the "incident," that is. Why could I not forget? Why were those years, those visits, still so significant to me? Why were they etched on my mind with Sharpie-like indelibility? When I organized this trip, this caper, my hope had been that once my scheme to deal with Ömer had been played out, all those memories would be erased and I would finally be free.

But Paz's revelation made me realize there was more to this game than I had realized. Or so it seemed. I needed to find out what.

I could not tell what Paz was thinking, but he was walking briskly, so I figured he had some kind of idea. A more "private" place to go, for

43

instance, in order for him to finish telling me why he was here. Because I was sure there was more to his going to all the expense and trouble of flying out than telling me he had spotted Ömer at his workplace. Or perhaps he was buying time, during which I might calm down. As well as he knew me, or had known me once, I did not think he realized the inferno that was blazing in me now.

"Wait up, Paz," I shouted, and forced myself into a light trot to catch up with him. "Where are we going?"

Paz stopped and turned to face me as I approached, panting mildly.

"Well, *arkadaşım*," he whispered. His head wagged back and forth in rhythm with each syllable of the Turkish word for "my friend." Was he being sarcastic? I could not quite tell. If so, why? Was he suddenly irritated with me? Had I said something to anger him? Well, whatever the case, I did not get it. But I was relieved that at least his voice was low, so that it did not echo loudly in the empty, silent street. According to Paz, you never knew who might be listening. Or why.

Paz continued, no longer exactly whispering, but still in a hushed tone, all traces of sarcasm gone as abruptly as they had appeared. Strange.

"I was thinking we could go back to the Beşik, after all. It's late, it's closer to here than my room is, and maybe we could get some *rakı* at the ol' Beşik bar while we continue our chat. I could use some. What d'ya think?"

I shrugged. "What about Mustafa? Or the other guests? Aren't you afraid they might overhear us? It's so *secret,* after all.*"

I bobbed my head to each word in mock satire of Paz's own sarcasm a moment ago. To me, all this clandestine hugger-muggery seemed overblown. Really, who the hell in Istanbul would care a jot about Ömer or Adrian or us or what we were talking about? Paz's over concern struck me as either paranoid or, should I think it?, suspicious.

He lowered his head, his focus still on my face as if he were peering over the top of spectacles and gave me a piercing stare. It reminded me of how my father had looked when reproaching me for some misdemeanor or stupid remark. After a moment, Paz lifted his head and looked up toward the slit of black sky above. His lips pulled tightly to the left side of his face in that particular habit he had. A kind of comedic grimace that I knew meant he was loosening up.

"Nah, it's okay. We'll have our *rakı,* or cherry juice for you if you want—I assume you still don't drink?—and then we'll finish talking. I know the walls are thin there, but it's late enough now that I don't think anyone will be listening. Okay?"

I chuckled inside. What a joke, the notion of anybody eavesdropping on our conversation with any seriousness. But I went along with Paz's plan, so we could get moving.

"Sounds good to me," I said. Relief flooded through my bone-weary body, beginning to drown out the fiery thoughts that had been consuming me the last few minutes. I looked forward to being back "home," even if it was only the temporary digs of my homely *pansiyon.*

At that moment, a cat meowed nearby, as if in agreement, and Paz and I both broke into constrained laughter.

"That makes three of us," he said. "Okay, let's go. I think I know the way."

ಹ   ಹ   ಹ

Tuesday, June 21, 2005 – Çalış Beach

"What's going on?" shouted Mallie, bursting into my room like a balloon whose valve had suddenly come loose. "I just saw that guy Murat flapping around downstairs like an angry goose on speed! He could hardly talk and just, I don't know, waved me up here. What's happening?"

"Mal," said Paz, pressing his palms downward several times in the air. He reminded me of a traffic policeman slowing down disobedient cars. "Chill, okay? Sit down on the bed and we'll fill you in."

"Chill" was the operative word. It was eighty-five degrees at Çalış Beach, and it seemed the breeze was on holiday as much as the tourists. Even the usually ubiquitous mosquitoes dared not venture outside. Fortunately, we were inside where the air con worked and was now blasting the center of the room.

"Fill me in on what?" cried Mallie, as she threw her daypack down on Adrian's single bed and plopped herself onto the bright rose and purple duvet.

The map she plunked onto crinkled up under her and, distracted for a moment from the current drama, I thought: *Damn, now we have to get to the tourist information kiosk tomorrow and buy another map.* After adjusting herself into a comfortable position, Mallie placed a hand, palms down, on each knee. I could not help noticing that her jeans were ripped where her hands lay in just that right amount of shabby chic that was popular with young Americans. Like us. And, at this moment, the sight

45

gave me a momentary relief. Mallie was here. She had old jeans on. They were ripped. All was normal.

But it was not.

Mallie's glance darted around the small, third-story room.

"Where's Ade?" she asked, her eyes screwing up into small holes. "I thought you guys were together," she added, turning to glare at me.

"Me?" I said, pointing to my chest. Her accusing tone put me immediately on the defensive. "What's your problem, Mal? You don't even know what's going on. So shut up for a sec, okay?" The air con might be in cool mode, but the mood was heating up.

I was on the far side of the room, in this case, only a few feet from Mallie and Paz. I had been leaning against the white laminated dresser where my smaller travel gear lay cluttered around the top. At her verbal attack, I pushed away from the dresser—a kind fight-or-flight physical reaction. Something clanked loudly on the floor. Paz and Mallie's heads jerked toward the door as if they were expecting someone.

"Crap!" I said, jumping to the side of the dresser. "Sorry, guys, I'm jumpy. Just knocked my frickin' travel clock off."

The impact of the plastic clock on the floor caused its battery compartment to unhinge, and two AA batteries started rolling toward my bed. I bent down to scoop up the offending items and placed them brusquely back on the shelf. I did not bother to replace the batteries inside the clock. The time would be off now. In light of what was happening, maybe it did not matter. Time seemed to be slipping off the edge of reality. A little like the Dali painting.

When I stood back up, I saw that Paz was sitting close to Mallie with his left hand over her right. His head hung forward and the breeze from the air con was blowing his forelock back. He looked dejected. Paz inhaled deeply then exhaled very slowly through his nose with a long, exaggerated humming sound, his nostrils flaring slightly. After the hum faded off, he lifted his head and turned toward Mallie.

"It doesn't look good, Mal," he said, squeezing her hand. He blinked.

Watching him, the debacle facing us now beginning to sink in, I felt my eyes start to water. I wiped quickly at them with the back of my left hand, hoping the others had not seen. It would not help matters if I began to cry.

"What d'ya mean, Paz? You guys are being hella mysterious," Mallie said.

Her large brown eyes were clear and focused as she locked them onto his. Mallie was our battle axe, our Boadicea. And, slight as she was, strangers might mistake her for a delicate type of lass. They did not know the tough creature that lurked behind that misleading facade. In some ways, we were all afraid of Mallie. Because when she latched onto something, she really latched. Like a vise. Beneath that soft, lithe-looking exterior, she was fierce. We loved her for it. Most of the time.

Paz opened his mouth to answer her when a loud knock shattered our stillness. We all three twitched like mice when the queen cat enters the room.

No cat, just Murat. He knew us better now, so he was less formal than when we first arrived. Nevertheless, he performed his small head bow facing the center of the tiny room, at no one in particular.

"He is here now, guys. Waiting for you in our lobby. Please." And his right arm swept toward the open door. I stifled a fleeting inward grin at Murat's use of "guys."

In this part of Turkey, the locals were much more casual. Maybe it had something to do with the lazy turquoise Mediterranean Sea beckoning from down the street. What a world away from the bustling cosmopolitan mania of Istanbul. Here, tourists, mainly from the United Kingdom, flocked for fun and sun—and a lot of alcohol—not so much history and culture and *çay*. Formality was not on the menu. Restaurant, bar and hotel owners catered to their customers' endless demands with incredible patience and aplomb. They even went so far as to learn British slang—like "mate," "chips" and "absobloodylutely." As with faces, their collective memory of words was astounding. And I got a jolly laugh from it, hearing the Brit's bastardization of their own language, of which they were so proud, delivered in a Turkish accent. What a turn-up for civilization, I thought.

Now, however informal Murat might seem in employing English jargon, I could see there was an edge in his demeanor. His voice sounded tighter than usual.

"*Who's* here?" barked Mallie, springing to her feet. I cringed to see our map rip in the center. Paz's hand, which had been holding hers so tightly a second before, flopped to the bed. He hardly seemed to notice.

We all waited for Murat's reply. I could feel small objects, like chickpeas, bounding around and up and down behind my ribs in a dance of anxiety. I had chowed on chickpeas, in the form of creamy hummus, earlier in the afternoon. I wondered if they were mutinying now. I wondered if Paz and Mallie had similar sensations in their own chests.

Stop! I commanded, silently. *This is not the right time for this nonsense,*

47

got it?

"Please, *lütfen*, you come to lobby and all will be okay," came Murat's answer. His mustache twitched above his thin lips and his eyes pleaded.

"'Okay?' What do you mean, 'Okay?'" cried Mallie. "What the hell is going on here?" The normally jovial, lighthearted girl had switched to incandescent mode. (It was a characteristic of hers that led us to joke that "Mallie" was short for "malevolent." But, of course, we never let her hear that.) Murat opened his eyes wide in what I was sure was astonishment. He had never seen this side of Mallie.

"Please, please to calm down, Miss Mallie," he entreated, his hands clasping together at his chest, prayer-like. "The other guests..."

"I don't care a flying Turkish fig about the other guests!" shouted Mallie. "I want to know, before we head down to Mr. Fucking Whoever in the lobby, what the problem is. If there *is* a problem?"

Mallie was facing Murat, her whole body taut, legs apart and her hands akimbo on her hips. A fighting stance I recognized in her, but rarely witnessed. Clearly, she was on edge. None of us had slept well the night before, staying up late, carousing at our new favorite beachfront haunt. Otherwise, I did not understand why she was so upset, since she did not yet know what the trouble was.

Whatever had caused her to react so vehemently right now was not helping us, though. For one thing, Turks hated the 'f' bomb. It was one of the worst things an English-speaking person could say to a Turkish person. At least, that is what we had discovered before, and I hoped not to discover it again. The last thing we needed now was for Murat, our obliging proprietor and indispensable gofer, to over-react to Mallie's curses and throw us out of the Mavi Dolfin Evi. It was high tourist season and Fethiye was heaving with tourists. We might not find another hotel.

I decided to step in, hoping my interference might diffuse some of her anger. I used my quiet voice.

"It's Adrian, Mal. Something's happened to Adrian."

          ~o   ~o   ~o

Chapter 5

"Listen to the story told by the reed, of being separated." – Mevlana (aka Rumi)

Wednesday, August 14, 2013, Night - Istanbul

"So, I still don't understand why you dropped everything to fly out here and tell me about Ömer, Paz. I'm seriously confused. For Christ's sake, why was it so urgent?"

We had woven quietly through several side streets, the so-called *sokaks,* of the south section of the Sultanahmet. Now that it was full-on nighttime, they verged on eerie, and I had questioned the soundness of Paz's plan as I drew my thin shirt collar close. I wished I had brought a light jacket, after all. But Paz was right, he knew the way and was spot-on at every turn.

As we walked, I glanced up to the slit of sky between rooftops and saw the partial moon, whether waxing or waning, I was not sure, observing us. The moon, I felt, was a reliable force. It was always there, keeping watch, even if it was hiding. But seeing it there tonight, guarding our way, made me breathe a little easier.

We made it back to Mustafa's, slash, the Yeşil Beşik Pansiyon, in short order. I wanted to genuflect in gratitude at the sight of the front entrance. It had been several hours since I threw salt over my shoulder, planning to return after a quick repast. So much for superstition. I had never envisioned such a lengthy evening. Nor could I have anticipated the surprise reunion with Paz. Was this what was meant by "returning like water?" I certainly did not feel like water at that moment. More like lead. But it had been a relief to be back, anyway.

"Thank God," I muttered under my breath. I hoped Paz did not hear me.

"Oh, shit." I stopped inside the foyer and caught Paz by the shoulder.

"What's wrong?" he asked.

I suddenly remembered that Mustafa did not recognize me on my arrival earlier today—was it really still the same day? Was he going to make the

49

connection between Paz and me now if we entered the bar together? Did I want him to? I thought perhaps not. It would be awkward, to say the least, especially as I had intimated that I had never been to the Beşik before. Or rather, I had not divulged my previous stays. Nor even said "good to see you again" to Mustafa in the way a past acquaintance normally does.

So, I decided to come in separately a few minutes later and make out that Paz and I had just met and decided to share a drink, as fellow travelers often do. Hopefully, my plan would work. Should have stayed at another *pansiyon* or a B & B, after all. In another section of the city. I would have avoided this awkward predicament altogether. But then, I could not have foreseen Paz's waylaying my day as he did. This incognito thing was not going the way I had anticipated.

Dang, why has everything gotten so complicated? As if it weren't already before.

"Oh, nothing. I just need to grab some more lira from my secret stash upstairs. If you want me to pay for your drink, that is," I said, aiming for a casual tone. "Be back in a few. You go ahead inside."

I nudged Paz toward the bar in front of us. Then I left him to himself.

Through the open door, I caught a glimpse of the now calm Mustafa standing behind the old bar cleaning a glass with a thick cloth, and as I sprinted my way across the tile floors to the stairs beyond, I heard his nasally voice above the mild din of customers.

"Oh, Mister Paz! *Nasılsın?* How are you, mate?" I imagined him slapping Paz on the chest or giving him a high-five.

Things would have been less tricky if Mustafa had not remembered Paz. But my instinct had told me he would. These guys had incredible memories for faces. Good thing I thought of that just in time. Well, let them have their reunion while I delayed my entrance. If I was lucky, Mustafa would soon leave the room to one of the other bartenders who worked there, and I would not have to worry about him spotting me and Paz together. Fingers crossed. A lot of that today, it seemed.

I ran up the stairs, in my energy rush, taking two at a time. By the time I arrived on the third floor, I was sucking air and trying not to panic. Things had taken a decidedly unexpected turn and up until now I had not had a chance to process any of it. I quickly opened the door to my room and flopped down on my bed, leaning back on my arms and staring at the high dingy ceiling. A spider crawled across it toward some unknown destination. I laughed to myself.

"Kind of like me, my friend. Good luck to both of us."

I pondered the evening's events one-by-one. First, Mustafa had accosted me on my way out to dinner and thrust me onto the mercy of the inscrutable Barış. Then, we took our death walk through town to the mysterious building where Paz shocked the bleep out of me. Third, I found out that he had been stalking me, for some as yet undisclosed reason about which he was being very cagey. And now, we were back at the place where it had all begun years before and I still had no idea why.

I had lied to Paz about needing to fetch more lira. I learned long ago never to leave anything valuable, especially money, in my hotel room. Ever. Anywhere. But especially in Istanbul. I had used lira-fetching as a foible to get distance from Mustafa, but also to have a few moments alone. On my way out, I encountered my reflection in the cloudy dresser mirror and I saw how disheveled I had become during the course of all these bizarre events. Taking advantage of this small opportunity, I grabbed my brush off the bed and hurriedly swiped at my hair. I might not be exactly the same person I used to be, but I still had my standards. More, maybe.

I walked slowly back down the dark, coiling stairwell to the bar.

ॐ   ॐ   ॐ

Now Paz lounged in his wooden slat chair, leaning back in his standard casual pose that I remembered. His right hand was on the tabletop, curled around a small, straight-sided glass of milky *rakı*. Judging from the level of liquid in the glass, I figured he had already taken a few swigs. My lips automatically curled up in disgust. I had never taken to *rakı* myself. Fortunately, Mustafa had vanished, a discovery that added another relief to my decidedly short list.

"Man, I needed this," sighed Paz. "Thanks, Molo. *Şerefe.*" He lifted his glass in salute.

"*Şerefe,* Paz. Cheers," I said, lifting my own glass of *vişne* soda. Paz must have ordered it for me. Since 2005, I preferred the non-alcohol-based cherry juice drink to any of the Turkish liqueors, basically shunning alcohol altogether. Besides being more refreshing, it helped me keep my head clear. And now, thanks to our *lokanta* visit, my headache had dissipated and I wanted to keep it that way.

I eyed Paz's aniseed-infused drink, in anticipation of him relinquishing the much-awaited information about Ömer. He tended to talk when he was in his cups. Well, he tended to talk a lot of the time, but alcohol inspired him to greater eloquence—and divulgence. At this moment, I did not feel

51

guilty for bribing him in this way. Plus, he was my friend whom I had not seen in eight years. I was happy to indulge his *rakı* whim. And he had paid for my *kebap*. Fair is fair. I vaguely wondered if there was a Turkish saying about that, as there were on so many subjects. But then I returned my focus to the matter at hand.

Time to hear Paz's story.

"So?" I asked, my shoulders lifting in query. From its tilted back lolling position, Paz's face now returned to the horizontal. He looked at me.

"Alright, kid." He sighed and plopped his glass onto the table. "Here's the deal. Or some of it, anyway."

"I can hardly wait."

"First of all, I never told you everything before..." began Paz.

"'Before?' What do you mean, 'before?'" I interrupted.

"Just hold on, Mole, don't interrupt. I have to figure out how to say what I'm going to say."

"Didn't you figure it out before you came here? Like, on the twelve-hour-whatever flight over? Like when you were plotting with Barış to abduct me? C'mon, Paz. You're driving me crazy already. You came after *me*, remember? You must have known you were going to spill some beans when you found me."

"Yeah, you're right. Okay. Background. Our man Ömer is a creep. A *herif*. That's common knowledge. At least as far as we're concerned. A given."

"Yep, true enough. Go on..."

"*But* there's more to it than that." Paz's mouth twisted into a strange shape and he had a sheepish look on his face.

"Yeessss, I'm all ears." I pulled mine out to emphasize the fact.

"The thing is, what you never knew...Oh, man, this is weird. I don't know how to say it."

"You said that already, Paz. Out with it."

"The thing is," he puffed his lips and blew an emphatic sigh out of them. Then he snatched at his *rakı* glass and took a quick gulp. "The thing is...Ömer knew Adrian." He thrust his glass back onto the table with a thud. "There. I said it."

I stared at him. I felt my own mouth gape open in shock. After a few seconds of silence, during which I questioned whether I had heard Paz correctly, I found my voice again.

"What? Ömer knew Adrian? No way, dude. Not possible. How could he? What are you talking about?" I heard my old voice again and was not sure if that was a good thing or not.

"It's true. Sorry, Mole." And he lifted his shoulders in apology.

I held my soda glass in my lap and blinked. Something was not right. I had not had any alcohol, and yet I felt dizzy. Was this what vertigo was like? The earth spun around me as I stared into my glass, hoping to find stability there, at least. I waited several seconds for the spinning to stop before I dared look up at Paz.

"I don't get it. How do you know?" I asked, now carefully placing my glass on the table. I was no longer thirsty.

"First, let's get this straight, just so you don't blame me. I didn't know back then. Not at first. I kind of figured it out. It's hard to remember now exactly. And I still don't know everything," Paz replied.

I shook my head in disbelief. Suddenly, everything I thought I had known started to shift. I was now entering the proverbial Twilight Zone. I did not know how to respond, so I just sat there, staring at the ubiquitous reproduction of an Atatürk photo, the great man clutching his equally ubiquitous glass of *rakı,* on the wall in front of me. I wondered what he would do in such a situation as I now found myself in. He was a problem solver, after all.

"And that's why I'm here," Paz continued. "When I saw the 'O' man at the school, I knew something was very *çok* not good. I was messed up the rest of that day, actually. And the more I thought about it, the more I realized I needed to find out what was going on."

"And that's when you decided to fly to Istanbul to tell me," I said, trying to keep my sarcastic tone under wraps. "Huh. Right." I looked up at Paz. "So how long ago was this?"

"A couple weeks ago. Maybe three. First, I tried to find Ömer, to see if he was still hanging around."

I leaned forward, my hands on the table in front of me. "And was he?"

"Nope. I checked with the clerk who had helped him, to see if he'd left a contact address or a phone number. Nothing. Smart. Then I looked online to see if he had a local listing. Just in case, even though it seemed unlikely. Still nothing. He just...vanished." He paused. "I guess."

"I don't understand, Paz. Why would Ömer be in Santa Cruz? I mean, what possible reason could he have?"

"Fuck if I know," Paz answered.

I looked around to see if any Turks were in the room listening. They might object to Paz's use of the dreaded English expletive and confront us, which was the last thing I needed right now. But the room was nearly empty. It had to be getting on for ten o'clock. Even Mustafa's replacement was lounging in a chair staring at the retro-style television mounted in the corner near the counter. Maybe the tourists wanted an early night if they had a long day of sightseeing ahead. Good for them. I suddenly wished I was one of them.

"Okay, so Ömer *Bey* was nowhere to be found in Santa Cruz, but I don't get why you had to find *me*. I mean, maybe he just decided to visit northern California. Maybe he has relatives there."

Chewing on my pinkie finger, I considered this possibility. But it did not seem likely. Ömer was pretty entrenched in his Turkish life, as far as I could tell back in 2005. But it was not inconceivable for him to travel. Many local people I met in Turkey had visited the States, which they called "Amerika," or "ABD," which they pronounced "ahbayday." And they often had gone to see a relative, usually an uncle. Or so they said. I wanted to believe that Ömer's presence in Santa Cruz was innocuous. Knowing his penchant for deception and skulduggery, it did not seem his style, but you never knew. My dealings with him had been so long ago, it was possible he had turned over a new leaf. So to speak.

But then again, if I was still harboring ill feelings toward him, it seemed only logical to assume he still had something up his sleeve, too. We had not left on the best of terms, after all. I had had very few dealings with him in person, but what there had been were unpleasant. More than unpleasant. And perhaps with people like Ömer a vendetta, like revenge, might best be served cold. You did not have to be a French history scholar to grasp that concept. I did not quite see that he had any reason to bear ill feelings toward me; after all, it was he who was the perpetrator. But these kinds of things did not necessarily follow a logical thought process. I had already experienced in my life situations where those who had committed an offense became resentful of the very people upon whom they had committed the offense. It did not make sense, but the human response mechanism did not always. More often than not, humans were unfathomable and unreasonable. I had studied some psychology. And I had been around.

I was willing to bet that Ömer could be one of those who did not forget. For that matter, neither did I.

While I was absorbed in this train of thought, Paz ran his fingers through his thick, black hair and scratched his head. And then I remembered something.

"Paz?"

"Yeah, Molo?" His hands paused mid-scratch.

"How did you know I would be here? I hardly told anyone. And I definitely did not post it on Facebook or Twitter or anything. In fact, I hardly ever use them."

Paz's face suddenly looked contrite. Almost like a little kid caught stealing a cookie from his baby brother.

"I..."

Despite his legerdemain tendencies, he was not the best liar. Never had been. Or so I had always believed.

"Yeahhhhhh..." I encouraged, smiling grimly at him.

"I asked Mallie to check up on you. You know she works at an IT company, right? In Los Gatos." He raised his eyebrows. "A lot of times they let her telecommute because of Caria. It's kind of a new thing."

"No, I didn't know that. But go on," I said.

"Well, at first she told me she didn't want to do it because it's unethical." I nodded my head in understanding. I could see Mallie responding in that way. Good ol' Mal. I would have done the same.

Paz continued. "But then I told her about me seeing Ömer at the school and she felt like I did. That there was something fishy about that. So, she said she would try to find out where you were. We lost touch with you, as you know, so we figured you didn't live in the same place."

"It's true. I don't," I agreed.

"So, she got on the computer to try to find you. We both thought that you should know about Ömer. Just in case he was up to something. Just to warn you."

"That was thoughtful of you guys, thanks." I smiled wanly.

"It took her awhile 'cuz she has the kid and work and everything. But then, lo and behold, while she was searching one day, she found this Intel about you buying a flight to Istanbul. Even she was surprised she found it." Paz looked jubilant for a second.

"I'm surprised, too," I said. "Doesn't say much about the whole privacy thing, does it?" I rolled my eyes and shook my head.

"And we decided, she and me," Paz continued, "that I should just come find you. Before you did something you might regret. Because we both kind of realized you probably weren't going to Istanbul for a reunion tour by yourself. And if Ömer had come back to Istanbul, and figured out that you were here, too, no telling what he might do." Now Paz smiled. "And that's it. Here I am." He reached across the small table and patted my shoulder.

"Yes," I chuckled. "Here you are. My savior."

"Ha ha," he smirked. "And now we've come to my big question for you."

"Oh? What's that?"

"Why *are* you here, Molo?" And both his hands gestured in a questioning way.

"Ahhh...yes, hmm. Good question. I have been asking myself the same thing," I replied. "Seems like my whole plan just collapsed. And now I need a new one. Not only that, I need to hear more about Ömer and Adrian."

ಞ   ಞ   ಞ

October 25, 1922 - Constantinople

Ayşegül scurried in her pointy slippers to the door. Her yellow kaftan dragged on the floor and, in her haste, she almost tripped over the hem. Catching herself, she grasped for the door handle, only a few feet away. Because she had recently been elevated to the status of *ıkbal*, she was entitled to her own room. It was not nearly as spacious as Sazkar Kadın's, of course, since a *kadın* was like a wife to the sultan and she, Ayşegül, as an *ıkbal*, was merely one of his many favored consorts. At this moment, she was glad. The smaller space allowed her to scramble across the apartment quickly. Ayşegül's curiosity surged in the few seconds it took her to reach her door.

There was no lock on it, but the handle was firmly in place. No one had jiggled it, as far as she could tell. She put her right ear against the hard wood. There was no noise, no disturbance in the hall outside.

Who had knocked? Why so loudly? And why did no one answer when she called out?

Ayşegül felt her heart pound under her blouse. Maybe she should call again. Maybe the person on the other side had not heard her before.

"Helloooo?" she whispered tentatively, her voice croaking despite her effort to sound subdued. The *saray* was unusually hushed in the twilight that now descended like the unfurling of the heavy draperies that adorned the walls of the grand guest hall. Where was everyone? It would soon be time for the *İncesaz* concert, an evening of "graceful" music. That usually meant a flurry of activity from the staff as they prepared the large concert room for guests and bustled like over-sized beetles down the corridors.

Ayşegül pressed her head even flatter against the thick door, just in case her own loud thoughts had muffled any sound of someone standing on the other side and they were still lingering, waiting for her response.

Hayır. Still no hint of anyone. Whomever might have been there was no longer, so there was no reason to open the door and check.

Hmm, she thought. *How odd.* Ayşegül shrugged her shoulders, grabbed her skirt and the edges of her baggy blue *şalvar* trousers with her hands, and trundled toward her loom, which she had neglected so abruptly a few moments before.

Even in the fading evening light, she could see that the normally ordered work area was littered with small bits of yarn in colors that matched those on her fledgling carpet. Her hand-drawn pattern had flown into the far corner by the window while her metal scissors and heavy, carved *kirkit,* with its sharp edges, sprawled discarded and dangerous to the right of her stool, where they had fallen earlier. Sometimes she worked barefoot, so it was lucky she had her slippers on now. The *kirkit,* if stepped on, would no doubt bang her ankle with its heavy metal teeth, bruising her skin, and surely cause much pain.

She could not afford to waste time waiting for an injury to heal. She needed to work hard and fast if she was going to complete this *halı* before anyone could see it. This one would be hers. She would not sell it. And she would have to hide it from prying eyes. Including Zeliha's.

"*Aman*! What a mess," Ayşegül groaned.

She reached toward her lantern and lit the candle with the wooden "safety" matches she kept in the lantern's narrow tray. The *saray* was fitted with electricity, one of the first places in Anatolia to have it installed, but she sometimes preferred the softness of candlelight. After lighting the wick, she stooped down, the long tips of her kaftan sleeves drooping, and placed the candle on the floor. Then she began to gather her carpet tools. As she worked, her mind still pondered the mystery of the vanished knocker.

"If it was Zeliha, or any of the other girls, they would not run away. Would they?" she mused out loud. She paused, looked toward the now dark window, and saw that her guide, the moon, had moved on to her next position in her celestial path, wherever that was, and was no longer visible. "Oh, well, when I go down to the concert I will ask around. Perhaps she knocked on my door by accident, realized it and left."

But it would have been polite for her, she supposed it was a "her," to have at least said something. To apologize.

And yet, the knock had sounded so urgent. And that was why Ayşegül was anxious to know.

જ   જ   જ

Tuesday, June 21, 2005 - Çalış Beach

Mallie's hands dropped to her sides as if in defeat. I watched the seething ball of fire she had just been deflate, flames extinguished.

"Adrian?" She regarded me for a second, then turned toward Paz. "What do you mean?"

Paz took over.

"He's at the hospital. That's about all we know right now, Mal." He looked at me, beseechingly, palms raised in question. He seemed at a loss, as if he wanted me to fill in. As if I knew any more than he did.

Mallie spoke. "Why the hospital? What hospital? You mean here in Çalış Beach?" She shook her head in disbelief.

I said, "Yeah. Well, actually, in Fethiye. Near town. This private medical center. It caters to tourists. One of the paramedics told me it's really good."

I knew what was coming next.

"The paramedics," said Mallie, in an upward lilt, almost a question. "Sooo, there was an accident, or what?"

Paz and I both looked at each other and then started to speak at once.

"Well..." said Paz.

"Uhhh..." I said.

Normally we would have chuckled at our conversation colliding, and egged each other on. But this was not a laughing time. We stopped and I gestured to Paz. I wanted him to continue because he had been there first. Of the three of us, he had been at the scene when it happened. I arrived just after.

Mallie gave Paz a hard stare.

"Well?" she said. "Tell me, Paz."

"Okay. I don't really get the whole thing, it happened so fast, you know."

"What happened, already? Why are you stalling, Paz? Our friend is in the hospital and it's like you're both trying not to tell me about it. I want to know. Now!"

Mallie's hands flew back to her hips. I had never seen anyone who could turn a moment of desperate pleading into a battle maneuver. Not like Mallie. If the circumstances had not been so grim, I would have laughed.

In my peripheral vision I saw Murat's face. His eyes were bugging out with that panicked look cattle have when they're forced up the slaughter ramp—I had witnessed that, and it was unnerving. His body was tense, and I realized he wanted us to leave the room and follow him downstairs. Someone—in authority, I assumed—was waiting there to talk to us. And the longer he or she or they waited in the foyer, or even in the bar, the more potential there was for agitation in the hotel. Again, I found myself impressed with the Turks—for a culture that sometimes seemed so haphazard, the people responded with rapid-fire efficiency during emergencies.

I felt sorry for Murat at that moment. It was not his fault that four Americans chose to stay in his establishment and that one of them ended up in the hospital. The fact that authorities had come to talk to us meant nothing good. Not for him or for the hotel. He would not be able to bribe his way out of this with *rüşvet* money. We were going to have to comply sooner or later and speak with this official entity, and the sooner, I realized, the better for Murat. And for us. But it would not be pleasant.

I hoped to tamp Mallie's temper down to at least thirty-five miles per hour before we entered the public area and dealt with the inevitable. At the moment, she was revved at seventy-five. Murat could see that, too, and he looked worried. I wanted to assure him that we would not make a scene. So, I concentrated on willing him to look my way. It worked. He glanced in my direction and I nodded calmly and closed my eyes briefly. Then I smiled a thin smile, raised my eyebrows and looked at him with what I hoped was a kind of serenity. As if.

He stared at me for a moment, then blinked and nodded his round head. All this happened while Mallie waited for Paz to answer her.

Then I turned to Mallie myself.

"Mal." I sighed. "He's in a coma. Adrian is in a coma, okay? And we don't know why. Not yet, anyway." I shrugged. Then I sat down on the edge of my bed and plonked my head into my hands. For suddenly it really dawned on me.

Adrian was in a coma. And no one, not even my best friends, knew how cataclysmically my world had crashed. But apparently it had for Mallie, too.

"Oh, my God," she cried out. "Oh, my God!"

She clapped her hands onto her forehead as she threw herself back onto the already tattered map. Despite my despondent state of mind, I could not help but mope over the fact of our map being terrorized by Mallie's butt.

That was mine and Adrian's map. Not hers. Something he and I had shared. And she had desecrated it without a single thought to what she was doing. I wanted to shake her. And just when I was thinking this, she lifted her body slightly, tore the poor thing out from under her, and threw it to the floor. It was a crumpled mess now. Irredeemable. Unusable. Just like Adrian. The whole idea of us trekking around as tourists with our map now seemed ridiculous, impossible. The idea of doing anything fun again was out of the question.

Adrian was gone.

ಶಿ   ಶಿ   ಶಿ

Chapter 6

"If you wander around in enough confusion, you will soon find enlightenment." – Turkish proverb

Two Weeks Earlier, June 7, 2005 – On the Road to Fethiye

A nd *why* exactly did we come down here?" asked Mallie, swabbing her forehead with a purple bandanna. "It's hot as Hades!"

We were in a surprisingly modern tourist bus, Mallie by the window and Paz beside her, on wildly patterned, plush seats near the back. Adrian and I sat behind them, leaning forward so we could confer without the other passengers, most of whom were Turkish villagers with boxes and bags of all sizes and colors on their laps, hearing us. Our novelty having worn off, it seemed, I found it unlikely they could decipher our rapid discussion, which was in English and not their native tongue. The near non-stop assault of Turkish pop music playing on the bus speakers would seem to make it impossible for anyone to overhear our conversation, anyway. But one never knew.

Adrian spoke in his measured voice. When Mallie was distressed I found it usually best to let him respond. He had a calming effect on her. On all of us.

"Oh, Mal, c'mon," he soothed. "It's gonna be fantastic. That's what Zeynep said. We all agreed to it. Just wait, okay?" He leaned even further forward and tousled Mallie's short-cropped, mussed up hair.

"Was that her name? Zeynep?" Mallie asked, gently pushing Adrian's hand away. She rubbed her head, making her hair even wackier than before. "For a tourist agent, she seemed pretty young, don't you think? Maybe she doesn't know what she's talking about and we're heading to the back of beyond. Maybe it's going to be just hot and shitty." She slumped in her seat.

Paz looked at Mallie, then at us, and shook his head.

"No, really, Mal." I jumped in. Adrian needed back-up and Paz was being uncharacteristically mute. "Zeynep told us 'You will love it, absolutely,'" here I put on my best female Istanbul accent, "and I believe her. I mean, she must know what foreigners like if she's in the tour business. Don't you think?" I turned toward Adrian and we both shrugged our shoulders, hoping our goodwill ambassador spiel would work its magic.

"Not necessarily. Not in this country, anyway. You guys should know that by now," responded Mallie. After a pause she added, "She might have been a *gözleme* maker last week. You know, flipping pancakes on those moundy hot plates."

I chuckled under my breath. I knew exactly what she meant. Now on our second round of Turkey travel, we had seen several instances of just such anomalies. Once, a young shopkeeper at the Grand Bazaar who had tried to sell Mallie a knock-off Gucci bag turned up later as a DJ at a Galata dance club. Another time, Paz and Adrian pretended to be interested in renting an apartment and the proprietor of the estate agency told them he used to sell fish with his father down at the Beyoğlu fish market.

"Just sayin'..." Mallie added.

Now she stared out the large window to her left. That prompted me to turn and glance out Adrian's and my window.

The bus was cruising at speed down a steep, snaking highway. From our height, I could see the switchback below. To reach it would involve a very tight curve ahead. Guard rails must have been on back-order, too, as the edges of the road lay perilously *un*guarded except for the odd boulder and swatch of dry grass and wildflowers. Silently, I hoped the maintenance guys had recently checked the brakes on our bus. I also hoped Mallie could not read my thoughts. Her brooding outbursts, often followed by an even broodier silence, could dampen our holiday spirits. Any hint that our bus might veer off the road into the abyss would have sent her into a blazing tizzy.

On the plus side, the sky was brilliant. It was as if Van Gogh had flown by brandishing a giant airbrush filled with his famous Arles-inspired blue paint. Not a cloud, not a hint of fog anywhere in sight. Clear sailing then, presumably, lack of guardrails notwithstanding. With a small sigh, I leaned back in my seat. I considered Mallie's questions.

Perhaps she had a point. Why, indeed, *had* we agreed to this last-minute trek? Up at the crack of six for a quick, tepid coffee and hard-boiled eggs and toast and then schlepping our ill-packed backpacks from our third-story rooms at the Beşik to the bus station a couple blocks away was not our usual style. Somehow, somewhere, yesterday, someone corralled us all into a cramped tour office outlet where the chubby, winsome Zeynep sweet-talked us into splurging on a trip down to the Mediterranean. We had never thought about it before. At least I had not. Not on our first trip to Istanbul in 1998, that was certain.

Maybe since then someone in our foursome had done some research about the Med and just never wanted to come out and say, "Hey, let's all check it out." It was possible. We all have our secret desires, I thought. Just because we were good friends did not mean we shared every single idea in our heads.

Maybe one of my chums thought we had to be talked into this venture by a disinterested third party to make it more legitimate. After all, we each paid a few hundred dollars, which was a small fortune for all of us. And, more to the point, we had never heard of Fethiye. Or its surroundings. What could possibly be there of interest to four twenty-something travelers? And yet, here we were. Zooming along mountain roads with nothing but uncertainty ahead. I could definitely see what Mallie was getting at.

The bus was air conditioned, but just barely. It was still stuffy, making my head dizzy from the institutional smell of the new bus furnishings. Not to mention the stale odors of dried sweat emanating from the myriad passengers, commingling in my olfactory nodes. Deodorant was clearly not a high priority on the shopping lists of Turks—at least, not the ones here.

Still, the seats were comfy and the driver pulled over every hour or so for a pit stop. These took place at designated facilities that were bigger and cleaner than the bus depots I had been through in the States, that was for sure. Yes, the hole-in-the-ground toilets were still cause for consternation, but Mallie had informed us there was usually at least one modern toilet in the women's rooms. More bonuses than not, I had to conclude. If only I were a woman.

"So," said Adrian, with somewhat forced cheeriness. It occurred to me he might have been the one who had secretly wanted this escapade, had somehow stealthily manipulated it into being. He was the one who had talked us all into coming to Turkey in 1998, after all. "How much longer before we get there? I'm ready for a dip in the famous Med. What about you guys?" He made a fist with his left hand and punched it lightly into his right palm. His abject enthusiasm reminded me of some of my YMCA day-camp counselors.

"I don't know," said Mallie. "We might as well be going by camel caravan. Seems like we've been in this bus for a century. So, we must be close, right?"

She peeked through the slit between her seat and Paz's to peer at Adrian. He winked at her. And she smiled back. I felt relief that he had, true to form, managed to pull her out of her sulky mood.

"Yeah, I guess I'm ready for that dip, too, especially after this ride," she conceded. "I hope the sea's as awesome as everyone says."

While Mallie, Adrian and I discussed the potential merits of sun and sea in the southern climes, Paz threw in the odd "hmm" and nodded his head occasionally. He sat still, staring fixedly into the back of the seat in front of him. Was he not well? I did not spend a lot of time speculating. I was beginning to daydream about life on the Turquoise Coast.

As we neared Marmaris, or so the road sign said, I glanced out the window again to see stuffed toy sheep of all sizes standing side by side on the dirt shoulder of the winding mountain road. Beside these were tables stacked with *nar*, or pomegranate, plastic juice bottles, neat pyramids of honey jars and bags of shelled and unshelled almonds. I marveled at the tenacity of these roadside salespeople. Who in the States would park their bodies and their wares on top of a mountain with nothing else around for miles, just to make a few bucks? Or, in this case, lira.

A few harrowing switchbacks and hair-raising turns later, our driver made a wide left onto a thankfully straight, flat road. Mallie turned around and high-fived Adrian and me. I saw Paz's head turn left, so I assumed he was looking out Mallie's window and had seen the bus's maneuver. I could not see his expression, though. *Why are you so quiet, Paz?*

Adrian hummed beneath his breath. It was faint, but if anyone had asked me, I would have sworn the tune was "by the sea, by the sea, by the beautiful sea." His head bopped side to side and a big grin took residence on his fair face. I wondered how he could keep rhythm, what with the hyper-beat of Tarkan booming overhead. But I leaned back in my seat, a kind of lazy contentment subsuming my previously exhausted being.

Mallie busied herself gazing at the view, I supposed, while beating the back sides of her hands on her thighs. Clearly, Turkish pop was more her thing than mine.

As our bus rolled on eastward, I began to pay more attention to the sights beyond. Trees were thicker here than on the mountain, for sure. Some were a dark, leafy green, others, sage gray. What they had in common, besides being plants, was the dust, which coated each like a kind of speckled over-skin. Either this was dry terrain or the exhaust from passing motor vehicles had cloying power. I suspected both.

Every few hundred meters, makeshift stands with equally makeshift banana leaf roofs, displayed pyramids of round, yellow melons or fire truck red tomatoes. Pile after pile of intensely bright oranges and lemons, artfully segregated, threatened to tumble onto the well-trodden dirt under the plastic folding tables that supported them. Figs, almonds and apricots were stacked into low, rectangular boxes laid out in neat, short rows, covering every inch of available space.

One stand posted a sign, *Vitamin Deposu Café*, whose specialty seemed to be fruit smoothies. That was the last thing I expected to see on the roadside in rural Turkey. Another sign read, *Çay ve Mısır*, or tea and corn. Tea and corn? The unlikely combination reminded me of 7-Eleven's advertisements for pantyhose and milk a few years back. I snickered under my breath. Commerce was commerce in any country, apparently. American or Turkish, it did not matter.

Other stalls sported multi-colored umbrellas, the kind usually erected outside casual cafes, advertising *dondurma keyfi* or *Efes bira*. "*Bira*" was a word I knew well: beer. I was pretty sure that *dondurma* meant ice cream. Cleverly covering all the possibilities, as usual. *Cold beer, cold ice cream, take your pick*, they seemed to say. *We've got you covered. And your whole family, too.* This culture was gifted in the vending trade like no other. Even the most humble merchant knew how to snare a potential buyer.

Sometimes it seemed as if the Turks would do anything to make money. This tour of ours was making some Turk a lot of it, for sure. I hoped it would be worth it. To my pals and me, anyway.

"Adrian," I said, turning to face my friend and seat partner.

He stopped humming and looked at me, his green eyes glittering. "Yeah, Mole?"

"What d'ya think?" I gestured toward his window.

He glanced to his left and sighed. "I think...hmm..." he mused. I could almost hear his brain clicking for a few seconds and then he finished. "I think this is the road to paradise. That's what I think." Then he smiled, flashing his glaring white teeth, and clapped me on the shoulder. "It's all good, my friend. All good."

I prayed he was right.

☙   ☙   ☙

October 25, 1922 – Constantinople

Her workstation tidied and clean, Ayşegül strode to the far corner of her room where her trunk hunkered in the gloaming. Pushing back the heavy lid, ornately decorated with silver clasps and tulip designs, she stuck her hands into the trunk's depths. It was getting dark, but she knew where everything was. Ayşegül rummaged through the assorted textiles piled neatly inside and dug out her best turquoise-colored, silk *şalvar* trousers, a hand-embroidered *gömlek* and a violet *zıbın* jacket with long sleeves. A little old-fashioned, but she preferred the traditional designs to the more fashionable European ones, especially for formal events like this one. After shedding the garments she was wearing, and tossing them onto her small divan, she hurriedly stepped into those chosen for tonight's *İncesaz* concert. She was late.

She picked up her *saz* case, jostling it in her arms as she headed toward her door, blew out her candle on the way, and managed to open the door without dropping her instrument. She wondered why she was made to play in these concerts, as everyone knew she was not particularly skilled on the *saz*, had only learned it because it was part of her training. Carpet-making was her real talent. Well, she muddled through. Thank Allah, the concerts occurred only once a month.

As she closed her door behind her, she wondered briefly if the sultan would attend. She had not seen him in three months.

"Oh, well. It doesn't matter," she said under her breath. "Soon I will ask Sazkar Kadın to get me an audience with him. I'm sure he will grant it to me."

ϡ   ϡ   ϡ

"Davulun sesi uzaktan hoş gelir." Or... "Distance lends enchantment to the view." – Turkish saying

June 7, 2005, Later in the Day – On the Road to Fethiye

The tour bus rumbled on at speed for a half hour or so.

Then it was time for the ever-requisite pit stop. Apparently, riding on a bus for more than an hour was considered exhausting, so there were frequent breaks.

The four of us stepped down onto the asphalt surrounding a large petrol station, equipped with an institutional-looking, sit-down *lokanta*, as well as a more informal snack bar. We chose the quicker, easier snack bar. I grabbed a cold *ayran* from the refrigerated open-top container and a Snickers bar from a burgeoning snack shelf. I had learned in Istanbul that Turkish people like junk food as much as the rest of us: name-brand candy bars, Doritos tortilla chips, crisps and the like, as well as the standard-issue *leblebi* dried chickpeas (which tasted like dried sawdust to me), Ülker pretzel sticks and (never shelled) sunflower seeds in small cellophane bags one could find at any food outlet up north. And always, always, the *simit*. Turkey's answer to the bagel, it was thinner, crispier and coated with white, toasted sesame seeds. Best eaten plain. This was not lox and cream cheese country.

The only difference between northern snacks and southern, it seemed, was none. As above, so below, they say. And here that adage bore out a truth so immutable, I chuckled out loud. For starters, just as in Istanbul, here there seemed to be only three flavors of Doritos. Ever. The same three. Most Americans would be aghast at their lack of choice in these parts. Apparently, the same items were sold in this neck of the woods, as up in the city. Not surprising. I had long ago discovered that despite the incredible culture the Ottomans produced, and the ensuing dishes and treats, innovation was not at the top of the list for the modern republic. At least in the culinary category. Nevertheless, I was glad to see what they did produce here, as my stomach had started rumbling many kilometers hence.

The other three picked out a few nibbles, and we headed up to the cashier. The whole set-up was remarkably similar to gas stations in the States. And possibly nicer. The cashiers themselves responded with grins and hearty "*merhabas*" when we greeted them. The clean, modern and friendly facilities were definitely something to tell the naysayers back home about. Many people I knew thought of Turkey as a backwater country with few, if any, amenities. One of them had even asked me if there were paved roads here. I was sure their prejudices would be dispelled if they could experience the modernity of our bus and the quality of roads it traversed (despite the dearth of guardrails).

Not long later, all settled in our seats, the bus carried on. The driver's ebullient, but bedraggled assistant slowly perused the aisle pouring lemon scented cologne out of a clear plastic bottle onto the outstretched hands of expectant travelers. This custom occurred every time the bus left a station. As odd as it might seem to us westerners, I found my skin quite relished the fresh feeling that the cologne bestowed. As a bonus, the strong citrus fragrance helped mask the acrid coalescence of unwashed clothes and bodies in the closed bus.

After splashing my hands and face with the refreshing potion, I noticed some new faces on board. First, I spotted two older couples, carrying large, white polypropylene tote bags that seemed to be popular here. Then, further down the aisle, but closer to us at the back, sat one male, maybe fifty years old, rather short and sporting a thin mustache and CIA-style sunglasses, more than likely knock-offs of some popular brand or other.

Most of the passengers were quiet. As were we. The driver had yet to pummel our ears with the cacophony of electronic violins and undulating vocals of local radio tunes. Now the only sounds were the chugging of the powerful bus engine, the whirring of the almost useless air con as it shifted hot air from one part of the compartment to the other, and the crunch-crunch-crackle of food wrappers. No conversation. Was it considered vulgar to talk on public transport? Or were we all too absorbed in eating to chat?

As I munched, I observed the other travelers on our bus. These people were shorter and rounder than the tall, sleek Turks we were accustomed to seeing in Istanbul. Not only were the ones here rather squat, but many of the men had thick heads, flat down the back, with no real differentiation between the base of their skulls and the top of their necks—they simply ran one into the other. Were they of a different genetic stock than the northerners? Musing on this possibility kept my mind active as I sipped my *ayran* and bit into my *über*-sweet candy bar.

Well, whatever the DNA story here, our bus friends are remarkably polite. I noticed that, almost to a person, they nodded at us as they shifted their odd-looking boxes and parcels, the plastic-striped shopping bags stuffed with Allah-knew-what, and adjusted their headscarves and caps. We might look different than the passengers they were used to, but they did not treat us so. That was heartening.

The dress code, too, seemed to have shifted somewhere after leaving the big city. Gone were the women's solid black trousers, silky one-hued blouses with pearl buttons and fancy headscarves. Instead, scarves were plainer and of cheaper, usually white, fabric—obviously hand-embroidered. Trousers were replaced by baggy, cotton *şalvar* pants with their crotches hanging down to the knees and blousy legs tapering at the ankles, a distinct leftover from Ottoman times. I got a kick out of their startlingly garish, crowded patterns of flowers and clashing tones. An oversized tunic of opposing color scheme to the *şalvar* completed the discord. It was not an elegant ensemble, but it was homey. This must be the local costume, I decided, which made a kind of sense. These were village women, with close ties to their ancestors' customs. And they were clearly not rich. If the scenery had not already suggested to me that we had entered a different milieu of life, the outfits of our fellow travelers made it evident. We were not in Istanbul anymore.

But I had no idea what that would mean for my friends and me. If anything.

I watched the sights roll by and marveled at another difference between the towering concrete metropolis of the far northwest and this bucolic, tree-festooned region of the southwest. A few kilometers to our left, towering limestone mountains defended the shores with an austere, but magnificent presence, which seemed to keep look-out over us as we trespassed through their domain. Small, unpaved detour roads branched off to south and north, with small, chalkboard-green signs in Turkish explaining where the roads led: places like Köyceğiz, Ortaca and Güzelyurt. I had never heard of them. Of course, there was Dalaman, too. That, I knew of because of its airport. We would have flown into it if we had not opted, instead, for the more economical bus trip.

Few villages were visible from the highway, but I spotted the occasional dilapidated stone cottage vying with more modern concrete structures on the verge or partway down a rutted track. Three-foot sticks of rebar stuck out of their unfinished top floors like some kind of bizarre homage to Stonehenge. Others were completed, with slanting red-tile roofs topped with large solar panels, their black screens appearing almost white in the relentless blaze of the sun that reflected off them. Yards, if you could call them that, were scrabbly and unkempt. Not so much as a cut-grass lawn or a flower bed as we had in California. And yet, there was a humble charm to these premises that spoke of years of care and tending. These were not investment properties owned by the middle-class or wealthy; they were family homes, probably the same family of generation upon generation. I wondered if they were comfortable inside.

"Ade, can you imagine if Santa Cruz houses looked like this? Would they still cost a fortune, do you think?" I asked my seat partner.

Renting a small apartment in the southern San Francisco Bay Area made the first of every month a time of high anxiety for me and many others I knew, despite often working multiple jobs to keep up. In addition to my full-time job as the manager at Castaways Thrift Store, I moonlighted as a window decorator for the sundry small shops on and around Pacific Avenue, the main drag in downtown Santa Cruz. Not exactly the high-income career choices my parents had envisioned for me when they scooted me off to university. I could not imagine a time when I would ever be able to buy even one of the older bungalows in the area. I did not know how anybody could. And yet here, it seemed, even fruit stall proprietors had a house to call their own. Maybe I should quit my low-pay jobs when I got home and move here to open my own stand.

"Yeah, who knows?" answered Adrian, squinting his eyes in the dappled sunlight that refracted through our window. "I mean, they are near the sea. That means big bucks in our 'hood. But I don't think it's the same mentality here. Capitalism doesn't hold the same sway."

"God, I hope not," I said. I blinked my eyes and changed my mental focus from housing to water.

That is, the Mediterranean.

It was somewhere off to our right: the shimmering, shining mega-sea of history and legend. Was it as beautiful as the stories chronicled? Was it as vast and magical as we had read and studied in our school years? I found myself almost jumpy in anticipation of getting to it to find out for myself. And it occurred to me how incredible it was that I was actually here, on a journey of discovery, to experience at last a remnant of the ancient past, a puzzle piece of antiquity. It would have, perhaps, been a bit more romantic if we were on a camel caravan instead of a Kamil Koç tour bus, as I imagined Mallie might point out, but I assuaged my daydreams of eastern-style adventure with the realization of how much cooler and more comfortable this modern mode of transport was in comparison. Although I could have done without the piped in music.

Far from the jangling sounds of the new Constantinople we had left behind, and the glistening minarets and domed palaces of its celebrated, but defunct, empire, here the odd mosque was constructed of concrete block or plain white tile with only one minaret and sometimes a solitary, bedraggled fountain with dull metal faucets, instead of brass or polished chrome. Here, there was little clamor, save that of the bus chugging along and, no doubt, the twitting sounds of different birds outside our soundproofed vehicle. I spotted a few flocks and watched them fly in formation out toward the southern climes. I imagined them heading to an unknown island or some secret nook, rather than hovering in circles around a swarm of Sultanahmet tourists strewing breadcrumbs on a paved and ordered walkway. Speaking of walkways...

The historic Lycian Way beckoned. And it began in Fethiye. We were almost there.

ॐ   ॐ   ॐ

Chapter 7

"Nazar değmesin." Or..."Don't let the evil eye touch you." – Turkish saying

Wednesday, August 14, 2013, Late Night - Istanbul

P az left.
I gave him a bear hug, more genuine than I would have thought myself capable of earlier today—was it really today?—before our unexpected, at least on my part, reunion.

It was now close on midnight. I was the only patron left in the empty foyer, so I put my hands in my pants pockets and slowly headed back up the stairs to my room. Mustafa, thankfully, was nowhere in sight. No one was in sight. The Beşik was silent, save for the buzzing of the naked compact fluorescent light bulbs in the stairwell's sconces on the wall at the bottom of the staircase. The sound irked like an annoying insect, mosquitoes, in my ears. Or was it my bone-tired brain cackling with fatigue? Each step I took felt as if an anchor—or Jacob Marley's ball and chain—was tied to my ankles. It had been an interminable day and the outcome was nothing like I had expected when I arrived here. If it were true that Ömer was not in Turkey, what had started out as my covert retribution expedition would no longer be possible. I stopped at the first turn in the spiraling stairwell's semi-dark and leaned against the cold wall.

Now what?

Before leaving, Paz agreed to meet me outside on the street the next morning at ten, so we could continue our colloquy. So much for the early start I had originally planned. But what was the hurry now?

I pushed myself off the wall and resumed my slow trudge upwards. Well, if nothing else I might get some decent shut-eye. That would be good. Nothing clouded one's thought process like sleep deprivation.

I switched on the light in my room.

Standing in the open doorway, I could not exactly have said what

72

bothered me, but something was off kilter. I was generally exacting about how I laid out my things, both at my apartment and wherever I went. Something to do with my obsessive compulsive tendencies. And I did not remember noticing anything odd when I had been in my room earlier pretending to pick up lira for Paz.

No, something was not right. But what?

My eyes were blurry from the long day and all the flight fatigue and drama, but still...

Blinking profusely, I forced my eyes to focus. Then I scanned the tiny room. My roller suitcase was on the floor in the corner where I had left it. My daypack was on the bed, also where I had left it. So far, so good. But the room still did not look right.

Now entering the room, I shut my outer door quietly, locked it from the inside with the old-fashioned metal key I kept in my front pocket, walked to the bathroom and poked my head in. My towel was hanging on the tiered radiator rack. I touched its edge; it was still damp from my earlier attempt at showering. Toiletries were laid out on the narrow glass bathroom shelf as normal. I did not sense any human presence. In any case, if someone were still in the room, I would have seen them straight away. It was not as if the room had any hiding places. Not even a closet. At this moment, I was very thankful for the humble space.

So, what was wrong?

Shit, I really don't need this now, you know?

I backed out of the bathroom toward the bedroom.

Just in case, I walked slowly around the bed, knelt down and lifted up the hanging edges of the coverlet, trying to make out if anything—or anyone—was underneath the bed itself. No one. Nothing. Well, nothing but a few vagrant balls of white-gray dust loitering on the tile.

Hmm, this is very weird.

I stood up again. I had read about this phenomenon in mystery stories, but I had never experienced it myself: as I looked across the room, the hairs stood up on the back of my neck.

Because I saw it.

My book. *The House on the Strand.* It was Daphne du Maurier's 1969 fictional exploration into the world of the supernatural. A time-travel piece with romantic overtones and an unresolved ending. Right up my alley. I knew the story, had read it at least twice before. The main character, Dick, becomes addicted to an unnamed hallucinogenic drug his buddy, Magnus, has invented. The two end up, separately, time-passaging into fourteenth century Cornwall at a site called Tywardreath. Tywardreath means "house on the strand" in Cornish. I googled it once. Eventually, both men become obsessed with the events and characters, like Isolde, in this past era—with disastrous consequences. The parallels to my own plight were not lost on me. Perhaps because the tale reminded me of my own struggle. With Adrian. With Ömer. With everything that had happened eight years before.

And everything that had not.

I had purchased the book for a dollar at Castaways as an homage to my earliest forays into du Maurier mania. This version was an old paperback whose front cover depicted a watercolor country scene. In the bottom left corner, a rider in a black shirt sat atop a standstill horse facing a copse of deciduous trees surrounded by a low wall that occupied the center of the cover. Diagonally to the left, loomed a white manor house or castle within a green field, presumably unseen by the horse and rider because of the trees. The rest of the scene depicted a slice of sea edged by dark sand, low-lying hills and a blue sky. Mine was only one of many versions of covers publishers had printed over the years.

The book itself now lay at a precise right angle to the edges in the center of the dresser top. As I myself might have placed it had I placed it there. But I had not. Of this, I was certain. I had left it with the other flotsam and jetsam from my daypack lying on the bed earlier in the evening. Admittedly, in a certain disarray, which was not my usual style. And so, it came to me, whomever had put the book there was either like me or was trying to make me think I had put it on the dresser myself.

And that could only mean...*they know me. Or they know what I am like.*

The realization pummeled me like hail.

Someone was following me.

Suddenly, the events of today did not seem like coincidences. Not at all. Especially my meeting with Paz. I began to wonder. Had Paz really come to Istanbul because of an Ömer sighting? Was he here to help me figure out why Ömer had been, or still was, in Santa Cruz? And if so, why would he come out of hibernation after all this time just for that? Was there something else going on? Something more insidious? Paz could, after all, be very mysterious and elusive. And he was even more so now than he used to be. Today's meeting was no accident.

I thought back over our evening together. He had been very cagey about divulging information. At the time, I figured he was tired from the long journey over from the States and was also trying to mitigate the shock of the news he had given me. We were getting reacquainted, after all. One had to allow some latitude. But other than that, I really could not figure out what his true purpose for being here might be.

I had assumed he was going to tell me more tomorrow, after we had both rested and our travel brain fog had evaporated.

But maybe I was wrong. Maybe I was really wrong. *Think!*

Okay. Resolving my Paz dilemma was certainly paramount. But of more immediate concern was cracking the mystery of the walking, climbing paperback novel. Someone had been in my room while I was in the bar with Paz and I wanted to know why.

And what was the deal with *The House on the Strand*?

ॐ   ॐ   ॐ

October 25, 1922 - Constantinople

Ayşegül rushed down the long corridor with its high, white walls and priceless oil paintings.

At the end of the passage, she descended the wide, double staircase and turned the corner into the music room. It was large, though not nearly as large as the Grand Ceremonial Hall, or Muâyede Salonu, which she and the other girls were not allowed to enter. Instead, they sometimes watched official ceremonies there from behind screens on the upper balcony and marveled at the immense crystal chandelier that hung from the center of the domed ceiling.

Here, though, they could mingle as they pleased.

By the time she arrived, Ayşegül's breath came in short gasps. It did not help that in her haste she had tied her sash too tightly. On the far side of the hall, the other musicians, all female, were positioned in their places and re-arranging their skirts and *şalvarlar* around their chairs or their small satin cushions on the floor. Ayşegül ran over, blushing. Everyone would notice her late arrival.

"Where have you been, Ayşegül-*hanım?*" asked Yasmin, a mock-scolding tone in her usually pleasant voice. "Saskar Kadın is put out that you were not here at half seven."

"I know, I was working on my new carpet and forgot to check the time," said Ayşegül, finding her pillow and sitting down.

She quickly retied her sash. Then she placed her instrument case on the floor beside her, undid the latches, opened the lid, and pulled out her *saz*. It was a traditional Anatolian instrument, similar to a lute, she had been

75

told, with a bulbous, pear-shaped body and a long, thin neck. Hers was made of maple wood and had seven strings. The movable frets were always a challenge and she was glad that she sat in the back, so her face would not show while she struggled with the pieces the group would play.

Sazkar Kadın caught her eye and scowled. But at least she did not come over to reprimand Ayşegül, who was not in the mood for an upbraiding.

She settled her *saz* in place and then tapped Yasmin on the shoulder.

"Is the sultan expected tonight?" she asked her friend, in what she hoped was a casual tone.

"Why?" asked Yasmin, grinning. "Do you want him to admire your excellent musicianship?" She chuckled.

Yasmin knew how self-conscious Ayşegül was at these events. But she also knew that almost every girl here wanted to be noticed by His Highness, or "*Şahbaba*," "Emperor Father," as so many people referred to him. Even though he was old, being noticed was how they attained status. And special privileges. Yasmin's words were meant to tease Ayşegül and Ayşegül knew it. But, as they were friends, she did not take offense. She flicked her right hand over her shoulder and pursed her lips into a mock pout.

Then her moue morphed into a small smile. "No more than you," she responded. "I was just curious, that's all. I have not seen him here in several weeks. Have you?"

Yasmin cupped her right hand to her mouth. These walls had ears. Big ones. Speaking in a whisper now, she leaned in toward Ayşegül and said, "No, I don't think so. I heard that he went to Rumelihisarı with Nazikeda Kadın. She wanted to visit Sabiha Sultan—you know, their youngest daughter who got married three years ago? Nazikeda Kadın wants to see the new baby girl, her first grand-daughter, Fatma. *But* I also heard that because of the Greek uprising in Thrace, the sultan had to go to there instead. To join Refet Pasha, you know, the commander of the Western Front? He is there to oust the Allies, they say. Who knows what the truth is? I think it's getting crazy, though." Yasmin paused and examined her friend, whose attention seemed to have drifted. "Haven't you been paying attention, Ayşegül?"

Feigning indifference to Yasmin's question, Ayşegül busied herself arranging her music sheets. After a moment, during which the din of hovering concert patrons became louder, and still preoccupied with her sheets, she shook her head and remarked, "Not really. I mean, I heard some rumors but nothing serious. Who did you get that gossip from? Estreya?

Anyway, I mean, what could happen? Isn't the sultan in charge again? What is there to worry about?"

Yasmin stared at Ayşegül. Ayşegül's casual tone held no hint of guile or intrigue, unusual enough in this place, so she smiled sideways and shrugged. "I guess you're right. I mean, whatever is happening out there, we're in the palace. So, we are safe. I should stop listening to gossip."

Distractedly, Ayşegül nodded and replied, "Yes, that would probably be wise. The less we know about about the *politikalar*, the better."

But as she uttered the words, she was not so sure she believed them. There had been those problems with the Young Turks and that treaty two years ago. Things had not been quite the same since then. She still hoped to get an update from Estreya herself when next she showed up. She wanted some confirmation—or denial—of her already growing sense that something was changing. And it seemed only prudent to be aware of it before it happened. If her life was going to crash down on her again, as seemed possible, she wanted to be prepared. She would not let the course of her life be dictated by others ever again, if she could help it.

But she did not tell her friend these thoughts. If she started to confide one thing, that would lead to her confiding the other. And that, she was not ready to do.

Just then Zeliha rushed over to where Yasmin and Ayşegül sat, cross-legged, on their silk pillows. Her perfect oval face was flushed, and she held the bottom of her saffron-colored kaftan in her right hand, as if afraid of tripping in her hurry. Zeliha, like Ayşegül, loved more traditional costumes, especially at gatherings such as this one.

"Ayşe. Ayşegül," she whispered loudly. Guests and other residents started to fill the temporary seats arranged in a semi-circle around the short stage platform. Yasmin and Ayşegül looked up.

"Oh, *selam*, Zeliha-*hanım*, I was looking for you," said Ayşegül, her mouth upturned and her small teeth gleaming. "I did not see you before."

"I was in the hallway talking to Hande-*hanım*. I saw you come in, but I couldn't get away. You know how she can be." Zeliha rolled her gray-blue eyes.

"Yes, it is sometimes hard to get Hande to stop yacking, that's true, but her name really does suit her. She always seems so happy," said Ayşegül, and Yasmin nodded up and down vigorously.

"That's true," agreed Yasmin. "She is a good-natured *kız*."

"Anyway," continued Ayşegül. Then a movement in her peripheral view caught her eye. "Oh, there's Saskar Kadın now. I think the concert is about to start. But I'm glad you are here. I have something to ask you later."

Zeliha knitted her brows together. "Really?" she asked. "How strange. Because I have something to tell you."

From the corner of her eye, Ayşegül saw Saskar Kadın sashay over to the small band of young women and their various instruments. She watched the head woman clap her hands three times. Three loud cracks resounded through the salon. That was her signal.

The girls stopped chatting. Now Emsalinur Kadın, a portly, middle-aged woman with gray-streaked hair, made her way slowly toward the small band. She raised her arms to conduct the first piece of music of the evening. Appropriately, it was an old folk song well-loved by all Turkish peoples, "*Kâtibim.*" Even Ayşegül liked this tune. It was about a clerk traveling to Üsküdar in the nearby north. And it reminded her of home.

❧   ❧   ❧

June 7, 2005, Even Later – On the Road to Fethiye

After Adrian's happy prediction, I settled back in my seat for the remainder of the ride. From time to time during that hour, I glanced out the window across the aisle at the view toward the west. There were fewer trees now and the vegetation grew sparser. The sun hovered at its high point, suffusing everything in its domain with a heightened glare. In addition to the occasional, but far fewer, fruit stands and a smattering of half-built, rebar-adorned houses, I began to see road signs for Çalış Beach. That was the starting point for our local tour. But the bus station was in the main town of the area, Fethiye, a little farther on, according to the signs. We would go to the end of the line where someone (I hoped) would pick us up and escort us to our *pansiyon.*

Mallie must have seen the signs, too, as I noticed her fidgeting in front of us. Paz stirred slightly, his tan outback hat spread over his face, and was flattened down as far in the seat as it was possible to be without actually oozing onto the floor. He must have been snoozing since we left the last rest stop. I wondered how. The bus was comfortable as buses go, but spacious it was not. Nor quiet, what with the perpetual pop and folk music blaring. Personally, I would have preferred taking a train for the thirteen-hour ride, but Zeynep, our vivacious travel guide in Istanbul, had informed us that Turkey did not have a passenger train culture. The bus was the way to go. If you were on a budget, that is. Otherwise, driving a car or flying were it.

Many of our fellow passengers certainly had the look of budget about them. I ran a thrift store; I knew budget. If it was good enough for them, it was good enough for us.

And yet, I was relieved to be on the last leg.

Next to me, Adrian closed his travel book with a papery smack. He carefully slid the inch-thick Turkey guide into the outside pocket of his cobalt blue daypack. Then he rubbed his palms together as if he had just devoured a seriously satisfying meal instead of a small pack of crisps.

"Well, this ought to be interesting," he mused. He leaned back in his seat, folding his hands behind his head. "You know, Mole buddy, I think this might turn out to be one of the best decisions we've made, coming down this way. According to *Lonely Planet*, there's tons of stuff to do here. A lot of history, too."

He crossed his legs at the ankles. Their length must have made the interminable ride even more uncomfortable for him than for me. My mind flashed back to the day we first met—at the Santa Cruz roller coaster— and how he struggled to find a place for those long limbs in the ride's little car. At times like now, I mused, there were distinct benefits to being medium height.

I bent towards my feet. I was tying my hiking boot laces to be ready for our imminent disembarkation, and realized I was excited at the prospect of more rugged sight-seeing than what Istanbul offered. Still hanging forward, I twisted my neck to look up toward Adrian.

"Yeah? Sounds good, Ade. I'm ready. I remember Zeynep telling us about some canyon that was recently discovered. Remember? Isn't that on our itinerary?"

"Saklıkent. Yep. I think it's full of water and we actually hike through it. Sounds awesome." Adrian puckered his lips and made a continual swishing sound, one of his idiosyncrasies when excited.

"What's that?" came Mallie's throaty voice through the seat crack. "What are you guys talking about?"

"Oh, hey, Mal. You're back from the dead," joked Adrian. Mallie tilted her head to the left and grimaced.

"Haha. Yes, and I'm sooooo ready to escape this coffin." She poked Paz. "Paz! Wake up! We're almost there." I saw his right shoulder slide off the seat back toward the aisle at the same time his right arm grabbed the seat back in front of him.

"What?" he asked, shaking his head. "What's up? Why are you jabbing

79

me, girl?"

"We're almost in Fethiye, Sleepy." She blew him a kiss and smiled. "We already passed that beach we're staying at. So, get ready. Show time."

Paz raised both arms to shoulder height, his fisted hands punching the air above his head in rhythm with his words. "*Yes! Yes! Finally!*" And on "Finally!" he thrust both arms into straight beams, a gesture that might well have punctured the ceiling fabric above him if the ceiling had been a few inches lower. Paz's ability to go from zero to sixty without a lapse always amazed me. It was a trait he and Mallie shared.

"Well," said Adrian, laughing. "I guess you're not dead, after all, Paz, dude. We've been wondering if we were gonna have to borrow a body bag from the driver."

"Not bloody likely," said Paz, still shaking his fists, though now with a more subdued enthusiasm. "If anyone is going out in a body bag, it's not gonna be me."

Truer words were never uttered.

After a few more kilometers of cruising down the main highway our bus careened off to the right onto an arterial road. At first, I thought the whole vehicle would topple as my face banged onto the back of Paz's seat. But the bus stayed the course and I pushed myself back to sitting, rubbing my forehead.

My friends were antsy, I could tell. So was I. We craned our necks, gaping out our windows as we tried to take in the new scenery.

"Oh my God, did you see that?" squeaked Mallie.

"See what?" asked Paz, his voice still thick with sleep, despite his exuberant expostulation a moment ago.

"Four people on a scooter! How could you miss it? A man was driving, his wife was sitting behind him, and she was holding a baby—on her hip! Then there was a little boy standing on the floorboard in front of his dad, holding onto the handlebars. And guess what else?"

"What?" asked Paz again, and he peeked around his seat with a conspiratorial wink at me.

"Surprise, surprise, the only person wearing a helmet was the father. Figures," said Mallie, shaking her head. "Obviously, no helmet laws here."

"Wow," said Paz. "That is truly horrible, Mal." He winked at me again.

Adrian and I both rocked our heads side to side, raising our eyebrows at each other while trying not to laugh. Mallie was clearly offended by the sight of the scooter family, and it would not help anyone if we fanned the fire of her wrath by laughing. Four people on one small scooter would never happen where we came from. Mallie was right, it probably was not the safest way to travel but, hey, it was things like that that made me appreciate the different culture we were in. What would be the point of traveling if everything were just like home? If everything were "safe?"

"It's, like, really funky here," Paz continued. Was he talking about the scooter menage, or changing the subject? I guessed the latter; more than likely he did not want to get wrangled into a repartee with Mallie so soon after waking up. "All those little shops crammed into each other." He sounded a little disappointed. "A lot more developed than I thought it would be. But not quite as chockablock as Sultanahmet, at least."

Adrian, always the chipper, cheerer-upper, interjected. "I think this is the big town in these here parts, and this is probably a main drag if the bus is taking it, right? So it kind of makes sense it's going to be a little more dense. Oh, ha! I rhymed. Get it? Sense and dense?" He grinned, fanned his palms toward the ceiling and shrugged. The other three of us rolled our eyes and shook our heads.

"No, seriously," he continued. "But I don't think the whole area is like this. The maps show that most of it isn't actually built up. Don't worry, buddy."

Paz nodded. "Hope you're right, Ade. I was looking forward to not being in a megalopolis anymore."

"We aren't," Adrian said in a soothing tone. Then he pointed. "Hey guys, look, we're here. The *Otogar* station. At finally fucking last."

We high-fived each other over the tops of our seats and shouted, "Yay!"

A few of our headscarved and be-capped traveling compatriots turned our way. Some smiled, some shook their heads. The lone guy with the phony Ray-Bans glanced at us for a second and, with no other hint of reaction, returned to his former forward-facing position. As the bus pulled into its marked spot in front of the long, single-story station, everyone stood up, stretched their legs or arms, and began to gather their belongings.

"Party time," said Adrian.

"Beer time," said Paz.

The four of us lurched along the tiny aisle, juggling our various packs. One by one we jumped off the vinyl steps to the waiting asphalt of the *otogar's* parking lot and began the search for our escort.

Despite the hustle and bustle all around us, during which I lost interest in the other travelers, it did not take long to find him. A bear-like young man approached us holding a small, white poster-board sign on which a black felt pen had written:

81

ADRIAN AND FREINDS

"Hey, that's us!" shouted Paz, with a whoop. "There can't be too many Adrian and 'freinds' in these here parts. Vamoose!"

Still clutching our various gear, me helping Mallie shift her over-large Gregory pack higher onto her left shoulder, we all but ran over to our driver. He was standing behind a scrupulously clean, white Ford minivan.

"Are you Genghis?" asked Adrian, stopping just in front of the upheld sign. He pronounced the name with hard "g" sounds.

With his free hand, the bear man began to push up the van's rear door, revealing a black, cavernous interior. He frisbeed the sign inside then gestured toward the empty space. As we began to throw our packs in, he answered Adrian's question.

"*Evet*, I mean, yes. Is 'Cengis,' like Genghis Khan. You know, in Turkish language the letter 'C,' it make a sound like your English 'J.'" He chuckled. "But call me George. It is more easy for you." He bowed his head and closed his eyes for a second. Opening them again, he scanned each of us in turn. "Come, we get into to my van now. Then you say me your names."

"Sounds good," said Adrian, shaking Cengis's, aka George's, hand. "Thank you for coming to get us. Can we just call you Cengis, though?"

"No problem," answered Cengis, not George, airily, with that lilting, sing-song emphasis on the "no" that we often encountered in Turkish locals' speech. It seemed to be no different down here in the south than in the north. I found that continuity somewhat comforting. Perhaps our limited Turkish would not be as troubling as I had feared. It was one thing to travel in a major tourist destination where locals expected to speak other languages if they wanted to exploit the would-be spenders, quite another to veer off the chosen path into the distant backwaters.

I was soon to discover most definitively that language barriers would not be our problem. That would be reserved for trouble of an altogether more sinister nature.

82

The five of us climbed into the van from its two sides. Adrian, of course, took the passenger seat up front. I ushered Mallie into the back middle seat and plopped by the window behind the driver's. Paz grabbed the opposite window seat. Glancing over my shoulder as I settled in, I saw our packs lying crumpled in the back compartment, as if exhausted and ready for a long nap. I empathized.

Cengis, meanwhile, had slipped into the driver's spot and started the engine. The van proceeded towards the parking lot's exit. My heart raced into my throat, all traces of travel fatigue forgotten. We had finally made it to the Mediterranean.

"Okay, now I ask your names," announced Cengis, as he pulled out of the *otogar* lot.

From my backseat window, I saw that the road we turned onto was narrow, but adjacent to an embankment at the bottom of which an urban stream flowed, its olive-green water dotted with tiny white ripples. Access to the stream was barred by wooden fencing, like that I used to see in horse country in the States. Except this was not made with flat, white two by fours. Instead, the slats were rounded and painted a viridescent green shade. *Does this stream flow to the Med?* I wondered, feeling a ripple of adrenaline course through me.

Adrian, sitting next to Cengis, introduced each of us in turn. He called me Molo, which rather surprised me. But I was glad. I was so accustomed to my nickname by now, that my real name did not seem to fit me anymore. Sometimes, even when I saw it in my passport or other document, I wondered who that person was. It suddenly occurred to me that I was transforming. Whatever that meant. One thing was certain, though. I was more and more becoming aware of a shift in my sense of myself.

These reflections I kept silent. As always. If the others were aware of them, they did not divulge any of that awareness to me. For the most part, they seemed to see me as the same old Molo I had always been for them: reliable, quiet, game. Maybe a bit eccentric. Because I did not myself quite understand the nature of this shift, it was easier for me to keep the status quo. No need to voice my thoughts aloud.

"*Ecdanını sikiyim!*" yelled Cengis. I had to brace myself when our van screeched to a sudden stop. "Sorry, my friends. This idiot pull out in front of me. No problem. It is happen all the time here." Then he laughed, exuberantly banging his right hand on the steering wheel.

"It's more crowded than I thought it would be," remarked Adrian. "Is Fethiye a big place?"

"Fethiye is biggest town on this coast until Antalya. But not so big. Just many idiots here." Again, Cengis laughed. He seemed to enjoy the idea of living in a city full of idiots. *Curious people, these Turks.*

Adrian turned around in his seat to face us.

"Antalya's a couple hours east of here," he said. "I read it in *Lonely Planet.*"

The three of us in the back just nodded. Our windows were closed, so the air conditioning, which seemed to be working at full blast, could do its job protecting us from the Mediterranean late spring heat. Its loud thrum made it difficult to hear the conversation up front.

Instead of talking, I eyed the people bustling along the streets, the women in those long coats, the men in their pointed leather shoes. They seemed almost as intent on their business as the people in the Sultanahmet. And yet, there was a different air about them. I could not quite pinpoint what that difference was. No doubt I would figure it out over time.

"How far is it to the *pansiyon*?" Mallie asked Cengis in her sweetest voice.

"Maybe fifteen minutes more," he responded. "Don't worry. We will not get in accident. Fethiye drivers is crazy, but not dangerous." He paused, then continued, "You will love Çalış Beach. Not so crazy. And very beautiful. Many people come there."

"We heard about it from Zeynep. In Istanbul?" said Adrian.

"Yes, yes," said Cengis, nodding. "I know Zeynep. She is very nice lady. Sends us many tourists. Like you." He blinked and bobbed his head.

Cengis was one of the burlier Turkish guys I had come across. Though similar in age to us, I figured—mid- to late twenties—he looked older. For one, he was almost as tall as Adrian, but compared to Adrian with his thin, sleek stature, Cengis looked overly fond of *pides* and baklava. Turks loved their desserts, I knew. And their heavily sugared *çay*. Weight aside, another contributing element to Cengis's preternaturally aged look was his hairstyle. Adrian, Paz and I all let our hair grow, though not past our shoulders. Cengis's on the other hand, was cropped close. This short look accentuated his round face and that distinctive flat back of the head I had already noticed on many of the men on our bus. Cengis did not sport a mustache, as so many Turkish men did, but the dark circles under his eyes detracted from the youthful appearance his otherwise smooth skin might have given him. He probably worked impossible hours. Zeynep informed us that guys down here only had a few months to make most of their year's wages, and they would do almost anything and everything to

84

accommodate the tourists who were paying them. I vowed not to ask too much of Cengis once we were situated.

As he made a sudden sharp right turn, I spotted a chalky blue mosque behind a group of shady trees. In the spaces between branches and leaves, I noticed several older men pacing nearby. I was surprised to see them with yarmulke-like caps on their heads, despite the heat. This mosque, as much as I could tell in that flash moment, was a much paler version of anything I had seen in Istanbul: smaller, shorter, only one minaret, and nestled quietly in a secluded park-like setting. Nothing like the giant, gilded, multi-minareted mega-mosques erected on large esplanades we were accustomed to. It occurred to me it had been a while since I had heard a call to prayers. Not since we had climbed aboard the Kamil Koç. I wondered if the prayers would be as loud here as in Istanbul, their transcendent words mingling and clashing down the streets like dueling chants.

I hoped not.

Fascinating and mesmerizing as I often found the prayers, they could be disruptive, especially at five in the morning, waking me prematurely. After two nights on a bus, I was ready for a quieter brand of sleep. Something, I hoped, reflecting the peaceful calm of the mythic sea we had come down here to investigate.

As I was thinking these placid thoughts, I glanced to my left. A two-story McDonald's made me raise my eyebrows, as I had not expected to see one here, but after that, all regular buildings on that side vanished. Jacaranda trees, most of their purple-blue blooms now withering, took their place. They stood sentry over trellised wooden benches spaced some thirty feet apart along a wide promenade. Now I noticed the occasional, what looked like, white and brown-painted food kiosks with their backs to us. In between them, I spotted pedestrians, mostly young couples, sauntering along a salmon pink walkway. Some had small children in tow, drinking juice out of cartons through almost invisible straws. The odd single man in pointy-toed leather dress shoes, as well as black-haired teenage girls in school uniforms, ambled in the opposite direction, toward the town behind us. And then...

"Hey. Guys," I shouted. "There it is. The Mediterranean!" I found myself edging closer to my window, practically pasting my face to its cold, air conned surface. "We're here!"

"Oh, yeah, you're right, Molo. Awesome!" exclaimed Mallie. Suddenly she perked up in her seat next to me, almost knocking my face out of the

85

way when she nudged her body next to mine for a better view out my window. "Paz, look!"

Paz, on the opposite side of the back seat, peered past Mallie's shoulders. "Sweet," he said. "Can't wait to dive in there."

From the front seat, Adrian added eagerly, "We should be able to swim today. I mean, it's not even two o'clock." Then, turning to Cengiz, he asked, "Our tour doesn't officially start 'til tomorrow morning, right?"

Cengiz nodded. "Of course. You swim today, no problem. Very soon we are at hotel."

Now our van drove along a straight, two-lane road. On our left, we had a nonstop view of the famous Mediterranean, sparkling and bright and spanning out to infinity. Or at least to where sea and sky merged into one perfect semblance of infinity. To my novice's eye, its beauty equaled that of the Pacific—perhaps even outdid it. For here the water, unlike the often-olive cast of our beloved California ocean, shone an iridescent kind of blue I had only ever seen in travel brochures. Its brilliance and heightened color were almost surreal. Not only that but, also unlike the roiling, dramatic surface of the northern Pacific, here it was as calm and serene as bathwater. The temperature would be warm and soothing and inviting. I found I just wanted to melt in, perhaps never to come out.

As the four of us ogled the giant expanse of watery heaven, Cengis took another right and the mirage-like view was suddenly lost. We slumped back in our seats, all of us with a kind of daze in our eyes. At least, I could see it in Paz's and Mallie's and just assumed Adrian, in the front, bore the same bedazzled expression.

Cengis laughed. "Here we say '*Akdeniz*.' It mean 'White Sea.'"

"Oh, wow, cool. 'White Sea.' I like that," said Adrian in a far-away voice. "How lucky for you that you live here and have known it all your life."

"No, no. I come from north. Kayseri. We do not have any sea there. Only desert," and he hooted quite loudly. "Desert and carpets!" He chuckled. "I come here only three years before. To make money. From tourists. Like you!"

His sudden guffaw was infectious and the four of us joined him.

"And now, we are here," he said, jovially. He pulled the van over to the side of a narrow dirt road and parked it under a gigantic, dusty fig tree. "Welcome to Mavi Dolfin Evi. It mean Blue Dolphin House. *Hoşgeldiniz!*"

In my excitement and relief, I never expected anything but smooth sailing ahead.

Chapter 8

"When you're a traveler, ask a traveler for advice, not someone whose lameness keeps him in one place." – Mevlana (aka Rumi)

Wednesday, August 14, 2013, Still Late Night - Istanbul

I slowly approached the dresser and stared down at the book. Should I pick it up? Could there be something dangerous on it? The British crime series I had watched taught me that poison could be placed on paper and, if touched, would cause illness or even death. Neither of those options were part of my agenda.

I compromised.

Turning around, I headed toward the bathroom and unrolled some toilet paper from the roll sitting on the sink shelf where I had moved it earlier, before my shower. I folded the paper into a five-inch square, placed it in my right hand and retraced my steps to the dresser.

A book is just a book. Inanimate, lifeless, dead. And yet, looking again at the printed volume lying on the dresser, a thought came to me. There is a story within its folds that is dramatic and stirs up one's senses with characters and plots. Could it be that it has another kind of life, too? A life that is made up of those who have touched its bindings, thumbed its pages, absorbed its printed words through their eyes? Does it hold secrets or mysteries beyond the words themselves? Is it, in fact, alive?

Okay, now you're really out there. You need sleep. Just pick up the thing already.

Squinting my eyes and recoiling my body slightly backward, and with the toilet paper firmly in my hand, I reached forward, cautiously.

DO IT!

My hand grabbed at the paperback's corner that was closest to me, and I started to slide the book in my direction. But my grip was tenuous, and it slipped out of my grasp, flopping back onto the dresser top.

Damn.

I tried again, reaching toward its center for more traction.

Gotcha, sucker.

Now, toilet paper still protecting my skin, I slid my fingers and thumb farther along the cover's surface, both on top and underneath, until I had a better grasp. I started to raise the whole volume off the dresser and then...

Thud!

It fell onto the floor tiles.

Good one, you clod.

As I bent forward to pick it up again, a thin piece of beige paper floated to the floor at my feet.

What the...?

Leaving *The Strand* where it lay askew before me, I crinkled up my eyes and mouth in confusion and gently placed the toilet paper on top of what looked like a little note. I did not recognize it. How had it gotten there? I picked up this note and brought it close to my face, scrutinizing its makeup. The scrap of paper was four inches by five inches or so, slightly rectangular, and I could make out tiny splashes of different colored fibers embedded in it. *Hmm, homemade?* What else? I turned it over.

There, in a scratchy kind of artwork executed in black ink were, not words, or a printed message, as one might expect on a note stuck inside a book, but this:

"What?" I asked out loud, somewhat disappointed. I do not know exactly what I was anticipating, but certainly not this. "The hell?"

Blinking, I carried the small rag with me and sat down on the edge of my bed, staring at it. I turned the paper around, this way and that, trying to make sense of the curious picture inscribed there. For better focus, I brought it closer to my bleary eyes again and blinked. Still, I could not make it out. Whatever this was, whether or not it was indeed some kind of a message to me, I had no comprehension of its significance.

What does it mean?

I reached over, carefully placing the scrap on the lamp table by my bed and laid the toilet paper on top of it. Just in case. I did not want to touch it by accident, nor did I want it to blow away. Though I had not a clue as to why this little picture should be in my book, in my room, on my trip, I realized that staring at it all night would not make anything clearer to my already befuddled mind.

I was utterly exhausted and needed shut-eye. Whatever this was about, it would simply have to wait until the morning.

After ensuring the piece of paper was securely nestled on the little wooden table, I got up, kicked off my shoes, and then removed my Hawaiian shirt and khaki trousers, folding them over my rolling case. I turned off the overhead light from the switch above the table, and, enshrined in darkness at last, collapsed on top of the mattress.

This was surely the longest day I had ever experienced.

જ   જ   જ

Early September 1922

Demetrius placed the battered red fez on his head, bent forward into the wind, and began to walk.

જ   જ   જ

October 25, 1922 - Constantinople

"What was it you wanted to ask me, Ayşegül-*hanım*?"

The concert was finished at last, and with great relief Ayşegül sat on the long divan under the room's largest window, sipping a rose *şerbet* out of a tall crystal glass. Glancing out the window for a moment, she noticed the cloudless sky was fully black now and the moon's partial visage shone bright and immutable.

Yasmin had joined a small group of other musicians across the room, but Zeliha sat next to Ayşegül, fanning her face with a piece of sheet music.

Turning back to face the room, Ayşegül lowered her glass into her lap and looked intently at Zeliha.

"Nothing important. I was just wondering...did you knock at my room earlier this evening? Before the concert? It's just...someone banged on my door, but when I opened it, they were gone. I thought it was you. Maybe to tell me to hurry for the concert?"

Zeliha's lower lip protruded. She lifted her thick eyebrows and shook her head slowly side to side. "No, Ayşegül, it wasn't me." She shrugged her shoulders.

"Oh," said Ayşegül. "That's peculiar. I wonder who it was. You don't know, do you?" And she took a quick sip of her drink while waiting for her friend's reply.

"I'm sorry." Zeliha paused as she took a moment to think. "No, I don't. Perhaps it was Yasmin." She flicked her head in Yasmin's direction.

"I already asked her. She doesn't know anything about it. Well, whoever it was, it sounded urgent. But I guess it wasn't, after all."

Ayşegül set her glass down beside her on the thin, hard cushion she and her friend occupied. She studied the arabesque design in its fabric and briefly considered that she might work a similar design into her next carpet.

"Oh well. It doesn't matter. Must have been a mistake." She lifted her arms and stretched them overhead. "*Tanrım*, I am tired now. So happy that silly concert is over. I didn't make too many mistakes, did I?"

Zeliha put her left hand on Ayşegül's jacketed shoulder and chuckled. Her laugh was silvery and high and full of good humor.

"Oh, Ayşegül-*hanım*, you are funny. No, I think you did okay. At least Saskar Kadın did not glare at you this time! Remember last year that time she came over and ripped your *saz* out of your hands? I thought she was going to break it over your head!" Bringing both her hands up to her mouth, she began to laugh out loud. "The look on your face when she came up to you. You turned purple. I was so anxious what was going to happen to you. But now it does seem a little bit hilarious, don't you think?"

Ayşegül threw her hands onto the top of her head. "Oh, Zeliha, I had forgotten about that night. How horrible Saskar Kadın was. I was so embarrassed. I'm surprised she still forces me to play at the concerts."

"Maybe she thinks it will make you play better," said Zeliha. Her expression showed she did not believe it.

"Oh, yes," giggled Ayşegül. "But we know the truth. '*Balık kavağa çıkınca!'* I will get better when the fish climbs the tree."

She grabbed Zeliha's upper arms and they collapsed into each other in a fit of hysterics.

Zeliha chortled, almost choking. "Better stick to carpet weaving, Ayşegül. You're better than anyone here. Even the fish."

The two girls burst into another short round of laughter. Then Zeliha paused and looked up toward the plastered ceiling. "Except for Maryam, of course. She is the master." Ayşegül nodded in wordless agreement.

After a few more chuckles, the two friends broke apart, wiping the tears from their faces. Others in the room turned to look at them and their stern faces showed disapproval.

Ayşegül immediately feigned a serious demeanor, picked up her now warm *şerbet* again, took a sip, and asked, "Now what were you going to tell me, Zeliha-*hanım*? Remember, before the concert you mentioned you had something to say."

As Zeliha opened her mouth to speak, a loud clamour erupted in the hallway outside the concert salon. It was like a stampede of large herd animals. Ayşegül remembered that sound from the farms surrounding her old home where many people kept horses. And yet this was somehow more frightening because she was certain it did not come from animals, but from men. Men who were not in a peaceful mood. The thunderous disruption of the previously peaceful atmosphere was reminiscent of her own past, and she shook inside.

All chattering in the salon halted abruptly. The women in the room stood still, like the background characters in a shadow play when the main characters emerged onto the stage. A few girls glanced wildly around them, their eyes wide with fright.

Zeliha's mouth still hung open. Ayşegül shifted uncomfortably on the divan, spilling some of her pink *şerbet* onto the large blue carpet underneath her. She stared at the closed double door leading into the salon and clutched her glass to her chest.

The door burst open. A statuesque military man with a thick, curling mustache and the front half of his scalp bare of hair, strode into the room. His knee-high boots thudded on the wooden entrance floor, but deadened as he himself stopped dead on the carpet. He wore a uniform that Ayşegül recognized as the one worn by the Caliphate Army. This was the army that supported their sultan, Mehmed VI, in his fight both against the European Allies and the Turkish nationalist army led by the upstart general, Mustafa Kemal. His high collar was blood red. Gold-colored epaulets and thick ropes draped across his chest, while flower-shaped medals adorned the front of his coat. It was an impressive array; he must be important, Ayşegül thought. She recognized the man from the formal ceremonies she had witnessed in the Muâyede Salonu. Because she and the other women had only been allowed to watch, secluded, from the second story balcony, she had had a very good view of the man's bald pate.

"That's Süleyman Şefik Pasha!" gasped Zeliha, her mouth finally shifting out of its shocked position. "What is he doing here?"

Ayşegül wanted to ask her friend how she knew who the pasha was, but she also silently prayed he had not overheard Zeliha's outburst.

Two men in similar, but less decorated, uniforms flanked the pasha as, now stopped, he surveyed the room. Other soldiers waited, at stiff attention in the hall outside.

Saskar Kadın was the senior lady in the room. She gathered her skirt hem and strode purposefully up to the pasha commander. Then she performed a slight bow as she placed her right hand gently across her ample chest.

"How may I help you, Süleyman Şefik Pasha?" she asked, her low, stern voice echoing across the silent room.

The pasha bowed to her in return. "I am sorry to interrupt your gathering, Saskar Kadın, but I have come to have an audience with the sultan. I hoped he was here. It's quite urgent." His voice sounded high and strained. Something had happened.

During their exchange, Ayşegül watched the two eldest members in the room with interest. Because the palace was strictly segregated, men from women, she was surprised that the two knew each other. On the other hand, Saskar Kadın had lived there for many years as a liaison between the sultan himself and those—such as Ayşegül—who were trapped in the harem. It was likely she was familiar with all the important male—and female— visitors to the palace.

Saskar Kadın pursed her lips tightly. Ayşegül was sure she was not pleased with the sudden intrusion of these men, important as they were, into the harem. It was not the accepted way. But Ayşegül watched as Saskar Kadın's face softened a little. *Çanak yalayıcı,* thought Ayşegül. *Suck up.*

Immediately she was ashamed for her disrespectful thought. It could not be easy for Saskar Kadın to be in charge at such a moment. Was she scared? Ayşegül had never witnessed Saskar Kadın display fear of any kind.

Saskar Kadın spoke again. "The sultan is not here, I'm afraid." She looked around the room at the sea of women's faces intent on her and the three men in front of her. Then she nodded toward the door and said, "Please, come this way. I will tell you what I know, Pasha Bey." She curtsied.

The pasha nodded brusquely, turned on his heels and, after Saskar Kadın swished by him, took one long stride to catch up to her departing figure.

His two officers, in stiff unison, moved aside to let the pasha and the lady pass and then, like curtains closing at the end of an act, fell into place behind them.

When they were gone, one of the older girls closed the double door and after a second or two, a bee-like buzz began to infiltrate the silence in the salon.

"What was that all about?" asked Zeliha.

Just then, little Hande trotted over to where Zeliha and Ayşegül waited.

"Allah, Allah," she piped. "Did you see that? Something is happening, something big is really happening. Don't you think?" Her normally squeaky, animated tone was even more so now.

"*Evet*, you are probably right, Hande-*hanım*," answered Zeliha. "I am sure you are right." She put her hands on her hips and cocked her head. "But what?"

Ayşegül stared at her friends. She could hardly move. For after this surprise incident, and the pasha's urgency, she, too, realized Hande was right. Something was happening. She could no longer pretend that all was as usual at the palace of the sultan, could no longer bury her head in the sand, knowing what she knew. About herself, her predicament, what she had done. She was not privy to affairs of state, but it was obvious that the country was in more turmoil than she had realized. She could not stand by and let the dice land where they might. She had a decision to make and she would have to make it immediately. Time was no longer on her side. She did not have the luxury now to wait for *eşref saati*, for the stars to be aligned.

Allah karhetsin, she thought. *Damn it*. She looked toward the uncurtained window, out at the big night sky. *Oh, Moon*, she sighed. *Please, please. You must help me. I need you now.*

    ชิ   ชิ   ชิ

Thursday, August 15, 2013, Morning - Istanbul

Should I tell Paz about the weird sketch? This was my second thought upon waking the next morning.

My first thought was, *What did that djinn, Naji, say to me, again?*

Through all the strange events and surprises of the day before, my post-flight dream—or whatever it was—had lurked in the recesses of my mind.

94

I still had a niggling sense that Naji's words held some significance for me, if I could only recall what they were. The only thing I could really remember about him was the disturbing image of his strange, swirling shape and those disgusting teeth.

Morning light filtered through the slits in the curtains above me. I stretched my arms and felt the stiffness in my body ease a little. Yawning, I reached for my flip phone where it lay behind the toilet paper-wrapped art diagram. My eyes were crusted over, but even so, I could just make out the the time. Nine o'clock. Yikes! I must have slept hard. So hard, I had missed the five a.m. muezzin prayer calls. That was something, at least.

I flopped back onto the rock-like mattress, trying to decide my next course of action. Everything had changed since Paz had shown up. Now I did not know why I was here. If there was no Ömer, my plan of retribution for what he had done—to Adrian—was dead.

Paz.

What was he up to?

Ömer.

What was he doing in Santa Cruz?

Christ. Just get up and get dressed. You've got a date with The Paz Man in less than an hour. Maybe, at last, he'll actually tell you what is going on.

I glanced over at the mystery paper. *Questions three, four and five. Who came in my room and why did they put that thing in my book? What is it about?*

I shook my head and rapidly opened and closed my eyes to jog the night crust apart. I felt as if some unknown entity had usurped my trip. My agenda. My life. It was all beginning to feel like too much. But I forced myself to sit up. Then I untangled my legs from the too-thin coverlet and swiveled my body so that my feet touched the cold tile floor.

"Carpe diem," I said out loud. "Remember Robin Williams." Even as my other self, I loved that movie, *Dead Poets Society*. "Seize the day" and all that. Well, I had better *carpe diem* and get my ass moving. I now had only forty-five minutes before my meeting with Paz. And I needed to prepare for it, not only physically, but mentally.

The room was stifling. I opened the curtains and blinked several times as the glare of day assaulted my half-closed eyes. I felt like the released prisoner in the Plato's Cave allegory. Freed at last and introduced to the sun, he is so accustomed to the shadowy illusions of fire projected on the inner wall of the deep cave where he has been imprisoned his entire life, he cannot accept this new reality. What was my reality now? Paz's sudden

95

reappearance had caused everything to shift.

Stop thinking about it. "Boşver," the Turks said. "Let it go." And get going.

To that end, I padded to the bathroom for my morning splash in the device that pretended to be a shower. My towel had finally dried. Its roughness got my skin tingling, at least. After all that, but still slightly groggy, I tread naked back over to my suitcase, rolled it to the bed as quietly as I could manage and hoisted it on top of the crumpled bedclothes. The sound of the zipper as I opened the main compartment of the case jangled in my ears.

Dang, kid. You've got to get it together. This is undoubtedly going to be another hairy day, because Paz is surely up to something and you need to be ready.

I rustled around inside the case, grabbing a pair of beige cargo pants and my favorite, turquoise-colored tee-shirt. Paz would chuckle. For old time's sake, and because the design reminded me of happier times, I had managed to get a silk screen shop to copy the mola design from my old, worn out shirt onto this one. The design featured a jaguar with the head of a bird, a phoenix maybe, flanked by two opposing crescent moons and twinkling stars. The intricate, parallel layers of varying vibrant colors rendered the main subject difficult to discern, as it seemed to be camouflaged behind all the color. I always felt that was part of a mola's mystique. When I had the new shirt made, I had never expected Paz to see it. Again, it occurred to me that strange coincidences were happening all over the place. Never in my life had I experienced such a phenomenon. Until now.

I completed my ablutions, even applying a fresh coat of mascara. Then I stood over the night table, removed the toilet paper from the mystery note, and stared at its curious design. Indeed, it was quite as abstruse as my mola. Really, did I think someone had poisoned that paper? I must have been whacked out last night. All the dramatics with Paz had distorted my thinking.

I wadded up the toilet tissue and tossed it into the small wastebasket beside the table. Gingerly, I picked up the note between my thumb and forefinger, making sure not to crumple or tear it. Grabbing my travel pouch with my free hand, I lodged it under my chin and zipped open the longer side pocket where I kept my passport. Carefully, I slipped the note between two pages in the booklet, zippered up the pocket and clipped the wallet around my waist under my tee-shirt. I did not know why someone had left me the mystifying picture, but I had come to the conclusion that I did not want anyone to see it. Not even Paz. In fact, it might be best if I did not mention the incident of the intrusion at all. I would see how things progressed and revisit my options later.

I scanned my small, meager room, shoved my feet into my rubbery Gezers, grabbed my bag and left. This time I double checked that the door was locked.

ॐ　　　ॐ　　　ॐ

"Second, whatever I was looking for was always you." – Mevlana (aka Rumi)

June 1997

"I've gotta go on, again," I screamed, trying to make myself heard above the clacking machine mechanisms. "Are you two coming?"

The three of us, Paz and Mallie and I, had just stumbled out through the openings of our red compact cars and onto the waiting ramp of the ride. They had shared a car and I had had the front one to myself. The way I liked it.

Now, as I rushed down the exit ramp, panting, I glanced back and saw Paz and Mallie clasped onto each other. She was bent over in laughter, and he was rubbing her hair with one hand as he held onto her right arm with his other hand. I smiled. The evening of the bizarre tent performance was a couple months past now. Since then, the three of us had cemented our bond with an almost daily outing of one kind or another. I was surprised that Paz and Mallie spent so much of their time with me. It seemed their love was inclusive. One of our favorite haunts was the Giant Dipper roller coaster at the Santa Cruz Pier. Or, it was mine.

"Well? You guys coming, or what? Hurry, the line's filling up!" I called out, still running. To re-embark, you had to exit the ride area, go back to the boardwalk and join the usually long line outside. Fortunately, I had bought several tickets already, so I did not have to dash across the boardwalk to the ticket counter again.

Paz and Mallie paused their canoodling for a second and looked toward me. Then they turned to each other. Suddenly, their expressions became serious. I noted it, but did not take much heed, anxious as I was to get back on the ride as soon as possible. Mine was almost an obsession.

"Nah," yelled Paz. "You go ahead. We'll sit this one out and take a

97

breather." Freeing his hand from Mallie's hair, he waved me on.

I shrugged my shoulders, grimaced in disappointment, and hurried forward. "See ya at the end then!" I assumed they would wait for me outside the exit as usual. More often than not, I took a few more turns on the ride than they did. They were good sports to humor my addiction.

It was a late morning Sunday in July. School was out. On Sundays, if none of us were working, we got together for breakfast and coffee at Pluto's then headed down to the pier. We tried to get there before the *après*-church crowd. We would buy our tickets at the ticket booth and spring across the wide pavement to the Dipper as quickly as possible, skirting bike riders, kids with skateboards, pedestrians with kiddies in tow. This Sunday was no different. By now we were on a first name basis with the weekend train operator, Bob. We called him Bobski. He was not much older than us, a skinny, otter-shaped guy with a light brown goatee that seemed to be missing a few hairs. Once in a while he would wave us through without a ticket. I would later bring him a burger and fries.

Now, after a quick wave in the general direction of the love doves, I made my way to the roller coaster entrance, digging furiously in my pocket for the row of paper tickets.

"Aha, gotcha," I said, relieved. At four dollars a pop, I could not afford to lose any tickets. I sidled up to the person in line in front of me. Fortunately, since the Double Shot ride had opened a few months before, the lines for the Giant Dipper were shorter than they used to be. Of course, I had checked out the Double Shot not long after it opened, and it was scare-worthy, but just shooting up twelve stories did not appeal to my more three-dimensional nature. The Dipper was still hands-down my favorite thrill.

Today, the crowds were sparse, thank goodness. But there was still a short line of mostly teenagers to get on the Dipper. As I stood there, basking in the late morning sun, I glanced up at the sign farther down the sidewalk over the park's entrance gate and read:

SANTA CRUZ: FUN IN THE SUN FOR FAMILIES AND CLUB-GOERS ALIKE

"Yep, I guess," I mused out loud.

"You guess what?" asked a lilting voice behind me.

I started. Who was that?

One of those strange ironies of life is that your fate can be both opened and closed at the same moment. And that is what happened when I turned around.

"Uh," I said, embarrassed. The person who had interrupted my truncated monologue was about my age, maybe a little older, hard to tell. Taller than me, and lankier. His sandy blonde hair wisped down toward his shoulders.

"I was just agreeing with the entrance sign," I explained. "You know, down there," and I pointed toward the gate. The guy's gaze followed my finger. And then, to make it clear I was not one of those homeless people who rambled out loud to no one in particular, I added, "Just hangin', you know. Talking to myself."

"Curious sign, definitely," he agreed. Then he smiled.

My stomach looped. Almost as much as it did when the Dipper lurched into action. Had he noticed? No, how could he?

I smiled back. But just a little. I did not want to give myself away. In fact, what had just happened? No dude had ever made me nervous before. I was confused. At myself. About this person I had never seen before whose expressive eyes, like two tiny planets, glimmered with light and at the same time seemed to pry into my soul.

Shit.

"Adrian," he said, brightly. And reached out his right hand.

Taking the hint, I nervously switched my wad of tickets into my left hand and grabbed his right with mine. We shook. He had a firm, but not rough, grip. And I felt a small shock wave sizzle up my arm. *Jesus, what is happening?*

"My friends call me 'Molo,'" I responded, disengaging my palm from his. He opened his eyes wide. "Yeah, I know, it's different," I continued, wondering where to put my now sweat-damp hands. *Why did you tell him that?* "But..." and then I stopped. I did not know what to say. My mouth just stopped working. Seized up.

His mouth, on the other hand, turned up in humor and he nodded, his light hair falling around his almost hollow cheeks. I felt a flutter in my chest, a hummingbird of happiness.

"Molo. I like that." He stared off into the cloudless sky for a moment, musing, I guessed, about this odd name I had thrown at him. Why hadn't I told him my real name? Tongue-tied, I could not assemble an intelligent response. I stood there like a dork.

Adrian, as I now knew his name to be, turned back to face me. "Yeah, that's really cool. I've never known a Molo before." He smiled again.

I nodded in fast motion, a moron on speed. "I know, kinda stupid. But I've gotten used to it."

"No, it's great. Don't apologize. You're lucky you've got creative friends," he said, reaching his hand toward my arm. I thought he was going to grab me, but he let it drop back to his side. I sighed. I do not know how I would have responded if he had held onto my arm.

"Oh, yeah, they are that, for sure. My ffff-riends," I stuttered. Geez, what the hell was wrong with me? "Creative, I mean. My friends are very creative."

Oh, my God, what a frickin' jerk I was. If there had been an exit sign near me, I would have bolted toward it. But there was no exit. Ha, I almost laughed out loud as, in my ridiculous predicament, I thought of the Sartre book. *No Exit*. I had read it in one of my literature classes. His observance "hell is other people" seemed particularly apt. Although, in this case, it was not Adrian himself who was "hell," it was my unexpected reaction *to* him. Like Sartre's three miscreants, I was stuck. Stuck with my embarrassed, goofy inability to figure out what to do or say to this creature, this unlikely being who, out of the blue, had changed my own being in just three words: "You guess what?" How trite. How maddening. I was a cliché. A moronic, lovestruck cliché. I took a deep breath and prayed this Adrian guy would not notice my discomfiture.

If he did, he gave no indication. I sighed again, this time with humongous relief.

Adrian just nodded. A congenial, friendly nod. "Like I said. Lucky you. It's great to have creative people in your life." Then he tilted his head toward the ride. "You go on this a lot? I see you have a few tickets, so, you know, I just wondered." And he nodded toward my left hand.

"Oh," I answered, looking down at my now somewhat crumpled wad. "Yeah, I guess. I do come here pretty often." I paused. "I'm kind of a roller coaster fanatic." I shoved both my hands, tickets and all, into my Levi's pockets.

"Me, too," he said, still smiling. "I love this old thing. It's my favorite of all the roller coasters I've been on."

"Really?" I grinned. Now here was something I could talk about. "Mine too! It's great. Did you know it turned seventy-three years old this year?" Uh, oh, me and my trivia. I had to be careful not to turn this person off with my propensity for rattling off random facts. It was a nervous habit.

"Yep," he said, nodding. "I did know. I was here for the celebration.

Were you?"

"Nah, I didn't make it. Work. Or something. I don't remember. But that's excellent you were here. If I'd made it, I might have met you then." *My God, stop talking, you cretin!*

Adrian still did not seem to notice my ineptness. He did not display any tell-tale signs of abhorrence or dismay, like backing away from me or smirking, at least.

"Well, we've met now," was all he said, and winked.

While we had been chatting, we had also slowly inched forward as the other thrill-seekers in front of us boarded their open cars in turn. Each car held two passengers and was connected to five other cars in a kind of train. There were only two. While one train zoomed around the 2,680-foot track, the other loaded its next victims. I prayed for the front car again. The thrill increased when you could see the track in front of you as you crashed forward along it.

Suddenly I was first in line. Bobski, a master of understatement, silently gestured for me to enter the platform where the next train of empty, red cars waited to be boarded. Adrian followed me as I headed for the lead one. Bobski always tried to work the line for me that way. I nodded a silent appreciation, and he blinked back, nodding his head almost imperceptibly. Understated, as usual.

"Hey," I said, turning to face Adrian. My nerves bounced up and down like pogo sticks in my chest as I gathered myself to ask, "Do you want to share the front car?" I prayed he would respond "yes," surprising myself to realize I wanted him close to me.

Adrian's full lips pursed in a friendly way. In fact, he seemed to smile often. *Good sign.*

"Sure," he said. "That'd be great. I love the front."

Bingo! He loves the front!

I scrambled into the miniature car through the cut out door and scooted over to the far side while Adrian followed, his knees almost banging into his chest as he climbed in beside me. Even after he had settled into the seat, I noticed that his knees just missed the front wall of the little car. Mine were inches away. Other passengers filed into their cars behind us. I felt my armpits begin to sweat. And it dawned on me: I had just met this guy. And his body being crunched against me in the cramped train car was making me more anxious than the hairy ride that was about to launch.

The automatic security roll bar folded down over our laps and we glanced at each other. His face was clear and gentle and kind, and I could not help beaming at him. Then the clicking of the coaster's mechanism disrupted our tableau and the small train of thrill-seekers edged forward. I turned my face from Adrian's to the track ahead. The anticipation of the first few moments of the ride was always exhilarating. But now, with Adrian sitting beside me, it was almost unbearable. My heart beat wildly, not just one hummingbird now, but a small flock.

Once the ride began in earnest, the red track before us was visible for only a few seconds. We slowly jerked forward, inch by grinding inch, and then, suddenly, a giant open maw gaped menacingly and we were swallowed whole by the hungry black tunnel. Inside, we were immediately enveloped by dark. The small convoy of connected cars picked up speed and momentum and we hurled down the first steep plunge in pure blackness. My stomach crashed into my throat. As if in total sync, both Adrian and I threw our arms up into the cold air above and screamed,

"Yeaaaaaahhhhhhh," at the top of our lungs.

And that was when my friendship—or my fixation—with Adrian began.

Thursday, August 15, 2013, Morning - Istanbul

"*Günaydın*, Molo, my friend!" called Paz. "How's it going this fine morning?"

He stood leaning against the wooden stair railing outside the Yeşil Beşik, wearing beige seersucker pants that tied at the waist and a loose, blue and white striped cotton shirt. A Panama hat and huaraches would have completed the picture of a European gentleman going native. But there was no hat. Or huaraches. Just Teva water sandals. And Paz was no European gentleman.

The glare of the mid-morning sun was blinding, and I put up my hand to shade my eyes. *Damn.* I had forgotten my backpacker hat. Well, I had my sunglasses, at least, so was not about to go back to retrieve the errant head covering. Coffee was calling.

I was desperate to get this show on the road. Paz's show, as it had become.

Shoving my uncertainty about Paz's involvement in the book incident to the back compartments of my mind, I heard myself croak, "*Günaydın* to you too, Paz."

In response, he blinked and leaned back slightly, his chin receding toward his Adam's apple. "Is that...?" he pointed at my shirt.

I chuckled. "I wondered if you'd notice. No, it's not the same shirt, but I had the same design copied onto a new one."

"Good ol' Molo," Paz nodded. "Glad to see *some* things never change," and he gave me a funny look, as if to say, *unlike some people I know*.

Changing the subject, I said, "You're chipper. Must've gotten your beauty sleep. Too bad it didn't help your looks, though. So...where're we heading? Tell me coffee is first on the agenda."

He snickered, good-humoredly ignoring the "looks" insult. "Coffee, I wish. You mean, Nescafe? You'd think in all these years this country would have gotten with the program and started importing the real thing. And I don't mean the Turkish stuff."

I threw my head back in frustration and thwapped my hand on my forehead. "Oh, man, I forgot about Nescafe. Nasty. Surely, there's somewhere around here with an Italian espresso machine. It's a tourist mecca. And it's 2013, for God's sake."

Paz shrugged nonchalantly. "We'll walk around and see what's here. Some joe would really help kickstart this day, you're right about that." He put his arm around my shoulder and started veering me down the short flight of steps to the narrow street below, saying, "C'mon, let's do it. I'm hungry. Americanos and some *kahvaltı* are waiting."

Breakfast would definitely hit the spot, I agreed. As we touched the pavement in front of the Yeşil Beşik it suddenly occurred to me: *I don't even know where Paz spent the night.*

"Paz," I said. "Where are you staying? Is it close by?"

He stopped for a second and removed his arm from my shoulder. His eyes shifted from mine. "Oh, didn't I say? I'm staying with Barış. Well, him and his family." He started walking briskly, threading between the nearest passersby.

"Really?" I knitted my brows together and hurried to catch up to him. "Oh. So, you guys are friends then." I was fishing, though his relationship with Barış was really none of my business. Or, rather, I wanted it to be my business, but I was not sure Paz would agree it should be.

"Well, not exactly." He glanced over his left shoulder at me and winked. "Not like you and me." And then he turned forward, picking up his pace. "So, where should we suss out this elusive Americano?"

Was he being cagey, or just messing with me? Whichever it was, Paz's abrupt change of subject away from Barış meant it was effectively closed—for now, at least. I had no choice but to let the thing drop. I did not know then that the subject would re-open soon, without my instigation, and in a way I could not have anticipated.

We spent a frustrating ten minutes or so trekking down Kadırga Meydanı Sokak and winding around the impossible to name one-block side streets of the south area of The Old City, peering in windows or at menus posted on sandwich boards. Finally, we stumbled on a small establishment that boasted an espresso machine.

"Eureka!" shouted Paz. "We're saved!"

The cafe's "haggle meister," a term we four—Paz, Mallie, Adrian and I—had long-ago coined for the men who lurked outside of shops to lure unsuspecting tourists inside, waved us in with gusto. "Yes, yes, come in!" We trudged up the gray stone steps to the cafe's streetside patio and found a small, round metal table under a red and green-striped awning with the name "Cafe Cennet" painted on it in white, Ottoman-style letters. "*Cennet*" was Turkish for "paradise," I remembered. But the place itself was more reminiscent of a bistro than the heavenly abode. And probably busier.

"'S good enough for me. What d'ya think, Mole?" asked Paz, settling into one of the two seats nudging the table.

"Yeah, I'm okay with paradise. Hope its coffee lives up to its name," I responded. I collapsed into the empty chair across from Paz, wiping the sweat from my forehead. My stomach growled at the pleasant odor of fresh-cooked food wafting our way.

A young woman approached almost as soon as we sat down. Her thick black hair was held in place by a bright purple scarf wrapped tightly around her head. The small gold designs on it reminded me of the scarf Mallie wore during our 2005 trip to Fethiye. Shaking the memory aside I marveled, as I had in the past, at the creative folds and knots Turkish women employed on simple squares of cloth. I stopped myself from bursting into laughter as a bastardized version of a Paul Simon song popped into my head: "There must be fifty ways to wear your headscarf." The ridiculous image made me suddenly cheerful. I wanted to sing the lyrics out loud, but decided maybe that was not the best idea. Just in case I offended the waitress.

"*Günaydın,*" she rasped, her husky voice belying her ultra-feminine appearance. Her smooth, tan face was bissected by a long, acquiline nose, pierced through the left nostril with a garnet stud. Beneath swaddles of loose clothing, her shapely torso was apparent: cinched at the waist and full and curvy above and below. Her hips, when she walked toward us, swayed above muscular thighs. I noticed these things, but not in the way I used to.

As I enumerated her attributes to myself, she spoke again, uttering the standard Turkish restaurant word whose exact meaning had never been clear to me. But wait staff used it before taking your order and again when returning with it. It was a uniquely Turkish custom that did not exist in the U.S...

"*Buyrun.*" She did not smile.

"Uh, huh," muttered Paz, almost stuttering. I could see by his gawping expression that he was bewitched by the waitress's beauty. She even had a mole above her left lip. Classic. An Ottoman odalisque in modern Turkish clothing. I was rather amused to find Paz off his guard for once.

Taking pity on his plight, I decided to order for us both.

"*Iki tane Americano, lütfen.*"

Thankfully, a smattering of this deucedly difficult language was coming back to me, but the woman's sardonic half-smile smothered any notion I might have entertained of sounding like a local. Though I knew a few phrases, I was clearly not fluent enough to engage in a discourse on quantum physics. And my accent sucked. Nevertheless, I decided to test my skill a little more. I was in a better mood than I thought I would be.

"*Adınız ne?*" I asked, unsurely. The waitress gave me another half smile, which I interpreted to mean, "What's it to you?" But I was no threat to her, I was sure she realized that. So I was not particularly surprised when she responded to my question.

"I am Elif. What is *your* name?" she answered, smirking in faux politeness. I sensed she was bantering with me. "And what else would you and your boyfriend like to order?" Well, this girl was from a different planet than the ever-curious "haggle meisters," whose endless curiosity about where you were from and what you did for a living made us as anxious to dodge their queries as they were to entangle us in them. I coughed at her reference to Paz being my boyfriend.

Her inference shook Paz out of his lovesick reverie and he butted in, answering for me.

"That's Molo, I'm Paz, and we would like two Turkish breakfasts, *lütfen.*"

"As you wish," she replied, with a slight forward nod of her stately head before she turned from the table and headed toward the nearby door. I watched, fascinated, as she swayed into the cafe, her generous hips rocking side to side as she moved. I could not help thinking about *djinns* again. "As you wish." Wasn't that something they always say after their master has rubbed the magic lamp and made a command? If only.

I bet Paz would love to rub her magic lamp and make a few commands himself right now. If Mallie were here, there would have been hell to pay, that was for sure. The merest hint of infidelity, even if a mere fleeting thought, would have once set Mallie on a rampage. Or at least an angry kick under the table. Maybe she was different now, what with the kid and being older and all. Thinking about how much trouble Paz *could* be in if Mallie were sitting with us was somehow comforting. It made me feel as if I had a leg up on him, after all the shenanigans he was putting me through. I chuckled under my breath.

We did not wait long for our order, which Elif deposited in front of us with a suave brandishing of arms and flicking of scarf ends. I found myself now entranced by her winsome feminity and self possession, traits that still eluded my own deportment, despite my efforts. You definitely did not get such a display from American wait staff. This predilection toward theatricality was another one of the idiosyncrasies of Turkey that I found inexoribly enchanting.

After Elif sauntered off again, her hips undulating provocatively, Paz and I spent the next few minutes focusing on our breakfasts. Besides the steaming Americanos in giant, round mugs, there were warm *simits*, a bowl of various varieties of olives, a plate of sliced Persian cucumbers and wedges of tomatoes, two types of white cheese sprinkled with herbs, several jam pots and *sucuklu yumurta*, eggs with sausage. There was also a stack of the ever-present flat bread with black sesame seeds sprinkled along its crusty top. And goat butter. I gave my sausage to Paz.

When we had finally stuffed ourselves beyond redemption, I pushed my nearly empty plate forward and said, "Okay, time is up. You told me we have 'a lot to do.' So, what's the plan?"

I should not have asked. Or maybe it did not matter, as it was clear by now that Paz was running this show anyway. My own show, the one I had come to Istanbul to play out, had seemingly been cancelled.

Paz stretched out his body in the small chair and, pushing his plate into mine, said, "We're going to Fethiye."

A silence engulfed me. I thought my ears had clogged up suddenly. So I leaned forward, my hands clenched on the edge of the table, now warmed in the August morning heat.

"Sorry. I didn't hear you. What did you say?"

Paz, still leaning backwards, repeated in a maddeningly casual tone, "We're going to Fethiye."

I shook my head. "I was afraid that's what you said. Paz, why? What's in Fethiye?"

My old pal now pushed himself forward again, making a showy display of his movements. When he grinned impishly, I realized, not only did he relish the shock effect his pronouncement had on me, but he had purposefully strung me along for this moment. From his self-satisfied expression, I knew without doubt this scheme had not just occurred to him; it was always his plan for us to journey south. He could have told me last night, but chose not to. Why? Because he wanted to hook me by surprise and watch me squirm. Because he got a buzz from keeping me dangling. So Paz. So irritating. But was it out of deviousness, or just one of his pranks? That, I could not tell.

And did he know about the book stunt? If so, he kept annoyingly shtum.

Now pressed against the table, Paz said, in a tone so casual an outsider would not suspect he had completely usurped his friend's plans, "You'll see what's up when we get down there, Molo. And don't worry. We're not going on the bus. Takes too long. We're going to fly to Dalaman."

"What?"

107

"I've got two tickets on Pegasus Airlines."

"You do?" An alarm clanged in my head. When could he possibly have booked tickets, unless he had done it before coming to Turkey? This whole state of affairs was morphing into a labyrinth of twists and turns. All because of Paz, too, it seemed. Or was I missing something?

"Yeah, I got them this morning. Online." He checked his watch. "In fact, we've gotta get moving. We fly out of Sabiha Gökçen Airport in about four hours. That gives us time to get to our rooms, pack, and take a taxi to the airport." He slapped both of his flat palms on top of the table. As if this change of plans was a done deal.

"Paz, you're insane! I..." I protested, my hands grabbing the side of my head like the screaming man in Edvard Munch's painting. Not only did I feel like screaming myself, I felt as if my own sanity were melting and beginning to resemble the wavy, indistinct brushwork of the iconic picture. How more crazy could anything get?

"Not insane, exactly. Just," he lifted both his palms shoulder-height, shrugged, and continued, "a little bit nuts." Then he chortled. "Really, Molo, it's not that big a deal. You'll see." He paused.

Just then Elif arrived at our table with the tab for our meals and Paz and I both watched her. He did not seem as bedazzled with her now. She eyed Paz, then turned to look at me. Seeming to make a decision, she brusquely slapped the piece of paper, its reckoning written in red ball point pen, onto the table where my plate had been. Without a word, she jounced off again. I was sulking now, slumped back, hands listless on my lap. I stared at the bill, not really checking the numbers, and then pushed it toward my infuriating friend.

"You can get this."

Then I slowly extricated myself from the hard seat, unhooked my bag from where it was hanging off the chair back, and waited. Paz's mouth slid to the left in his famous sardonic grimace and he swiped up the check.

He made no retort. Just reached into his pocket, examined his lira collection, threw down a few bills, and shoved the rest back where it had come from. His metal chair screeched as he pushed away from the little table, stood up, and put on his hat.

"Okay, let's go," he said. I did not even feel like waving good-bye to Elif as I might normally do. But she was serving another couple, not paying attention to us, in any case. My emotions were deflated. Paz and I exited down the cafe steps and back onto the bustling street.

We strode for a few minutes in silence. By now, the shops were in full swing: large, handwoven carpets hanging from thick nails out front of open doors, books piled haphazardly on wooden tables under faded awnings, neon orange and purple duvet covers shouting from window displays. A mottled cat slurped surreptitiously from a milk-filled bowl on a restaurant patio. In other words, Istanbul was open for business as usual.

But I did not feel my usual self. Whatever that was. I felt sapped. And even, if I dared to admit it, betrayed. I dug into the side pocket of my bag, pulled out my phone and checked the time. Eleven thirty. If my original agenda had played out, I would have been at the bustling Grand Bazaar by now. Searching for Ömer. Hoping for redemption. Praying for solace at last. My sole purpose for coming here would be close to realization.

But everything had turned pear-shaped and I was no longer in charge of my own exploit. Paz had taken over and, much as I had been glad to run into him again after all this time, at the moment I wanted to push him off the curb and run. I felt the prick of tears about to erupt. How had things gotten to this point? And so quickly?

The crowds were thickening. I pushed ahead of Paz, my negative energy sizzling and spurring me forward. Let him catch up to me this time. I wanted him to realize his games were not amusing and were pissing me off. As I dodged the throng of Istanbul humanity, bustling off to work or school or shopping, I felt like a striker in that carrom game we used to play in Santa Cruz's student union basement, ricocheting off the sides, avoiding my opponent's maneuvers in the attempt to bag the targeted pocket. But in this case, where was I going? Everything I thought I had come here for, planned for, hoped to accomplish, just like a striker pocketing the wrong piece in carrom, had struck foul.

And so had my mood.

I heard Paz calling, "Molo, wait up!" I pushed and bumped my way down the street, eliciting angry glances and choice hand gestures along the way. For a few minutes I did not really care if Paz was on my tail or not. And then I stopped.

Paz smashed into me.

"Molo, please! What's the matter?" he cried out, peeling his body from mine and grabbing my right arm. "What're you doing?" His voice trembled.

I turned to glare at him.

"You, Paz. That's what's the matter."

His eyes widened in giant question marks. And I could see in his shocked expression that his distress was genuine. I did not care. I had not yet mastered the art of skidding from seventy to twenty in a second. It always took me at least several minutes to calm down after an angry outburst.

"Seriously, Paz? You don't get it?" We stood there face to face now, blocking the wide pavement, so that others had to deviate their course to avoid a collision. A few gaped sideways as they skirted around us, but their inconvenience did not deter me from my stand-off with Paz.

He spoke, wildly.

"I'm just trying to help you, Molo. I just want to make things right for you." He looked helpless, his compact body taut and his round face sheeny with sweat. "That's all! I don't know why you're reacting like this."

Seeing his genuine distraught state and hearing the urgency in his voice, I finally capitulated. I opened my fists and took a deep breath. Then I reached out and grabbed Paz's left shoulder, digging my fingers into the damp seersucker of his shirt.

"Alright. You're just helping. I get it." I paused and looked in his eyes. "I concede. If you have a plan, I'm willing to go along and see what happens." I paused, turning my head slightly and arching my brows. "*But*, if I'm not happy with it at any time, I'm done. Got it?"

Paz smiled almost shyly, and his eyes reclaimed some of their usual gleam. He put out his right hand and held onto my extended arm.

"Got it."

"Okay, let's head back to the Beşik so I can check out."

Paz grinned.

"What now?" I asked, in mock exasperation, dropping my arm and placing both my hands on my hips.

"You're going the wrong way," he said, and pointed to the street sign on the corner wall.

❧   ❧   ❧

Apogee
(Part II)

Chapter 9

"Backgammon is like life: You get what it has, not necessarily what you expect." – The Ölüdeniz Post

September 13, 1922 - Uşak Province

After hours of walking along the Uşak highway, Demetrius spotted a large, nearly flat-topped rock thirty meters off the road in the scrubby wasteland beyond and collapsed onto it, throwing his canvas pack down onto the hard dirt underneath his feet.

He whipped the fez off and rubbed his scalp, hot and itchy from the old wool the hat seemed to have seared into his head. How could anyone wear such headgear day in and day out? In the heat, they were insufferable. He would have far preferred his old fisherman's cap, but had lost it months ago in the turmoil.

Traveling incognito, it was wise to look as though he were one of them. He did not know what would happen if anyone discovered what he really was, but he did not desire to let such an event come to pass. In that case, there was nothing for it but to endure the fez's torture until he was safe again. No one would think to question his identity as long as he wore it. It was the national headgear. Every Ottoman male had one.

After his rest, he would continue a few more kilometers southwest and then find a place off the side of the macadam road to lie down for the night. His pack would serve as his pillow and the felted heat of the fez would keep his head warm.

It had been a strenuous two days trekking from Dumlupınar, almost thirty-five kilometers. It was no wonder he was exhausted. He would need a good sleep.

In two more days, he hoped to make it past Uşak. From there it was still more than two hundred kilometers to Smyrna and the glorious Aegean Sea. But if he traveled in the early and later hours to avoid the oppressive mid-day heat, and kept to himself, he could make it in less than two weeks.

Perhaps.

oo   oo   oo

October 16, 1922 – Constantinople

Back in her room, Ayşegül lit her taper candle with a fresh wooden match, and the translucent halo emanating from the tiny flame bathed her chamber in a soft orange glow. She could just make out her infant carpet crawling up her loom where it stood near the opposite wall. Carrying the candle by its curved handle, she tiptoed over to her *halı* stool and set the candle on the floor next to it. Then she settled down on the narrow seat. The rustle of her silk *şalvar* pants echoed through the stillness. She waited, frozen. What was that noise? Was someone else in the room? After a few moments, she realized it was her own clothing that had made the disruptive sounds and she hit her head with her hand, at the same time shaking her head at her own silliness. Clearly, she was spooked by all that was happening. She needed to calm down.

Instinctively, she turned toward her window to see if her guardian, the moon, was still looking in on her, watching over her. She was not. The three vertical panes were void of anything but the deep night sky. Even the stars had gone to bed. Ayşegül sighed. It was time she slept also. The day had been tiring. There had been the hours of weaving, the mysterious knock on her door, the anxiety of playing in the concert. But the most disturbing event of the day was Süleyman Şefik Pasha's thundering appearance at the after-concert soiree.

She slowly reached out to her carpet, brushing her right palm along the chopped fibers of its fresh surface. The wool felt smooth and rough at the same time, like petting a foal or a calf as she had done when she was a girl on her parent's large farm. That was ten years ago. Now she was twenty years old—or so she calculated—a woman, and her parents were no longer able to help her. It was they who had thrust her into this new life back then, and though she often wished she felt otherwise, she would not ask them for help now. In any case, perhaps they were no longer even at their farm. She was on her own, with only the moon for guidance. But the moon would not be back for another day.

Ayşegül pulled her hand back from her carpet and reached absently for the piece of paper on which she had drawn her latest carpet design. She

113

had placed it on the edge of her stool when tidying up her work area earlier. Now she stared at it in the faint light. The design was more intricate than her previous ones. And each of those were more intricate than the ones before. During the hours and hours of weaving in solitude, as she had done since moving into this apartment two months earlier, new ideas kept springing into her mind. With every row or two that she completed, came another inspiration—a tweak here, a different knot there, small departures from what Maryam had trained her to do.

Ayşegül's head was crammed with so many ideas that she often could not sleep. She did not think her thoughts were random. There was almost always a central idea around which they orbited. The patterns and colors she envisioned whirred around in her head the way Al-Biruni, the ancient scholar, described the planets twirling around the stationary sun.

The design she held now was good. But it would have to change.

There was no longer any doubt. The unrest within the Empire and throughout Europe threatened the sultan, the palace, and everyone in it. That included her. She was astute enough to realize it now, without Estreya's gossip, even if she had been hoping for months that everything would be resolved, and their lives would go on peaceably as before. It would be helpful, of course, to listen to what news Estreya might have to impart, as she was out in the city and would be privy to more information than those who resided in the palace. They were like children here, prisoners, with no connection to the world beyond. And this isolation, despite their privilege, made the palace inmates dependent on the sultan and the sultan's court—for everything. That, Ayşegül realized, would be the others' downfall. And hers.

She could not let that happen. She had to protect herself.

A plan, swirling and amorphous, was starting to solidify in her mind. This carpet would help her. Not only did weaving concentrate her thoughts, the outcome, her new carpet, could become a useful tool. That is, if she managed to bring it about. She thought of *a zij*, how it tabulated positions of the sun, moon, stars and planets. It was said that the idea of *zijes* used by astronomers originated from the way threads were manipulated in weaving. How curious that carpet weaving was so closely tied in with the study of celestial bodies. And even more curious, that she, Ayşegül, was a student of both. Well, not a formal student of astronomy, like those at Boğaziçi University, but a mentee. She bobbed her head like the eunuch attendants in the harem did when their minds were made up about something. Well, her mind was made up.

114

And now she would sleep.

Placing her now obsolete design back on her stool, she quickly stood up. At the same time, her wide pant leg brushed against the candle where it stood on the floor. Ayşegül watched in horror as its flame licked at the hem of her long kaftan and began to chew at the silk cloth, causing the flame to grow and spread up the fabric like a hungry demon. The candle itself had toppled over and, though dousing the flame as it hit the floor, a stream of liquid wax oozed into the crack of the floorboard beneath it, heading in the direction of the loom. Almost as quickly as the wax flowed, it began to harden into an opaque mound. But the ravenous fire on her kaftan consumed more and more cloth with each second.

"Oh, Allah," cried Ayşegül. Both of her hands flew to her mouth, stifling her expostulation. It would not be good if anyone heard her call out. The last thing she needed was Tanju the eunuch to send Saskar Kadın to her for an upbraiding. Or worse, a punishment. Tanju had never liked her and seemed always to be looking for any reason, even a small error, to get her in trouble. They might take her away from her room, her carpet. Ayşegül could not let that happen, for several reasons. And no one knew what those were except herself. She would not even confide in Zeliha. Not now, anyway.

As these thoughts tumbled through her mind, Ayşegül set to work. First, she quickly undid the fastening of her kaftan and threw the still burning garment onto the floor as far from the candle as she could. Grabbing her *kirkit* off the stool where she had placed it earlier, she bent over and bashed at the now dwindling flames until there remained only a few bright orange spots here and there and the black-toothed edges of the fire's destruction. Then she stomped on the soggy mass. She would not be able to salvage her dress now.

Despite her vigorous efforts on the smoldering remains, Ayşegül did not trust the orange spots that still lingered. They were like minuscule dragon eyes seething with ill intention. They might re-ignite any moment and lash out greedily to cause more destruction. She had to make sure that would not happen. Though she shared a bathroom with four other girls in this hall, she always had a large porcelain bowl and a pitcher of fresh water on a small table by her bed. It took hardly any time at all to cross the room to her bed in the opposite corner, snatch up the pitcher and rush back to the site of carnage. As she poured cold water over her ruined kaftan, she took note of the other damage her clumsiness had caused.

First of all, there was the smell. Fire was always followed by a thick, woody stench. No matter how much she cleaned, anyone with a nose would know there had been some conflagration in the room. She would have to open her window to air it out. And thankfully, she kept incense in her bedside drawer. If she lit her incense when she went to sleep, by morning the distinctive odor of flames and burning should be gone. Or at least well masked.

And of course, she would have to smuggle her burned kaftan to the incinerator in the kitchen when she got a chance. She was often there, anyway, begging sweets off Berkan the baker.

But there was another problem.

The wax. What a mess it would be to scrape it off the floor. She would have to dig up a small carpet from her wooden storage chest and cover that part of the floor until she was able to clean it completely. If anyone else came into the room and saw it, word would get around. Ayşegül knew she had the reputation of being clever and adept, and an incident like this would cause tongues to wag, spreading rumors about what she might have gotten up to that night. That, she could not afford.

An idea occurred to her. Perhaps the moon was out there guiding her, after all.

She quietly placed her pitcher on the floor and moved to the spot where the wax formed a semi-frozen stream and several tributaries. Crouching down, she touched the fattest blob with her forefinger. It was not completely hard yet. Her finger made an indentation in the blob. Perfect.

Standing up again, Ayşegül quickly moved toward the light switch by her door and flicked it on. The room was suffused with a dim glow from the four decorative light sconces, one on each wall. Now she scurried to her chest at the corner of the room nearest her bed. She squatted in front of it and, feeling under its front edge, waited for the click she knew would come. When it did, she pulled the edge toward her and a small drawer slid open. Feeling inside with deft fingers, she curled them around a small object, smiling to herself as she did so. Holding it tightly, she got up again, stepped in front of the waxy riverlet near the loom and crouched down by it, almost as if she were going to slip into its milky thick depths. Instead, she pushed the small object she had been holding into the still soft wax and submerged it until nothing of it could be seen.

"That is it," she whispered. "I think it might work. *İnşallah.*"

ॐ   ॐ   ॐ

The year blew by. Not long after my bizarre first encounter with Paz and Mallie, Adrian crashed into my orbit like an asteroid. I introduced him to the others that same day when we staggered out of our first of many trips on the Giant Dipper, laughing and comparing roller coaster notes. From then on, Mallie and Paz and I all gravitated toward Adrian, vying for his attention, basking in the glow of his scintillating light. We were minor planets dancing attendance on his fixed presence. Our Helios.

I never told anyone what had happened to me that first day, content to let Adrian's dynamism eclipse my own. I was good at keeping secrets. So, our friendship carried on, in a kind of syzygy, like the sun and the moon. Nor did I begrudge the other two their time with him. What did it matter? We were three wandering souls who had found our center. Our fixed orb.

Adrian was older than the rest of us. Not by much, two years or so. But he had already left the University of Santa Cruz, or so he said. None of us questioned this information. Did he have a degree? I never asked. None of us had ever seen him on campus either. But in June of 1998, Paz, Mallie and I finished our senior year there at last and were ready to take on the universe.

That's when the idea first arose.

"Why don't we go to Turkey this fall?" suggested Adrian. He and I were alone in my living room-slash-bedroom. I was reading. He was drinking coffee.

"Turkey? Who?" I said, my chin pressing into my chest, my left eyebrow upraised. I heard Adrian set his coffee mug down on the windowsill near him.

"All of us. You, me, Paz, Mallie."

"Why Turkey? It's…I don't know what it is, but it's far away. Why not Mexico, or something. Paris?" I replied, not even looking up from my current book obsession. I was pouring through *The Soul's Awakening*, by Rudolf Steiner. It was the final novel of his four-part mystery series and I was now engrossed in the chapter where Capesius refuses to use his thought power. I was applying that idea to my current conversation and, therefore, not really paying much attention to Adrian's words.

"'Cuz!" he almost shouted. I jolted. It was so unlike Adrian, always so good-natured and calm, to raise his voice. My own thought power now irretrievably disrupted, I shut Capesius and his theosophical concepts gently away and stared at my friend. My own soul's awakening would have to wait.

"Those places," he continued, "they're so predictable. You know. Everybody goes there." If I had not known him so well, or thought I did, I would have said he was on the verge of whining now. I decided to pay more attention.

"Okay," I ventured, unsure where this conversation was heading. "Yeah, they're a bit predictable, I guess, but *I've* never been to any of them. Have you? I mean, I kind of wouldn't mind checking out the Louvre, actually. Or the pyramid at Chichen Itza. If I were going to travel somewhere, I mean." Now I looked up and saw that Adrian was picking at a fingernail, his mouth twisted. Odd. It was unusual for him to be nervous.

"Not to mention," I added. "How are any of us supposed to pay for this adventure? I don't have, what?, six, seven hundred dollars lying around just to hop on a plane and gander around some far-off country to ride camels and shop in bazaars. I don't think Paz and Mallie do either. Come to think of it, do you? Mexico and France are much closer. Or so I've heard."

I did not usually engage in sarcasm with Adrian, but his pronouncement had caught me off guard. I felt as if he were toying with me, taking advantage of my devotion. A devotion I was sure he sometimes exploited. Even though I gave in to his whims as a rule, at this moment I felt that he had jumped to a new level of presumption that even for me might be a step too far. Travel to the other side of the world? What was he thinking?

While I was speaking, Adrian had started biting his nail, but now he stopped. For a moment, I thought he looked crestfallen. Lost. I found this disconcerting and changed my tone. I could not stand to see him forlorn or sad.

"So…" I said, softly, putting my book down on the small lamp table next to the folding director's chair I was sitting in, one of two in my apartment. "What's in Turkey then? You obviously have a particular reason for wanting to go there." I hoped my tone was encouraging, and I folded my hands in my lap to show him he had all my attention.

Adrian flashed me one of his shy smiles and I felt my heart vibrate. I was sure he now had me where he wanted. But I was okay with that.

"Well, I was reading the travel section in the Sentinel awhile back," he replied breezily, suddenly reverting to his default charming self. The Sentinel was Santa Cruz's daily newspaper. "There was this article about Turkey."

Adrian gazed off into the middle distance momentarily and then turned back to face me. "It sounds so fascinating, you know? The whole Ottoman culture and the ancient sites and the Silk Road thing. Turkey's on the map now. It's easier to travel there than it used to be." He paused. In the ensuing silence I could almost hear his brain cells buzzing. "Also," he continued, "for you poor loan-paying ex-students, it's really cheap once you get there. So, our money would go a lot further than it would in France." He winked. "For instance."

I shook my head in wonderment. Somehow Adrian never failed to bring me around to his way of thinking. This time, it was probably the wink that did me in.

"Wow, sounds awesome," I said, hesitantly. "I didn't think about all that." What else was there to say? Traveling had been the last thing in my consciousness, but now that the subject had come up, I had to admit, I was intrigued. And if Adrian was interested, so was I. Anything to stay orbiting in his sphere. "Have you told Paz and Mallie your idea?"

"Nope. I wanted to see your reaction first." Again, that smile. Why did it hold such power over me? A good strategy, telling me he was letting me in on the plan before he told the others. In spite of myself, this special treatment had the effect I was sure he expected. My full capitulation.

"Well, obviously I have to figure out how to pay for it and all. And I'd have to see if I can beg off work. But if those guys are in..." I pursed my lips, musing.

What would the characters in *The Soul's Awakening* do? As I concentrated on the tenets of Steiner's story, it occurred to me that reading about grand concepts was not the same as participating in them, taking risks. Riding roller coasters was one thing, but venturing out into the world to see what might come of that would be life changing. I was always reading. Always fantasizing about the exploits of Marco Polo, Ibn Battuta, even Gertrude Bell, the irrepressible English pioneer woman who traveled throughout the Middle East before it was called the Middle East, hobnobbing with the likes of Lawrence of Arabia.

Maybe now was the time to take my fantasies to the next level. What was that Nike slogan? Not the one for the ancient Greek goddess of combat victory, but the newer one from the athletic shoemaker of entrepreneurial victory: "Just Do It." I took a deep breath and held it. And then I surprised even myself:

"What the hey, so am I."

I could hardly believe I had uttered those words. What was I thinking? Where *was* I going to get the money? What with school loans and a minimum-wage job, I barely had enough for my upcoming rent, let alone an exotic adventure abroad. Asking my parents for help was out of the question. My mediocre performance in the academic arena, and my subsequent less-than-preferred career choice, had put me in the doghouse with them. We were more or less estranged these days. I was pretty much on my own.

Still, as I stood there looking at Adrian, his boyish exuberance radiating like a nimbus, I thought, *why not?* Those historical characters I revere did not become iconic by staying safe in their villages and towing the line. It is only because they bucked convention or the mores of the time and pursued a crazy dream that we even know about them. I wanted to be like that. Or at least die trying.

Adrian's eyes twinkled and he lurched across to where I was sitting. It was not far—my living room could hardly be equated with the terms "large" or "luxurious." He leaned over, put his right arm around my shoulders, and squeezed his fingers into my upper arm. I could feel myself blushing.

"Oh, Molo. That's great. Do you mean it? You'll go?"

He now stood back up, releasing his arm from me, and locked his eyes on mine. I blinked.

"Hey. Like I said. If we can work it out, yeah. Let's do it." I smiled at him. "Turkey, wow. Who would've thought? I guess I better start planning. Fall's not far off."

Adrian stepped back and beamed. "Let's call Paz and Mal now. I can't wait to get this rolling. Thanks, Mole. You're something."

I was not quite sure if I should read between the lines or not, but one thing was certain. Adrian was happy and that made me happy. Enthusiasm started to bubble up in me at the thought of an adventure.

We were all going to Turkey.

"Please. Paz. What *is* going on? You finagled me onto this stupid-ass flight to Fethiye and I still don't know why. Don't get me wrong," I added, "I like it down there. Just…what's the point?"

The two of us were hunched in our economy seats in the Pegasus Airbus A320 plane, Paz by the window, me on the aisle. Fortunately, the flight was slated to last only an hour and a half. Much easier than the thirteen-plus hour trek from the States the day before. Or was it two? I could hardly remember now. I felt utterly steamrolled by the recent turn of events. Though this flight was less grueling, I could feel another headache coming on, and my whole body jittered. Airplane peanuts would help, but the snack cart had not even rolled out into the aisle yet. Hopefully, we would not be hit up for money if we accepted something from it. You never knew these days with the economizing airline companies had instated. At the thought of money, it occurred to me that, so far, Paz had not asked me to reimburse him for my ticket on this flight. If he did, that would exacerbate my headache—my funds were already stretched to the limit.

Paz did not answer. His forehead lay pasted against the tiny oval window to his right and I saw now that his eyes were closed. So much for that.

Still edgy, and needing help to diffuse some of my nervous energy, I dislodged my daypack from under the seat in front of me and ruffled through it for my plastic bottle of ibuprofen. Still not there. But I did come across *The House on the Strand*, wedged into the front pouch. Of course, I knew it was there; I had packed it when Paz and I had gone back to the Beşik for my things and to check out. I had made Paz wait outside the building as I still had trepidation about Mustafa seeing us together. I did not want to jog his memory of me. He would not understand why I had not just told him who I was when I arrived, and the ensuing scene would have been awkward, a contretemps I was not up to in the circumstances. So, Paz had not seen me pack *The Strand* and I had not had the opportunity of gauging his reaction to it then. The ensuing hubbub of this morning and our sudden change of plans had temporarily put the question of the note I had found last night into the back reaches of my consciousness. Now, the juxtaposition of coming across the book while sitting so close to Paz brought the mystery back to the forefront.

As far as I knew, Paz was not a fan of Daphne du Maurier. Nevertheless,

121

would he have reacted at the sudden appearance of her novel? Would he have flinched, or displayed some other guilty tell-tale body language? In other words, would he have been able to disguise—or not—his knowledge of its being tampered with the night before?

I sneaked a sideways glance at him. Still sleeping. Should I extract the book from my pack? If I was noisy about it, that might cause him to look in my direction. At the tell-tale book in my hands. What then? Could I bring myself to accuse him outright if he looked guilty?

Maybe. But not here.

I shoved my daypack back under the seat in front of me. Later. When we were unpacking at our hotel in Fethiye, or wherever he was taking us, I would catch him off guard. I would nonchalantly unpack *The House on the Strand* and place it conspicuously on the bed or some other furniture and check his reaction at that time.

Until then, I should try to chill.

I pushed the round anodized seat button on my armrest and my seat eased back about one inch. God, I envied those who could afford first class. Fidgeting into as comfortable a position as possible in the cramped space, I closed my eyes, hoping to catch some zzz's for the duration of our relatively short flight. Maybe a nap would keep my headache at bay. As I brought my hands to my waist, I could feel the slight bulge of my travel pouch under my mola tee-shirt. The paper note with its strange artwork was in there. My fingertips moved slightly over the outside of my shirt as if decoding a Ouija board message. It occurred to me that my fingers were extensions of my consciousness, a consciousness mystified by the secrets lying under the surface, in this case, not a wooden "talking" board but a curious, silent slip of paper. There was a mystery there, and I hoped Paz would be able to solve it for me.

After a short while, even my palpating fingers stopped their inquiring movements, and I began to relax to the plane engine's steady hum. After a few moments of drowsing, a vague, shadowy image of a bizarre creature with ugly teeth and conical feet showed up on the dark screen of my semi-consciousness. I could feel my eyes twitch as my mind tried to focus on the apparition. As if it had something to tell me. The creature was getting larger and clearer, but when it opened its wide mouth to speak...

I jolted and opened my eyes. I turned my head side to side to see if the strange being was still hovering nearby. But now, fully awake, I realized I must have been dreaming. No unusual shadowy form in the aisle or anywhere in the vicinity.

But I did notice a carefully coiffed flight attendant patrolling the aisle a couple of rows down. Blinking, I realized she must have brushed my arm where it lay on my armrest on her way to the back of the cabin with the rattling snack cart. I was annoyed, first, because I had clearly missed getting my possibly free peanuts and, second, because the vision I had just been thrust from seemed on the point of revealing an important message that now was lost to the ether. Ah well. I could not really blame the airline hostess for that. If only there were a lost and found department for dreams, though. How revelatory that would be.

Paz, who must have been jarred awake by my movements, was rubbing his eyes. Suddenly turning toward the back of the plane, he leaned across me and barked out, "*Bakar mısınız!*" The attendant, a slight smirk pasted onto her light brown face, turned around and maneuvered toward us.

"*Evet?*" She sounded annoyed, before even seeing who had addressed her. When it was obvious it was Paz, her tone softened. He often had that effect on women. "Yes, sir. How may I help you?" she replied in stilted, formal English. Her navy-blue pill box hat bobbed as she walked. It was perched so precariously above her bun, I was afraid it would fall onto my lap. I noticed with disappointment that she had left the cart stranded in the aisle.

"How long before we land?" he asked.

Without thinking, I punched his arm. A stupid question. We had both reprogrammed our phones to local time last night and our arrival time was printed on our boarding passes. Was he confused after his nap, or did he just want an excuse to chat with another attractive female? I rolled my eyes, wishing I could apologize to the attendant on his behalf. The flight was full, being summer tourist season, and I was sure the poor woman had enough to do without Paz's intrusion. On the other hand, I was a bit miffed with her myself for the missed nibbles and at myself for not having the gumption to ask for some.

The attendant, whose laminated name tag read "Hulya," slowly lifted her left arm and checked the thin watch on her slender wrist. "In half hour later we land. You will hear announcement. Anything else I can do for you, sir?"

"No, *teşekkürler*," replied Paz, replacing his body back into his seat. "Thank you." He grinned and bowed his head slowly.

The attendant bowed back, scowling slightly now, then turned on her heel and continued down the aisle to her abandoned cart, her hat bobbing up and down again with each step. I watched for a moment then turned to

Paz.

"What was that about?" I asked, shaking my head. I was still groggy, and the movement made me dizzy.

"Oh, you know, just passing time."

"Well, I think you pissed the girl off."

"So what? Isn't it her job to help passengers?" Obviously, the nap had not improved his mood much.

"Well, yes, but why pester the attendants when you don't have to?" But then I realized if I had Paz's chutzpah, I could have asked for my peanuts. Maybe he had a point, after all.

Paz blinked at me. "Let up, Molo. I didn't do any harm. And we had a little light entertainment at the same time."

I shrugged. "Right. So, now that we've been entertained, how's about answering my question?" I turned to face him and glared.

"What question?" he said, with a blank look.

I almost hit him. "Stop the crap, dude. I'm tired of your games. Tell me *some*thing, for fuck's sake!" If I were not in public, I think I might have cried. "God, I feel like shit."

I flopped back into recline mode and put my hands over my face. Then I had an idea. Maybe once we landed, I could leave Paz to his rendezvous, or whatever it was, head to the ticket counter and book a one-way flight back to Istanbul right away. Just me. Once there, I could get that hamam bath I had promised myself, maybe take a ferry ride up the Bosphorus for old times' sake, order an *uskumru* mackerel plate to enjoy while watching the boats float by, check back into the Yeşil Beşik Pansiyon and relax in my crummy, stuffy, outdated room until my flight home. Give up the whole exploit and forget why I had ever come here. Forget my plans for revenge. How absurd, after all. What had I been thinking? Adrian was gone, he would always be gone, and punishing Ömer was not going to change that. It was time to get on with my life.

"Molo?" I felt a hand on my left shoulder. Obviously, it was Paz's. Was he suddenly trying to be conciliatory? If so, my inclination was to ignore him, let him feel what that was like. But, as always, I submitted to his gentle turnabout and, taking my hands from my face, replied,

"What?"

I cannot say my tone was particularly encouraging. Apparently, my nap had not helped my own mood either.

"I'm sorry," he said. His big, sad eyes reminded me of the Turkish kids "guarding" the rock tombs who tried to milk "*para*," or money, off us that first time we toured Fethiye in 2005. "Look, okay, I don't want to tell you everything right now." His eyes shifted back and forth, and I knew he was referring to the other people around us, his paranoia about being overheard clearly still in full force. "We're arriving there soon enough and then I promise I'll be more forthcoming. I will say this, though. We're going to Ömer's place."

I bolted upright in my seat, grabbing onto the armrests for support. I heard the tray table on the seat behind me rattle. "Ömer's place? What are you talking about? Ömer lives in Istanbul. That's why I went there in the first place."

I sat immobile, my nerves and sinews tensed. Paz stared at me placidly for a moment. Then he spoke, his usually thick voice now soft and slow. "You don't know?"

"Know *what*?" I asked, trying to keep my exasperation from escalating into a full-blown Cherokee yell. I certainly did not want to bring Hulya running to our seats and threaten to throw me off the plane at the eleventh hour.

"Ömer lives in Fethiye. His main business is there. That's why we're going. I thought you knew that's where he was from."

If an Ottoman turban had suddenly wrapped itself around my head, I could not have been more shocked by this latest bombshell. Paz was full of them ever since he had Barış summon me to his little hideaway in the back alleys of Sultanahmet yesterday evening. It was as if he had taken some post-college adult education course in shock tactics and was practicing his newly learned techniques on me.

I blinked, hoping I had not heard correctly. After a pause, I turned to face Paz. He was gaping at me, his eyes wide and expectant.

"Nooo," I whispered, dragging out the "o"s like a petulant kid. "I didn't know Ömer was from Fethiye. How did you?" I heard the faint whine in my voice. But I kept my eyes glued to his, hoping to be able to discern from his facial reaction whether he was being honest or not. I waited for his reply. I did not wait long.

He shrugged, nonchalantly. "Adrian told me. Back then. 2005. I'm sorry, I just assumed he'd told you, too. I thought you knew." He blinked, but otherwise his expression did not change. He did not look up to the right, or shift his body, or seem in any way agitated. I decided he was telling the truth.

"Nooope. Not a word about it from Adrian." I tried not to sound too disappointed. "Maybe he planned to tell me, but had the accident before he could. Not that it would have meant anything to me at the time. But I wonder why he said anything to you. I don't get it."

Paz shrugged again, benignly. "I don't either. But that's what he said. So...I thought we'd check it out. I have an idea."

"Of course you do." I smiled a wan smile. "Did you bring your bag of magic tricks with you, just in case?"

Paz laughed out loud. The couple across the aisle craned their necks to see, I supposed, where the sudden noise had come from. Perhaps they were praying it was not an engine exploding or a drunken American making another scene.

"That," Paz replied, "You'll just have to wait and see."

ॐ   ॐ   ॐ

I was alone, digging in the desert. All around me rose the endless sand, blowing here and there in isolated swirls of sirocco. My digging tool was a small shovel, a trowel, the kind you might use to transplant seedlings in a garden.

Ahh, garden. Lush and green and full of life. Water.

But here, nothing. Nothing wet. Dry and hot and the sand filling my mouth, my nose, my mind with a choking, dirty premonition of disaster...

Suddenly, from across the sea of sand loomed a large boat, a cruise ship or some such vessel. Its massive bulk cut through the dunes like a Spanish galleon. Strange as that sight was, even stranger was the large Santa Claus hat perched on its hull. What did it all mean?

Was I going to be saved?

ॐ   ॐ   ॐ

Chapter 10

"Dimyat'a pirince giderken eldeki bulgurdan olmak." Or..."Run out of bulgur at home while trying to get the rice in Dimyat." Meaning: Go farther and fare worse. – Turkish saying

Wednesday, June 8, 2005 - Çalış Beach

I pulled the double pane glass door toward me and stepped onto the concrete balcony. A searing light pummeled my eyes and I held my hands up to ward off the assault. Then, squinting, I leaned my stomach forward onto the black wrought iron railings. A sharp tang of rotting citrus assailed my nostrils. A cockerel, presumably the same one who had woken me up a few minutes earlier, crowed in the background. Looking down into the yard below our room, I saw the source of the acrid stench: a weathered blue milk crate full of moldy oranges and lemons. The white and black dotted cockerel strutted near the stone wall at the edge of the property. Perhaps the moldy fruit was his breakfast.

"Bastard," I called out to him.

It was our first morning at the Mavi Dolfin Evi. I had not been summoned to prayer at five as I had feared, but our friend the cockerel was louder and even more persistent than the recorded muezzins I was accustomed to in Istanbul. At last, I could no longer pretend that sleeping in was an option. I had rolled stiffly off my hard mattress. And as my bare feet curdled on the cold tile floor, I had uttered my first curse at the offending cockerel, inwardly invoking the evil eye to bring about its untimely demise.

Now, from the balcony door, I looked over toward my friend's bed. Typical. His lanky form was sprawled across the sheets, seemingly undisturbed by the cacaphony of the crowing bird outside.

"Adrian?" I whispered. "You up yet?" He stirred.

As in our previous escapades, we decided to share a room to save money (although for me there were other reasons, too) and, in this case, our twin beds were squeezed into opposite corners. By the tranquil appearance of my roommate, tousled though he was, I figured he had spent a more restful night than I. As usual. Sleep did not come easily to me, and this country seemed intent on depriving me completely. Each time I hit the sheets was only the beginning of a long night's journey into day.

Adrian never tossed and turned as I did, never groped toward a window in the wee hours to stare out at a moon bright sky and pray to the heavens for reprieve. What seemed a natural consequence of nighttime for him was a constant source of torture for me. Why, I never could figure out. But it did not seem fair. I felt, not for the first time, a kind of envy at his imperviousness to the hiccups of life.

Now, though he squinted at first, and rubbed his eyes, he suddenly jumped out from under his sheets, landing on the same cold tiles as I had, but with greater aplomb.

"Hey. Morning, Molo!" (I rolled my eyes.)

"Morning, Ade. How did you sleep?" (as if I needed to ask).

"Fantastic! You?"

I grunted.

"So, I guess we should go down to breakfast. Our tour guide is picking us up at nine, right?" He reached over to the faux birchwood nightstand between our beds and picked up his phone, flipping it open gingerly. "It's seven-thirty now. That gives us enough time."

"Yep," was all I could muster.

"You gonna shower, or not?"

"Nope."

"Okay, I'll get to it then. Wonder if Mal and Paz are up yet."

"Doubt it." They tended toward sleep-ins as much as I craved them.

"Yeah, you're probably right. You wanna go check on them? We don't want to be late for our first adventure in Fethiye."

"Sure." As I answered, Adrian grabbed his cargo shorts and started ruffling through his pack for a clean shirt, I guessed. Just watching him enervated me. I would need a lot of coffee to get through this day. Even Nescafe would do.

"See ya in a few. God, this is gonna be great." He rubbed his hands and did a little jog in place. I resisted striding over to smack him.

Fortunately, our room was an "en-suite," so we did not have to share a bathroom with other guests. Adrian practically dashed into it and shut the door with a jaunty kick. Hardly a pause later, I heard water splashing. And humming.

"Dang, what *is* it with you?" I said out loud, shaking my head. *Ugh.*

Reluctantly, I trudged the few steps it took to reach the chair where I had deposited my backpack when we had taken possession of this room the day before. I had been more enthusiastic then, unzipping zippers, rummaging through pockets and compartments, digging for swimming gear and hot weather clothes. Now, my trunks were still draped over the balcony in the sun. But my other clothes from the day before lay strewn haphazardly on top of my pack. At least I would not have to expend any energy to retrieve them. I changed, taking my time, blinking every few seconds, tripping into my shorts legs.

Now dressed, I wiped the heat-induced moisture from my cheeks and swiped my hands on my shorts. *Already scorching. Damn. Mallie's not gonna like this.* But I knew even the excruciating heat would not deter her from an outing. I should go check on her and Paz, nudge them into action.

As I passed Adrian's and my bathroom, the shower was still splashing. I heard Adrian humming merrily along and sighed, grudgingly. I opened the door to our room and veered left down the empty hall. Where was everyone? Our landing was square-shaped, skirting the eight or so guest rooms on this floor. An aluminum railing kept guests from hurling into the three-story atrium around which the hotel was centered. Surprisingly modern, in an ancient Rome kind of way.

In front of Mallie and Paz's door, I hesitated. It seemed cruel to wake them up. But Adrian commanded and I obeyed. Just like a devoted Roman slave, I supposed. I smiled and my head throbbed.

"Knockee, knockee," I called. "Wake up, guys. Time to rumble."

From inside a muffled voice shouted back at me.

"Shut up. Go away." And I chuckled. It was going to be a fun day, after all.

෧ ෧ ෧

September 13, 1922 - Uşak Province

A low rumble caused Demetrius to stop in his tracks. What was that? Was it thunder? A vehicle? The sky surrounding him was pale blue, wispy cirrus clouds sweeping across the vista. Thunder did not seem likely. A vehicle then.

Holding the fez with one hand so that it would not slip off his head, he used his other hand to shield his eyes as he surveyed the scrub-laden territory around him. A small flock of alpine swifts with their white bellies and black wings veed toward the rocky pinnacles on the horizon. Otherwise, all was still. In the distance, from the direction he himself had just walked, he spotted the front grill, like a blunted masthead, of a battered lorry. He watched, mezmerized, as it moved slowly toward him, parting the jagged heatlines like waves of roiling water. Its metallic bulk sliced through the horizon, which shimmered and oscillated in its wake. Demetrius rubbed his eyes with his free hand. The long trek in the sun was making him hallucinate.

He had already been on the road for three hours and his feet, inside his weathered infantry boots, throbbed with fatigue and the sharp sting of blisters. He had eaten only a chunk of stale bread and some hard cheese. Two weeks like this would be very rough going. Perhaps he should take the risk.

He eased the straps of his pack off his shoulders and let the pack drop to the macadam road. It sank slightly into the melted bitumen. He then fixed his unshaded eyes on the oncoming truck, continuing to watch as it came closer to him, appearing bigger and bigger with each advance. The mirage-like ship became a tanker in his fantasy. But in reality, Demetrius could see that the truck was not army-issue, thank God, but like one used by farmers all around this part of Anatolia. He had seen similar ones before. So far, so good. But, even so. Would it stop? Would the driver be obliging?

The metal behemoth with its slat-wood sides was close now. Demetrius could make out the shape of a human head wearing a hat at the wheel and another matching shape next to it. He took off his fez and waved it high above his head like a semaphore. Back and forth. An arc, a white flag. Inside his head, he muttered a short prayer. "*Stop. Please.*"

Against all odds, his entreaty worked. Lumbering though its approach had been, the truck crept even slower now as it came within fifty meters of Demetrius, waving and hopeful on the side of the road. A drowning man in the sea. He heard the screech of the hand brake as the driver brought the vehicle to a standstill. Its engine continued to grumble. Demetrius waited for a moment. No one got out of the vehicle. What should he do?

Time stood still. The air around him ceased to flutter. The grumbling stopped now. Or had it? Was he imagining this tableau? Was he like a man floating for hours in freezing water having the vision of a lifeboat coming for him?

Just as Demetrius thought he must be immersed in such an illusion, after all, and the truck—or boat—a figment of his heat-tired mind, an arm reached out of the passenger window and beckoned in halting, jerking motions. *Thank Christoper*, not an illusion. He briefly touched the medal hanging from his neck in gratitude. Quickly, before the hatted figures changed their minds, Demetrius leaned down, grabbed his pack straps and ran over to the waiting vehicle. His speaking Turkish was limited, but if he kept his conversation simple, perhaps he would be all right. In any case, what was done now, was done. He had made his choice. He would ride with these men.

With luck, he would be in Uşak before dark. With more luck, the truck was heading even farther—to Smyrna.

ھ   ھ   ھ

October 26, 1922 – Constantinople

Early the next day, Ayşegül sipped her morning *çay*, amber-colored and sweet. Reviving. Now she felt ready to put her plan into action.

She carried her *çay* glass across the slatted floor, bypassing the place where the hardened candle wax, mostly scraped up now but stubborn in spots, still threatened to expose her carelessness of the night before. She had covered it with a small carpet to disguise its presence. *İnşallah*, no one would think to lift its edges and peer underneath. Anyway, she had few visitors in her room as she had only moved in recently and her few friends did not often have the opportunity to roam around the huge palace. This crude cover-up must do for now. She would work on the wax later.

The thought of visitors brought to her mind again the mysterious caller of the night before. Who had knocked in such a vehement manner and then vanished? As no one had yet approached her about the incident, it must have been a mistake. Whoever had knocked had realized their error and felt no reason to tell her. She shook her head as she walked across her room.

Now Ayşegül opened her wall cupboard and, after setting her empty glass down on an unoccupied area, from the top shelf pulled out a fresh piece of drawing paper. In a drawer below, she found her ink and pointed calligraphy pen. Her hands were full, so she left the cupboard open. Having no table on which to write, she chose a place on the floor near her window and, clutching her implements in her hands, sat down, cross-legged. She then laid the sheet of paper on the floor in front of her and placed the small ink pot to the right of it. It was her habit to create a design freehand before inking it into the small squares that made up the graph she would use as her weaving template. The design, when redrawn onto to the graph, must account for each and every strip of wool she would knot onto the *çözgü* skeleton in order for the final picture to look complete. It was a time-consuming and complicated process.

Ayşegül set to work.

ॐ   ॐ   ॐ

Thursday, August 15, 2013, Mid-Afternoon - Dalaman

Our Pegasus flight landed at the domestic terminal of Dalaman Airport and Hulya ushered us out of the cabin with a sardonic grimace. Paz smiled at her winningly and then we rushed to collect our travel bags from the baggage carousel. We were not alone. All around us, a melee of men, women, children and teenagers, all in shorts, scrambled to heave their heavy suitcases off the carousel. The skin on their legs was so translucent, it might never have made contact with a sun particle. British tourists.

A smattering of more solar-skinned Turks grabbed their own luggage, which I hesitated to call suitcases. Instead, theirs were an assortment of the plastic woven bags we had encountered in the past on our various bus trips with Turkish passengers. These bags bulged and ballooned in all manner of shapes that caused one to wonder. What could they possibly hold? Why would travelers from Istanbul have such a different array of paraphernalia than those from Merry Old England? In these times could there really still exist such culture clash? Apparently so. Confusing and frustrating as it could sometimes be, the anomaly between western and eastern traditions was also bewitching. Disparity in luggage styles was a mere microcosm of a more looming and intrinsic incongruity.

It was precisely this incongruity of cultural ideologies that had gotten us four into the pickle we found ourselves in back in 2005. I had never doubted that.

My rambling thoughts, rather than riling me up, calmed me. Somewhere between exiting the plane and retrieving my own western-style gear, I nixed my retaliatory plan to fly back to Istanbul sans Paz. In fact, my curiosity about his scheme now superseded my frustration with his quixotic attitude. I realized that with all that had happened over the course of the last twenty-four hours, less even, I wanted, no, *needed*, to see where all these bizarre turns of events would take me, if there would be resolution, if my questions would be answered.

132

And more than that, if I could still find a way to avenge Adrian.

Following Paz out of the small terminal, I noticed his ease and confidence at finding his way. This mildly surprised me, as he had only been here once before. At least, as far as I knew. That was when we had all been heading the opposite direction in 2005 after Adrian's accident, when we three, Mallie, Paz and I left southern Turkey, bereft and bereaved, and then flew home. It was the last time any of us had been in this inscrutable country. I could never have imagined then that I would find myself back here ever again.

But here I was.

"Hurry up," called Paz, without stopping. "The bus leaves in fifteen minutes."

I opened my eyes wide at this bit of unexpected information. "How in the world do you know that, Kimosabi?"

"I looked it up online last night. Pays to research, eh?"

"Right. I guess so. Well, we better leg it then. I definitely do not want to hang around this place longer than necessary."

Even as I dashed behind Paz, I could not resist the temptation to check out the terminal we rushed through. For one thing, the place was cavernous. And disconcertingly, most of the overhead lighting was switched off. I knew why from past experience and inquiry. In Turkey, the cost of using electricity is prohibitive, so it was not unusual for lighting to go unused. Another reason was the almost daily occurrence of power outages. Even in public spaces. Why turn on the lights if they were just going to go off anyway? Made sense.

Besides the dearth of light, not a lot was happening, as airports go. No comparison to, say, San Francisco or Atatürk International where the hordes of humanity darted and zipped along like alien automatons, seemingly inured to the imminent danger of an asteroidal collision. No clamor of excited voices, just the intermittent thwap, thwap of a few roller bags, including mine and Paz's, on the shiny tile floor. The space itself was wide open. A handful of stragglers waited at currency exchange booths or loitered near the glass exit doors. I noticed only a couple of food counters, too. Really, then, no reason to stick around unless one wanted a cool reprieve from what threatened to be a shocking heatwave outside its protective walls.

The exit door opened automatically as we approached it and the heatwave no longer threatened. It attacked mercilessly.

"Yikes!" I blurted, turning my head to my right to avoid the onslaught

133

full-on.

"C'mon, you wimp," Paz called, grabbing my arm.

We rushed across the two-lane terminal road to get to the parking lot beyond, weaving in and out of the way of other tourists searching for their rides. The difference between the number of people inside the building and those outside was striking. Clearly, most of us were ready to hightail it to our vacation destinations. Paz headed toward a row of surprisingly modern buses parked diagonally side by side. The sight reminded me of our first bus trip down to this area as a group of novices in 2005. Now, the contrast between the upmarket quality of these buses with the homespun travel gear at the baggage carousel could not be more glaring. Turkey never failed to astonish with its anomalies and inconsistencies.

"This one." Paz pointed.

Number 3. The long placard propped in the over-sized front window announced its destination: Çalış Beach/Fethiye. We hoisted our packs and bags over our shoulders and started up the steep steps into the cool, nearly empty, bus. As I did, I turned around, just to survey the hubbub outside. Suddenly, my insides lurched. A short man with a round head and wearing dark sunglasses slid into the back seat of a black Mercedes sedan. Could it be? Was I seeing things?

I stopped to try to get a better look, but a heavily accented British voice behind me barked, "Oi, you getting in that thing or taking a siesta?"

"Oh, sorry." I turned back to the bus steps and made my way up. But I could have sworn that the man I had just seen entering the nearby Mercedes was my nemesis. The sole reason I had come to Turkey this time at all.

Ömer.

The question was: why would he be at the airport the same time as we were? Coincidence? Surely not. Another question was: had he seen me? Had he seen me see him?

I hoped not. Confused and a little suspicious, I followed Paz down the dim-lit bus aisle and plonked beside him on the seats he chose mid-way down. We did not speak. I was too preoccupied by what I thought I had just seen. He was looking out the window, a vacant expression on his face. A few minutes later, after vaguely watching the bus fill up with other, mostly British, vacationers, I saw the bus driver board and take his seat up front. Revving into action, he slowly backed the giant, throaty vehicle onto the inter-airport parking lot road, and we began to move forward. I hardly noticed the palm-specked scenery beyond. Instead, I thought about Ömer.

And I prayed my possible sighting of him was just the conjuring of my over-tired, over-active mind. Something Paz might pull out of his old bag of misdirection tricks.

The bus headed down the highway toward Çalış Beach. Paz, reveling in his role of irrepressible tour guide, had already booked a hotel there. I vaguely wondered whether he had chosen our old haunt, the Mavi Dolfin Evi. But then, it held such sad memories, I figured even Paz would have the delicacy to choose somewhere fresh, somewhere without the taint of tragedy. So, I sat quietly throughout the hour and a half ride, my head pressed against the large, air con cooled window, and revisited my hatred for the man whom I believed had ruined my life, who was responsible for destroying the one thing that had brought true joy to my existence.

Adrian.

Was it possible Ömer could be here? Would we find him at the office Paz said he owned in Fethiye? The answers were: possibly and hopefully. But then what? What did Paz have in mind, really, for coming down here? He must have some plan, or he would not have gone to so much trouble to search me out in the Sultanahmet or to book that last flight, I was sure of that.

And how did all this link to the bizarre ink scratching I still had in my passport pouch? Was now the time to tell Paz about it? Should I reveal my own secrets to him? Should I tell him about the Ömer sighting?

Peeling my cheek off the window, I turned my head to the right. Paz's own head was now flung back against the gray and purple velour headrest, his mouth slightly open, his hands quietly crossed across his arms on his stomach. Against the hum of the bus engine and the purr of the air con, his breath rasped and snorted in a kind of rhythmic counterpoint. He was asleep.

I decided to leave him that way.

Chapter 11

"There is no past, there is no hereafter, everything is in a process of becoming." – Bedreddin the mystic

August 26, 1922

*T*he man called Kemal launched a daring attack on rival Greek defenses in Anatolia and captured Afyon. This attack is hailed as "The Great Offensive" by Turkish people and marked the annihilation of the Greeks' long-desired goal of achieving Megali. They had dreamed of reclaiming Constantinople from the Ottoman Empire. But Field Marshall Kemal was not going to let that dream be realized.

Greek morale waned. Their hope, the British, French and Italian Allies, had abandoned them now after deeming the 1920 Treaty of Sèvres no longer enforceable. The Greek army was on its own. To top that off, Commander-in-Chief Anastasios Papoulas butted heads with the Greeks' Venizelist government officials and was fired at the eleventh hour. His replacement, General Georgios Hatzianestis, proved to be blazingly incompetent.

In the meantime, the fighting intensified. Would it ever end?

After the twenty-sixth, Mustafa Kemal and his men drove on and destroyed the Greeks at the Battle of Dumlupınar on August thirtieth. The result? Nearly 50,000 losses for the beleaguered Greeks and less than 15,000 for the Turks. Kemal's army pursued the Greeks as they retreated to their stronghold of Smyrna on the western coast. It was a move the Greeks should probably not have made, but it is doubtful whether they had an alternative.

The Sick Man of Europe was making a comeback. And it was relentless.

Afterwards, the man called Kemal would be renamed "Atatürk," father of the Turks. And he would change the course of Ottoman history.

ॐ   ॐ   ॐ

September 13, 1922 - Uşak Province

After their initial gruff greetings, the three men rode along in silence. Demetrius was wedged onto the bench seat next to the passenger window, his fez on his lap and his pack thrown into the truck bed atop burlap sacks overflowing with dirt. The less said, the better. Fortunately, his rescuers were quiet men. He had not yet asked where they were heading—for the moment he was content to sit.

His window was open, and he gazed at the passing scenery with a mixture of relief and wonder. The gray green scrub and occasional stone bridges seemed more picturesque from the truck window than if he had been trudging by them, slow step by slow, painful step. Occasionally, the truck passed stragglers slogging along the wide road. Demetrius could not make out whether any of them were Greeks like himself, trying to escape the interior of Anatolia for safer territory, or Turks setting off from their villages for work at some nearby field. But he thought the latter was closer to the truth; by now most Greeks would not expose themselves to the potential danger of being on public display. In fact, Demetrius realized, he was probably the only one stupid enough to do so.

He had started walking two days ago. That meant that today was the thirteenth day of September. And the second day of his new life. He was lucky to be alive. If he survived the trek to Smyrna, he could rejoin his compatriots and arrange to go back home. To Alexandroupolis.

The truck lumbered along. The driver with his lined, tough face and long mustache was not in a hurry. The horrors of the previous days did not seem to affect him. Perhaps the village he and his friend lived in was far from the raging skirmishes. If that were the case, Demetrius, despite his own convictions, was glad for them. What was it all for? Lives lost and ruined. Families destroyed. Grievances festered. And now it was all over. His side had lost. That was that. He was almost relieved.

After an hour or so, Demetrius spotted a small, makeshift road sign off to the right with the words:

Uşak 20 km

Another fifteen minutes at this pace. He allowed himself a small smile.

Uşak was still a long way from Smyrna, perhaps 225 kilometers. Unless this truck was going farther, which seemed doubtful, he would ask the driver to let him off in the Uşak town center and search for a cheap *konak* for one night. It was risky, but he needed to rest and clean up. To look like a vagrant—or even worse, a Greek vagrant—meant trouble. The war had deepened the rift between the Turks and the Greeks, but Demetrius was sure the battle of Dumlupınar, and the Turks' victory there, would cause all Turks to view even the local Greeks as combatants to be detained, perhaps imprisoned. Or worse. Demetrius could not let that happen. He had not escaped Dumlupınar to be taken down now.

He tapped his feet nervously on the metal truck floor, his eyes furrowed in concentration.

He would, of course, be happy if his companions' cargo was headed beyond Uşak. In such a case, he would try to travel as long as possible in the truck. The less he was seen walking on the road, the better. Less risk of being identified by passersby as the enemy. And the quicker he arrived in Smyrna, the better.

But this was not to be his destiny.

ॐ   ॐ   ॐ

Wednesday, June 8, 2005

Those first few days in Çalış and Fethiye were an adventurer's dream.

Day one of our tour of the Fethiye hinterlands took us first to the Lycian home of Bellerophon and his legendary horse, Pegasus. This was the rocky outcroppings of ancient Tlos and its celebrated citadel. Not only was it our introduction to Lycian rock tombs, impressively carved and decorated into cliff sides all around the area, but exploring its environs was when I realized that a large percent of what I had learned as ancient Greek history, actually took place in Anatolian Turkey.

For lunch our group of ten, including two Turkish lads from Istanbul and two thirty-something British couples, dined alfresco at a trout farm in the nearby hills. The heptatonic strains of Turkish folk music filled the open-air restaurant with haunting voices and rhythms. A stream wove through the wooden bar where live trout fries wriggled by, like piscine belly dancers seemingly unperturbed by the captivated humans sipping lemonade and beer above them. Watching the small fish undulating their way along their narrow water path, it occurred to me that my life was not so different from theirs. I might think I was a free agent, sightseeing, riding roller coasters, cavorting with my friends, but was it not possible I was merely following a route planned out for me by some destiny of which I was not even aware? Perhaps this tour had less to do with my own desire for adventure and was part of a bigger plan. The thought was depressing; I gulped my *ayran* to drown it out.

After our drinks, we lounged on hard, flat pillows set on the floor of a slapdash platform called a *köşk,* a cross between a wooden deck and a gazebo, where our food was placed on a low round table in the middle. Adrian was beside himself with excitement, with the uniqueness of everything we were being exposed to. We all were.

"God, I'm glad we did this, Adrian," chirped Mallie. "Thanks."

"Cheers, Adrian!" We clinked our glasses.

"*Şerefe!*" called out the two Turkish guys, and clinked across the tiny table.

Stuffed with trout and salad and bread, our group climbed back into our four by four tour jeep. Deniz, our intrepid guide, then drove us to Saklıkent, the canyon Adrian and I had discussed on the bus down to Fethiye. We sloshed through its ball-curdling water surrounded by vertical walls of sheer, black granite. Japanese women screeched with delight and Paz slipped on a slimy, hidden boulder, cutting his knee.

"I love it," called Mallie, sopping wet, and scaling a mini waterfall.

"I bet you do," said Paz. "Love to see me hurt, I mean. Because then you get to help make me better later on." He winked.

"In your dreams," replied Mallie, blushing.

I caught their banter in between sliding around on slippery rocks and squelching through waist-high water in my Teva waterproof sandals. I did not think any of us had been on an outing as fun as this in a long time. Even the Giant Dipper ranked as boring by comparison.

After traversing a harrowing four kilometers of canyon, and back, we all flopped onto the pillows of one of the many weather-battered *köşklar* suspended precariously from the banks of the canyon near the parking lot. We sipped hot *çay,* gobbled Turkish-style Lorna Doone biscuits and exchanged guesses as to our next day's adventures. There would be six days altogether with this gang. Exhausted and euphoric, I was beginning to feel this small assemblage of people was as close to having a family as I'd ever experienced.

Over the next six days of thrills and sight-seeing, I also felt my feelings toward Adrian surge. Being so close to him all the time, the excitement of our adventures, the laughing and jostling we all engaged in, even the accidental brush of his bare arm against mine as we bumped along the dirt roads of Lycian Turkey, sent jolts of electricity through my body.

And yet, I could not let Adrian see or know how I felt, had to keep vigilant and constantly on my guard against myself and my reactions to his presence, to harden myself to my own feelings. My longing. Because I believed Adrian would find my desire revolting. Nevertheless, the tension of restraining myself was almost unbearable.

Though it was my choice to carry on as if I was merely his good pal, I questioned my secretiveness, too. Really, what would be the harm in letting him know how I felt? Was I afraid of his rejection, his ridicule? Of crossing the barrier between platonic friendship and...something else?

If anyone else had an inkling of what I was going through, they did not let on. Once in a while, a knowing look from Mallie made me wonder, but she never said anything to me. I did my best to act as any best friend would, joking, slapping, laughing and pretending to have zero cares in the world. Would I have told Adrian what was really going on in me if I had known what was to come? If I had foreseen the tragedy that would soon rob me of the most fulfilling relationship in my twenty-eight years of life? If I could have seen into the near future, would I have acted differently throughout those few days?

Would I, in fact, have disclosed to Adrian my emotions and let fate take its course?

Looking back, I wish I could say, "*yes*." That I *had* the strength, the conviction, to let go of my fears of rejection and reveal my true feelings to him. Because Adrian was more than my best friend. He was my other half.

Despite my inner conflict, those days continued on like an otherworldly dream.

Until the dream evolved into a nightmare.

ॐ   ॐ   ॐ

October 27, 1922 – Constantinople

As she concentrated on her new design, Ayşegül's thoughts strayed to her predicament. She would need to act quickly; if she was right, there would be little time before she would no longer be able to act on her plan. She would be swept up in the politics of the palace and her life would become even less her own than it was now. And who knew what craziness was coming, what with the turbulence and fighting increasing all the time in the empire?

Estreya. Where was she these days?

She should seek her out, find out if the Jewess was still venturing to the palace. Not only would she gain more knowledge of what was happening in the city beyond the palace walls, but Estreya was brilliant at *fal*. It was taboo in her religion to read coffee grounds, but she did it anyway. For a fee, of course. She knew the girls in the palace loved to hear what her interpretations of the gloppy leavings at the bottoms of their cups predicted about their futures. It was something to do, to help them look forward to a better life down the road. Perhaps if Estreya gave her a session, Ayşegül thought, it would confirm her suspicions about the possible upheaval in the palace and give her confidence to forge ahead with her intentions. She stared at her loom, considering.

On the other hand, because her intuition was uncanny, if Estreya *did* read the coffee grounds for Ayşegül, she might uncover her secret. Ayşegül could not afford that to happen.

"Hmm, I'll think about it," she mused aloud.

Biting on the end of her pen, she shifted her mental gears back to her paper and studied the shapes she had already drawn onto it: running water, rams horn, wolf's print, hands on hips. No, this was not right. It was too much like a design Maryam would make. It needed to be unique, to reflect her own life, not Maryam's traditional ideas about how carpets should look. But it would also need to be simple enough for her to complete the weaving before the week was out, if possible. Nine or ten days at the most, anyway. For, she figured that was all the time she had, though she was not sure exactly why she felt so certain about it. She picked the drawing off the floor, crumpled it and threw it across the room.

Ayşegül pushed herself up from her seated position, walked to her cupboard and grabbed several clean sheets to carry back to her floor spot. In case she made more mistakes and needed to start anew more than once. As she passed her windowsill, she flipped the large hourglass over. Its white crystals started to stream from the top bowl toward the bottom and, watching this process for a moment, Ayşegül was astonished at the quick passage of time as evidenced by the rapid running of sand in the glass. She would need to weave this carpet faster than she had ever weaved before, if she wanted to complete it in time. But how, if she could not even come up with a design for it?

She knit her brow. "*Allah*, think!"

She was about to resume her drawing position under the window, when her door opened. She felt the rush of cool air and then heard the hard thump of a body against its thick wood. She jumped, clutching her drawing papers to her chest.

"Ayşegül-*hanım,* Ayş!" It was Zeliha, grasping the outside door handle with white knuckles, and gasping. Perspiration caused strands of her usually impeccably combed chestnut-colored hair to stick to her cheeks in wavy formations, like the tendrils of new growth on a grape vine.

"Zeliha! What are you doing? You scared me!"

"I know, I am sorry, but Ayşegül, listen, I have to talk to you." Zeliha peered down the hallway in both directions, her head snapping to each side like that of a small panicked mouse. Then she stepped deeper into the room and quickly closed the door, clutching the inside handle as if it were going to break off in her hand if she let go. The sight of Zeliha's almost comic distress made Ayşegül giggle.

"Zeliha-*hanım,* what is wrong? You look like a crazed dervish after a long Sema dance." Ayşegül crossed her eyes, tilted her chin to one side and raised her arms outstretched, one palm facing up and the other facing down. Her blank sheets of paper fanned out from her hands.

Zeliha spurted out a single snort of laughter and let go of the door. "Stop, Ayşegül! Don't make me laugh." She crossed her arms in front of her chest. "Anyway, you have the hands wrong, you clown. The right palm is supposed to face up, not the left one."

Ayşegül uncrossed her eyes, lifted her shoulders, and looked up toward the ceiling. "Who cares? I had to do something, didn't I, you looked so ridiculous just now. Really. Why are you being so strange? Come over to the bed."

Together the two friends strode the few steps to Ayşegül's single bed in the far corner. Ayşegül sat down in the middle of the cotton mattress between the head and the foot, and perched on the edge. She placed the papers she was holding beside her. Zeliha, wiping the moisture off her flushed cheeks, took her spot on Ayşegül's other side. The bed frame underneath creaked as she sat. The two young women turned and faced each other.

"Ew, what's that smell?" asked Zeliha, crinkling her nose.

"What smell?"

"I don't know, like..." Zeliha sniffed a couple of times and rolled her eyes upwards in thought. "Like smoke? But that can't be."

"*Bok.* Crap," said Ayşegül. "You can tell?"

"What do you mean, Ayşegül? It's pretty strong. What have you been doing?"

"Oh, just a little accident," she said in a lilting tone.

Zeliha sniffed twice more and then said, "*Tamam*. Okay, if you don't want to tell me." Since her dramatic entrance a moment before, her breath had ceased its gasping intensity and become more measured. Ayşegül smiled. Her comic pose had done the trick.

"No, it's really nothing. Don't worry." Now Ayşegül touched her friend's shoulder lightly. "So, what is so urgent? You really did look like a crazy *fakir*."

Suddenly serious again, Zeliha leaned forward and seized Ayşegül's shoulders. Her long fingers dug into Ayşegül's blouse and, though it hurt, Ayşegül chose to ignore the pain. She knew her friend was not hurting her deliberately. Her fervor was a sign of Zeliha's obvious distress. Still clutching Ayşegül, Zeliha whispered, "*Canım*, I just heard something and I don't think I was supposed to. I'm scared."

Ayşegül twined her arms around her friend's and gazed into her eyes. "What do you mean? Who did you hear? What did they say?"

Zeliha disengaged her arms from Ayşegül's, placed her palms face down on either side of her, and leaned back. She sighed. "Remember last night—after the concert—we were all talking, and drinking our *şerbet*? Before the interruption of Süleyman Şefik Pasha, I mean." Her words came out in tight bursts.

"*Evet*, I remember. Of course. It *was* only last night, Zelihaciğim," replied Ayşegül, rubbing her shoulders. "So? What happened?"

Zeliha locked her wolf-like eyes onto her friend's and said, haltingly, "It was about...you."

Ayşegül burst into laughter. "Me? That's impossible. Why would anyone talk about me?"

"Ayş, you know how this place is. Everyone gossips. Even Berkan."

Ayşegül nodded her head. "True. He's the worst! Especially when he's in the middle of baking *su böreği* for His Highness, *Şahbaba*. Which I understand, because they're so complicated to make, and if he makes a mistake..." She drew her right hand, palm down, rapidly across her throat. "Really, he gets so frustrated, he can't help badmouthing anybody who comes into his head. It's almost funny. As long as you're not the one he's badmouthing." She smiled.

"I know. Berkan is terrible that way. But this isn't funny, Ayş. This was serious." Her small mouth was set in a tight line and Ayşegül stopped chuckling.

"What could someone say about me that is so serious? All I do is make carpets and play the *saz* badly."

"It was Gülizar and Shahinaz yammering, as they do. They were in that alcove near the chandelier in the Muâyede Salonu, you know? I was in our hallway on my way to see Hande-*hanım*. She wanted to borrow some thread from me. Anyway, I was coming around the corner and just before I turned into the alcove, I heard your name. And it was not in a nice way, either." Zeliha dipped her head and shook it slowly, her eyes cast towards the floor.

"Which one? Who said my name like that?" Ayşegül sat erect now on the mattress and scowled.

Zeliha looked back up at her friend. "I think it was Gülizar. But she was whispering, and I couldn't see who was talking. It's dark in there when the electric light is not switched on. I'm sure they did not want anyone to see or hear them. They were standing really close to each other. I mean, it was really furtive."

"Okay, so what else did they say besides my name? What made you so scared?" Ayşegül sat still for a moment. *Uh oh, maybe they know what happened. And that will make some people in the palace angry. But how could they know? No one does!*

"I couldn't hear very well," said Zeliha, interrupting Ayşegül's silent ruminations. "But I heard something about how you took advantage of the sultan because he is so old and all. That they heard you *stole* something! Which is ridiculous, of course."

Here, Zeliha shook her head vigourously and rolled her eyes toward the ceiling. "But," she continued, leaning forward intently. "I heard the name Tanju, too. I think they said he's going to come 'talk' to you. And you know what that means. You know how tight-knit he and Saskar Kadın are. So..." She shuddered. "I came as fast as I could to warn you. Do you know what this is about?"

Ayşegül's heart, on hearing Zeliha's report, had begun to beat faster under her white chemise. She hoped Zeliha could not hear the pounding. The mention of Tanju's name brought on a sudden internal panic. As the head eunuch, he controlled all the girls and was responsible for their ultimate fate. Or rather, he was the one in charge of ensuring that whatever decrees the sultan made were carried out. She had heard stories of girls disappearing, being thrown into the Boshporus inside a burlap bag, or smothered in their beds. But surely, that was in the old days. These were modern times. Nothing like that happened anymore.

Or did it?

Shut up, you're imagining things. Tanju is stern, but he wouldn't hurt you.

Or would he?

Say something. Don't let Zeliha see how you nervous are.

Ayşegül blinked. She sat still for a moment, gathering her composure. She must not let Zeliha think she had anything to be afraid of. That whatever Gülizar and Shahinaz had intimated, it had nothing to do with her, after all.

"Zeliha, my dear *arkadaş*. I'm so fortunate that you're my friend." Ayşegül smiled, just a little bit. Then she reached for Zeliha's right hand. "And I'm so glad you came to tell me this. Don't worry. Tanju doesn't have that much power. And Gülizar and Shahinaz are trouble-makers. Everyone knows that. They're idiots. Whatever it is they were saying about me..." she looked up to the plaster ceiling. "It's nonsense. Forget about it." She squeezed Zeliha's hand.

"Really? You're not worried?"

"Nope," Ayşegül lied. She hated doing it, but she definitely did not want to involve her best friend in her awkward predicament. "*But,* I'll keep an eye on those two. I don't trust them much anyway. Ever since that time that they purposely placed a bar of soap on the floor of the hamam when I was bathing, remember? If I had slipped on it after my bath, I would have smacked my head on the marble and I would probably be dead now. I am sure that was their plan. They're just *kaltaklar*." Bitches. She forced herself to laugh.

Zeliha sat for a moment staring at her friend. Then she let out a breath and chuckled.

"*Tamam*, okay, c*anım*. Well, I hope you're right. But I'm glad I told you, anyway. You might want to sleep with that candlestick under your pillow, though. Just in case." And she grinned, her beautiful eyes shining in the sunlight that streamed through the window.

"And my *kirkit*. The steel combs would do some good damage, don't you think?"

"I'd love to see Tanju with a few holes in his face. He's so vane, you know."

The two friends burst into laughter. After a few moments, they locked eyes and then, as if on cue, each reached toward the other in a bear hug, their pale cheeks brushing lightly.

As they embraced, Ayşegül uttered a silent invocation. *I was right. Something is up. Now, thanks to Zeliha, I know for certain that I must be careful. And quick. The faster I make my carpet, the better. Even if I have to stay up nights until it's finished.*

Help me, moon.

∿   ∿   ∿

Thursday, August 15, 2013, Mid-Afternoon - Çalış Beach

Two hours later, we dragged our bodies and our bags into the small foyer of the Lavanta Ada Apart Otel on one of the unpaved back streets of Çalış Beach.

I had so long harbored negative memories of Calış, since the Adrian incident of 2005, that mentally I had crossed it off my Bucket List forever. And yet, as we walked down the dirt *sokak* toward the hotel, I was surprised at the cozy wave of nostagia that washed over me. But I was also mildly dismayed to find the iconic "dolphin roundabout" had lost its eponymous statue, which we often used as a landmark instead of the street names at that main intersection. Now, the center of the roundabout featured bushes and flowers, as well as a bronze sculpture of the earth, defined by a few longitudinal and lattitudinal lines and two-dimensional depictions of the various continents. Inside the bronze perimeter was open space. I had preferred the dolphins, but the plants were a nice touch.

The roundabout was not the only change to the area. All the main roads we traversed en route to the Lavanta were now paved with brick. This was a decided improvement over the old, pitted asphalt at least. Most of the familiar restaurants were still there, though the Indian one had morphed into a bakery (which, hopefully, served Americanos instead of Nescafe— I would check it out when I had a chance), but there was a new *pide* place. In fact, I had noted a large Kipa supermarket, too, that had not been there in 2005. No doubt there would be other changes we would discover as we went about our business. Whatever that was going to be.

As we dropped our bags on the red tile floor of the hotel, a scruffy mutt with an oversized head and incredibly short legs scurried over to us, yapping enthusiastically.

"Do not worry, he is friendly dog," said a raspy voice, that of a heavy smoker, if I was not mistaken. It seemed to emanate from the shadows of the walls. Indeed, my nose detected a whiff of leftover tobacco vapor in the air.

"*Git*, Canavar! Lie down," the voice added.

146

Paz and I looked at each other and raised our eyebrows. This was going to be an amusing place to crash.

As the Corgi-esque canine sulked to its bed in the corner, a thirties-something woman with curly, voluminous hair, kept somewhat at bay by an orange and yellow strip of fabric tied behind her ears, stepped into view. Where she came from I had no idea. There were no open doors that I could see except for the one we were standing in front of, and I had not heard anyone enter the room. Her sudden entrance was a bit unnerving. Maybe she was a distant relative of Paz's. But she smiled, a crooked front tooth marring what otherwise would have been a brilliant display of browned enamel (evoking memories of Naji), and my trepidation about her vanished almost as abruptly as she herself had appeared.

As she reached out to take Paz's hand, she nodded at the banished canine and said, affectionately, "Canavar, it mean 'monster.' He is little monster, yes?"

Paz laughed. "If you say so." The creature in question curled his lips in a sinister smile that seemed to say, "Just you wait."

"I am Nevra," continued the woman. "You are Paz Lavigne?"

"Yes, *evet*. That's me!" responded my companion, shaking our hostess's hand vigorously. "And this is my friend, Molo."

For some reason, I nodded my head once and blinked in the familiar way that Turks do when they are agreeing with something. "*Memnun oldum*," I said. The old ways were returning to me in spite of myself.

"Nice to meet you, also. 'Molo.' I never hear that name before. Is it English?" Her gaze was intense and I sensed a keen intelligence behind her almond-shaped green eyes.

"Uh, not exactly. Just a nickname, really," I muttered, embarrassed. What *was* my name? Well, soon she would know when she took our passports. "It's what my friends call me."

"Ah, *evet*, I understand," she said, her round head bouncing up and down like a bobble head doll's. "A *takma*. Very good. 'Molo,' hmm." She turned her face at an angle and her thick brows knitted inwards. I had not experienced such interest in my goofy moniker since that day at the Giant Dipper when Adrian had congratulated me on my creative friends.

"Okay, Paz-*Bey* and Molo, we must check in now and then I show your rooms." I was mildly surprised to hear her use the plural there, as it had not occurred to me that Paz would book us separately. I sighed in relief. His relentless energy and scheming exhausted me, so I was glad I would get some time to myself on this escapade. And I was saving money by not being in Istanbul anymore, so my wallet would not be overburdened with this surprise. Definitely some private space in which to examine the curious note that was burning a hole in my pouch was more than welcome.

Which reminded me...

I must make sure Paz did not see my passport when I handed it to Nevra. While he followed her to the makeshift check-in counter at the other end of the foyer, I turned my back. As surreptitiously as possible, I pulled my shirt hem out of my pants, unzipped my travel pouch and rifled my passport pages to fish out the note.

"Mole, what are you doing? Let's get checked in."

Holding my breath, I pulled out my passport, stuffed the note back into the now empty slot of the pouch and zippered the pouch closed. Then I turned around.

"Here you go," I said, handing my blue booklet to Nevra. Without even perusing its contents, she placed it in a drawer behind the counter, locking it with a key she took from her pocket, and brushed her hands on her trousers. *Whew, good thing you retrieved that thing before she shut it away.* Why, I was not exactly sure.

Canavar, from his bed in the corner, opened one eye. Did he know something? *No, of course not.* Nevertheless, I peered at him suspiciously and placed my right thumb in between my first and index fingers, the fig sign to ward off the evil eye. Cengis had taught me in 2005.

Our rooms were on the second floor, which we accessed via two flights of narrow marble steps that were divided by a sharp right turn, and flanked by wooden banisters attached to the pale green walls. No atrium here as in Mavi Dolfin Evi. Lavanta Ada was altogether humbler. I found myself liking it better for that. In fairness, probably anything would have felt better than a return to the place I had shared my last days with Adrian.

Nevra chattered like a squirrel as we climbed, and then shoved keys into our hands as she indicated our rooms. Mine was to the right of the stairs and Paz's was on the opposite side of the narrow hallway. This extra space between us heightened my relief. It acted as the architectural version of a Red Sea after parting for Moses. A safety zone. Paz would have to cross it, knock on my door, and wait for me to let him in if he wanted to come in for any reason. After the incident in Istanbul last night, I promised myself I would double check my locks from here on out.

I rewarded Nevra with an ebullient smile and she grinned back.

"*Kahvalte* is serving at eight in the morning until ten-thirty, my friends. Turkish breakfast: toast and eggs and coffee, et cetera." She waved her hand airily. "You see dining room next to office when you come down. Anything more you need at this moment?"

"We're good, thanks, Nevra," said Paz. "We'll see you later."

Our buoyant hostess tipped her head to the right slightly, turned on her scuffed beige ballet flats, and bounced down the stairs. When she had turned left at the corner where the stairwell angled, Paz whispered, "That was easy, at least. C'mon, let's put our stuff down and get going."

"Going? Where? It's nearly eight o'clock."

"Aren't you hungry? I'm starving."

"You're always starving. But, yeah, I could definitely eat. Let's see if Can's is still open. We can walk there in about ten minutes, if I remember right. What d'ya think?" "Can" was the Turkish equivalent of "John," though to see it written that way always took me a moment of concentration to remember not to pronounce it "kan." I wondered if this particular Can would remember us from the few times we four had dined at his restaurant in 2005. Before Adrian's accident.

"Sounds good to me," replied Paz, turning the key in the lock to his room. "Just something simple like *pide* would be good."

"And *ayran*," I added, opening my own door. Paz flinched.

"*Ayran*, no. Beer, yes."

Without even turning on the lights, we threw our bags and packs into our respective rooms, closed our doors and almost bumped into each other as we dashed back into the hall.

"When we're chowing, I'll tell you what I'm thinking about for tomorrow," said Paz. He practically skipped down the steps.

"Why is it we're always talking about plans while we're eating out?" I asked. It was meant rhetorically, but Paz called over his shoulder.

"Because I like it that way!"

"Some things never change," I said.

"What?"

"Nothing. I can't wait to hear what's next on this charade."

"Oh, you're gonna love it. Trust me." I could almost feel Paz winking.

"I was afraid you'd say that."

By then we were at the bottom of the steps and heading for the open foyer door. I could see that dusk was just beginning to nudge daylight back to its nighttime lair. At this time of year it stayed light until almost nine. A sliver of moon glowed against the backdrop of fading sky and I wondered: was it waxing or waning? Was it on its way to fullness, or retreating? I was never good at astronomy.

149

A couple of Turkish boys in shorts kicked a ball across the street, but Nevra was nowhere to be seen. It was if she had been sucked back into whatever vortex she had first appeared from. Strange. This whole endeavor was strange. I thought again about the note in the pouch around my waist and shook my head. What this was all about, I could not glean. Well, perhaps I would get another sliver of insight at my late supper with Paz.

He and I dashed toward the street outside and Canavar raised his large head. As we exited his domain I heard him yap "careful."

But I must have imagined it.

ટ્ર ટ્ર ટ્ર

Chapter 12

"Carthāgō dēlenda est." Or... "Carthage must be destroyed." - Attributed to Roman senator, Cato, before the Third Punic War

September 13, 1922, Eleven in the Morning - Uşak Province

T he truck with the three silent men approached the town of Uşak. Demetrius hoped they would continue past the turn-off, following along the highway toward his ultimate destination. Smyrna.

At the Uşak turning, however, a man standing erect and grave raised his arm. His distinctive uniform hung loosely over his slight frame and his blood red fez sat imperiously atop his square head. Demetrius had seen plenty of these uniforms and he knew at once. The man was Turkish army. What regiment, however, Demetrius could not determine. His heart stopped.

"*Dur!*" The man on the road croaked. Stop.

The truck driver's mustache twitched on one side. "*Bok*," he said. The single syllable was barely discernible behind the thick curtain of fuzz that overhung his lips. Despite the quick curse, he nevertheless moved his left foot to the clutch, his right to the brake, and down-shifted, the metal stickshift grinding into first gear. Slowly, he pulled the vehicle to the side of the highway and shifted into neutral. He kept the engine running.

Demetrius's heart now began to pound in time to the throaty idling of the truck's engine. In the distance, a thrush chirped. Perhaps it was calling for its mate. Its notes were solemn and wistful.

The soldier marched to the driver's window, poking his fezzed head toward the open space. "Where are you going?" he asked, brusquely. This much Demetrius could understand. Not only could he translate the Turkish words in his mind, but the barking tone of the soldier's command left no room for doubt. He was not fooling around.

The sloe-eyed driver turned to look at the soldier. He tilted his head to the left, blinked, and said, "Smyrna-*ya*."

Demetrius stifled a whoop of relief. The truck *was* headed for Smyrna. *Thank the gods,* he muttered silently. He could not risk letting the other men, particularly the soldier at the window, hear his Greek utterance. They would immediately realize he was an imposter. The other passenger said nothing, only shuffling his buttocks on the seat leather and rearranging his shoulders, as if adjusting his own discomfort, trying to appear at ease.

"*Hayır!*" snarled the soldier, shaking his head side to side. "No Smyrna." His chin jutted sharply upwards and he thumped his right fist on the edge of the window opening. "It is not possible today."

Demetrius's heart stopped beating. No Smyrna? Why not?

The ever-calm driver looked the soldier in the eye and asked, "Why not? I must deliver this load there today. I have customers."

"Not possible. Smyrna is having big problems. You want to know what? Our army is throwing the stinking Greeks out. Finally. After Dumlupınar, no more Greeks in Ottoman lands. Mustafa Kemal is taking over."

Demetrius could hardly believe his ears. His Turkish was not fluent by any means, but he heard the words for "no" and "Smyrna" and "Greeks" and "Kemal."

And he understood.

If he went to Smyrna now, there would be trouble for him. His mind started to race with queries and worries. What was going on? Were his fellow combatants there and were they under siege? If so, what would happen to them? The Turkish general was known for his uncompromising tactics. Despite his trepidation, Demetrius still wanted to get to Smyrna. He wanted to see for himself what the situation was.

The soldier peeped his head around the driver's, trying to get a glimpse of the other two passengers sitting beside him. His brows knit together and he scowled, but then he banged the door with his hand and said, "You may stop in Uşak or Gediz, but you cannot go to Smyrna. No one will be allowed. You understand?"

The driver sighed and nodded his head. "*Evet.* I understand." Then he nodded curtly at the soldier as that man strode purposefully back to his position at the roadside.

The driver shifted back into first gear, then shifted again in order to reverse the truck. Making a three-point maneuver, he turned the vehicle back onto the highway. Only now it was headed in the direction from which it had just driven.

"*Başka bir yol biliyorum,*" he announced.

I know another way.

Demetrius understood. He smiled and uttered a short, silent prayer.

ॐ   ॐ   ॐ

Tuesday, June 21, 2005, Morning - Çalış Beach

"See ya later, Molo!" shouted Adrian.

I poked my head out from our bathroom door where I had just been brushing my teeth. Adrian's hand was on the open door and he was half-way into the hallway.

"You're going somewhere?" I asked, the residual mintiness of my toothpaste suffusing my mouth with chemical exhilaration. I wiped a spot of the paste off my chin and hoped that in doing so I did not also wipe my happy feelings away.

"Yeah, just going into town for a little while," said Adrian. His tone was casual, and yet I was confused. I had thought we were walking down to Çalış Beach for a swim. But the last thing I wanted was to seem too eager. Or to let him know how disappointed I was. The happy feelings had indeed been diminished by Adrian's announcement.

"Oh, right. Do you want me to go with you?"

"Nah, it's okay. I'm just gonna check out a couple things. Thanks, though." Adrian smiled that bewitching smile, which never failed to vanquish me. "You should go swimming while I'm gone. It's a superb day for it."

Yeah, and you were supposed to go with me, I whined inwardly. In spite of my attempt to seem nonchalant in the face of my disappointment, I felt a niggle of resentment. What was so urgent that Adrian would need to sneak into town instead of swim with me, as he had agreed? He had never reneged on his word before, so this departure from the norm waved in my consciousness like a red flag.

"What are Paz and Mallie up to, do you know?" I asked. Were they part of his new plan, or was he on a solo mission? Was he leaving me out on purpose? Were the three of them going on an expedition that they did not want me to be part of? It seemed unlikely. But at the moment, I felt anything was possible. And I wanted to know if I harbored intense feelings for a guy who was not what he appeared to be. Surely that was not possible. No way. Not after all this time. Adrian was the golden boy of gallantry.

"Nope," he said. "I think they're still sleeping. You know how they are." He winked. "Anyway, ciao, Mole. Don't drown in the Med, okay? That

153

would put a damper on our vacation." He chuckled at his bad pun.

"Haha, funny," I said. "Anyway, not sure if I'm going to the beach or not. I might go into town myself in a little while. I kinda want to get some souvenirs."

Adrian's brows furrowed. Then he said, "Really? Why don't you just go to the shops in Çalış? Just about anything you could want is down there, dude. Doesn't make sense to go all the way into town." He paused, and I could almost see his mind clicking. "Well, that's up to you. Anyway, I gotta go. See you later."

He smiled again and then the other half of him vanished beyond the door. It was as if some meddling *djinn* had swooped down and whisked him into the ether of ancient dreams. He must have been in a hurry, too. He left the door open.

I hovered another moment at the entrance to our bathroom, then hurried to the door Adrian had just disappeared through. I peered into the hallway and whipped my head to the right toward the three-story atrium, then left toward Mallie and Paz's room. Nothing. Not even a whiff of Adrian's deodorant or a swirl of specter dust. The whole floor was abandoned.

I ducked back into the room, closed our door, and walked over to the balcony window. Maybe I could spot Adrian on the street. I scanned the section of roadway that led to the Mavi Dolfin's entrance.

But Adrian was not there.

How could he have disappeared so quickly? Maybe he went out the back way and down a different *sokak* than the one we had gotten accustomed to taking, mostly because it was the one we knew. The town of Çalış was small, but its streets comprised a perplexing maze of alleys and alleys off of alleys, with no name signs except at the major thoroughfares. We had not been staying there long enough to familiarize ourselves with all the twists and turns. It was possible Adrian got confused and was even now searching for the direction of the main street that led to town, whatever it was called. I had forgotten to ask him how he was even getting to Fethiye, which was a good fifteen minutes by car. Surely, he was not walking.

More than likely, he would catch a *dolmuş*.

Cengiz had taught us the *dolmuş* bus system after our six-day tour had ended and the four of us wanted to explore the area on our own. It was quite a clever set-up. *Dolmuş*, according to Cengiz, meant "stuffed." And, indeed, the little buses looked like white loaves of bread puttering down their specific routes, stuffed with riders. If you were a pedestrian, the drivers beeped at you when they passed, to alert you in case you needed a lift. There were designated stops, but if a driver did not beep at you, you could just hail him (it was always a him), even if you were in between the official stops. That would never be allowed in the California transit system, but it was one of the major benefits of taking the *dolmuş.* Another benefit: the cost was only fifty *kuruş,* something like thirty cents. And they went everywhere. In short, very user-friendly.

The tricky part was asking the driver to let you off if you were not going to the end of the line. The complicated Turkish phrase I had tried to memorize from my Turkish/English travel booklet always eluded me. Fortunately, because these curious vehicles were widely used by locals and tourists alike, and almost always full, there was bound to be someone getting off where you wanted to—assuming you could figure out where that was!

The more I thought about it, the more I decided that the *dolmuş* was Adrian's ride into Fethiye. Still, why was he going there in the first place? He had never mentioned to me that he was thinking about it. That oversight—was it an oversight?—in itself was unusual. Adrian was always straightforward and forthcoming. And since we had become so close, I had never known him to leave me out of his confidence.

What is he up to?

I stood at the window quietly, looking out, and to an omniscient observer I would no doubt have appeared serene and calm. But I was not. My head was crackling with curiosity. What was Adrian doing that was so important he would break his "date" with me? In spite of my disappointment, I realized whatever it was was none of my business. For, in truth, just because we were best friends—and in my mind, even more—did not mean I was entitled to be apprised of everything he did. I knew that. And I tried never to cling. So, why could I not just leave it alone and get on with my own day? What was niggling me about his furtive departure?

I gazed out the window for a few minutes, trying to decide what to do with myself now that my day's plans had gone pear-shaped. Then I sat on my bed, slipped on my Teva sandals, grabbed my daypack and went out. Unlike Adrian, I remembered to close the door.

In the hallway, I turned left. If Adrian did not want to spend the day with me, I would pal up with Mallie and Paz. Chances were they would be thrilled to swim in the Med yet again. Maybe that was already their plan. Because, really, we could not get enough of the Mediterranean's balmy embrace, and had all spent quite a bit of our time there when not taking the *dolmuş* to the rock tombs or the ancient amphitheater or some such tourist site.

Maybe I could even persuade them to embark on the longer *dolmuş* trip to Ölüdeniz.

Ölüdeniz was to Çalış what La Jolla is to San Diego. In other words, the jewel in the crown of local beachery. I had never seen anything like it. The tiny town of Ölüdeniz itself was also redolent of Capitola, near Santa Cruz, quaint, but surprisingly crammed with overpriced eats and knock-off beach paraphernalia. Even so, tucked away on an isolated cove down an impossibly steep, vertiginous embankment, and surrounded by the imposing Taurus mountains, once there you felt removed from the rest of the world.

And the water. So brilliantly blue, so clean and clear and shining. We had all swum in it once already, and it had taken the threat of the last *dolmuş* back over the mountain into town to get us to leave. So, I was pretty sure I could talk Mallie and Paz into going again.

But when I knocked on their door, there was no answer.

∿ ∿ ∿

October 19, 1922 – Constantinople

After Zeliha's hug and departure, Ayşegül grabbed her abandoned blank sheets of paper from her bed where she had left them and hurried to her work place on the floor. If no one else barged into the room, she would have a few hours to create her new carpet design.

She stripped off her kaftan and settled down on the floor, arranging her legs in a crossed position again so that she could lean forward to draw. It was almost as uncomfortable as sitting on her stool when she weaved. But she was accustomed to both and did not think much about it as she concentrated on what she wanted her carpet to say.

∿ ∿ ∿

"Tell me about Ömer's business then," I said, between bites of my chicken and *peynirli pide*.

The white cheese *peynir* had a sour aftertaste that, though I did not always savor it, somehow spiced up the blandness of the boiled chicken on my boat-shaped *pide*. *Pide* is Turkey's answer to pizza. Which, of course, is a universally loved menu item, in Turkey as well as elsewhere. I scarfed enthusiastically. It had been eight years since I had had the opportunity.

The last time I had eaten at Can's place in 2005, I was different than I was now. When Can, wearing a frayed tee-shirt asking *Wassup Homies?*, exited his restaurant structure and came outside on the grapevine-covered patio to take our orders, he seemed to look askance at Paz and me for a moment. We probably seemed familiar but not perhaps the "homies" his shirt addressed. But as it had been eight years, and because I was not quite the same person I was back then, he might have thought he was mistaken in thinking he recognized us.

I saw him squint for a second, as if trying to work it out, but then he shook his head, ever so slightly, and politely took our order. Neither Paz nor I enlightened him. In my case, I decided to act as if I were a new customer, just as I had with Mustafa at the Beşik. Was it because I was embarrassed, or because I thought they would be embarrassed? Did I like being incognito, another version of myself? Perhaps. But mostly, to try to explain everything, to justify the change, my reasoning, my ordeal, was too complicated and too personal. I was not even sure that Paz and Mallie understood. If my two best friends did not, how could the proprietors of a hotel and a restaurant who hardly knew me begin to comprehend? In the end, I kept it simple. And safe. I said nothing.

Paz held a thin, rectangular slice of his own *sujuk* sausage *pide* in his hand, paused for a moment, then shoved it in his mouth. After chewing briefly he reached for another slice. I waited patiently. As before, I realized I was more likely to coax information out of him while he was engaged in his favorite activity—eating. So far, however, the information had been coming in small bites instead of large chunks. Hopefully that was about to change.

"You know he has a company in Istanbul, right?" Paz responded. Then he took a bite of the fresh slice.

157

"Well, I thought I'd heard someone mention it. That's why I went to Istanbul in the first place. I was going to look up the business before I arrived there, obviously." I stopped for a moment, remembering that this morning was when I had planned to do just that. So much had happened in such a short amount of time. "I probably should have done more research before I left the States. Then you came along and usurped my whole plan, anyway. I don't actually know what kind of company it is, now that I think about it."

"I thought not," said Paz, chewing. "That's why it's a good thing I *did* usurp. As you say."

"But why? I could've figured it out, you know." I took a swig of my *ayran*. Unfortunately, this version was from a plastic container. It did not have the frothy coolness of the home-made variety, such as the one I drank at the *lokanta* in the Sultanahmet the night before. But it was still soothing.

"Yeah, maybe," said Paz. "But it would help to have a little background. Ömer's a slippery oyster."

"You can say that again." I watched as he munched another slice of *pide*. A blob of white *peynir* slid off onto the plastic table. I rolled my eyes. When was Paz ever going to get to the nitty gritty of things? "Sooo?"

"So, *what*?" That blank look again.

"What kind of business is he into?" I asked, struggling not to scream bloody murder in my frustration.

"Oh, not one business. Several. And probably more." Paz leaned back, taking a breather, I guess, from all that sausagey, doughy deliciousness he seemed so intent upon.

"Such as?" God, trying to get any useful information from Paz was like trying to extract gold from a dead man's tooth.

"Gold, for one. That's the big thing in Istanbul. And he has a small gold shop in Fethiye, too." He paused. "But—and this is the pertinent thing—he also deals in carpets." Now, at last, it seemed we were getting somewhere. Or were we?

"Carpets?" I squished my chin back toward my neck and grimaced. This was probably the last thing I had expected Paz to say. Carpets?

"Yep. Carpets. You know, those wooly, rectangular things you put on floors." He winked.

"Yeah, haha. And?"

"But our Ömer is not into the ones at those bijou tourist shops we checked out back in the day. You know, where the shopkeeper would snap his fingers and his assistant would throw samples onto the floor all over the place. And then, remember? We'd get some free apple *çay* afterwards. Or *rakı,* if we were lucky."

"Okay, I remember. Forget the *rakı.* So, what other carpets are there?" My eyes screwed up in confusion. What was Paz on about? And what in the world did it have to do with Ömer? Or me? Or the Adrian incident (which was the real crux of this whole excursion to begin with)?

"Molo, have you been hiding under a rock or something? Don't you know that Turks are famous for their carpets?" Paz took a swig from his small bottle of Efes beer.

"Kind of. But I haven't really paid much attention," I replied, shrugging my shoulders.

"You can say that again." Paz chuckled.

"And?"

"Turkish carpets go way back. And some of the antique ones are really valuable. You can't just buy one and take it out of the country. You have to get a certificate of authentication and stuff."

"Really? That's weird. But what does that have to do with Ömer?"

"Ömer, *mi amiga,* or *amigo,* or whatever you are, is a major dealer in these antique carpets. And some of them are worth an extreme bit of bob. He trades worldwide."

"What do you mean, 'extreme bit of bob?'"

"I mean, like, thousands of dollars extreme. More, in lira."

"Wow, they must be pretty special then. I don't get it. I mean, who can pay that kind of money for an old carpet? Who would *want* to?"

"Exactly. Well, apparently, some people do. Obviously, not you and me. But there are people with money who like that kind of thing. It's considered art. High art, especially if it's also got some historical value."

"Yeah, I guess I can see that in a way. Some of the older carpets I saw in those shops in Sultanahmet and Fethiye were pretty amazing."

"And think about how they were made. I mean, the antique rugs, not the factory-produced ones they sell these days. Hours and hours someone sits in front of a loom, knotting one little strand of wool at a time. Turkish carpets use a double-knot technique that other cultures, like Persia and India, don't. It's a very distinct process. Very durable. And those intricate designs. Takes incredible patience, I would think. Can you imagine?" Paz took another, longer, swig of Efes. He set his bottle down, as if that last bit of intelligence and the subsequent beer intake had worn him out and he needed a rest.

"Nope," I responded. "Not really. It'd probably drive me nuts."

"Me, too," said Paz.

I looked up to the side for a moment, trying to picture a young Turkish village girl, or even an elderly one, poised in front of those low-lying looms hour after tedious hour, wrapping hundreds of strands of colored wool around the woof or weft or whatever it was called that they knotted onto. We had watched a couple of women demonstrate this process during our Fethiye tour in 2005. Deniz the tour guide had taken us to a place out of town where carpets were still handwoven. It seemed dauntingly time-consuming and difficult work.

"But, I'm still not following you, Paz. All this data about carpets notwithstanding. I mean, what does any of that have to do with Ömer? Or with me, more to the point? I've lost the plot." By now, I was stuffed, and pushed the remnants of my *pide* to the center of the table. I yawned. Another incredibly long day and I still felt no further along in my quest for retribution on Ömer. If Paz had a concrete plan for the next day, he had better tell me soon. Otherwise, I was going to crash.

I did not have the chance.

Because what Paz said next floored me. My exhaustion vanished in a flash.

"Don't *you* have a carpet, Molo? At your apartment, I mean?"

Goosebumps rose on my forearms. Where did those questions come from? His manner, almost as much as the words themselves, gave me the creeps. For suddenly, Paz's voice contained a guilelessness completely out of character with his usual brashy, theatrical tone. But, perhaps, this was theater of a subtler nature. I hesitated for a second before I responded.

"Me? A carpet?" I shook my head. Was he referring to that old rag my mother had begrudgingly thrown into a cardboard box of crap for me when I had moved out years ago? I had never known what to do with it, so it had stayed in the box all these years.

"Yeah, I remember Adrian said you had an old Turkish kind of rug that you never used. Or, at least, he thought it was Turkish." Here, Paz, made that left-sided smirk of his. I was not sure what to make of this sudden change of demeanor. Was he being innocently casual, or connivingly casual? Hard to tell with him sometimes.

I shook my head briskly in confusion.

"God, I don't know. I mean..." I stopped.

This conversation had taken a seriously unexpected turn, and I realized that, though Paz obviously knew something I did not, I was not sure now what my position with him was. The same hairs that stood up on my arms last night when I knew something was not right in my room at the Beşik—when *The House on the Strand* had been moved and I had eventually discovered the strange note stuck within its pages—now stood up again. That, along with the goosebumps, made me shiver.

Without knowing why, I sensed I was wading into murky waters and I was not at all certain whether Paz would help me out, or push me further in. Whatever the case, I was definitely in over my head. I had to think fast if I did not want to submerge.

And then a lightbulb switched on in my otherwise confused head.

The note.

That cryptic, ink-scribbled sketch on that curious homemade paper scrap was not some random jotting stuck in my Daphne du Maurier paperback unwittingly. Or even for a joke.

It was a careful, premeditated maneuver. A reminder. To me. But why? And by whom?

I dared not pull the item in question out from the zippered pouch clipped at my waist under my shirt. Not in front of Paz. But I wanted to. I wanted to take another close look at the scratchy inkwork. To scrutinize it more fully. Because, suddenly, its image did remind me of something. Something I had completely forgotten about. Forgotten, because it had never held any meaning for me and had lain hidden away from my sight—and my consciousness—since college.

As Paz sat there fiddling with his napkin, staring at me, I closed my eyes. The crunch, crunch of the paper cloth acted as background noise for my racing thoughts. I scrunched my eyes, concentrating, thinking, trying to recall the strange drawing I had found in my room last night. Using the inner wall of my shut eyelids as a kind of screen, I finally, consciously, projected the image of what I remembered from the drawing. And this is what I saw:

And all at once, it dawned on me. My carpet. The faded, worn, three-by-five foot rectangle of colored wool that I had completely ignored and forgotten had the same—or very similar—image to the weird note planted in my book.

I gasped.

"Molo?" asked Paz. I could hear the concern in his one word question, but I could not trust that the concern was genuine. Not if he knew about my carpet. Because if he knew about my carpet, he most likely knew about the note. And that would mean, he knew that someone had snuck into my room at the Beşik and put it there. Put it there to remind me? To confuse me? To warn me? That, I could not say.

Slowly, I opened my eyes. I looked down at my waist where the perplexing item lay hidden, snug and safe. Then I lifted my head and blinked at Paz.

"Sorry," I said. "Just giving my eyes a break for a second. I'm totally bushwhacked, dude. I think I need to go to sleep. Can we get the bill from Can now?"

Paz stared at me.

"Umm...yeah, I guess. Don't you want to discuss tomorrow's plan? I thought that's why we came here." Now Paz sounded distraught. Well, let him. I had had enough of his subterfuge and cunning. I needed to sleep, that was true. But I also needed to think. And I needed to think away from my friend. If, indeed, he was my friend.

"Not anymore. Not tonight."

Folding my own napkin carefully, I placed it on top of my partially eaten *pide*. I fiddled in my pockets, found a twenty lira bill and placed it on top of the napkin. Then I pushed away from the table, scraping the white plastic chair on the brick floor beneath us as I stood up.

My brain and body, once again, were jittery with fatigue, but now that jitter was compounded with excitement that I was no longer completely at

Paz's mercy. For now, I had discovered something. I knew he knew something that he did not think I knew. That was power. I chuckled out loud.

"What's so funny?" Paz asked, in a plaintive tone.

"Nothing," I said. But if a heart could be said to be grinning, mine was now.

I could not wait to retire to my room and study that curious ink drawing, the replication of my old rug's design. I did not exactly know what it was all about, but I did know something.

What I knew was this:

The carpet was the key to the whole mystery. It was the answer—or at least, a link to the answer—to what happened to Adrian back in 2005. I was sure of that.

Another image popped into my head. This time, it was Naji the *djinn* again. Again, he seemed to be trying to tell me something. To remind me what he had said to me in that dream—or vision—yesterday as I lay on my bed at the Beşik after my interminable flight to Istanbul.

If only I could remember.

I strode thoughtfully toward the restaurant's exit gate, hearing Paz scurrying behind me. It was a luscious sound. Let him scramble in my wake for once. I grinned as I walked. And then, in the shadows of the hanging vines and *camellia* trellis that loomed over the empty tables and chairs of Can's outdoor eatery, two large, black rats scurried toward the street beyond.

Rats. Yes, they were definitely about. And it was my job to suss them out. I would do it.

I would do it for Adrian.

Chapter 13

"He mourns the absence of his guide for awhile, and then thinks, 'What can I do to save myself from these men and their nets?'" – Mevlana (aka Rumi)

*M*ehmed stood, deep in thought, on his balcony overlooking the Bosphorus. What now?

The Empire, his empire, and that of thirty-five sultans before him, was on the brink of collapse, an accordion of power folding in on itself. The Savior of the Sublime Ottoman State could no longer hold out against the tides of time. How had this come to pass? He had fought. He had argued. He had broken promises even, with Kemal Pasha and the Young Turks, as well as Celalettin Arif, the one-time parliament speaker, and Ahmet Tevfik Pasha, the Grand Vizier. He had dissolved the Parliament. He had colluded with the Allies. He had tried everything he could think of, everything Ahmed Izzet Pasha, Minister of Foreign Affairs, had advised him to do, to remain sultan. To keep the dynasty alive. And yet, the 1920 Treaty of Sèvres could not be ratified. And the nationalists persisted. All was crumbling.

Soon, he would be deposed and the Grand National Assembly of Turkey would take over. The House of Osman, established 1299, ruling Asia Minor and nearly half of Europe and the Balkans in grandeur and supremacy, was about to slide into the backstory of history.

And what would happen after that? What would happen to his daughter, Fatma Ulviye, his son, Şehzade Mehmed Ertuğrul, his wives and other children? His little grand-daughter, Neslişah?

The sixty-one-year-old leader placed his hands on the railings in front of him. He had reigned as head of one of the most awe-inspiring and successful empires of all time.

And now it was ending. He was the last of the sultans.

He sighed and turned his back to the outside world.

෭   ෭   ෭

September 13, 1922, Afternoon - Aydın Province

The trio of men spoke occasionally—and then only in monosyllabic grunts—as the truck ambled along a dirt track, over bumps and ruts, pebbles and ditches. They seemed to be the only beings alive in this abandoned region of the world. They had only themselves, the road and the dusty maquis vegetation for company. And the endless sky.

Where are we going? Demetrius asked himself. He did not voice his question aloud. The driver, clicking his tongue in his mouth, as if speaking another language, drove on. He seemed content. Demetrius had to trust the man knew what he was doing.

He had no choice.

The sun was high now, casting shadows of prickly pear cactus and the occasional black pine onto the one-lane track. The blood red poppies had dropped their petals months ago, before the skirmishes, leaving their own blood red stain on the desolated earth.

The man in the middle, the one with the drooping mustache, reached behind him and pulled a sack onto his lap. Digging inside the sack, he soon presented a small, dappled apple to Demetrius, only nodding his square-shaped head. Demetrius nodded back and accepted the fruit, which was bitter and sweet when he bit into it. The man handed a similar apple to the driver and, after taking one for himself, quietly placed the sack behind him again.

The three men crunched and chewed, but said nothing. They threw their white fleshed apple cores out the windows for the goats and burros who might happen by.

On they drove.

Some time later, but perhaps only an hour—it was difficult to tell in this time-eluding wilderness—the driver turned left onto a flatter, straighter track. Demetrius crossed his sticky fingers on both hands, where they lay in his lap. He dared to hope that Smyrna was not far ahead.

Now the driver began to whistle, no doubt some Turkish folk tune with which Demetrius was not familiar. Why would he be? In any case, he took this whistling as a favorable sign. *We must be close.* Uncrossing his fingers, he began to tap them on his thighs in rhythm with the driver's airy notes. The mustached man wagged his head side to side.

What a funny orchestra, Demetrius thought. And smiled. He would be done with this journey at last, reunited with his Greek comrades, and on his way home. Soon.

But events were not destined to pass in that way.

Through the flat glass windshield he watched the road ahead for a few kilometers more. The little orchestra now took a break from its curious concert. All three members surveyed the landscape before them, hoping, it would seem, to glimpse the outlines of the city they sought. The place where life teemed, where children played, where women scrubbed their floors and men stood outside their shops calling to passersby to come in and appraise their quality goods.

Smyrna. The sprawling, popular port town on the Aegean Sea.

But though they hoped and watched, what they saw was nothing that they had expected to see. There were no buildings tottering on the skyline, no children throwing balls into the air, no women with their rags and buckets or men in their shiny shoes hawking their vegetables and household wares.

Where the sprawling western seaside town should have appeared, should have shown itself vast and welcoming on that sunny afternoon horizon, there was nothing.

Only smoke.

It curled gray and black, like storm clouds, but thick and tinged with flashing orange streaks. Threatening storm clouds did not display this kind of menace. This was a spectacle altogether more ominous. Sinister. Destructive. The three men knew at once that this amorphous display of gas and vapor was not clouds at all.

It was fire.

     ᄅᄅ   ᄅᄅ   ᄅᄅ

SMYRNA, Sept. 14 (Associated Press). --A fire of serious proportions is sweeping Smyrna. —The New York Times, 1922

     ᄅᄅ   ᄅᄅ   ᄅᄅ

October 28, 1922 – Constantinople

"Ayşegül-*hanım!*" called Yasmin, popping her curly head through Ayşegül's door. It was after Asr prayer time, late afternoon, and Ayşegül had ignored the summons. Indeed, she had hardly noticed when the first restrains of "*Allahu Akbar! Allahu Akbar! Fawwwwww...*" drifted through her open window. She was engrossed in her design and now, after hours of drawing and concentrating, felt a headache begin to form at her temples

166

and her resolve waning.

She sighed. Perhaps a visit would restore her spirits.

Hurriedly, she flipped her drawing upside down. She did not want Yasmin, or indeed anyone, including her friends, to see it. The design was nearly complete. Another half hour or so should do it.

"Yasmin, is anything wrong?" she asked her friend, wrinkling her brow. Yasmin, a *câriye*, a new recruit, did not often come to Ayşegül's room. Not an insider yet, she did not have as much freedom of movement in the palace as Zeliha or Ayşegül. She had not earned her own room, and lived in a dormitory with several other *câriyeler* on the lower story. For her to come to Ayşegül was unusual.

"*Hayır,* nothing is wrong, but I wanted to tell you. Estreya is here. I know you always like to visit with her when she comes." Yasmin smiled, her olive green eyes crinkling at the outer corners.

"Estreya? Here? Now?" Ayşegül felt her heart quicken. Perhaps this was her chance to find out what all the turmoil the palace was experiencing was about. Sometimes Estreya also divulged gossip about the Imperial Mabeyn, on the opposite end of the palace, where the sultan performed his administrative duties. Information like that was worth its weight in gold lira, and could prove invaluable at a time like this. Ayşegül needed as much of it as she could glean and Estreya was her best source.

She pushed herself to standing.

Yasmin, meanwhile, was staring at the floor.

"Is that one of your carpets, Ayşegül-*hanım?*" she asked. "It's beautiful." She crouched down and reached out her hand toward the small rug in the middle of the floor.

"Stop!" shouted Ayşegül. Immediately, she apologized. "I'm sorry, Yasmin, that was not kind of me. I just did not want you to trip on your skirt."

What she really meant was that she did not want Yasmin to shift the carpet and see the waxy goop beneath. It was unlikely Yasmin would think much of it, but in this place an accidental utterance could lead to unintended, unpleasant consequences. Especially now that she knew Gülizar and Shahinaz were talking about her in the shadows. Yasmin herself might not have any malice toward Ayşegül, but if she mentioned the mess on the floor, Ayşegül's enemies—whoever they were—might use this knowledge as ammunition against her. Just to stir up trouble, not because there was any real problem with a bit of wax on her floor.

Yasmin's eyes clouded over for a moment, but then she smiled again.

167

"No problem, Ayşegül, I understand." Then she motioned toward the open door. "Are you coming?"

Ayşegül approached her young friend, nudging her gently toward the door. "*Evet*, yes, thank you, Yasmin. I just have to get ready. I will see you in the hallway in a minute."

Yasmin nodded, then bowed out of the room.

As soon as Yasmin was out of sight, Ayşegül snatched up her design from the floor and hurried over to her bed. Fortunately, during her conversation with Yasmin, the ink design on her paper had now dried. She lifted up her mattress and slid the paper between the mattress and the wooden divan on which it lay. No one would be looking for it. But ever since the mysterious knocker had banged on her door last night, she had felt uneasy. She felt safer hiding her design away from prying eyes.

In this place, anything could happen.

৵   ৵   ৵

Light, golden light. Translucent.

She gazed at the dust floating down from her latticed window. No, not floating—suspended—twirling, bouncing in place. The afternoon sun beyond managed to sneak through the bars in her darkened room, creating a glittering triangle stage on which the particles danced and flickered. Lit from behind by the luminary sphere of all light, the sun, each piece of dust displayed its own halo: brilliant, flowing, transcendant. As if each were alive and resplendent in the joy of it.

She sat at her loom, her own being suspended in the moment of observing. What if these beings, so ebullient before her, were alive? Avatars of another place beyond this realm? Was it possible?

She thought of Tevfik and Tagir, her brothers. But also her mother and father and all those who had been left behind when her body, her identity, was stolen and forced to come to this place. This palace.

What were they doing now? Were they alive? Would she ever see them again?

Time ticked by. The silvery moon soon pushed the golden sun into the wings of the fading sky's perpetual proscenium. As if on cue, the twinkling motes of dust and light settled and exited the stage. Nighttime had begun.

৵   ৵   ৵

Wednesday, June 8, 2005, Still Morning - Çalış Beach

"Mal, Paz? You guys in there?"

I kept my voice low, hoping not to awaken any other guests who might still be trying to recover from a late night of carousing and drinking. "It's me, Molo. Open up!"

I waited, but not patiently, shifting back and forth on my feet as if in a kind of bird dance. The odor of eggs and other breakfast foods wafted up from below and my stomach began to growl.

"Guys!" I knocked louder. "What's up? Why don't you answer?" *Damn what's with everyone this morning?*

After a minute, I gave up. *Shit, where are they? Maybe already down at breakfast. I'll go check.*

I dashed back into Adrian's and my room to grab my daypack, into which I had already stashed my beach gear, closed and locked the door, and took the nearby stairs two at a time.

At the bottom, I collided into Murat, about to make his way up the way I had just dashed down.

"*Merhaba*, Murat," I managed to eek out between gasps. "Sorry to bother you, but have you seen my friends this morning?"

I would not have blamed him for cursing at me, but instead he nodded his head politely and said, "No, Mister Molo, I not see them. Very sorry. You look in breakfast room?"

"No, but I am going now. Thank you." I paused, still gulping air. I ought to match his civility with some of my own by at least trying out some of my Turkish. "I mean, *çok teşekkür ederim!*"

He nodded once, a slight upturn on his thin lips, and headed up toward the second floor. I turned on my heel and all but ran to the dining room on the other side of the foyer. I already knew its location from previous mornings, but even if I had not, I would have been able to find it by the clank of utensils and chattering of voices. As I poked my head into the door, I scanned the small wooden tables scattered about the floor. Several couples and a family were either eating there or clumped at the long buffet table at the farther end, loading their plates and filling their coffee and tea cups.

But no Mallie and no Paz.

Hmm. Where are *they? Why is everyone avoiding me today? Did I miss something?*

Since Mal and Paz had vanished and Adrian had deserted me to go into town on his mysterious escapade, I decided to grab a bite of food at least. I would use the time eating to figure out my next step. I selected a clean white plate from the stack at the right end of the buffet and worked my way down the line, piling the plate with hard-boiled eggs, cucumber slices, fried tomatoes, chunks of white cheese and, my favorite, the puffy bread. I skipped the Tang-like orange drink and decided to brave the freeze-dried Nescafe, scooping dark brown crystals out of a glass jar, filling my tea cup with hot water from the spout on the metal water dispenser at the edge of the table. Then I poured in milk from an already opened carton.

There was one free table in the corner. Energized from all my jogging around, I yanked the wooden chair out from the table, making a loud scraping noise on the tile floor. The other diners in the room stopped eating for a second and stared at me. I shrugged, bestowed on the room one of my apologetic smirks, and the clanking and chatter of the other breakfasters continued as before. Then I plunked down on the hard chair and started shoveling the morning's offerings into my mouth. Thankfully, the eggs were already shelled, that would save time.

But for what? Where was I going?

Think.

First, what did I know? I took a bite of most of an egg and chewed, starting a mental list.

I knew:

1)   That Adrian had decided to blow off our beach outing to go to Fethiye for some errand he did not divulge,
2)   He probably went alone,
3)   He was in a chipper mood, as usual,
4)   Mallie and Paz were not in their room...

I plopped the rest of the half-demolished egg into my mouth, munching rapidly. Knitting my brows in concentration, I continued my mental list:

5)   ...Or at breakfast (which was obvious because here I was, and my two friends clearly were not),
6)   They had decided to do whatever it was they were doing without me,
7)   I was pissed off at all three of them,
8)   And a little bit hurt, though I would not admit it to them when I found them,

9) What could be so urgent or important for Adrian, in particular, to venture forth without me?

I tore apart a section of the air-filled *ekmek* bread and mashed a dollop of butter and another of honey onto its coarse, white inner surfaces. My elbows on the table and clutching the bits of bread in both hands, I glanced out the nearby curtain. Outside, my pal the cockerel was chasing one of his coy concubine hens around the yard. Watching him terrorize his mate, and hearing his—I could only surmise it was "triumphant"—squawk, he seemed more in his element than I was in mine. I almost envied him.

Bastard.

I watched the antics of the chicken flock a few seconds longer then began to wolf down the bread in my hands. My curiosity about my trio of friends fueled my hunger, it seemed.

But now what? Should I go swimming, or try to find my companions? Were they avoiding me intentionally, or had Mallie and Paz assumed I was with Adrian and just casually headed off on their own? After all, there was no agreement between us that we had to be together all the time.

I scooped some cheese onto cucumber slices. As I spooned, something jarred my elbow and the cheese on my spoon took flight and crash landed on the floor. I leaned forward to wipe it up with my napkin, but before I could do so I heard...

"Excuse me," in a pleasant voice. "I am sorry about that, Molo."

Still bent over, I craned my head toward the voice and immediately recognized the face it had come from.

I stood back up, napkin in one hand, just missing smacking my skull on the edge of the table. I brushed my hair out of my eyes with my free hand.

"Oh, you're Emre, right? From the tour?" I blurted out. I could feel my cheeks turning red. Emre had caught me off guard—and in a rather embarrassing pose.

"Yes! So good memory. How are you?" He grinned. The Istanbul Turks always seemed delighted to practice their English skills. "You are alone today?" His grin morphed into a frown, as if he felt suddenly sad about my solo status, though he himself was breakfasting without his pal.

"Me?" I pointed to my chest. He nodded. "I, uh, well, I'm not sure." To gain time, I leaned to my right and stabbed the cheese, which had just done its best lemming imitation, with my fork. Bringing both cheese and fork up to my lap, I dislodged the errant blob from the fork tines and finally squished it into my napkin. Emre watched with amusement.

171

"Sorry," I said. "Just...you know." I shrugged. God, what an idiot I was! His mouth re-morphed into smile mode.

"Anyway," I continued. "Actually, I *am* looking for my friends. You know, Mallie and Paz. The couple."

"Oh, yes. Miss Mallie and Mister Paz. I like them very much. So funny."

"Hmm, yes. Funny." Where was this conversation going?

"Do you mind if I eat at this table with you?" Emre asked suddenly.

Did I?

"No, of course. Eat away," I responded, gesturing toward the seat opposite mine. I took a bite of cucumber and cheese, hoping to appear casual. Emre's interruption had disturbed my train of thought and, though I did not want to seem rude or unsociable, I really wanted to figure out what to do about my mislaid friends.

The amiable young Turk put his plate on the table in front of the vacant chair and then scooched onto the chair itself. He tucked a paper napkin into his open shirt collar.

"Thank you, it is a pleasure to see you again. That was a very good tour, do you think? Altan and I are so happy to come to Fethiye. Unfortunately, we must return to Istanbul tomorrow." He frowned.

"Really? That's too bad. Work?" I cut up some tomato and took a bite, watching him the while.

"No. School. We are both at university."

"Oh, yes, I remember. Engineering, right?"

"Of course. Ha! You *do* have a good memory!"

Speaking out of the side of my full mouth, I muttered, "Not really. But it was only a few days ago. Even I can remember that far back." We both snickered. I marveled at Emre's command of English. Much better than my Turkish.

For a few minutes, we concentrated on eating instead of conversing. Then Emre surprised me.

"You know, I saw Mallie and Paz this morning."

I stopped in mid-chew and looked straight at Emre's eyes.

"You did?"

"Of course!" He placed the ends of his fork and knife downward on the table. They looked like Tuareg spears sticking out of a sand dune.

"Can I ask where?" I tried to sound nonchalant. I did not want my eating companion to think I had been abandoned by my friends.

"Of course," said Emre. "They were walking to that dolphin—how you say?—roundabout."

172

Thursday, August 15, 2013, Night - Çalış Beach

Back in my own room at last.

In the distance, I heard the last calls to prayer for the night, their garbled summons squawking out of the tannoy system. I had first discovered this modern method of muezzin chants in 2005. Gone were the days when a caller had to ascend the slender minaret tower and yell his lungs out off the balcony at the top. I did not know where tannoy headquarters were located, but the puke-green, old-fashioned speakers with their splayed spouts hung almost inconspicuously from lightposts or telephone poles all around town.

So convenient was the tannoy for getting Allah's summons out nowadays, that it was also used for other announcements: urgent weather warnings, local news, political updates. With my limited understanding of the Turkish language, I could not make heads or tales of the muffled voices. I was surprised anyone could. But Murat and other locals I met the last time I was here would fill me in. Usually they laughed as they interpreted the messages. But I thought it was an ingenious system. Why did we not have something like it in the States?

Why wasn't it used when Adrian had his accident?

It was late. Tannoy din aside, I knew I would not be able to sleep until I had explored the latest peculiar development. Regarding my carpet. The carpet I had utterly forgotten about until this evening.

Paz had given me an odd stare before he disappeared into his own room, leaving me—at last—the chance to scrutinize the scribblings on the peculiar scrap of paper that was burning a hole in my money pouch.

I threw my shoulder bag onto my bed, plonked down beside it, and yanked the hem of my mola shirt from its tucked in place in my cargo pants. Reaching around my back with both hands, I unclipped the pouch and dropped it onto my lap.

Now, the unveiling. Again. Only this time I would not be so confused by what I was going to see. This time I *knew* what it was. I just did not know why. Or how.

I unzipped the pouch and carefully extracted the curious paper.

Whew.

It was still there.

For a moment, I had worried that somehow someone might have abducted it without me realizing. Some Turks were expert pickpockets. But then, whoever knew about the note *wanted* me to have it or they would not have gone to so much subterfuge and trouble to hide it in my room in Istanbul in the first place. Had it been Barış, by any chance? Was he working with Paz?

The note had gotten somewhat crimped in its journey from Istanbul to here, so I smoothed it out on my knees.

"What are you trying to tell me?" I asked the little drawing. Its presence loomed so large, it seemed to have a personality of its own.

I rubbed my eyes. Could this strange creation be a *re*creation of that old rug my mother had given me? If so, what could it mean?

I stared at the characters on the paper before me. Then I turned it over to see if I had missed something on the back last night when I had first examined it. Nothing. Nothing I could see, at least. I turned it back to front and brought it closer to my eyes. What was I missing?

Think.

Okay. I first found the thing hidden inside *The House on the Strand.* Was that significant, or just a convenient hiding place to get my attention? Maybe there was something else inside the dog-eared paperback that I had overlooked before.

I carefully placed the note onto the bed beside me, stood up, and strode over to my daypack where it lay on a table. The book with its sepia pages was peering out of the front pocket where I had left it. That at least was a relief. I pulled it out, carried it back to my bed and sat down again.

Now I examined the aged dust jacket. Nothing there but the same somewhat amateurish painting reproduction that had always been there since the 1970s.

I turned the book over, as I had the note, to see if there was anything on the back of the dust jacket. Nope. Just the usual commendatory blurbs and a few reviews.

Next, I thumbed through the entire book, turning the flaps to face the floor in case that would dislodge whatever might be inside. Again, nothing.

I pursed my lips and squinted. Now what? I guess the drawing was all there was. Well, that was enough. What more could there be, anyway? I started to put the book aside.

Except. Wait.

What is that?

Wedged toward the back, between pages 202 and 203, and stuck deep into the crevice of the binding, was another slip of paper. Had it always been there? I did not think so. I had owned this book for a long time and would surely have noticed it before. As I opened the book more fully in order to extricate this new mystery note from its hiding spot I saw, first, that it was smaller than the rug drawing, maybe two by three inches, and whiter. It was also jagged on two adjacent sides, as if it had been hand-torn from a larger sheet of, what seemed to be, modern typing paper. It was blank on the side facing me. I turned it over.

And on it, handwritten in blank ballpoint, were these words:

SILK ROAD CARPET SHOP, SAN FRANCISCO

ॐ　　　ॐ　　　ॐ

Chapter 14

"Do this or the snake will eat you." - Ali Pasha, the Albanian, of Janina

October 28, 1922 – Constantinople

Ayşegül, poised to take her last gulp of the Turkish coffee Berkan had brewed for her in his copper *cezve,* glanced at Estreya, who was sipping her coffee and watching Ayşegül intently. Yasmin sat opposite them, grimacing as she placed her cup down onto the table. Until that moment, Ayşegül had assumed Yasmin liked her coffee *sade,* barely sweetened, while Ayşegül always preferred hers *tatlı,* with extra sugar, as well as a sprinkling of cardamom, to mask the bitterness of the unfiltered beans. The coffee was so potent, it sometimes gave her jitters. But she was prepared to go through the uncomfortable physical aftermath of drinking the concoction today because she was most interested in what the *fal bakmak* reading would tell her. Or rather, what Estreya's interpretation of the left behind grounds would reveal.

"Be careful, *tatlım,* sweetie," Estreya warned. "Leave two or three sips in the bottom. You need them for the swirling."

Estreya's large brown eyes had not lost their gleam, though she must be well into her fiftieth year, Ayşegül thought. Her paisley-patterned *tichel* was pulled tight around her head and the knot that held the ends together was like a twisted bun at the nape of her neck. Today her large bosom was covered modestly with a loose blouse, striped in alternating browns, blues and orange tones, while her ample chin slid towards her ornate silver choker. With its many filigreed tassles and coins dangling over Estreya's upper chest, it reminded Ayşegül of the tribal jewelry that the harem girls used to wear. More than likely Estreya had owned this necklace for many years. Ayşegül found herself riveted by its burnished glow, as the fire from Berkan's oven reflected off its metallic surface. She could feel herself being drawn in by that glow, as if it had something to tell her.

A loud clatter shattered her absorption. Berkan must have dropped a

176

metal pan onto the brick floor nearby. Ayşegül blinked and looked back up at Estreya. By now her penetrating gaze had lightened and her lips were turned up, revealing a row of gray, even teeth. The moment of intensity had vanished. It was time to start the reading.

Suddenly recalling Estreya's admonition from a moment before, Ayşegül smiled behind her cup as she drew it to her lips. "*Tabii*, of course," she said. "I remember from last time."

"Good," replied the Jewess. She was sprawled atop her usual stool at one end of the large food preparation table where the three women, Estreya, Ayşegül and Yasmin, sat drinking and chatting. Berkan, solid and stocky in his starched apron, stood by his beloved ovens, stirring a large pot out of which streamed a thick cloud of steam. The fez that had once adorned his round head had been replaced by a tall, white chef's hat that billowed at the top like one of his puffed pastries. Ayşegül almost laughed at the sight.

Berkan and Estreya, both in their middle years, had been friends since Berkan had first come to the palace. Ayşegül sensed he liked hosting the women in his domain from time to time. The sprawling kitchen could be lonely, he had told her, despite his large staff and the constant cooking and baking for the palace. He had also revealed that he found Estreya's way of performing entertaining. His own mother read coffee grounds and it was she who had predicted he would one day have a position here.

"Don't forget to make your wish, Ayşegül-*hanım*," Estreya reminded her protégée. Ayşegül nodded, pulling her thoughts away from the two elders, and her lips away from the delicate porcelain cup.

"What did you wish, Ayşegül?" asked Yasmin. She was perched on the edge of her stool, absorbed in the ritual unfolding before her. She was not the prettiest *kız* in the harem, but her smiley, pink lips and generous nature made her one of the most popular.

Estreya gave Yasmin a mock stern look. "You know she cannot tell you, Yasmin-*hanım*. It's her secret." Estreya winked at Ayşegül.

Yasmin frowned slightly, a tiny pout. "I know, but I get so excited at a reading. I always want to know what the other person is thinking."

"Well," responded Estreya, touching Yasmin lightly on the arm. "We will chat for ten minutes about this and that while the grounds settle and form, and then I will read them. And you will find out everything. Yes?"

"I know," said Yasmin. She started squirming. "I'm too impatient, aren't I?"

At last Ayşegül, holding the cup in one hand, carefully picked up its delicate matching saucer and placed it upside down on top of the almost empty cup, making sure there was no opening between the two. When she felt sure there would be no spillage, she held the curious ensemble in front of her chest and began to move it in a clockwise circle, keeping it parallel to the floor beneath her.

"Two more rounds," prompted Estreya in her hoarse, thick voice.

Ayşegül repeated the circle twice more, concentrating on not letting the saucer disengage from the cup.

When she was done, she quickly flipped the ensemble upside down. This was an important part of the reading process. Now the grounds would cool and resettle to form the tell-tale patterns for Estreya to interpret.

Ayşegül concentrated. She wanted to be sure whatever patterns emerged would be to her utmost benefit. *Please*, she said silently. It would not do to let the other two women guess how desperate she was for a positive outcome. So much was at stake. Anything that might help her would be a bonus.

The cup and saucer, with their white background, Baroque blue fleur-de-lis design and gold trimming, sat inert on the table in front of her. She stared at them for a moment, willing the coffee they held to form shapes of a tree or a door. These were good omens. A "tree" formation could mean your life was evolving the way you wanted it to; "doors" opened your life to new opportunites. But, she knew, even good omens at certain times could be foreboding. It depended on the circumstances. And Estreya. How she interpreted them.

Hopefully she would not get the "eye." It was bad energy and almost always portended trouble. She had enough of that already.

If only she had brought her ring to place on the back of the cup. That would signal the grounds that she was interested in finding out about relationships. And she was. But she did not want the others to know about the ring. If they saw it, they would most certainly ask questions that she would feel obliged to answer. And that would reveal a secret she was not prepared to divulge.

The women, and Berkan raking over ashes at the open wood-burning oven nearby, waited for the grounds to settle. To do their magic.

Islam frowned on the practice of *fal bakmak*. No one should attempt to usurp Allah's will or wisdom. Judaism also rejected the practice. But the ancient custom persisted despite the taboos. And most of the females in the harem practiced it. Religiously.

You should not try to do a reading on yourself, though. That was why

Ayşegül sought out Estreya. But, she also trusted her more than she trusted the others. Jealousy and intrigue were rampant among the palace residents, especially now with so many unanswered questions about the state of the Empire.

"Estreya..." asked Ayşegül.

"*Evet*, little one."

"I need to know. What is happening outside? In the city? We're so isolated here, but it is obvious that since that treaty failed the palace is in turmoil. And with *Şahbaba* away at Rumelihisarı, it feels like we have been deserted. We are inmates in a giant prison." Ayşegül was wringing her hands.

Estreya leaned forward on her stool, her wide thighs spreading to make room for her generous stomach. She nodded solemnly. Then, after taking a deep breath, she spoke, hushed, almost in a whisper. Her raspy voice was somewhat softened by the hushed tones.

"*Sevgilim,* my darling, hmm, how shall I say? Do not worry too much, but you are right. There is unrest everywhere. The sultan wants to hang onto the dynasty, but Kemal, you know, the Major General, he and his new congress, they have a lot of power."

Yasmin's eyes turned large and frightened. Ayşegül sat rigid, her heart pumping.

"So, what is the story? Will the sultan stay in power?" Ayşegül asked. She hardly dared. She was not sure she wanted to know the answer. For whatever it was, it was sure to create havoc on their lives at the palace. She would rather take control of her destiny than let political rivalries usurp it from her.

Estreya leaned back, folding her plump hands over her pudgy abdomen. She turned her face up toward the soot-stained ceiling, cocking her eyes to the left. After a moment, she brought her head back to its normal angle and regarded, first Yasmin, then Ayşegül. Berkan, busying himself with his pots, stopped what he was doing and watched Estreya. One had to be careful in this place about what one said. Estreya knew that. Berkan knew that. Both young women knew that.

The three others stayed completely still, hardly breathing, while they awaited Estreya's response.

She blinked slowly. Then she said:

"What makes you think *Şahbaba* is at Rumelihisarı, Ayşegül, *canım*?"

Ayşegül, her eyes wide, had not expected a question. She hesitated. "Well...someone mentioned it. Last night. We had an *İncesaz* concert—I hardly made any mistakes, by the way—and someone told me."

Estreya's eyes twinkled. "Well, someone is wrong. The sultan is here."

Yasmin and Ayşegül turned to each other and each raised their eyebrows.

"Here?" asked Yasmin. "But no one told us. We thought he was with Nazikeda Kadın."

"He was at Rumelihisarı with Nazikeda Kadın, but he came back. Two nights ago."

"How do you know?"

"Oh, I know." Here, Estreya smiled secretively and touched her temple with her right index finger. Then she glanced quickly at Berkan. "But, it is not really a secret. He just came back early."

Ayşegül caught Estreya looking sideways at Berkan. Of course, Berkan would know. He was the sultan's head chef. She would have to remember in future to search out Berkan for information. "But why? Is there something wrong at the palace?"

"Not so much in Dolmabahçe. But there is big trouble down south. In Smyrna."

"Smyrna? Why Smyrna?"

"Because of the Greeks. Don't they tell you anything here?"

"Not really. I mean, sometimes we get reports, but Tanju makes sure we only get information that is sifted through first."

"Yes, that's true, Tanju—ach! the man who is not a man—is very loyal to our sultan. But it seems impossible that you would not know about Smyrna. It is such big news."

"So? What about it? What should we know?"

"First of all, as I said before, try not to worry. The sultan still has power and a lot people support him."

"Yes...?"

"But. It's true that since the Second Battle of İnönü last March, many Turks have become angry with his highness. Quite a few have switched over to Kemal's side. To the nationalists."

"What does 'nashunist' mean?" asked Yasmin. Her forehead crinkled up in confusion.

"No, 'nationalist.' It means, they want to keep Turkey for Turks. They don't want the Allies to take over part of Anatolia. That is what the Treaty of Sevre was doing. What Sultan Mehmed agreed to."

"I remember. The treaty was carving up our country and serving it out to Britain, France, Italy and some other country." Ayşegül clasped her hands together.

"Yes, you're right. The other country is Greece. In the treaty, the Greeks were supposed to get a lot of territory that are our Ottoman lands. They want to take back the places that they occupied in ancient times. They call it '*Megali*.'"

Yasmin and Ayşegül clapped their hands to their mouths.

"But..." Estreya continued. "The treaty was never ratified."

"What's 'ratified'?" asked Yasmin. Her eyes screwed up in uncertainty.

This word Ayşegül knew. She turned to Yasmin. "It means that there were not enough votes in our parliament to make it a law. So it was never official."

"Exactly," said Estreya with a nod, crossing both hands on her chest. "And that is where General Kemal comes in. He wants to keep Anatolia for the Turks. No Greeks. He wants to kick out all the Greeks. It's causing a huge uproar, I can tell you." She shook her head from side to side.

Ayşegül suddenly bolted up straight and held out her right index finger.

"And most Greeks live in Smyrna! Ah, yes. I see."

"See what?" asked Yasmin, shrugging her shoulders.

"Because..." continued Ayşegül, now balanced on the edge of her stool, "because, if General Kemal is going to kick out the Greeks, that means that Smyrna is a stumbling block. How is he going to get so many people to leave? It's their home!" Her eyes dimmed for a moment as she thought of her own home years back, and how she herself had been forced from it.

"Exactly," said Estreya. "Bravo, Ayşegül." She winked at her young friend.

"But also..." here Ayşegül paused. She blinked.

"Yes?" asked Estreya, with a slight grin on her face, as she watched Ayşegül thinking.

"Kemal wants the Greeks and all the Allies out, right? But the sultan wants to keep the Empire for the Ottomans. I'm confused. Why does the sultan want to bargain with the Allies? To do so would mean that our country does not belong to us anymore."

"Yes, it's confusing. You must know that the sultan made terms with the Allies that if the treaty was carried out, even if the other countries got part of our country, he would stay sultan. He wants to keep the dynasty." She nodded. "I suppose I can understand that. He does not want to lose his power. He wants to pass on the Ottoman heritage to young Mehmed Ertuğrul Efendi."

Ayşegül and Yasmin nodded in agreement. They both liked the friendly,

181

round-faced prince.

"And the Young Turks and the nationalists and a lot of people around Anatolia are angry. They have lost faith in our *Şahbaba* and they want him out because they don't want him to compromise with these other nations. Turkey has already lost so many territories in the last few years."

"What a mess!" said Ayşegül, throwing her hands to her head. "No wonder there is chaos everywhere! What is going to happen, Estreya?"

The older woman shrugged. "Who knows, *tatlım*. We must be patient." She looked at the clock hanging on the wall beyond. "But it has been ten minutes, and we have talked about troubling things. It is time to do your coffee reading. Perhaps we shall find out something. Maybe it won't tell us what will happen to the Empire, but we will find out something about you, Ayşegül-*hanım*. And that is the most important thing. Are you ready?" She smiled and spread her hands out to take Ayşegül's cup and saucer.

Ayşegül, with some trepidation, nodded. She slid the ensemble across the table to Estreya. Estreya smiled brightly as she placed her hands around the sides of the cup.

"Don't worry, *canım*. Now let us see what we have for you."

⮑   ⮑   ⮑

The two younger women edged forward on their stools, their elbows on the table and their heads in their hands. This was the most exciting part of coffee readings, when the reader described what they saw in the muddy grounds.

Estreya took a deep breath.

Ayşegül's stomach somersaulted. This was the moment the reading really began and, in spite of herself, she realized she was nervous. Would the omens be good ones, or bad? Positive or negative? She gritted her teeth.

Estreya slowly began to pull the upside down cup from its stuck position on the saucer. Ayşegül knew this was an important part of the ritual. She hoped a large chunk of the grounds would fall onto the saucer first. That was a very positive sign and would mean that her worries were leaving her. She also knew that if the grounds formed a pile it meant that money was coming her way. She did not really care about that. A third possibility was if the saucer and cup were stubborn and refused to disengage when Estreya was pulling them apart. That outcome was known as a Prophet's Cup. And then you would not need to continue the reading because all your wishes would come true.

182

Of course, Ayşegül hoped for the Prophet's Cup. But it was rare. And she was not even sure what all her wishes were. She almost stopped breathing.

Suddenly, there was a sucking sound and Estreya saying, "Ahh, here we are. Lucky girl, Ayşegül. A nice chunk on the saucer. A good beginning, yes?"

Ayşegül nodded and breathed a sigh of relief. *İnşallah,* the rest of the omens would be so felicitous.

Now Estreya touched the delicate, curved handle of the extricated cup.

"Are you right-handed, Ayşegül-*hanım,* or left-handed? I can't remember," Estreya asked, looking toward her young friend.

Ayşegül lifted up her right arm and waved it around.

"Good. Our starting point is at the handle of our little cup. Since you are right-handed, we will move around the cup starting from the right here and go clockwise." She drew a finger clockwise in an invisible circle above the cup and saucer.

"Now we look into the cup. As you know, it represents the world outside." Estreya squinted at Ayşegül. "You also already know some things because we have been discussing them, but we will find out how they pertain to you, personally, Ayşegül-*hanım,* yes?"

Ayşegül nodded once. She felt slightly less apprehensive since the chunk of grounds had fallen into the saucer. At least the process had started in a positive way.

"After we do the cup, we will check the grounds in the saucer. And you know that the saucer represents your home. Maybe even your love life." Ayşegül's lips twitched. She was not sure she wanted to hear about that.

"I'm ready," was all she said.

"I can't wait to hear about your love life, Ayşegül," said Yasmin gaily. "Everyone wants to know about that."

"Humph, we'll see," said Estreya. "Now let's concentrate on the cup. I'll start near the handle. That's your love life." She chuckled. "Well, there can't be too much to say about that, can there?"

Ayşegül did not respond.

"Hmm," mumbled Estreya, concentrating on the grounds just inside the rim of the cup near the delicate handle. "I'm seeing a horse, you see, here?" And she pointed at a tiny, strange shape inside the cup.

The two younger women craned their necks toward the muck-lined vessel.

The shape that Estreya pointed at did not look much like a horse to

Ayşegül, but Yasmin screeched, "Oh, yes, it is a horse, definitely."

"And that means," continued Estreya, "a love adventure. Well, that surprises me." She peered intently into the cup again. "And I'm seeing a boat. Someone, a friend, is going to help you. But I don't know with what. Maybe you do?"

Ayşegül shrugged her shoulders and smirked. Love adventure? What could that refer to? The other part, about a friend helping her, that made more sense. She would probably need help soon and hoped Zeliha or Yasmin or someone would be there for her.

"There are other small things I am seeing, but I will try to create a bigger picture for you after we've completed the circle," said Estreya. "Next, ah, I see a *hortum*, a tornado."

"A tornado?" asked Ayşegül.

"Is that good?" asked Yasmin. "It doesn't sound good."

"Yes, well, mostly it is, surprisingly," answered Estreya. "In this case, I would say that our friend Ayşegül will have some difficulties ahead." She patted Ayşegül's arm, the one closest to her. "But it's okay, *canım*. Everything will smooth out. It isn't always a bad thing to have troubles. It makes you stronger in the end. Helps you get through tough times."

"If you say so," said Ayşegül, wincing. She hoped that whatever these so-called troubles would be were not overwhelming. But she had survived before, so she would just have to do so again.

"Oh, now moving along, I see a house. Unquestionably. You will move to someplace else."

"I will? Is that good?" asked Ayşegül.

"I think so. Especially with what's happening around here. Let's go further." Estreya turned the cup to the left slightly. "I am in the right side of the cup now. This represents the future. Let me see," Estreya studied the insides of the coffee cup. Then she pursed her lips. "Hmm, yes, well, here we have the knife. That is a little trickier. You see, here?" And she pointed to the mysterious shape with her fat finger.

The girls craned their necks forward.

"I can't tell," said Ayşegül.

"I can't either," said Yasmin.

"Okay, don't be alarmed, Ayşegül, but there might be some physical danger in your future. But, here is the most important thing of all. To the left of the knife is...here." She pointed at a roundish shape in the brown mess inside the cup. The girls stared at it.

"What is it?" asked Yasmin, almost whispering.

184

"That, Yasmin-*hanım*," replied Estreya, "is a moon. Without a doubt." She grinned. Then she reached out and patted Ayşegül's shoulder. "And you are a lucky girl, indeed, Ayşegül."

"I am?" Ayşegül asked, blinking. "Why is that?" She hoped Estreya would tell her that the moon was her special guide and, as such, would protect her through all life's obstacles, as she herself believed.

But Estreya's answer was not what she expected.

"Because the moon, my dear, means love. You will find real love. And that is the most wonderful thing of all, is it not?" She removed her hand from Ayşegül's arm and wrapped both her own arms across her chest, like a paunchy old pasha after a satisfying meal. Then she nodded deviously, a *djinn* in a Jewish woman's clothing.

"I am most satisfied with this cup reading, girl. It's a good one. Overall."

Ayşegül sat still, thinking. *Love*? What love? An adventure, she could see that might be imminent, but love? In this place, that was almost impossible to find. She was surrounded by women and they were hardly ever allowed to venture outside. Especially not on their own. Where would she ever meet anyone who would fall in love with her? Or she, them? It was a dream that could never come to pass. She closed her eyes.

And yet. Adventure, yes, that was more likely. An adventure might refer to something outside the palace. With everything in turmoil, something new was bound to occur. Love *and* an adventure? That would be something. Her inner being glowed with the possibilities. Then she thought of what else Estreya had said.

The moon. Ah, maybe she is watching over me, after all. Wouldn't that be the answer to my prayers? Ayşegül smiled to herself. Then slowly, slowly, she opened her eyes, automatically turning to face the kitchen's latticed window. Just in case her celestial mentor was looking in on her at this moment. In case she, too, was smiling.

"Now you must stamp the grounds, *tatlım*."

Estreya's coarse voice interrupted Ayşegül's reflections. She turned her attention back to the table. "You must not miss this step if you want the reading to synchronize with your personality," added Estreya.

Ayşegül nodded once again. She shifted her stool closer to her cup-reading counselor, lifted her right hand and then plunged her right thumb into the bottom of the coffee cup, twisting it gently clockwise in the murky sediment.

The three ladies leaned forward and peered into the cup.

"Is it good?" asked Yasmin.

Estreya concentrated for a moment. "You have created a 'net,' Ayşegül. Danger is around you."

Yasmin gasped. "No!"

Ayşegül sighed. *There's more?*

"But," continued Estreya. "It says your personality is strong. And smart." Here she looked at Ayşegül and smiled. "The net will close in on you, but you will figure out how to escape it." She placed her right hand over the back of Ayşegül's left, where it lay on the table. "I believe you will survive. As you have already survived so much. It is up to you."

Yasmin yawned.

As is the way of yawns, Estreya and Ayşegül followed suit without even trying.

While on the downside of her contagious exhale, Ayşegül spoke, her voice distorted by her gaping mouth.

"*Teşekkürler*, Estreya-*hanım*."

When her yawn had passed, she continued her short speech. "Thank you so much for my reading." Then she smiled and held out a few coins, which she had just pulled from the deep pocket in the lining of her *şalvar*. She dropped them into Estreya's upturned palm. "I have much to think about now, don't I?"

"*Evet*, my dear. And thank you."

Estreya lifted her hand, the one holding the round gold pieces, in a salute. "But shall we do the saucer now?"

Ayşegül shook her head. "It's not necessary, Estreya. Anyway, it's late and I feel content with what you have told me. Let's give Berkan his kitchen back."

Estreya tilted her head to the side and shrugged her shoulders as if to say, "If you say so, but..."

Then all three women turned toward the massive wooden food preparation table a few feet beyond. There was Berkan, the top of his balding head leering at them, his chef's hat crumpled to the side. But his face was smashed onto his arms, which were folded on top of the table. And Berkan himself was fast asleep.

ﻬ   ﻬ   ﻬ

September 13, 1922, Afternoon - Aydın Province

What to do now?

186

That was the question burning through Demetrius's mind, as the three men sat side by side in the old truck's front bench seat, gaping at the scene of destruction before them. Even the driver, so recently confident that his backroads route would lead them to their destination, frowned. His thick mustache drooped.

Then he downshifted to neutral, braked, and turned off the engine.

Demetrius wished he could communicate better in the others' native tongue. His accent and his hesitations would give him away. If they abandoned him—or worse—out here in this no-man's land, he was doomed.

He waited.

"*Bok*," said the driver. Demetrius wondered that this man of few words preferred this one in particular. As the ever-quiet driver uttered the one syllable expletive, the hairs on his upper lip blew softly outwards. His friend beside him sighed.

Again, no other words were spoken. What could they say?

A moment later, the driver stepped on the clutch pedal, turned the rusted key in the ignition, and cranked the gearshift into reverse. The truck's engine spluttered back to life. But Demetrius wondered if the cranky beast was tired now. Tired of all the reversings and retracings of the just-traversed track. Their course was as circuitous as the Jericho Labyrinth.

And would they run out of petrol?

Please, no, he pleaded, in the silence of his head.

Another black-winged kite screed above. The sound had a desperation about it, Demetrius thought. He turned his face to the door window on his right and saw the lone bird, its serrated wings spread in a wide 'v' shape, circling overhead. *It must have found its prey.*

The idea was somehow depressing. Demetrius had no grievance with the hunting raptor, but his sympathy sided with the poor creature who was about to be ripped from its familiar territory and torn to pieces. Hadn't this wretched country seen enough destruction and death?

He watched, anxious, as the predatory bird circled and swooped. And then he lost sight of it when the truck changed vantage point and turned to face the direction they had come. Just as well. He, too, had seen enough.

But his journey away from the destruction and pain, en route to home and safety, to his parents and siblings, was disrupted yet again. The world was indeed unfair. Unjust. It was as if he himself were the prey, waiting to be caught and devoured, as so many others had been these last few months.

So much slaughter. So much blood.

He kept his brooding to himself. He wondered whether his companions would agree with his assessments. After all, this was their land, their home. And it was raging with violence. They seemed like passive men, intent on their business and their livelihoods. Yet, their reaction to the smoke and fire beyond was as shocked as his own. Yes, they must wish it all would end. As did he.

Where would the truck take them now? Did the driver know a third route? Even if he did, what would that matter? It was impossible to go to Smyrna now. The officious lieutenant on the main road at Uşak had been right.

What to do now? he asked himself again.

The sun in the rear window of the truck cab warmed the back of the three travelers' heads. It was mid-afternoon. If they stayed on this track, they should arrive in Uşak within the hour. And then what? Was that even the driver's intention?

Demetrius could wait no longer. The constant upheaval and delay gave him a headache. So, after a few moments of bumping and rattling over the dirt track, he translated the words in his mind, summoned his courage and spoke.

"*Uşak'a mı gidiyoruz?*" Are we going to Uşak? He had not used his voice in so long that it sounded like a croak. A frog would have been more eloquent. Did the men understand him?

He waited.

Both of them turned slightly to face him and lifted their bushy eyebrows. The driver turned back to the road in front of him, and his friend shrugged his shoulders.

"*Kim bilir?*" he said. Who knows? Demetrius nodded. He understood this simple response.

The day was slipping away now, as the three men sat in silence side-by-side on the truck's bench seat and drove back the way they had just come.

Demetrius sighed. It had been a long day.

And it was not over.

ಹ   ಹ   ಹ

Wednesday, June 8, 2005, Later Morning - Çalış Beach

The dolphin roundabout? Where were those two going?

I gulped down my last mouthful of honey and bread, grasped Emre's brown, long-fingered hand and rushed out the front door of Mavi Dolfin Evi. Maybe if I ran, I could catch up with Mallie and Paz.

Maybe if I caught up with my two friends, they would lead me to Adrian.

It was a long shot.

At that time, I did not exercise much. Okay, I was still pretty young, only twenty-eight years old, so you would think the five street-block sprint would have been a cinch. I tried. With my daypack secured on my back by its padded straps, I used my arms to catapult my body through space. And, though my Teva water sandals were not designed as running shoes, they were comfortable and malleable, at least. I flew.

Seven minutes later, according to my watch, I arrived at the intersection of the dolphin roundabout with its iconic bronze cetaceans corkscrewing up from their concrete platform. By then, I was almost wiped out. At the northwest corner where the two main streets of Çalış Beach converged, I bent over, my hands on my knees, and sucked air.

Several gasps later when my breath approached normal, I stood up and scanned the intersection. A family of abnormally red-faced tourists (I assumed they were tourists—they did not look Turkish), had their already blown-up lilos under their arms and were crossing the street toward the beach. They had clearly spent too much time there the day before. A large woman in a white tunic stood with her hands on her hips outside the Indian restaurant kitty-corner from me and gazed across at the *pide* restaurant opposite. For what purpose, I assumed only she knew. On the southwest corner, wait staff at the eating establishment with the blue awning was putting out its sandwich boards announcing the day's specials. A skinny black dog sniffed in the gutter near it. On my corner, a wizened Turkish man wheeled by with his bright red *börek* cart. Cars and motorbikes whizzed around the roundabout. The resulting buzz was not deafening exactly, but certainly put paid to the concept of a quiet day at the beach.

It seemed everyone was at this intersection. Everyone but Mallie and Paz.

Or Adrian.

He was probably in town by now.

I planted my own hands on my hips and observed the microcosmic meanderings of my fellow beings as they went about their business. So much bustle. So much fuss. A veritable hive of humanity. Who would have thought it in this virtually unknown coastal backwater of rural Turkey?

And still, I could not locate my friends.

189

Shit!

Okay, now what?

Beep! Beep!

The cartoon-like bleating of a horn made me jump, so focused had I been on my own thoughts. I turned to look behind me, almost expecting to see The Road Runner and Wile E. Coyote chasing each other in their mad-dash comic fashion. But it was merely a *dolmuş*.

Strangely, I had not seen it in the distance moments before. It seemed to have manifested out of the mists, as if a genie had summoned the little white bus just for me. *Djinns*, as genies were called here, could do that kind of thing. My mind flashed on the Ali Baba stories I used to read, where *djinns* appeared out of bottles or lamps and grudgingly agreed to grant wishes. But it was too sunny out for mists now. Not so much as a wisp of cloud in any direction. So the bread-shaped vehicle must not be a figment of my imagination.

I waved my hand back and forth vigorously and the bus pulled over to the curb. *Yes!*

Digging in my front pocket for some small change, I dug out fifty *kuruş* and handed it to the driver who, without a word or a glance at me, threw the coins onto a shallow metal tray sticking out of the dashboard. I nodded "thanks" and, as the driver headed into the fray of traffic, fumbled down the short aisle for a seat. As usual, the bus was stuffed. Hence its name. Women, mostly, held their purses and shopping bags tightly on their laps, though there were a few local men standing at vertical posts, a couple of thin, handsome teenage boys pecking at their flip phones and two obviously British couples clutching daypacks, presumably on a daytrip to explore the local scenery. I plunked down next to an older local woman wearing a thin headscarf that reminded me of a larger version of my grandma's handkerchiefs. She smiled and nodded at me and then turned to stare out her window.

I had no idea where this *dolmuş* was headed, but I hoped it was going into Fethiye. I hoped I could figure out how to get off it if I saw something I recognized. Such as the mosque on the main drag that I had discovered from the van window when Cengis drove us from the bus *otogar* to the Mavi Dolfin Evi on our first day here—was that only fourteen days ago? Or the chain supermarket where the four of us had purchased cold beverages a couple times.

I crossed my fingers under the bag on my lap.

My aisle seat was on the side of the road opposite the sea. Still, I kept a look-out for my friends. Maybe they had decided to walk. I scrutinized the shops and cafes, the occasional open field, and a few petrol stations as they streaked past. Several pedestrians sauntered by in both directions. The *dolmuş* kept its course on the busy street, not veering off onto some obscure arterial, thank goodness.

But no Paz or Mallie or Adrian.

I shook my head and sighed. My seat companion must have heard me, and turned to give me an apprising glance. But, just as quickly, she turned back to her window.

Where are you guys? I was beginning to doubt the sagacity of this bus ride since the sole purpose of it was leading me nowhere.

But I decided to stay on the *dolmuş* to its destination. For one of the drawbacks of these curious conveyances was that there was no laminated cord to pull or yellow strip to push. If you wanted to exit at a particular point, you had to shout out some Turkish phrase that I could not understand. It sounded like gobbledy-gook to me when the locals called it out, but the drivers always complied. Or you could hope that another passenger was getting off at your stop and would yell the magic words for you.

Meanwhile, my heart beat erratically and drops of sweat trickled down my cheeks. The only open window was near the front of the *dolmuş*, a few rows down, and no one seemed to mind the stifling heat inside. Was it only me who felt it? Perhaps my imagination was working overtime. Or, more likely, my anxiety at being alone for the first time in this foreign place was getting to me, was making me nervous.

Keep your head on, kid.

Finally. After numerous aggravating stops and starts, and rumbling slowly for what felt like an eternity, the *dolmuş* turned left at an intersection I recognized, the same one Cengis had driven us through that first day, only in the reverse direction. I glimpsed the familiar mosque behind the overgrown shrubbery that served to conceal the building from the manic activity on the streets surrounding it. Soon, we turned right and headed up a slight hill where a number of shops displayed their myriad wares outside under large, yellow umbrellas.

The *dolmuş* stopped.

Thank God.

As all the remaining passengers shuffled to the front door, I slipped out the side one. I had no clue where I would find my deserting companions, but I had an idea I should head to the old part of town. The so-called

Paspatur. Adrian had looked it up in his ever-ready guidebook and regaled the rest of us with its background. It was one of the few places I could identify. And it was a hubbub of activity.

The historic area was only five minutes' walk from the bus depot, and I figured I could easily find it by following the posted signs. We four had skulked around it twice before. It was famous for having survived a major earthquake years before and was the only section of the city still redolant of an Ottoman bazaar. Conveniently, it was near the bustling Fethiye harbor and teeming with tourists, traders and trinkets of all kinds.

I was sure that was where my errant pals must be lurking. Whether they were together or not, I did not know.

But I was going to find out.

~ ~ ~

Thursday, August 15, 2013, Night - Çalış Beach

"Silk Road Carpet Shop? In San Francisco? What the heck is that?" I asked the note. "Surely it's related, right? Carpets?"

My eyes were swimming with fatigue, so I could hardly focus. But I placed the new note on top of the small carpet drawing and pulled my outdated phone from my pocket. After eleven. This was one time when I wished I were not so Old Skool. A few people I knew had recently forked out big bucks for iPhones and "androids," affording them constant contact with the cyber world. Up until now I could not see the point of it.

Damn.

I was not even sure if Paz had taken the dive into modernity. Come to think of it, I had not seen him look at any phone in all our hours together during the last couple of days. That in itself was strange. Was he hiding his from me for some reason? Or was he more like me than I thought, shunning the latest must-have gadgets?

Well, even if he had one, I could not ask him for it. He would be suspicious or, at the very least, ask me what I wanted it for. I could lie, of course. But I was not very good at lying. So that was that.

In my book, holding back what you knew (or suspected) was not the same as lying. My conscious, so far, on that score was clear.

Too bad about the phone, though. I would have to wait to locate a computer somewhere tomorrow to search the web for "Silk Road Carpet Shop, San Francisco." And I would have to be sly. I definitely did not want

Paz to know what I was up to. If he was part of this hidden note scheme, I wanted to catch him off guard. If he was not, it still seemed wiser to keep him out of it. Until I knew more, anyway.

I yawned.

In the meantime, I hoped sleep would envelop me and my ever-racing thoughts. Tomorrow Paz and I were heading into Fethiye to spy on Ömer if he was there. I needed to be sharp.

In the end, I never made it to a computer.

࿐   ࿐   ࿐

Friday, August 16, 2013, Morning - Çalış Beach

"Yo, Mole, open up, will ya?"

I cracked an eye. The one that was not smashed into my pillow.

"Hello? You in there?"

The loud boom that followed those last two staccato queries shocked me into sitting up. What was happening? In the sudden silence following the fruckus, I shoved the light bed coverlet aside and rubbed my eyes.

"Molo! Jesus! Come alive already!"

Definitely Paz. I guess he wanted me to get up. I extricated my half-dead self from my hard mattress and forced it to pad to the door, barefooted.

As soon as I unlatched the lock, Paz pushed in.

"Damn, kid. It's getting late, you know. We gotta get a move on," he bellowed. I could see by the exasperated expression on his face that he was none too pleased with me at the moment.

Still groggy from that transition consciousness between Neverland and reality, I shook my head and blinked. Paz pushed me toward my roller bag.

"Get your stuff and get dressed. We're gonna miss that opulent Turkish breakfast our benevolent hostess Nevra promised. And I, for one, need it."

I shrugged Paz's hand off and rubbed my arm.

"Okay, okay, I'm going. Give me a few secs, will ya?" Paz rolled his eyes.

"Right. You do your thing and I'll meet you in the dining room, okay?" Paz started for the door and looked back. "Right?"

I nodded, my brain going one way, the rest of my head the other. A cold shower was definitely called for to help shock me back to consciousness. Maybe I could take a quickie and still make breakfast. I had no idea what time it was.

"Fifteen minutes," I said, as Paz slipped out of my room, and the door latch clicked.

❦　　❦　　❦

"So? What's the plan?" I asked my veteran companion, sliding into a seat opposite him. I reached across the square table and stole a chunk of bread from his plate. As I shoved it into my mouth, he glared.

"Go. Get your own. I'll wait," he barked.

"Ooh, sensitive this morning, eh?" I grinned as I stood up again. No response. Obviously, Paz had not had as good a night's sleep as I had. That was certainly one for the books. The thought brightened my spirits.

After piling up my plate with cucumbers, olives, fried egg, bread and sliced tomatoes, I almost skipped back to my spot. I had not felt this chipper since my arrival in this enigmatic country. 'Bout time.

"The Knights at the Round Table," I cooed, popping an olive in my mouth. Paz gave me a look, eyebrows knitted, then picked up his fork.

"Whatever," he said. He must have sensed me watching him dig in. "You gonna eat, or what?"

"Righto, Sir Pazelot. Eat. I will." And for a few minutes neither of us spoke as we quickly emptied our plates.

Finally, as we both put our forks down, I braved my question again. The truncated version.

"So?"

"Yeah, yeah, I know. What's the plan?" Paz grudgingly responded. He crossed his legs. Stalling as usual, I was sure.

"And?"

"We're gonna catch a watchamacallit *dolmuş* to Fethiye and check out Ömer's carpet shop."

Carpets. What is all this all of a sudden about carpets everywhere, anyway? A ping sounded in my now mostly awake brain. Paz definitely knew something he was not telling me. Sinking my fingernails into my bare thighs where my shorts did not quite reach to avoid spurting out what I was thinking, I opted for a more naive approach.

"Oh? Like an Arthurian reconnaissance mission?" I winked. "That sounds exciting."

Paz's expression was quizzical. In a "what's got into Molo?" way. *Ah ha, I've got him! He has no idea why I'm being so flippant this morning.*

Then I had a brainstorm. *Wait. If he put those notes in the book, he wouldn't be so confused by me right now, would he? I mean, he's no dummy. He would get that I was on to him, wouldn't he? Or would he?* My glibness slipped down a notch. Maybe I should think about this a little more before I headed down the wrong pathway, before I convicted my old friend of an action of which he was not, in fact, guilty. *Damn, this is getting complicated.*

"I thought you were into this," he said. He chewed his latest morsel of bread furiously, then continued. "Why are you being so weird?"

"Me?" I pointed to my chest. "*Me,* weird? What about you, so cagey and illusive every step of the way? Appearing out of nowhere, sabotaging my plans, never telling me what's really going on. Who's the weird one?" Suddenly, frustration again had gotten the better of me. And my previous good mood, like a half-devoured omelette, slid off the plate of my good intentions and melted onto the floor.

What happened next completely surprised me.

Paz placed his meaty hands into the edge of the table and pushed out of his chair, which scraped noisily so that the other diners stared in our direction. Once he was standing, he shouted,

"Okay, buddy. 'Molo,'" and here he put both his hands up to made quote marks in the air in front of his chest, "Whatever you want to call yourself. I get it."

Now he jabbed at the same air with his right hand. But in my direction. I had never seen him so angry. I could feel my mouth stretching out into a wide grimace of shock.

He continued, "I only wanted to help you, you know? I spent a shitload of money, which, by the way, I don't really have to spend, and I hightail it across a couple of contintents and an ocean to find you *and*, when I *do* find you, I try to let you in on stuff you never knew about..." He stopped talking, but his body started to shake. His face was turning purple and sweat started to drip down from his hairline. Watching this incredible transformation, I could feel my eyes widen. It was as if our two beings had switched places. By now, all other noise in the busy breakfast room had ceased. Everyone looked at Paz and me.

I waited. We all waited. Paz's lips tightened and he shook his head. While we watched, aghast, Paz grabbed his daypack from where it hung off one post of his seatback and marched out of the room.

Wow. The atmosphere of the previously cheery, bustling dining room shifted to a level of intense silence that used to be called "pregnant" in the nineteenth century novels I had read in school. But "pregnant" did not really fit this situation, as the word suggested something full and happy and dying to be born into a beautiful new world. This silence felt more like a gathering of mourners at the funeral of a small child.

I did not know what to do. Or to say. I felt as if each person was staring at me, waiting for a response that would free them from this agony of awkwardness.

"Sorry," I said. That was all I could think of. I assumed most people, even the Turks, understood, if not my word, at least my contrite demeanor. Hangdoggedness is universal.

How did this happen? My good mood had gone the way of so many good moods. Down the toilet. And without even a chance to flush.

So, in true coward's fashion, I swiveled in my chair, grabbed my own bag, jumped up and, without looking back, exited the scene as quickly as I could.

When I catapulted into the foyer, Paz was nowhere to be seen. I had an unpleasant flashback to the day he and Mallie and Adrian had deserted me in this town in 2005. The day of the disaster. My flashback was interrupted. At my abrupt entrance into his den of serenity, Canavar the monster dog perked his head up and tilted it sideways as if to say, "What is it about you busybody humans always disturbing my peace?" I smirked.

"Sorry, Canavar."

Sorry had suddenly become the morning's byword. Normally, I would have reached over to pat the beleaguered creature on the head by way of apology, but now I was in a hurry to find Paz.

"See you," I said. "Thanks for not biting my head off."

I scurried to the door as the now mollified canine settled back onto his dingy mat. So much for the monster.

Hovering briefly on the plastic threshold of the Lavanta Ada's front door, I looked right and left, saluted Canavar, then ran out.

And I spotted him.

Paz was hunkered down on a low brick wall in front of a flowerbed of red camellias with his head in his hands. His daypack lay in the patch of dirt by his feet.

I slowly approached. If I had included a white kerchief in my kit, I would have pulled it out at this moment and cautiously waved it over my head. Instead, I had to rely on my charm and wit. And our longtime friendship, which had heretofore survived so many challenges. Perhaps it could pull through one more.

196

Paz surely heard me creeping toward him, but he did not move.

"Hey," I ventured, carefully placing my bag on the ground. Then I sat beside him.

Still nothing.

"I'm sorry, Paz." There it was again. The "S" word insinuating its way into another conversation. "I was just, you know, in a weird mood this morning. That's what happens when I get too much sleep."

Was this banter working? Paz was as still as a playacting possum.

"Earth to Paz?" I tried to imbue the question with some levity. He usually responded to that. But not this time. I tried another tack.

"Look, I mean it. I didn't realize how much all this meant to you. And I am really grateful for all your help. Please, let's forget what happened at breakfast and go to town. Let's do whatever it was you had planned." Still no response.

"Seriously, dude. Come on!" I nudged Paz's shoulder with mine, the kind of gesture that I would have used as a kid on the playground to get someone to play ball.

He shifted away from me, but then he lowered his hands, clasping them between his knees. He stared at them for a few seconds, sighed and said,

"Just shut up, Molo, okay? And promise you'll stop apologizing. It doesn't suit you."

I could feel the left side of my mouth turn up in a half smile. His grudging acquiescence was a good sign and deserved a corresponding good faith concession on my part. I swiped my right hand from my left shoulder towards my right hip, and then the opposite direction, in the way that I had seen characters in movies perform a cross-my-heart vow.

As I did, I happened to glance toward the glass door I had recently exited. Canaver stood on the inside gazing out at me. He had an uncanny expression of approval on his face and as I nodded at the curious dog, I uttered the words, "I promise." I swear the anomalous animal winked before he turned and sauntered away from the door. But he could just as easily have been warning me.

My reflections on Canaver were interrupted when, without looking at me, Paz pushed himself off the brick wall, retrieved his pack from the ground, and started toward the hotel's side gate, the one closest to us.

"Let's go then."

"Right. Let's go. Ready when you are."

And I was. Ready, that is. I realized now more than ever that whatever was up Paz's sleeve, I owed it to him to let him do his thing. After all, he

197

was the magic man. And I needed some magic, some intervention, to get to the bottom of the Adrian debacle. And, though it was an unexpected development, I needed to find out what the story behind the two mystery notes was, determine who had snuck them into my du Maurier paperback. But most importantly, though Paz might not be fully aware of the real reason I had come back to Turkey in the first place, I myself had never forgotten. No twists or turns of events or thickenings of plot could make me forget. And my possible sighting at Dalaman airport the evening before underscored my resolve.

I still wanted my revenge on Ömer.

᠊ᡱ   ᠊ᡱ   ᠊ᡱ

Chapter 15

"If you cause injury to someone, you draw that same injury toward yourself." - Mevlana (aka Rumi)

*T*he white heron propelled itself off the large flat rock and flapped into the beckoning sky. Its wings beat furiously, yet emitted only the whisper of sound, like wind rustling gently through grassy reeds. The water bird's long, tapered body and trailing stick legs soon merged with the other objects painted onto the canvas of blue beyond to become a tiny smudge on the otherwise pristine view. Blessed bird. Off to new lands, possibilities.

Would it remember where it came from? Or was this moment, this reptilian reaction, merely an inevitability of its primordial origins paying homage to the infinitesimality of time?

As the last vestiges of the feathered forager faded into a distant, mystical realm, the ghost-like image of the rising moon began to take its place. We say "rising," but that is not the correct expression. For the moon is always there, is she not? She does not disappear, as herons do when they have finished fishing, and fly off toward a more favored spot. The moon is constant. She has a designated path and she does not deviate from it. For this reason, she can not really be said to rise at all.

What changes are her moods.

Sometimes, as now, she wisps onto the afternoon scrim of sky, like a hint, a white shadow, hovering quietly and shyly while the sun still claims his dominance in the daylight heavens.

But when Apollo bids goodnight and slips off the western edge of earth, and the darkness pours itself onto the stage of purple heavens, the moon sheds her shyness and dons her showy, silver costume of night. At first, she exposes only a tidbit. Each night of the month she adds something more, tantalizing us, her adoring audience, with just a bite at a time, baring only a sliver of herself, waxing from our right and leaving a black mass of infinity to fill in the derelict brightness. Day by twenty-four hour cycle, she

199

reveals a bit more so the crescent of light that shines out to us grows fatter and fuller until it eventually morphes into an icosahedron, a giant, glowing football in the firmament. The gibbous moon, she is known as then. When this occurs, our awe increases. She knows this, the moon, she is a show-off. She likes to keep us in thrall.

The process of her dressing is slow and takes her fifteen days, give or take one or two, to unveil her entire ensemble, to display herself in the full regalia of her majesty, a great round orb of silvery gold that outshines all other celestial spheres.

Down below, grounded on the prosaic predictability of planet Earth, we gasp in admiration. We gape at her astounding beauty and the reverence it inspires.

And when that night has segued into a new morning, when we are sufficiently succumbed to her power, she slips off her exotic plumes. It is time for her to rest. She hangs her silver cloak deep within the folds of fathomless space and sleeps soundly until, a few hours on, the deep dark night returns again.

After her one night of glory in fullness, the whole show reverses and an opposite crescent, like the other half of a lunula, evolves from left to right. This procession, too, lasts fifteen days.

We call it her waning.

But the moon is a complicated creature. Waning, she certainly is not. She is merely playing with us. She does not content herself with this sideways slide show of crescent evolution. She is on the move always, gliding along her elliptical orbit, a cosmic conveyer belt, to keep a watchful eye on all her subjects wherever in her realm they may reside.

Sometimes her path takes her farther into the abyss of the eternal universe. This is her apogee. When she roams to this most distant point of her migration, her influence on us weakens and diminishes. But, ever peripatetic, ever kinetic, our mistress moon slowly steers her course back toward Earth, toward her dearest subjects. Us. And when she is closest, when her presence looms largest and most impressive in the nighttime arena of stars and planets, she glories in her perigee.

Her perigee is our refuge. For this is when the moon's ascendency is the most powerful, most intense, when we ourselves are most affected.

It is the time of growth. Transformation.

The moon understands this. She bows and curtseys and entreats us to applaud and to obey.

We, meanwhile, are the herons on the flat rock. We flock to the shoreline *of possibilities through no will of our own. It is our destiny to stab with our long, curved beaks at the still water underneath for our sustenance, ephemeral and deficient. And then, the moon looms on the horizon, close, commanding, and we must submit—flap our diaphanous wings and take flight.*

࿔   ࿔   ࿔

September 13, 1922, Evening - Aydın Province

In a little town near Ödemiş, some hundred or more kilometers east of ill-fated Smyrna, the hard-working truck began to gasp and snort.

"*Bok*," squawked the stalwart driver. His vocal chords were rusty from so little usage over the last hours. "Petrol."

He pointed at the metal dashboard and Demetrius realized they were about to run out of gas. So lost were they all in their thoughts and in their circuitous detour, none of them had paid attention to the fuel gauge. Well, Demetrius could not see it from his side by the passenger window. Nevertheless, he should have wondered. Should have remarked on it.

The hours had drifted along, as had the three companions, and now it was early evening. They had stopped twice along the way to stretch and share a loaf of bread the driver's helper had dug out of a sack, a different one from which he had earlier retrieved his apples. Each stop had been near villages so small as to be hardly villages at all. The three travelers would not be noticed, thankfully. As they perched on rocks alongside the intrepid truck, Demetrius had managed to utter a few phrases in his halting Turkish. He spoke simply about the strange detour they were taking and asked few questions. The other men either did not notice his awkwardness in speaking or, if they did, they did not care.

No one mentioned the fire. It was as if the sight were too outrageous, too monstrous, they dared not give it credence with words. Any utterances they might wish to make were inadequate to express what was, surely, a mutual sense of mortification, of incredulity. It was, therefore, better to be silent on the matter.

Now, this time when the driver pulled the truck to the side of the small dirt track, he strode to the truck's rear, to the flatbed full of burlap bags. Demetrius watched him in the rearview mirror mounted outside his window. He saw the man shove aside some bags, heard him grunting with the effort, and finally haul a red metal can from underneath them.

Petrol.

Demetrius nodded in approval. They would not be stuck here for the night at least.

When he stepped out to assist the driver in his task of filling up the tank, the wiry, wizened man waved him aside and shook his head. So Demetrius leaned against the bed's railings and watched him attach a spout to the can, lift it up and pore the liquid contents slowly down the thirsty maw of the gas tank. After all the fluid had disappeared into the truck's belly, the driver unscrewed the spout, wiped it on his battered, faded trousers leg and carefully returned it to its place in the bed. He trudged back to his side of the truck, climbed in and shut the door with a clunk.

Demetrius repeated the same movements on his side.

The driver's friend, meanwhile, had whistled and picked at his teeth throughout the diversion. He had known that his help would not be needed.

Now the vehicle, quenched and revived, spurted into action and the three men, like a small delegation of missionaries who have just survived an unexpected raid, barked out expressions of glee.

Their triumph was to be short-lived.

ॐ   ॐ   ॐ

October 28, 1922 – Constantinople

"*İyi geceler,* Yasmin, good-night," Ayşegül whispered. She and her friend stood outside Yasmin's first story dormitory room. Ayşegül leaned in to give Yasmin a quick hug. "And thank you for coming to get me earlier." Yasmin's face lit up.

"Oh, *birşey değil*, Ayşegül. I'm so glad you got your reading at last. It was very..." Here she paused, her mouth twisted in a grimace and her eyes glancing toward the dim-lit hallway ceiling. Then she returned her gaze to her companion. "...revealing. What was all that about a tornado and a horse? I was confused."

"*Evet*, I am too." Ayşegül chuckled. "And the net, don't forget." She winked.

"Well, at least you got the moon. That sounded very encouraging." Here Yasmin waved her head around, dreamily. Then she chuckled. "Looovvvveee. Ooooo." She laughed.

"Shhhh, you idiot," whispered Ayşegül, slapping Yasmin lightly on her upper arm. "Can you honestly believe that I'm going to find love? In this place?" She waved her arm around in the air. "What a joke. A big *şaka*."

Yasmin brought both her hands up to her mouth, stifling a giggle. Then she dropped her hands to Ayşegül's shoulders and said, tittering, "I know. A *şaka* for sure. No one finds real love here. Except for Gülbahar and Neslihan. Remember when they ran off to Salonika? In Greece? *Şahbaba* was furious. He does not like his girls to be with anyone but him, right?"

The two girls moved farther away from Yasmin's dormitory so no one could hear them gasping with laughter. After a moment, they glanced around them, shrugged their shoulders, then tiptoed back toward the door, holding on to each other's arms.

"See you tomorrow, Yasmin. Thanks again." Ayşegül kissed Yasmin's cheek. "Next time we'll do *your* reading and see what's in store for you." As she pulled away from her friend, her eyes bulged with a kind of merciless glee.

"Right. Well, I guarantee it won't be as exciting as tornados and moon-lit love!" Yasmin's whisper was louder than it should be and Ayşegül shuffled away from her.

"Shhhh, Yasmin. Don't wake up the flock. Anyway, I must go. I'm exhausted."

"Oh, I know," said Yasmin. "Exhausted by all the exciting things about to happen. Lucky you!" Yasmin had her hand on the door and began to enter her room. "Sweet dreams, Ayşegül-*hanım.*"

"*Tatlı rüyalar,* Yasmin." She touched her fingertips to her smiling lips and then, moving them slightly away from her mouth, blew on them toward her friend and watched her evaporate into the darkness.

As Ayşegül crept down the hallway to the stairwell beyond, it never occurred to her that she would never see Yasmin again.

         ~ø   ~ø   ~ø

Friday, August 16, 2013, Morning - Çalış Beach and Fethiye Town

Paz was still in a funk, staring out the *dolmuş* window at the passing butcher shops, veterinarian clinics, restaurants and markets. The odd man or woman, sometimes couples, strolled along the sidewalks, down the side streets, or *sokaks*, that led to the Mediterranean two or three blocks away. I glimpsed snatches of its iridescent radiance, tantalizing teasers that made me wonder why I was on this bus to hunt down Ömer when I could be floating in that glorious sea. The scene reminded me of that ill-fated day in

203

2005 when I had grabbed a *dolmuş* into Fethiye town, desperate to locate my three friends after their disappearing act. Perhaps I should have gone to the sea that day, as well. On the other hand, it is likely that would not have changed the outcome. Had fate (in the form of Ömer) already decided its course of action? Had Adrian always been slated for disaster?

Strange that that fatal day eight years back was so inextricably linked with this moment. And yet I felt much calmer than I thought I would, despite the contretemps with Paz a few minutes earlier.

The bus beeped and pulled over to the right. A couple of school girls in their skirted uniforms ascended the steps up front and flashed cards at the driver. I watched them vaguely, as I did other assorted passengers when, every two blocks, they either boarded or exited. But my mind kept wandering back to the two notes: the one with the scratchy drawing of the carpet my mother had given me, which I had stored, forgotten, in a box, and the one with the carpet shop name written on it. Why had they been given to me? And in such secrecy? The theatricality of it all did really smack of Paz. He was still my number one suspect. Him or Barış, Paz's henchman. But if so, why?

If it was not Paz or Barış, since Paz really did seem quite insulted that I had implicated him in having nefarious motives, I racked my brains to think who else:

1) Had known I would arrive in Istanbul the other night,
2) And that I would be staying at the Yeşil Beşik Pansiyon,
3) Could possibly know anything about that old rug, let alone enough of its design to make a crude rendition of it,
4) Or that I, indeed, even owned such a rug.
5) Most importantly, what was the connection between the carpet, the name of that carpet shop, and *me*?

In addition to all those questions, where did Ömer fit in? If at all? It hardly seemed a coincidence that he was at the airport the same time as our arrival there.

My brain was crackling with questions. God willing, Paz would lead me to some revelation today. I could hardly stand the suspense anymore.

Suddenly, I wondered about Mallie. Could she have something to do with this caper? She did the research, after all, to find out where I was. She knew about Ömer. She had been as much a part of our group as any of us—back then.

"Paz," I ventured, keeping my voice low. "Can I ask you something?"

Without moving, he grunted, "What?"

"How's Mallie? I mean, you haven't mentioned her since that surprise attack from Barış the other night."

He looked up slowly. "Mallie? What do you wanna know?" I had trouble hearing his response, so low did he speak. Maybe he had taken offense at my tone.

I shrugged. "Nothing in particular. I mean, have you talked to her? Is she okay?"

Now it was Paz's turn to shrug. "Yeah, I've called her a couple times. On Skype, I mean. She's fine."

"And Cara, your little girl?"

"Caria, not Cara. Great, I guess. Keeping Mal busy, as usual." At last he turned his head and looked at me. "Why are you asking all of a sudden?"

"I don't know. Just, we're on this Ömer mission and Mallie was here when the whole thing blew apart. I feel like she's part of it, even though she's not with us now." I was part fishing, but everything I said was true. I did feel like Mallie was part of it, whatever role she may have played. Suddenly, I realized that I wished she were on the *dolmuş* with us right now. I was curious about their daughter, too.

"So, what's Caria like? Why did you name her that?" I hoped my voice sounded sufficiently casual, luring Paz back to my side after our conflagration.

He leaned back in his seat and a radiance filled his eyes. Bingo, I had hit the spot.

"Caria? She's incredible. My fireball angel. I miss her."

"Yeah, I bet. But what is she *like*?" I put my hand on Paz's shoulder. "Besides being a fireball, I mean. Is she like you or more like Mallie?"

Paz snorted. "Oh, 'fireball' wasn't enough of a hint? She's a mini-Mallie, that's what. Strong, clever, a little on the smart-ass side. But..." He shook his head, a bemused look on his upturned face. "She rocks my world. I can hardly believe she's real sometimes." He closed his eyes for a second, daydreaming, I supposed, about his prize child and probably wondering, too, why he had left her and his whippersnapper wife to come on this ill-advised escapade. With me.

"What about her name? It's kind of unusual. How did you guys come up with it?" I thought if I kept Paz on a subject that obviously jazzed him, his spirits would continue to improve. Maybe he would forget he was angry at me.

205

"Oh, that was Mallie. She was intrigued with the whole harem thing when we got back from Turkey the first time, remember? And after the second time, after Adrian and everything, she became obsessed. Started doing all this research, like she was going to write a paper on it. Or join up!" He chuckled. "Really, it was bizarre. But anyway, to answer your question, a '*cariye*,' spelled differently than Caria's name, by the way, was basically a lady-in-waiting in the harem."

I pulled my head back in surprise. I remembered how indignant Mallie had been when she discovered how women were treated during the Ottoman Empire's hegemony.

"Really? That's curious." I felt my eyebrows rise in surprise.

Paz chuckled again. "Yeah, isn't it? There's more to it than that, but Mallie's the expert, not me. When she was pregnant, the word just stuck with her. So when Caria was born, it was a no-brainer. Like she was meant to be called that." He shrugged and crossed his eyes goofily. "Don't ask me. It's a woman thing, I guess. We could have called her 'Apple Dumpling' for all I care."

I laughed. "Yeah, I get it. What's a name, anyway? 'A rose by any other name...' and all that."

Paz shook his head in agreement and smiled his usual good-natured smile.

Inwardly I congratulated myself. *He's back.* Now we could approach our reconnaissance mission with equanimity at least. It never pays to go into battle angry at one's fellow combatants. At least, I did not believe so.

Paz and I chatted amiably for a few minutes until the now nearly empty *dolmuş* approached the McDonald's intersection I had noticed when we had come the other direction on arriving in Fethiye for the first time. The day Cengis had driven all four of us from the *otogar* to the Mavi Dolfin Evi.

It seemed a lifetime ago.

Paz shouted out some unintelligible words, the driver pulled over, and we exited the little bus.

Time for business.

આ   આ   આ

Wednesday, June 8, 2005, Almost Noon - Fethiye

"Hey, hello, come, come."

I was jogging down the twisting pedestrian alleyways of the charming historic quarter of Paspatur, praying that if I hurried perhaps the hawkers would not pester me. I was not in the mood for shopping. Obviously, this guy was not buying my ploy.

"Cheap as chips! Cheap as Salvation Army!"

As I approached I pretended not to hear his exhortations. Really, did these fellows think this hassle-happy banter worked? It must, or they would not bother. Same tactic as in Istanbul. Obviously a Turkish thing. As when I stalked the streets in the Sultanahmet, I had a flash of vision: ancient narrow, winding passages lined with open-air shops, bright-woven kilim carpets festooned overhead for shade, while turbaned hawkers impeccably swathed in their pantaloons and silk sashes called out to passersby in an incessant sing-song babble.   Bulletin boards Middle Eastern style. This was my imagination's version of life at the bazaar in a *caravanserai,* the oases of commerce and comfort for travelers and traders on the bygone Islamic "Silk Road." Obviously, in those times there were no Salvation Army or French fries to flog, but I had no doubt the verbiage was otherwise the same. Old habits die hard.

I kept my face forward and waved dismissively at the shopkeeper. He was not deterred.

"You can look, you can try, if you like, you can buy!"

His voice had gotten louder. Poor man, I should at least give him some response for all his effort. After all, he was rather entertaining. So I turned around, still jogging by, and shouted, "That was a good one, mate. Keep trying!" We were both laughing as I faced forward again and continued running. Well, not exactly running. It was too hot for that. Trotting, more like.

"Next time, you come in," he yelled. I waved my arm in the air above my head. *Bye, buddy. Better luck next time.*

The heat was stifling. Fortunately, the backstreet I found myself on was protected from the harsh glare of the noon-time sun by awnings and triangle-shaped canvases suspended up above, between the buildings. Once I reached a neutral zone, that is, a spot without any shopkeepers hovering outside, I slowed down to catch my breath.

Where are those guys? Think.

Where would they go? Well, Paz and Mallie might have needed to exchange more dollars to lira. I could try the money changers. We had been to one before, down some street or other nearby. Or maybe they wanted a cup of almost American coffee at a westernized cafe. There were a few of those about.

And what about Adrian? Was he alone? Or was he with the others? I would just have to keep searching.

As I hovered in the middle of a Paspatur crossroads, whirling in all directions in the off-chance I might spot my pals in one of them, another barrage of talking sandwich boards assaulted me from a nearby sidestreet.

"Two for a Tenner!"

"Turkish Tescos!"

I paused to listen. I was somewhat comforted to realize I was not the only victim of these dauntless dealers. They must be harrassing a hapless tourist sauntering down one of the arterial alleys. Perhaps it was Adrian. I decided to head in the direction of the voices in spite of my dread of encountering another pushy peddlar.

"Cheaper Than Primart!"

Whatever Primart was, it must have incredible discounts to be included in a jingle. Maybe a British store? Everything was about Brits here. We had not encountered any other Americans in this town. In any case, I was not really concerned. I was not here to shop. Or to meet any of my fellow countrymen, necessarily. So, bracing myself, I entered the street from which the Primart ditty had issued.

The restaurant on the corner to my left was gearing up for the lunch rush, with a couple of waiters flinging light pink linen tablecloths onto the patio tables and smoothing them down. Despite my haste, I could not help but notice the day's humorous offerings written in fluorescent pink pen on the sandwich board out front: "'Sheef" Salad," "Mountain Chicken Things on Spinach Bed" and "Lamb Shank with Democratic Sauce." I realized I was hungry, but not that hungry. Shaking my head at the unsavory translations of today's no doubt delectable fare, I poked into one of the open doorways, looking left to right inside the dark dining room, just in case Adrian, or one of the others, was inside. A tall, thin waiter waved me in, but I managed to mutter "*Hayır, teşekkür ederim,*" as politely as possible. I was definitely not up to "Democratic Sauce" at the moment. He merely tipped his head and continued carrying out his tasks.

I passed a ceramics shop crammed with colorful bowls and plates and candleholders handpainted with ornate Turkish designs. I decided to pass it by, as I did not think my friends would be buying overpriced ceramics. We could snag better deals at the farmer's market, or *pazar*, never mind their competitors' promises. Next, was a narrow *kebap* stall, reeking of lamb fat, where a chubby proprietor, his face gleaming with moisture, wiped his hands on his apron. The plastic lime green stools out front were empty. Then I passed by a women's underwear store, its window displays arrayed with surprisingly scanty, lacey unmentionables for a Muslim town. If I had not been in such a hurry, the sight might have made me blush. Obviously, Paz and Adrian would not be inside. Mallie, probably not. I was sweating now, a front lock of hair pasted onto my forehead and drops of salty wetness tickling my cheeks. I swiped my forearm quickly across them to remove the drops, only for them to be immediately replaced by more. Despite the unpleasantness, I continued on my quest.

By now, my heart was pounding, more from anxiety, I thought, than exhaustion. If I did not find my comrades soon, I would abandon my search, head toward the harbor for a quick snack (eschewing the irreverant McDonald's for more local fare, though certainly avoiding "Chicken Things" if possible) and then flag down a *dolmuş* to deposit me back at Çalış Beach. Maybe take a swim, after all. I could do with a cool down.

Near the end of the darkened corridor of boutiques and eateries, I stopped in front of yet another food stall and realized I was too hungry to wait. I stood in the middle of the passageway, trying to decide whether I wanted a simple chicken *dürüm* wrap or a slice of *lahmacun* pizza for lunch. A glass of hand-squeezed orange juice would be refreshing, too, after all this darting about. I remembered seeing a tiny juice shack a block away. After a quick jaunt to get there, I realized I could not stomach meat in this heat. I perused the short menu. In the end, I opted for a plate of hummus and pide bread with sliced cucumbers.

As I munched the soft bread and creamy sauce, I noticed I was sitting across from a carpet shop featuring traditional weaves draped outside. Suddenly, my eardrums were pummeled by a strident, wailing racket.

"*Rrrr-eee, rrrr-eee, rrrr-eee...*"

The siren, for surely that sound must mean the same in Turkey as in the States, was so shrill and loud, I threw my hands to my ears for a moment in an effort to muffle its piercing effect.

"What the...?" I asked out loud. Around me, diners stopped chewing and pedestrians stopped window browsing. We all listened. I saw that their eyes bulged like the puffy bread I loved so much. Only, in this case, the puffiness was decidedly unappetizing.

I stood up, abandoning my lunch. Others did as well. As we sat with our half-eaten food in front of us, our touristic tranquility traumatized, a white van with red parallel stripes painted on its sides pulled up at the curb just twenty yards away from me. On its panels was painted the word "*ambulans*." My Turkish speaking ability was in its infancy, most definitely, but even I could decipher that word: ambulance. Uh, oh, had someone fainted in the heat? Or over-indulged in a pre-luncheon tipple? Forgetting my friends, my hunger, my thirst, I found myself unexpectedly eager to find out why this ambulance had been summoned. Its arrival was a welcome distraction from my own troubles.

I had already paid for my food, so I left the cafe and inched toward the carpet shop for something solid to lean on while I watched the proceedings unfold. Just before I smacked into the stone wall of the modernized Ottoman-style building that the shop was located in, my eyes drifted to its large front picture window. The room beyond was unlit, typical of most Turkish enterprises, but residual light from outside poured through the glass. When my eyes adjusted to the store's shadowy light, I was able to discern human shapes. Curious, I stuck my face closer to the warm pane and gasped. Was I dreaming? Was I having heatstroke?

I shook my head in disbelief. Surely, I was mistaken. Rubbing my eyes, I stood staring through the sun-streaked glass.

And there, without a doubt, was Adrian.

But something was not right.

Instead of being delighted at finding the object of my morning's hunt at long last, I felt a violent punch attack my solar plexus. The punch did not come from a person; it came from the shock of the sight before me.

For Adrian was not fingering the worn edges of an antique kilim, admiring its flatweave beauty and craftsmanship. Nor was he perched on the edge of the wooden bench by the wall sipping elma *çay* and chatting with the proprietor. No. I would have been thrilled to find him in either of these poses, immediately run in and shouted, "Adrian!" in an ecstatic voice.

What I saw instead was altogether beyond belief. My friend lay on his back, prostrate. Lifeless even, or appearing so. Not a twitch of movement. A squat, but vigorous-looking, middle-aged man hovered over him and a young woman kneeled by his side, holding his right hand.

My heart stopped. What was Adrian doing on the floor?

Then, stunned as I was, my eyes drifted, surveying the room around his recumbant form. It was as if seeing Adrian lying there was too much to take and I needed a distraction. But what I saw next was nearly as astonishing as the sight of Adrian lying down.

It was Paz.

Paz?

What was he doing here? And where was Mallie? I scanned the room, trying to discern her presence. But she was nowhere to be seen.

My eyes went back to her partner, my black-haired Artful Dodger. He was sitting on the floor cross-legged, a few feet from Adrian's head. His own head was bowed forward. He did not look mischievous now. In fact, I was sure he was crying.

All of my observations had taken place in a matter of seconds, though I was not aware of time. I floated in a miasma of disbelief. But I was thrust back to hideous reality when, with no warning, a swarm of paramedics pushed past me and stormed the carpet shop, flinging their medical kits onto the pile of folded up rugs near Adrian, and shouting unintelligibly.

Without thinking, I ran in behind them.

"Adrian! Ade!" I shouted. "What are you doing? I'm here. It's Molo!" His stillness was unnerving and his face looked pale and cold.

Before I could get to him, one of the emergency technicians stepped in front of me, blocking my access to my prostrate friend. He was a young man, younger than me, I thought, but his demeanor was surprisingly authoritative. He shouted something to me in Turkish, but his words came too quick and complicated for me to grasp.

"That's my friend. Let me by," I screamed back. He frowned.

"Please," I added. "*Lütfen.*"

"I am sorry, mister. You cannot go. Your friend needs medical help. Please to move over now." Astonished at the guy's ability to switch so quickly from Turkish to English, I grudgingly sidled a few feet away toward a tall stack of kilim carpets folded into large squares. The stack was almost as tall as I was. I slumped against it, folding my arms across my chest. I had almost forgotten about Paz.

Suddenly, I heard my name called out in an almost agonizing query.

"Molo? What are *you* doing here?" I followed the voice with my eyes and as I did so, I caught a flash of someone moving, shifting quickly from behind a large pile of carpets toward a wooden door in the back of the small showroom. Something about the form was vaguely familiar. Where had I seen it before? A short, rotund man with a square head, crowned with a pair of dark, CIA-style sunglasses. Who was he? Why was he so eager to disappear all of a sudden?

Well, whoever he was, he was not my concern.

"Paz!" I pushed away from the leaning tower of carpets and staggered toward my erstwhile buddy. "What am *I* doing here? What about you? I've been looking for you guys everywhere." I stopped and turned toward Adrian, still lying supine and inert on the floor nearby. Four or five men

211

and women in fluorescent yellow jackets were busy at work trying to revive him, or so I assumed. They barked commands at each other and fiddled at Adrian's chest.

Still in a miasma of shock, I hardly knew what else to say to Paz. But I came out with, "What happened to Adrian?"

Paz sat disconsolately on the floor and lifted both his arms, palms facing the beamed ceiling above. "I don't know, Molo. We were standing here talking to somebody and suddenly he just collapsed." He let his arms drop listlessly to his lap. "We didn't know what to do, it all happened so fast." Then he nodded to the trim man I had first seen when looking in the shop's window. "That man finally dialed 911, or whatever it is they call it here. Thank God."

"Fuck." That was all I could think to respond.

Paz continued. "Molo, do you think he'll be okay? I mean, he has to be, right?" His brown eyes were appealing to me—as if I had the answer.

I shook my head and grimaced. "Geez, Paz. What do I know? I hope so. I mean, shit, what happened to him? I can't believe this."

Paz blinked, as if he were attempting to block another onslaught of tears. "Me either."

I looked around the room. Sunglass man had vanished. But where was Mallie? Why hadn't I seen her in all this fruckus?

"Paz, where's Mallie?"

"She's in Çalış. She went to the beach."

"What? Really? Oh, man, I assumed she was with you." I paused for a second. "And that you both were with Adrian. He took off without me this morning. We were supposed to go to the beach, actually. But he changed his mind. And he was really cagey about why. Did you guys come into town together?"

Paz shook his head slowly. "Nope. Believe it or not, I ran into him by accident."

"You mean you came into Fethiye alone? Why?"

"I needed to get some money changed and I remembered that exchange booth we went to a few days ago. Thought I'd get it done and then go back to Çalış and find Mallie." So, I had been partly right about something, anyway.

"How come you didn't come get me? I could've come with you."

"I was going to, but Adrian told me you'd already gone." Paz looked apologetic.

"What? That doesn't make sense. He talked to me. Before he took off. I

212

don't get it." Despite my effort to disguise it, I heard the whine in my voice.

"Beats me. I guess we can ask him about it when he's awake. Or whatever."

"It's not looking so good at the moment."

We both stared at Adrian's prostrate form. The technicians seemed to have stopped prodding and poking it now, and a couple of them were heading toward the shop's front door, which someone had closed during the mayhem.

"What's going on?" I asked one of them as he brushed past.

He did not even turn to look at me, but responded, his voice breathy and quick. "Your friend is not waking. We taking him to hospital."

"Hospital? Is he okay? Will he be okay?"

But the man had rushed off without hearing my last questions. Paz and I watched him run out and then dash toward the ambulance vehicle, trying to catch up with his partner.

We did not speak. Two minutes went by, judging by the aged plastic clock on the wall behind the wooden bench. But it seemed longer.

Suddenly, the door crashed open and the techs entered through it again, this time pulling a shiny, metal stretcher on wheels.

"Oh, my God," I said, under my breath.

"Shit," muttered Paz.

It took all five paramedics to lift Adrian's inert body onto the gurney. Someone had fitted his mouth with a breathing apparatus. The sight was surreal. It seemed as if I were watching the entire scene from somewhere outside my body. How could this be happening?

As three of the paramedics began to wheel the gurney toward the door, I drifted back to earth.

"Paz, get up. We have to do something."

"Like what, Mole? What can we do?"

"Well, for one, we have to find out where they're taking Adrian, right?" As I spoke I was vaguely aware of my hands twisting around each other like wrestling snakes.

Paz gazed at my hands, his eyes glassy and vague. Then he stretched them wide and shook his head like a cat shaking off water. "Oh, right. Yeah."

I gathered myself together and plunged after the retreating medics before the last one filed out the front door where our friend's stretcher clanged along the cobbled street.

"Excuse me," I called. "*Bakar mısınız!*"

The pony-tailed woman turned. "Yes?"

"Where are you taking our friend? What hospital?"

She frowned for a second and then took a huffy breath. "We will take him to private hospital. On water front." She jerked her head toward the stocky man I had noticed when I arrived. The young woman I had seen earlier holding Adrian's hand stood next to him. "Ask him. He knows it."

Then she called out to the man, whose earnest expression was somewhat calming. He seemed to be taking the situation seriously. He seemed to be concerned about Adrian's fate. The woman next to him was completely still, unsmiling, her thick eyebrows knit together in consternation. Now the female paramedic blurted out some Turkish words to the man and he nodded. His eyes looked sad.

"*Tamam*," he answered. Okay.

But it was not okay.

The paramedic gave me a stern look that said, "Why do you foreigners come to our country and cause these problems? Can't you just stay home?" Then she bolted out the door to catch up to her fellow rescuers. And Adrian.

The room was silent. After all the ruckus, no one remaining seemed to know what to say. An awkward few moments later, the man the paramedic had spoken to edged toward Paz and me. Paz slowly eeked to standing.

The man stood in front of us with a serious look on his face. Then he placed his right hand over his heart and bowed his head.

"I am sorry about Mister Adrian, your friend," he said. "It is tragedy."

We stood quietly for a moment, neither of us knowing how to respond. Then Paz reached out his right hand toward the solemn man and said, "I'm Paz." He nodded toward me. "And this is Molo. Thank you for your concern."

The man took Paz's hand and, still clasping it in his, said, "My name is Bulut. I am owner of this shop." He nodded toward the young woman who seemed about my age. She did not look like most of the Turkish women I had met, with her light brown hair, green eyes and fair skin. "That is my daughter, Gulya." Then he released Paz's hand and shook mine. "Please, come over to my desk. I am writing for you name of hospital and address on a piece of paper. Then you must go find your friend. I hope he is okay." He bowed ever so slightly.

Paz and I glanced at each other, then followed the earnest Bulut to the back of the room where a small wooden table on black wrought-iron legs was tucked into the corner. On top of it were assorted papers, carved boxes and an old-fashioned blotter. Bulut removed a small sheet of thin notepaper from the top of a stack nestled inside a desktray and scribbled some words on it. He handed the sheet to Paz.

"There is your friend."

"Thanks," said Paz and I in unison. "*Çok teşekkürler*," I added. It seemed only right to acknowledge the man in his own language after all his troubles. Adrian's fall must have lost him some customers, after all.

We took turns shaking his hand again, mine juddering slightly in his warm, firm palm, and then turned to exit the store. For the first time, I noticed how crammed it was with kilim, the brightly dyed rugs of the form called "flatweave." That much I had learned in Istanbul. In the corner were giant pile carpets, akin to the Persian rugs I had seen in shops in Santa Cruz, rolled up and leaning against the walls, like defense fortifications constructed of wool instead of stone. Numerous ornaments, some of them also woven, some carved out of wood and others forged out of metal filigree, adorned the walls. If I had not been so distracted and stunned by the calamity of the last half hour, it seemed a place I would have enjoyed moseying around. All the wool and wood evoked comfort and solace, both of which I sorely needed at that moment.

"Come on," urged Paz. "We need to find Adrian."

We pushed the door open and headed out into the insufferable heat.

It was only when we were dashing down the Paspatur's labyrinthine corridors, trying to locate the main street leading to the waterfront, that I remembered.

I had forgotten to ask Bulut what happened, what caused Adrian to collapse.

ɶ   ɶ   ɶ

Chapter 16

"Geçti Bor'un pazarı, sür eşeğini Niğde'ye." "Passed Bor's market, take donkey to Niğde." Or... "It's too late to do anything about it, so let's think of something else." - Anatolian proverb

September 13, 1922, Afternoon - Aydın Province

D emetrius watched the town of Ödemiş, celebrated for its delicious potatoes, the ones he and his fellow fighters were sometimes served for supper, if they were lucky, retreat in his rearview mirror. He could happily devour one of those potatoes now. He was famished.

"Are we heading back to Uşak?" the man in the middle asked his friend the driver. He had begun to fidget next to Demetrius. It was understandable; they had been bumping along rocky roads to nowhere for hours. For the whole day, in fact. And now it was late. The trees and shrubs guarding the roadsides were silhouettes now, backlit by a violet sky.

The driver shrugged. "*Belki.*" Demetrius knew that meant "maybe." By now, he realized the driver had run out of ideas of where to go. Perhaps it made sense to retrace their tracks to Uşak. There would be *konaklar* there, inns where they might all find a night's reprieve from the disappointments of this day.

But where would he go after that?

Suddenly, the driver turned his wizened head slightly to the right and craned his neck toward Demetrius. "*Şimdi nereye gitmek istiyorsun?*" Where do you want to go now?

Demetrius at first was too surprised at the question to answer. He had not expected anyone to be concerned about his destination. He stared ahead through the windshield at the open expanse of nothingness before them. Meanwhile, the driver had faced his pickup forward again, concentrating on the darkening road. Demetrius furrowed his brows. Where should he go, now that Smyrna was no longer possible? His entire plan had been forced to alter course and he should have spent the last few hours planning a new one.

"Constantinople," he finally blurted out. "*Oraya gitmek istiyorum*." I want to go there. His abrupt decision surprised even him.

The driver and his partner chuckled. The partner said, "It's a long way." Then the two men whispered between themselves while Demetrius drummed his fingers on the metal sill under his window.

"*Tamam*. Tomorrow we drive to Manisa and leave you there. You can find a ride to The City. Tonight we sleep in Zeytinlik." The driver nodded, seemingly pleased with his decision. Pleased that a plan was now in place.

Demetrius, not interpreting every word the driver had said, but understanding the basics, responded softly.

"*İyi, teşekkürler*." Good, thanks.

Where was Zeytinlik? Would his journey never end?

ॐ   ॐ   ॐ

Friday, August 16, 2013, Late Morning - Çalış Beach

Over time, you would think that you become inured to the pain of losing someone you love. Yet I can tell you with certainty it is not true.

When I learned in that desultory August of 2005 that Adrian had lapsed into a coma from which he would never recover, the sadness hurled through my body like a relentless, raging sirocco, leaving in its aftermath a kind of desecration of my soul, a dry desert, and a longing that clung to my rib cage like a vise grip. In the eight years since, that grip had never really let go. I had never found an oasis in which to take refuge. I had let the sandstorm of desolation subsume me and eventually, in desperation, I had made the decision to wipe out the old me, to transfigure into something other.

Or, at least, I had tried. But, as I was discovering, as this trip was revealing, changing what you appear to be on the outside does not necessarily alter who—or what—you really are. Behind the facade of re-fashioned hair, new clothing, eye make-up and a different walk was...me. None of the external revisions could change that.

These were my thoughts after Paz and I had disembarked from the *dolmuş* and scuffled along the seaside walkway that led into Fethiye. I watched the white, wide-winged seagulls encircle the battered fishing boats moored all along the waterfront. It occurred to me that these aviating

217

animals probably never questioned their birdness. They continued arcing and diving as if that behavior was everything that could and ever would be. Why would they even want to change it?

At the moment, I envied their complacency. At the same time, their dissonant cawing, eery and familiar, summoned up memories of the pier at Santa Cruz. For a moment, I felt homesick. I shook the feeling off. I could not allow homesickness or nostalgia to overtake me; I was here for a purpose. I was here to wreak havoc on the man who was responsible for my predicament, my crisis of consciousness. I felt as if the grip on my heart would never loosen if I did not carry through my plan. If I did not punish Ömer. Wherever he was.

"I thought you said Ömer's shop was in town, Paz." I winced at the querulous edge in my voice as I spoke.

Paz kept walking. "We're taking the scenic route."

"Oh, whatever. I guess I could use the exercise," I quipped, in an attempt to dislodge my brooding thoughts. "Then what?"

"Then what, what?" he asked, still hurtling along. I could barely keep up.

"What's the plan? Jeeeesus, how many times have I asked you that now?" My frustration with his endlessly yo-yoing game plan was like a sore that would scab over but then reopen, reinsinuating its irritating presence. I wanted to snatch the hypothetical yo-yo and stomp on it.

"I dunno. Haven't been counting."

Paz continued to amble forward with a great sense of purpose and I struggled to keep up. I called to him, "And how do you even know where this den of iniquity is? I never heard anyone talk about it."

He stopped abruptly and swiveled to face me. I had to swerve my body sideways to avoid him. Why did I keep bumping into people lately?

"Molo. Crikey, stop asking so many questions. I told you last night. Adrian told me. There. Now you know."

I cringed. Paz's earlier revelation clearly had not registered. "Adrian? He *knew*?" Now I could feel the words enter my throat, strident with disbelief. But, piercing as was the emotion behind them, their sound barely passed my lips. The shock of Paz's revelation had almost put a chokehold on my vocal chords. Could I really have heard him correctly?

"Oh, yes, he knew. You don't think him being there was an accident, do you? Remember, that day we visited Bulut, he told us."

"Told us what?"

"That he'd seen Adrian and Ömer at the shop together. C'mon, after all

218

these years, you must have thought the whole thing was too bizarre to be a coincidence."

"What whole thing?" I asked, still hardly able to push the words out. "What do you mean?"

Paz shifted his daypack to his other shoulder. I could tell he still harbored some residual resentment from our earlier clash. "The carpet shop, the accident, the fact that he was there!"

We were standing quite close to each other now. Paz peered into my eyes with an intensity that almost made me want to turn away. Then he placed his hands on my shoulders. Pedestrians sauntered by. I could feel a slight breeze from the adjacent sea ruffling my shirt. With the breeze came a whiff of salty water and fried fish. Goosebumps rose on my forearms.

Had I known?

"Right?" Paz shook my shoulders gently. "Molo, for God's sake! Maybe it's time to face up to the truth."

What I uttered in response came haltingly. "What truth? What am I supposed to know?" I could hear my pleading tone and felt like a nagging fishwife. But even as the words finally poured out, I knew that somewhere in me, somewhere buried beneath the gravestone of my grief, I *had* known. Something.

Paz ushered me over to one of the wooden benches and pushed me down onto the slatted seat before perching onto its edge near me. Only a few dessicated flowers buried amongst long serrated leaves were still visible on the sheltering jacaranda boughs, which seemed to be recuperating on the latticed trellis around the bench after all their springtime efforts. A leaf blew onto my arm and I brushed it off brusquely.

A nearby gull screeked, hauntingly.

I could see that Paz was about to speak, but he stopped himself. I egged him on with my eyes. I wanted to know, was desperate to know, what it was I had been hiding from myself all these years. For hiding it was. I realized that even my current incarnation was a kind of concealment, a camouflage. After a moment, Paz seemed to make up his mind, and grimaced. Then he cleared his throat. He was clearly uncomfortable.

"Adrian was not as 'innocent' as you thought." At the word "innocent" he made air quotes with his index and second fingers. Then he gazed up to the jacaranda shading us, and I could tell he was contemplating, deciding what to reveal. He turned slightly and surveyed the sea. There was a glassy expression in his eyes as he spoke again. "As *we* thought."

I stared at my hands. What could I say? What was there to say?

Paz waited, patiently. Some birds twittered in the branches above us. But I was otherwise hardly aware of my surroundings. Everything went suddenly silent. The passersby, people intent on their daily business or simply enjoying the seaside attractions, moved in slow motion, their voices muted. Even the background noises of harbor life dissipated. My head filled with some kind of chimerical helium and I felt my inner self drifting away from my body, like a balloon untying from its tether. The part of me that was still a human, still me, wanted to grab onto the balloon's steadying string and pull it back. Another part of me wanted to float on forever, sail into the blue, blue atmosphere of the beckoning beyond.

"Molo? You okay?" My friend's concerned tone broke the spell. The balloon popped and I was back in my body. It took me a second to shake myself free of the weirdness I felt on returning, but at last I heard the sounds of Fethiye and the lapping sea in the background.

"Yeah." I shrugged. I still felt deflated. "Yeah, I'm okay. I don't know what to say. I don't understand. I mean, maybe Adrian wasn't as 'innocent' as I thought, but surely, he did not poison himself."

Paz, my Galahadian companion, did that sideways mouth thing and reached out to touch my shoulder. "True. Adrian didn't poison himself. But about the rest...I'm sorry, Mole. I really...I was hoping you wouldn't find out all this."

I nodded slowly. I could only stare at the ground.

"Thing is," Paz said, "I guess you were bound to." I turned away from the ground and stared at him. He continued. "I mean, when I found out, when Mallie found out, that you were heading back to Turkey, I realized you were on a mission. Even though I didn't know exactly what you were up to, I was pretty sure that if you kept digging stuff up, you were going to find out things."

"Like about Ömer being in Santa Cruz."

"Yeah, maybe. But that info came from me. I still don't know why he was there. And I definitely want to find out." He rubbed his chin. "But I mostly mean the other crap, about Adrian knowing Ömer and him being at Ömer's carpet shop..."

What did he say?

"What did you say?" I swallowed. My saliva tasted like bile.

"What do you mean?" Paz was looking at me strangely.

"About the carpet shop. Are you telling me that the carpet shop where Adrian, you know...*that's* Ömer's shop?"

"Yeah, that's what I've been trying to tell you!"

"Shit. I don't believe it." I slapped my forehead. How could I have been so stupid? Damn. "I..."

"Feel like you were duped? You were. Kind of. Sorry, kid." He looked genuinely empathetic. "But, the truth is, we all were: you, Mallie, me. We all loved Adrian. Trusted him. But, yeah, you especially. I know he changed your life. I know what happened crushed you." Here, he blushed. "I'm sorry Mallie and I weren't there for you. You became unapproachable. And we didn't know how to handle the changes you went through." Now it was Paz's turn to stare at the ground.

I grasped Paz's forearm and squeezed. "I know. I kinda went off the rails. I mean, look at me." I let go of his arm, gestured both hands along the length of my torso and legs, and then put both palms face up in the air. I smirked. "What a dufus."

Paz watched me for a moment, our eyes latching onto each others' and then, as if a release button were suddenly pushed, we both burst into laughter. Our mirth mingled in the breezy atmosphere around us, and I caught glimpses of people turning their heads to see what the noise was about. When they saw us, some of them smiled and shook their heads, then continued benignly on their paths.

"Oh my *God*," I gasped. "What was I thinking? What have I done to myself?" I had a sudden flash of that annoying creature, Naji. Something, again, that he had been trying to tell me. I shook away the memory and turned to Paz.

He had his hand over his mouth, trying to stop the flow of chuckles. His eyes went wide, but they exuded a kind of light.

"Buddy, I don't know. That's your thing. I don't care what you look like or what clothes you wear, or even how you cut your hair. Although," I could tell he was stifling a snicker, "this ain't your best look. No wonder Mustafa didn't recognize you."

We both let out another volley of laughs.

"I know," I blurted out. "But I was so scared that he would. I thought it would blow my cover. So I went a little overboard just in case. But mostly, I knew I wouldn't be able to explain."

Paz nodded. "I get it. It would be difficult. Especially in this culture."

I sighed, deeply and steadily. The straitjacket encasing my lungs was loosening.

"So now what? Are we still going to O's shop? Now that I know where it is."

"Up to you. It's pretty much your call, if you still want to get your revenge. Or whatever."

"Fuckin' A. Absolutely. No matter what Adrian was up to, Ömer is still a creep and he's still responsible for what happened to Adrian. He deserves to be punished, especially since the police here never even investigated him. But before we go, you have to tell me everything you know, Paz. I don't want to go on blind anymore."

"Okay, you're right, Molo." He lifted his right arm and, extending it toward me, curled his hand into a vertical fist. I echoed his gesture, reaching my right arm out toward his with my own fist. Our knuckles bumped and the vise that had calcified over my heart during eight years detached at last, allowing an embrace of happiness to take its place.

I smiled. For the first time in an epoch, it felt real.

ฉ   ฉ   ฉ

October 30, 1922 – Constantinople

Bang, bang, bang, bang!

Ayşegül stopped humming and cocked her head to the side. *Not again.* The mystery knocker, it seemed, had returned, making a bigger racket than five nights before. This time, instead of surprise, she felt anxious, as if unshelled almonds were ricocheting from wall to wall inside her chest. She was not sure now that she *wanted* to know who was trying so ferociously to get her attention. It could not be good.

It was a shame to be interrupted now; she had made much progress on her revamped carpet today. Because it was only one meter by one-and-a-half in size, she was completing one row in less than an hour. The sooner she finished, the better. She quietly placed her *kirkit* beside her on her *halı* stool. Then, pushing herself to standing, she skittered across her small room, grabbed her silk *paşmina* shawl from where it lay draped over the wooden rail at the end of her bed, and threw it over her loom. She did not want anyone to see what she was creating.

Before she could make her way to the door, it burst open, slamming onto the wall behind. Instinctively, her hands went to her hips, akimbo. *Elebelinde.* It was her room, and she did not appreciate anyone invading her privacy. This had always been her fighting stance, even as a child.

"Where is it?" a resounding voice boomed. Tanju. Who else? Zeliha had warned her he was on the war path. Tanju-*Bey* was nominally in charge of the younger harem women, though he did not wield the kind of power that

222

the eunuchs had in earlier times. Ayşegül knew this and held her position. Still, she was shaking. Tanju was a large man and gloried in what little power he possessed. It did not do to cross him.

Now he came hurtling into her, pushing brusquely against her upper arm, and she nearly fell onto her loom. "Where is it, I asked?"

When she recovered herself and had shifted away from him, Ayşegül's hands automatically returned to their former position and her face flushed with anger.

"I have no idea what you are talking about," she shrieked. "Get out of my room. You have no right to barge in like this, Tanju-*Bey*."

Tanju did not answer. While she spoke, the thickset eunuch paced the perimeter of the space, thudding his fat feet toward her various pieces of furniture, pushed against the four walls. He picked up garments, shook them, threw them on the floor. When he approached her tall cabinet, he flung open the double doors and rifled through the shelves. Ayşegül watched in horror as he crumpled up and ripped her special design paper and tossed her pencils aside.

"Stop! What are you doing?" she called out. Still no answer. Instead, Tanju mumbled to himself, cursing in vulgar Turkish. Ayşegül could not believe what was happening.

And yet, she could.

She knew exactly what he was searching for.

Tanju continued around the room, peering under her bed, throwing up her mattress to inspect beneath it. Then he stopped in front of her large, carved wooden chest.

"Open it," he bellowed.

Ayşegül shrugged, though her face was flushed and she wished she had the gall to punch Tanju in his ugly paunch. She pulled her key out from the deep pocket of her *şalvar* pants, the ones she liked to wear while weaving, placed the clunky key into the horseshoe-arched keyhole of the chest and slowly turned it. Then she stepped back. Tanju marched toward the trunk, cranked open the lid with a loud thwap, and immediately bent forward to inspect its contents.

Kick him!

But she did not.

She watched, remembering that Zeliha had overheared Gülizar and Shahinaz in the shadows talking about her. So, they were right. Tanju was coming for her. But how did they know? How had they stumbled upon such damning intelligence? Surely, Tanju would not have told them. No doubt they had spied on him, as they spied on everyone.

Well, the two bitches might have conspired in some way, but they would not get the satisfaction of seeing her hauled away or punished. Because Tanju had nothing on her. She watched, feeling smug inside herself—small compensation for the insult his behavior and the girls' scandalmongering was bringing on her—as he rummaged through her few possessions. The more he rummaged, the more smug Ayşegül felt. Her trepidation began to melt away like the snows off Alemdağ Mountain in the spring.

Because she knew he would not find what he was looking for.

    æ   æ   æ

New Moon
(Part III)

Chapter 17

"Mark yonder, how the long laburnum drips
Its jocund spilth of fire, its honey of wild flame!" - Francis
Thompson, Sister Songs (1895)

September 14, 1922 - Manisa Province

He had thumped his fist on the outer edge of the passenger side window, standing outside the truck. Just inside, his spot on the hard bench seat by the window had been taken over by the driver's friend. The apple giver. This fist thumping gesture was his good-bye.

The two Turks each put up a hand cursorily, their scarred, worn palms turned toward him, dropping them almost as soon as they had raised them. This gesture was their good-bye.

As they turned toward the highway in the clunky metal machine, Demetrius smiled a thin smile. He would never see them again.

They had spent the night in an old inn, sharing a room on the second floor. There were only two rickety beds, so Demetrius borrowed from the inn-keeper a straw-stuffed mattress, which he tossed onto the cypress wood floor. He had slept deeply at last. And in the morning, sipping *çay* and breakfasting on green, juicy *kavun,* or melon, farm eggs and bread, Demetrius had held out a few coins. The driver shook his head and put up his juice-sticky hand. A silent "no." No need to pay. You have been our guest.

After the driver had shifted his truck into first gear and his two companions chugged away from the inn, Demetrius stood watching them shrink smaller and smaller in the morning sun. The truck's throaty motor continued to clunk and grind as it drove, even as it had turned into a mere speck on the western horizon.

A mangy dog, whose fur might once have been white, sauntered by. Demetrius watched its slow progress along the dusty road. It looked lonely, desolate. Hungry. As he had the day before.

No doubt the driver and his sidekick had realized Demetrius was not Turkish like them. Most likely they had known he was a Greek. And yet, they did not seem to care. They had responded to his summons, stopping on the Uşak highway that bissected two battles, one of arms and one of fire. And they had taken him on, though there was nothing to force them. On the road, despite the long drive, the disappointment in Uşak, the short-cut to nowhere, the shock of Smyrna in flames, they did not blame him or chastise him. For being a foreigner. For being on the opposite side of the war's ambitions as they. They had accepted him as a man who lived in Anatolia and belonged to it as did they themselves. Their language and some of their customs were different, but they were brothers just the same.

Demetrius would never forget that.

At the edge of the road, a few meters from the inn's weathered door, he pulled his battered fez out of his battered bag and slowly, deliberately, placed it on top of his head. It still scratched and made his scalp itch. But he was glad to have it. The fez was his ticket to anonymity, he hoped.

He had made it as far as Manisa. But he was alone again. And now he needed to somehow weave in and between the lines of demarcation, the theaters of battle, the knots of ferocity and cunning and deceit, to slip behind the skeletal warp of war and go forward. He needed to somehow wend his way to Constantinople.

But the besieged metropolis was four hundred twenty-five kilometers north. And it was falling fast. Demetrius did not think he would be so fortunate a second time in finding two such samaritans to help him along as the two who had just driven away. He needed to be clever and he needed to be careful.

Smyrna was still burning and the Turkish army was a firestorm. Who knew what else lay on the path ahead? He wrinkled his brow and wondered if he was doing the right thing. The smart thing.

He placed his left boot in front of his right. The weight of his body on his feet reminded him of the painful, sharp blisters he had suffered from before. But thanks to two days in the truck, two days with his rescuers, his blisters had had a reprieve. They no longer made him wince. Thank God. Thank St. Christopher. As he had two days earlier, he fingered the copper icon hanging from the cheap, metal alloy chain around his neck. He would be able to walk. At least for awhile.

Dumlupınar had been brutal, but he had survived. He had escaped the worst, he thought, with the help of the truck men, and he would continue his journey with hope. He would slide through Constantinople, the gateway to Thrace.

Because he needed to get home. And he needed to get there fast.

ॐ   ॐ   ॐ

Wednesday, June 8, 2005, Afternoon - Fethiye

We sprinted as quickly as we could, Paz and I, bumping into afternoon daytrippers and school kids licking *dondurma* that melted down their cones in the post-lunchtime heat. I was ahead of Paz, and I could feel my daypack thwapping my back with each stride. I felt like Jack Lord cruising along the Pacific Ocean with The Ventures playing the *Hawaii Five-O* theme song behind the scenes. *Da-da-da-da-da-da, da-da-da-da-da.* Its driving rhythm and catchy surfer riff running through my head kept me from thinking too much about the reason I was running through the streets of Fethiye at all.

The song was still lingering in my inner television mind when I stopped at an intersection to catch my breath. Paz halted beside me and pulled out the piece of paper Bulut had written directions on.

"Book 'em, Danno," I said.

"What?" Paz gave me a quizzical look.

"Oh, nothing. Where do we go next?" I peered over his hairy forearm to check out Bulut's scrawls. Then I pointed to a spot on the paper. "Is this where we are, do you think? We've gotta be close."

Paz concentrated on the crude drawing. Then he looked up, his head swiveling around like Linda Blair's in *The Exorcist* to check out our coordinates. I was mixing movies now, but it was a distraction from my deeper feelings, at least. "It says '533 Sokak' and we're at 531. Come on. I see a big blue building down there. 'S gotta be the hospital."

I followed his pointed index finger with my eyes. "Yep, I see it. Let's go." Jack Lord aka Steve McGarrett would have been proud of our detecting skills. The realization spurred me on.

By the time we reached the Esnaf Hospital's entrance, sweat pored down my brow and into my eyes. I tried to wipe it off with my shirt sleeves, but because I was wearing a tee-shirt and the sleeves were short, my attempt had meager results, so beads of moisture merged into streaks instead. Paz was more successful with his trekking bandana, stuffing the now damp cloth into his back pocket. Only slightly less disheveled now, and inside the foyer, we followed red floor arrows and bilingual wall signs in Turkish and English to what we hoped would be the information desk. Supposedly, we would find it at the far end of a room sliced through here and there with decorative glass block dividers.

The place was heaving. At one end of the waiting area, apple-cheeked women wearing lightweight scarves tied under their chins bent forward on gray plastic and stainless steel stacking chairs, their own looks of steely wariness fixed on their lined faces. Perhaps the children they were leaning towards were suffering and their mothers—or grandmothers, I could not tell which—had come to this place as a last resort. Their expressions suggested this progressive approach to healing was something thrust upon them, but not entirely embraced. Rail thin men sat beside them, their caps hanging over their knees, staring into the middle distance or fingering their plastic worry beads. At the other end of the crowded room, flush-faced foreigners, that is, most likely British tourists, fanned themselves furiously with rectangular brochures or rolled up magazines. Overhead, garbled announcements blasted across the heads of the waiting patients, creating an aural cacophony that reminded me of a public sporting event.

These impressions came to me in flashes as we rushed by. But, despite the teeming mass of humanity around me, I also saw that the rubber tile flooring was shiny, the windows spotless and the direction signs fresh and bright. In other words, the place was much more modern than I had expected to find in a small town in southern Turkey. But it was a private hospital and maybe that made the difference. I sighed in relief. Adrian should be in good hands.

We made our way to the "Foreigners" counter. Fortunately, no one was in front of us.

"Yes? May I help you?" said a young, smiley Turkish man. He looked about twenty years old, and his chipper attitude further rallied my spirits. It helped that his English was perfect, though spoken with a slight London accent.

Paz leaned on the counter. "We're looking for our friend. He was brought here about half an hour ago. By ambulance." Paz drummed his fingers on the counter, which seemed a little rude, given the circumstances, but the youth behind the counter did not seem offended. He merely consulted his computer screen, clicking here and there methodically until he nodded to himself in what seemed to be some kind of affirmation.

"Your friend. What is the name?"

"Adrian McAllister," I said. "An American. He had an accident."

"Yes, I see," the empathetic clerk said, then added, "It is too bad." At this utterance, his brown eyes grew appropriately sad. "You are right, he is here in our hospital. But I am sorry. You cannot see him now."

"We can't? Why not?" I could feel the coolness of my Jack/Steve alter ego being supplanted by the more prosaic—and heated up—Molo me and then I almost shouted, "We're on holiday. He needs us!" Instead, in a purposeful attempt to gain the clerk's sympathy, I checked out the plastic nametag on his red uniform vest. "Ferhat? Did I say that right? We really need to find out what is happening to him."

Ferhat smiled wanly. "I understand." He blinked. "The problem is," and now he placed his hand over his heart. "Mister Adrian is in a coma. He is not able to do or say anything."

Coma? How could that be?

All at once, I felt the rubber tile floors fall away from me. Ferhat's smooth, bronzed face receded toward the back wall of the reception area and the clashing sounds of patients yacking, metal carts wheeling and machines whirring, suddenly became muted. Coma? No, it was not possible. The implications were too much to take in.

I felt someone grab my shoulder. "You okay, Mole?" It was Paz. His familiar, sonorous voice brought me back to the moment. I would probably have puddled onto the floor if he had not touched me. I might have preferred the puddle option.

I saw that Ferhat was shifting from foot to foot. By now, a few über-white-skinned people had formed a line behind us, anxious for information, too, judging from their shirking shoulders and glaring eyes. Ferhat, his own eyes bulging, looked past me to scan the growing queue. Before I had a chance to express my agitation at being denied access to Adrian, Paz took over. I let him, grateful for his commandeering calm. But I was sure he felt the shock of Adrian's predicament as much as I did.

"We understand about the coma. It's very difficult for us, as you can imagine. But Mister McAllister is our good friend and I am sure he would want us to see him, to talk to a doctor. Even if he can't talk. Please. We need to find out what has happened."

Ferhat listened politely to Paz despite the annoyed sighs of the assemblage of would-be patients behind us. A voice with a Cockney accent blurted out, "Oi, some of us would like to check in, too, if you don't mind." Ferhat pursed his lips, then picked up a phone. A few seconds later, he was speaking in Turkish, recurring "z" sounds buzzing like irritated wasps, to someone on the other end. As he hung up, he looked at us and said, "Okay. My boss say you must see your friend. The doctor will talk to you then."

He pointed down the gleaming hallway. "Go down that way and follow wall signs for 'Emergency.' Mister Adrian is there."

Dismissed, we moved away from the counter while an overweight man wearing cargo shorts and a garish Hawaiian shirt pushed his bulk into our place. The fabric on his colorful top stretched over his belly and its buttons seemed about to burst. As we rushed toward the hallway Ferhat had indicated, I heard the man say, "Hiya, mate. Can you help me?" The accent was definitely British. In spite of myself, that knowledge annoyed me. How dare this fat foreigner interrupt my efforts to suss out information about Adrian? Who did he think he was? I was about to call out some choice expletives in retaliation, but Paz, probably anticipating my reaction, intervened.

"Don't. It's not worth it. We've got more important things to deal with than that asshole." And he pulled my arm. I glanced back over my shoulder and mentally flipped the rude man the bird. He probably did not deserve it, but someone had to pay for Adrian's predicament and, as I did not yet know who the real culprit was, I might as well take it out on this guy.

Book 'em, Danno. If only.

❧ ❧ ❧

October 30, 1922 – Constantinople

After Tanju stomped out of her room, swearing under his breath, Ayşegül pushed her bulky, wooden chest in front of her door. No one else was going to barge into her room like that. At least, not while she was in it. But she did not know how to prevent it when she was out. She could not block the door from the outside when she was away. Unless there was a *djinn* she could summon. Despite the seriousness of her situation, the thought made her giggle.

Originally, it had not bothered her that there were no locks on the girls' rooms; now she wished there were. Before, she had nothing to hide; now she did. Who knew who might come in when she was in another part of the palace? Perhaps Tanju had even come that night after that first banging on her door. The more she thought about it, the more Ayşegül decided that he must have realized she was in the room when he rapped on her door so vehemently, and decided instead to return while she was performing in the *İncesaz* concert. That way, he could search to his heart's content—if indeed he had a heart—without her knowing. And it would explain why he had

231

knocked, but not answered, when she called out that night. Obviously, he had not found anything incriminating or he would not have come back. Had he also come last night when she was with Estreya and Yasmin for her *fal* reading? If so, had he noticed the melted wax under the little rug in the middle of the floor? She thought not; otherwise, he would certainly have said something to her, for he had been in a mood to call her out on any and all of her possible transgressions. If she was right, he had been in her room at least twice, and left—twice.

So, the worst was over. She hoped. Tanju had departed empty-handed. She could allow herself to believe he might not return.

It gave her great satisfaction that he had not succeeded in finding what he had been sent to find. She had taken a supreme risk, taking it in the first place, but it was her ticket out of this place and she had acted on impulse. What had Estreya read in the coffee grounds? There was the tornado, which meant trouble. Well, it looked like that part of Estreya's prophecy was coming true already. She realized she had probably brought some of the trouble on herself, but it was certainly exacerbated by the political turmoil throughout the Empire. But then Estreya said something about a horse and a love adventure. Hmmph. She could not see where that might come in, but what about the boat? Estreya insisted that meant a friend was going to help her.

"*İnşallah.*" She might need a friend soon.

Ayşegül closed her eyes for a moment and when she opened them, she walked over to her window and gazed out at the amethyst sky beyond. Absentmindedly, she picked up her large hour glass from where it sat on the wide windowsill, filled with pure white grains of sand. Still holding onto it, she flipped the device upside down. The crystal-like sand began to slip slowly through the narrow gullet of glass that acted as the conduit between the two tulip-shaped bowls at either end. It reminded her of the Bosphorus, the skinny throat between the Black Sea and the Sea of Marmara, through which boats of all sizes glided each day. Soon she might need to slip through its narrow banks, as well. She placed the hour glass down and turned again to her window.

The moon looked bigger than usual—near full—and hovered above the Üsküdar skyline, across the strait. She must be in the stage of her month-long journey where she was closest to the earth. Good. If Estreya's predictions were wrong and no horse or boat omen was going to come to rescue her, Ayşegül would summon her savior, her namesake, and the moon would step in, Ayşegül was sure. They were still sisters. She might be far away, aloof, but she was there. And she was bound to Ayşegül.

Quietened by this conviction, Ayşegül now turned to her loom. She pulled off the *paşmina* she had thrown over it when Tanju disturbed her work, then stood back, studying her composition. The different patterns she had drawn up the day before were taking shape, forming a picture. She smiled. Maryam might "tsk, tsk" over this unusual arrangement of symbols, but she knew in the end her teacher would approve. She would appreciate the nod to tradition in the design's overall symmetry, but Ayşegül had steered away from the elaborate, busy *mecidi* style popular at the palace and opted for simplicity and more open fields. To her, they suggested freedom. As she considered her creation she felt a kind of pride. Because this carpet told a story; you could see it almost as soon as you looked at it. "You have found your *sanat*, your artistry, Ayşegül-*hanım*," Maryam would no doubt proclaim. "And that means, you must not sell it to the carpet peddlars in the city for a few lira. You must use this carpet in a special way."

Maryam would be pleased to know that was what exactly what Ayşegül intended.

If only the wise, older woman were here now. Ayşegül could almost feel her mentor standing behind her, admiring her latest work. And she could almost see her wink with a twinkle in her eye. She would understand, Ayşegül knew. Understand why Ayşegül was making a carpet like this. Realize why Ayşegül had to do what she was going to do. It was possibly something Maryam herself had wanted long ago—long before she was sent last year to Hereke to weave carpets in jacquard instead of wool—but had never had the opportunity. This thought also strengthened Ayşegül's conviction. She was not only planning for herself, but for her fellow inmates. She would do it for them, too. Show them there was a pathway to liberation.

Because you had to take the chance. No, you had to *make* the chance.

She placed both hands over her heart, bowed her brooding head onto her chest and closed her eyes. After praying silently, she released her hands and approached her loom. For a moment, she glanced at her hour glass. The sand from the top bowl was now rapidly streaming through the throat toward the bottom bowl. Quietly, she sat down on her *halı* stool, picked up her *kirkit* and scissors, and set to work, furiously.

Time was running out.

❧   ❧   ❧

Friday, August 16, 2013, Late Morning – Fethiye

Ömer.

What was his relationship with Adrian, anyway? Why was Adrian in Ömer's shop that day eight years ago?

"That, I don't know," said Paz. I had asked him the same questions out loud while we walked.

We had made our way at last along the remainder of the waterfront, through the dense quarter of two-story shops, pharmacies and open-air *kebap* counters, retracing our path of eight years before between the Esnaf Hospital and Ömer's carpet place. I had not known then that it *was* Ömer's. My brain was still suffering jolts of aftershock from that bit of news.

Now we stood at the corner where the ambulance that took Adrian away had parked the day of his accident. The accident that surely was *not*, the "accident" that Ömer had conspired to commit and then carried out for some diabolical reason that none of us ever gotten to the bottom of. I was shaken out of my angry reverie when a surprisingly anachronistic yellow taxi honked nearby.

"What's next? Now that we're here, I don't know what to do."

Paz hiked his rip-stop nylon daypack higher up his shoulder. "Well, first, we need to find a decent place to keep an eye on the shop. I'm really hoping that Ömer will be there."

"What about Bulut and Gulya? What if they see us? I'm sure they'll remember us, even after all this time. Or, you, at least."

"Yeah, that's a good question, Mole. Not sure of the answer. I just want to see if the bastard is around, then we'll go from there, okay?"

I nodded. "Yeah, that sounds like a plan." I chuckled. "A plan that isn't a plan."

Paz harrumphed in acknowledgement.

Now seemed like the right time to brief him on something he did not know. For once.

"I saw Ömer at the airport." The words jumped out of me like oil from a hot skillet.

My friend stood completely still. He looked at me askance.

"You what?"

"I saw him. Ömer. He was climbing into a black Mercedes sedan when we were getting onto the bus. In the parking lot." I crossed my fingers discreetly. Was I doing the right thing, telling Paz this? If he was indeed in cahoots with Ömer, I might be tying my own noose. I had traveled a long way on the road of trust since the morning, but was it warranted?

Paz's thick brows squinched in the middle of his forehead, as if a set of calipers had just landed on his brow and its two ends were squeezing toward each other. "Molo, why didn't you tell me?"

I shrugged.

"Wasn't quite sure it was him at first. I thought he would be in Santa Cruz still." A slight lie. I knew it was Ömer, my sixth sense and the shiver that had zinged up my spine had confirmed it, but Paz would not know that. "But now that I think about it more, I'm sure it was him."

Paz shook his head as if shaking water out of his hair. "Shit. How weird. I don't get it." His eyes shifted upwards and his mouth twisted to the left in his usual way. "Well, our stakeout should prove successful then. Your sighting confirms that the man of the month is in the vicinity. So, I'm sure he'll come to visit his shop. Let's find a stakeout spot."

"Sounds good," I responded, uncertainly. I hoped we were not getting in over our heads.

After a couple of minutes searching, we leaned against an exterior wall in the cooling shade of grape vines growing over a metal trellis. The wall belonged to the lingerie store two shops down from Ömer's. I had not had a chance to get the name of Ömer's place in 2005; everything had catapulted to disaster so quickly. But now I could see the dark brown sign above the door. I had to do a double-take with my eyes, blinking in between takes to make sure I was seeing correctly. You could have knocked me over with a flyswatter when I read the words, painted in egg yolk yellow:

SILK ROAD CARPET SHOP, FETHIYE

I could hardly believe it. It was the same name, only substituting "Fethiye" for "San Francisco," that was on the little card I found in *The House on the Strand* last night. What the heck was going on? Clearly, there was a connection between Ömer and Adrian, my old buried carpet and this place. Should I tell Paz about the two notes? If I opened up now, he would wonder why I had not told him before. That is, if he did not know about it already.

I must have made some kind of sound in my astonishment at seeing the sign.

"What's wrong?" Paz asked.

"Me? Nothing." I swallowed a lump of phlegm that had formed in my throat. I pointed at my neck. Paz responded with a slight nod.

Then I remembered something. Something I had seen, but barely acknowledged, when Paz and I were leaving the dark room in Istanbul two nights before. When I had seen him pick up a small item from the desk he was sitting on and shove it surreptitiously into his pants pocket. I should clarify: what I thought I saw him shove into his pants pocket. It was dim as a monkey's bottom in that room, so I could not be sure. After all, I was in a mild state of shock at coming across Paz so unexpectedly. Not to mention, exhausted from my flight. All those factors combined, perhaps I had imagined the whole thing. Perhaps I had been a bit paranoid, too, wary of Barış's disagreeable demeanor and subterfuge.

I decided to tread lightly.

"Paz, is there something else I need to know that you haven't told me?"

He was picking at his nails and then turned to look at me. "Like what?"

"I don't know. That's why I'm asking." I shifted my own daypack on my back to create a cushion against the hardness of the stone wall we were leaning against.

"What could there be? I don't know what you mean."

I lifted both my palms, face up, standard "I don't know" gesture. Either my intuition had been wrong, or my inscrutable compadre was still hiding something. "Doesn't matter. Just wondered. These last two days have been a whirlwind, you know?"

"Let me ask *you* something." Paz shifted on his feet, removed his daypack from his shoulder and placed it carefully between his feet on the stone walkway beneath us. Then he looked at me pointedly. "Is there anything you need to tell *me*?"

Shit. He was actually turning the tables on me! I should have expected that. Paz was always clever that way. A veritable Artful Dodger of dissimulation.

I stared at my crotch, which happened to be in my line of sight when I bowed my head. I could not look Paz in the eye as I lied.

"Nope. Nothing I can think of."

"Cool. Well, there we are. All's out in the open. And now we can concentrate on Ömer of Oz."

That made me laugh.

"Right. Let's hope he shows up so we know he's actually here."

"And then, we can figure out what we're going to do to the bugger. At long fucking last."

"Amen to that," I said.

We fist bumped.

But even as we gestured in solidarity, like boys in the 'hood—another incongruity, considering my current incarnation—I felt a niggling in my gut. At the same time, I had another flash of Naji, my dream *djinn*, barking out some nonsensical phrase or other. A warning, a remonstrance. Something important.

Suddenly, two young women in long, beige *abaya* coats and toting light pink shopping bags with white rope handles, chatted loudly as they exited the lingerie outlet. Paz and I dropped our hands and watched the women saunter toward the shadowy regions of the back alleys of Paspatur, still blabbering away. The unbidden vision of the possibly provocative unmentionables lying folded and illicit in the bottoms of those bags made my torso quiver. I could never bring myself to buy such things even now. I wondered briefly if such thoughts entered Paz's mind. But after all, he was married and I had never had a partner. Not in that way. The girls faded out of sight and Paz and I both raised our eyebrows.

The interruption, fleeting as it was, was enough to erase Naji from my mind. It was not until later that the reason for his ethereal entreaty would make sense to me.

æ   æ   æ

Wednesday, June 8, 2005, Afternoon - Fethiye

I hurtled over to the steel-framed bed where my boon companion, my secret soul mate, lay inert. Corpse-like. Vertical slats, like jail bars, guarded both sides of the narrow, white-sheeted mattress, as if Adrian were a prisoner and might inadvertantly escape. In a way, he was a prisoner. A prisoner in his own inanimate body. If any escape was imminent, it was no doubt that of his soul vacating his physical self for the great Shangri-la of the beyond. As if to drive that point home, the blinking machine he was hooked up to by tubes and electrical lines loomed like a tombstone headboard above him.

"Adrian!" My hands gripped the steel bar guarding his sleeping form while a cold outrage gripped my chest organs, bits of glacier breaking off and plunging into bottomless depths. "Adrian. It's me, Molo. Can you hear me?"

237

Adrian responded as any comatose person would. He did nothing. There was no blink, twitch or even a slight heave in his torso. The stillness was unnerving, like that before a battle between a hungry cat and a tiny mouse. You knew what was coming and you knew, for the mouse, it would not be good. In other words, not much of a battle at all. In spite of what Ferhat had warned me, during my journey from the hospital reception to this sterile sepulchre, I had burbled with hope that Ferhat was wrong, that he'd accidentally read someone else's chart, not Adrian's. But now I was here, the sight of my best friend's drained face, the purple contusions under his eyes, his lank hair streaked with wet, and most of all, his life-ebbing, inanimate form, forced me to face reality. This was not a room of recovery; it was a death cell.

Paz, who had lingered in the doorway, now sidled up beside me. He stared down at Adrian and was so quiet, I wondered for a moment if he, too, had gone into a comatose state. But he must have rallied for he gently placed his arm around my shoulder. "Buddy, I don't know what to say. This really sucks. I can't believe it."

We both stood silently looking down on the being that once had been Adrian. Still was, in some way, but without the joy, the spark, the life force that characterized his essential self. When I could not take the silence any longer, I turned to the doctor. He had been patiently lurking on the other side of the bed, in the shadows.

"What's wrong with him, do you know yet?" I asked. My voice was hushed. Funereal.

Surprisingly, the doctor answered in English.

"We think he was poisoned."

"Poisoned?" Paz and I blurted out. I could feel his body tense up beside me. "What do you mean?"

"We are waiting for test results, but in my opinion, your friend," here, he nodded toward Adrian almost reverently, "has taken laburnum."

"Le-what?"

"La-burn-um. Ana-gy-roi-des," he replied, pronouncing each syllable with exaggerated precision. The first three sounded like "leh-BOORH-noom" in the doctor's Turkish accent. The rest was gobbledy-gook.

"What's that?" I asked.

"It is a tree. A very beautiful tree, in point of fact. But, unfortunately, every part of it is poisonous."

"A tree? How would Adrian get tree poison in him? It doesn't make sense. He was at a carpet shop."

"Ah," said the doctor, lifting his chin and eyeballs toward the acoustic-tiled ceiling. "A carpet shop. I see." Hugging his lilac-purple plastic clipboard to his chest with his left hand, he placed his right index finger above his lip and his thumb under his chin. Classic "Thinker" pose. And, indeed, he did look absorbed in deep contemplation.

"This is what I am thinking. You say, 'conjecture'?" His command of English was surprisingly adept. Perhaps he had gone to medical school in the States or in England.

"Yes...?" Paz and I asked, in unison.

"I thinking there was maybe laburnum seed or sap in his tea. Or something he drink at the shop. In my opinion, it is possible."

"Tea? Who would want to put poisonous tree seeds in Adrian's tea?" I heard my voice rise up the panic chart a few notches.

"I don't know," the doctor replied. "We will make test and find out for sure. It is unusual for someone who eats laburnum to get this sick. But it does happen. It has happen before."

"I don't believe it," I shouted. "Who could do this? Who would *want* to?" By now, I uncurled my white-knuckled fingers from around the cylindrical bed bars and began to pace the floor nearby. Paz watched me, a look of intense compassion in his nut-brown eyes.

"Please, give the nurse your information. Where we contact you. And as soon as I get test results, we let you know." Here, he wrote something on the his clipboard. "Here is my number, in case. If you think of something." He made to hand a paper chit to Paz across Adrian's bed, a sea of sadness in this cheerless, shadowy room. "I must go now."

Before the doctor could abandon ship, I blurted out, "Can you write the full name of this 'leboonum' tree down for us? I want to look it up."

The doctor tipped his head, said, "Of course," slapped the paper back onto his clipboard and dutifully scribbled. Then he passed the paper to Paz, who stood closest to him. And was, admittedly, the calmer of the two of us.

Paz read the note, then shook the doctor's hand. "Doctor Karatepe. I'm Paz Lavigne. Thank you for your help. We will wait to hear from you." I observed them both, stunned by their mutual calmness and civility. In contrast, my own inclination was to grab the good doctor around the throat and force him to tell us more. But I quickly realized that approach would probably cause more problems than it solved. After all, he was not the person responsible for Adrian's predicament. So I huddled by the bathroom door, saying nothing.

But who *was* responsible? That was the million lira question.

The doctor gave us both a curt nod, then turned and hastened out of the room. As he left, a young nurse with sleek, blue-black hair coiled into a low neck bun replaced him, as if she had just slid into Doctor Karatepe's place via some hospital floor conveyor belt. She handed me a different clipboard with a blank form on it and a black ballpoint pen tucked under the hinge. "Please to write name and information." Her English was stilted, uncertain, but she followed her short speech with a sympathetic smile. So I smiled back, thinly, and took the clipboard.

As the nurse checked Adrian's tubes and other hook-ups, I started to fill in the blanks on the form, my hand shaking all the while. Paz sidled up behind me and peered over my shoulder.

"Do you want me to do that?" he asked, quietly.

"No, it's okay. I'm alright. I think. I'll put both our names on, just in case."

He nodded in assent.

"I don't know the Mavi Dolfin's phone number, though. Do you?"

Paz fumbled around in his front pocket and pulled out a crumpled business card. "Here." He placed the card on top of the clipboard. "That should do it."

"I hope so," I said, completing the form as best I could. Fortunately, the questions were in Turkish and English. I silently and grudgingly thanked the British for their invasion of this small community.

"Okay," I announced. The tiny, coifed nurse gently placed Adrian's wrist back by his side and joined Paz and me. I held the clipboard out to her, but before relinquishing it completely, I said, "You'll make sure they call us, right? When they get the test back?"

She nodded exuberantly. "Of course," the Turk's most known and used English phrase, and put her hand out to take the board. I kept a hold of it.

"Do you promise? It's very important. We really want to know what has happened to our friend here," and I jerked my head toward poor, prostrate Adrian.

"Yes, yes, I am promise," she agreed. I released my hand from the clipboard, reluctantly. It felt like letting go of Adrian. Like leaving him to fend for himself in this helpless, diminished state. Abandoning him.

"Let's go, Paz," I said. "I guess there's nothing more we can do right now."

Paz nodded once, his lips pursed. And he patted my shoulder as we lodged one last glance at Adrian and walked out the door.

240

Neither of us knew whether we would ever see him again.

            ❧   ❧   ❧

It is known as the Golden Chain tree.

In late springtime, cascades of bright yellow blooms hang from its olive-green branches—long strands of cheerful party garlands, waving in the lusty wind. As on its cousin the pea, obovate petals open into miniature gloves, tiny and welcoming, ready to grasp offerings from leafminers and mealy bugs alike. The soft sepals glow, ablaze with light brighter than even the sun's, and their golden stamen, though short, are powerful and entrancing as they wriggle enticingly in the Mediterranean's briny breeze.

Oh, the aroma of this Anatolian angiosperm. Its seductive scent, so sweet and lingering, captivates its audience, seduces it, draws it near, lures it into capitulation. It is Myrina, queen of the Amazons, stunning and regal, her beauty unequivocal and alluring.

And like Myrina, who shocked the ancient world, conquering as she did the city-states of Phrygia and Samothrace, adjuring her warrior troops be merciless in their destruction—and pitiless—, the Golden Chain Tree possesses a sinister side, a separate identity, a face almost unrecognizable when it is turned the other way. Beware. This side is spurious and irascible. Threatening.

Its beauty may be unrivalled during springtime's happy flowering, but take heed. Take warning. Follow this advice: never sample of the Golden Chain Tree's entreating enchantments. If you do, you will be sorry.

For the Golden Chain Tree, in addition to its other face, possesses another name. That other name is the Laburnum Tree.

And all its parts are poisonous.

Chapter 18

"The soul is a newly skinned hide, bloody and gross. Work on it with manual discipline, and the bitter tanning acid of grief, and you'll become lovely, and very strong." - Mevlana (aka Rumi)

Wednesday, June 8, 2005, Afternoon - Çalış Beach

O ur *dolmuş* ride from the hospital to the Mavi Dolfin Evi seemed interminable. And then again, it was as if time itself had come to a standstill, a paradox that I had neither the skill nor the inclination to unravel. I sat next to Paz on the scratchy seats and stared out the window, unblinking. The people on the sidewalks were paper dolls, two-dimensional and inconsequential. The shops with their outdoor stalls featuring baby pink and blue plastic washing tubs or roasted chicken no longer elicited my interest, the usually enticing smell of the rotisseried birds, or *piliç*, failing to make me salivate. Quick shots of the Mediterranean between the streets and buildings as the *dolmuş* puttered along were nothing more than flash cards fanning before my eyes. The enchantment of its shimmering turquoise allure no longer registered. Even the road sign that cautioned: *"Hiziniz, cizbiz yirmi beş,"* or "Your speed, 25.50" (I had looked it up recently), with all its buzzy tonal hilarity, failed to make me snicker. In fact, all my senses ceased to function in their usual way.

It was as if I myself were lying alongside Adrian in that ghastly hospital bed, ghost-like like him and, for all intents and purposes, no longer sentient. If he was not there, I could not see the point of my own existence anymore.

"Mole? You in there?" Paz's voice was tentative. This in itself was unusual. I could actually hear his concern in the delivery, but I did not care. So I did not answer.

"Molo?" He jiggled my arm. "Talk to me. What are you thinking?"

I slowly turned my head to face him and just looked at his face, my eyes feeling as dead as the rest of me. His lips tightened in a pout and he turned his gaze down toward his thighs.

We road along in silence for a few more blocks, then he nudged me. "Hey. This is our stop. C'mon. We gotta get off."

I scooped up my daypack without a word, scooted after him into the narrow aisle of the cramped bus and, while I was dimly aware of the driver glaring at me from the reflection of his rear-view mirror, I took my time exiting. As soon as I was on the curb at the dolphin roundabout, no longer the beacon of hope it had been a few hours before, I felt the force of the dry, hot air on my skin and in my nostrils. The strength of it caused me to stir somewhat. I had to engage my muscles, anyway, if I was going to trek back to our hotel.

Paz urged me on. As we trudged up the main drag toward the Mavi Dolfin Evi, he continued to talk, his voice suddenly taking on a querulous tone. "What are we going to tell Mal, Molo? She's gonna have a fit. She'll blame me for what happened." He stopped whining for a moment, and then blurted out. "Shit, what a *mess*! What the hell happens here when a foreigner has an accident like that?"

I did not answer. What was there to say? I certainly did not know anything about how to deal with a comatose tourist in Turkey. We would just have to see what ensued.

"Molo. Say something, for Chrissakes!" Paz yelled. He sounded almost desperate and his plea must have hit a nerve, as I began to feel myself oozing out of the fog of self-recrimination in which I had been wallowing for the past hour.

We were at the corner of our *sokak* and automatically turned left down the dusty, unpaved road. Two more blocks. The guy who owned the corner market waved. This was the first time we did not stop in for a beer or an ice-cream. I thought I might never eat or drink again.

"I don't know what to say, Paz. The whole thing sucks and I can't wrap my head around it. Around what happened to Adrian. Or why. Can you?" I stopped in the middle of the road and turned to him. "It doesn't make sense. At all."

Paz stood next to me, fingering the strap of his small pack. He wagged his head, like a dejected puppy. "Sure as shit doesn't. I'm over my head with this one."

"Me, too."

"Well, we might as well go to the hotel and wait for the doctor to call. Nothing else really to do until then."

"Yeah, I guess. Let's go."

We plodded the rest of the way to the front gate of our current digs and lumbered up the three wide steps to its dark foyer. It felt like climbing the pyramid at Giza on a blistering afternoon with a sixty pound jug of water on my back. By the time we got inside the lobby, I was utterly enervated.

"Hang on, Paz. I've gotta take a second before I tackle the stairs."

"Okay, buddy. Doesn't seem like Murat's around anyway. Or anybody. I wonder if Mallie's gotten back from the beach yet."

"Mallie?"

"Yeah, you know, my girlfriend, our travel partner? Remember her?"

"Christ, you're right. How are we gonna tell her about all this?"

"I haven't a clue. That's what I was saying before. We might have to hire an arbitrator to do it for us, ya know? 'Cuz otherwise, I think she's gonna rip us each a new one."

In spite of myself, a chuckle burst out of me. "You're right about that." I took a deep breath. "Well, let's just do it. Might want to put on some kevlar though. You know, protective gear."

That made Paz laugh. "Ha, right. Okay, let's go."

We skirted the indoor atrium, making our way to the steel-banistered stairwell beyond and took our time going up the three flights. Passing mine and Adrian's room, I sighed. We headed straight to Paz and Mallie's instead. But when Paz unlocked the door and went inside, Mallie was not there.

"What'll we do now?"

"Just wait, I guess. Oh, shit..."

I hardly got the words out as I rushed out of his room, fumbling for my own room key in my front pocket as I ran. As soon as I barged through my door, I headed for the bathroom, barely having time to slide my pack off.

And then I threw up all over the bathroom floor.

ॐ   ॐ   ॐ

November 2, 1922 – Constantinople

Ayşegül weaved through the night and into the next day. She neglected prayer times, eyeing her small prayer rug with mild self-reproach. She had no time for prayers now. She was on a mission. In the morning, she slipped out briefly to ask Hande to bring some simple food up to her room to avoid meeting for breakfast with the others.

When Hande came to clear away the silver food tray, she entered Ayşegül's room after only a light knock.

"Ayşegül-*hanım*," she called. Her words flew out like a flock of house sparrows suddenly startled into taking flight. "Have you heard?"

Ayşegül quickly threw her long *paşmina* over the loom, as she had done when Tanju came and tore her room apart. The fewer people who saw what she was weaving, the better. That way, later on, they would not be able to recognize it if something went wrong and her plan was sabotaged. She would not want any of her friends, like Hande or Yasmin, or especially Zeliha, to be held accountable. Fortunately, Hande was not the curious type.

She stood up, wiping her sweaty hands on her *şalvar*. Working with wool made her hands hot.

"Heard what, Hande-*hanım*?"

"*Tanrım*, what's going to happen to us?" the younger *cariye* cried. "Everything is lost."

"What are you talking about, Hande? Here." Ayşegül steered her friend toward her bed and gently pushed her onto the mattress. "Sit down. Try to take a breath."

Hande collapsed onto Ayşegül's rumpled duvet, holding her face with her hands. To Ayşegül it looked as if the poor girl were trying to keep her head in place. She waited, holding gently onto Hande's arm as the girl's chest heaved. Her breath burst out in tearless sobs like ash clouds before a volcano eruption. After a few moments, she began to calm down. The eruption was stemmed.

"So?" Ayşegül prompted. "Tell me what's so upsetting that you have to barge into my room like some crazy *sufi*." Ayşegül's light sarcasm brought a slight smile to Hande's face.

"Oh, Ayşegül-*hanım*," Hande finally blurted.

"You don't need to be so formal right now," Ayşegül interrupted. "Just tell me what is so urgent and, obviously, distressing."

Hande looked at her senior with bulging blue eyes and a panic-stricken expression on her usually cherubic face. "It's horrible, Ayşegül. Really, truly horrible."

"*What* is?" asked Ayşegül, her voice rising. She was beginning to lose patience with the novice. Not to mention, wasting valuable weaving time. She shifted her weight on the mattress and gently turned Hande's torso to face her. "Out with it, girl."

Hande swiped at both eyes with her small, white hands and then placed them in her lap.

"I can't believe you haven't heard this terrible news already. It's all over the city. All over the world!"

"Really? All over the world? What can be so terrible that the whole world knows about it? What *is* this catastrophic announcement?" Ayşegül prodded. She almost shook the teenager in front of her in her frustration.

Hande gulped. "The sultan, our *Şahbaba*..." She hiccupped. "He..." She began and then paused, holding her hands over her mouth as if what she was going to say was a sacrilege. "He has been..." and here she lowered her voice to a whisper, "deposed."

Ayşegül stared at the young girl. Had she heard her correctly?

Ayşegül's silence seemed to unnerve her young confidante. So she continued rambling. "I'm not exactly sure what that means, except that he is no longer the sultan. Can you believe it? It's impossible. There's always been a sultan in Constantinople, right?"

Ayşegül's heart stopped, or so it felt. Despite her long discussion five nights before with Estreya and Yasmin about the political situation in their country, this was not the news she had expected exactly. It was worse. She put her hand over her chest and forced herself to breathe. Her thoughts began to spin.

If the sultan was deposed, that meant he would probably be forced to leave the palace. In one sense, that was good for her. She would have even more reason to carry out her plan. And it might be easier if the sultan—and maybe some of his loyal men, like Tanju—were forced to leave with him. It might mean they were not paying as much attention as usual to the women in the harem. And if Tanju had been ordered by the sultan to find what she took from him, and he did not succeed, the sultan would be very angry with her. It was only when she heard from Estreya that he was back that she really began to worry. His return would force her to move more quickly than she had originally believed she would need to. But this update changed the urgency a little. The sultan surely would be too upset, too preoccupied with the inauspiciousness of his situation, to even think about her. Let alone plot to destroy her.

Nevertheless, the palace would be in an uproar. Soon, if it was not already. She knit her brow. Strange, that she had not heard anything from Zeliha. Or Yasmin. Anyway, it was a good thing she had worked through the night. The sooner she was ready, the better.

"Are you sure?" she asked Hande, fretful. She could hear the high squeak in her voice.

Hande nodded her head vigorously. "Yes. It is certain. Everyone is talking about it."

"But what does it mean? How did it happen?"

"I don't know. Of course, everything here has been changing for awhile, up and down and all over the place, but Saskar Kadın has forbidden us to talk about it. As you know. She always acted as if these things were just little bumps on the road and that once they were smoothed out, everything would continue as always."

Ayşegül nodded in agreement. Yes, it was obvious that the sultan and the Empire were under pressure, but their superiors did not want the girls to know about it. It was only through leaks among the palace captives or from tradespeople like Estreya who visited that the girls had heard anything at all. Anything important, that is.

As Hande bit her fingernails in agitation, Ayşegül's brain began to strategize.

"Hande..."

The frightened girl looked up at her with beseeching eyes. "Yes, Ayşegül-hanım?"

"Did you hear anything about when the sultan will have to leave the palace? Anything like that?"

Hande thought for a moment and then slowly shook her head, her short bob bouncing from side to side. The bob was a new style in the harem, borrowed from European fashion, like much of the clothing these days, but Ayşegül had not followed the trend. She kept her hair long.

"Not exactly. But I heard Shahinaz say that it is going to be very soon. She always has the knack of finding out secrets, doesn't she? Anyway, that general—what's his name?"

"Mustafa Kemal?"

"Yes, that's the one. The one every one is talking about. The one who has caused so much trouble to the Empire. He's taken over everything. He won that big battle, remember?"

"Yes, I think so. You mean the one in Dumlupınar back in August?"

Hande's forehead furrowed in concentration. "I think so. I'm not sure. It was a major battle, though. And then there was the horrible fire in Smyrna right afterwards." She sighed. "So many terrible things happening in our country. I don't understand it. What is going to happen to us, Ayşegül-hanım? What are we going to do? Where are we going to go?"

Ayşegül glanced up at the ceiling and shrugged. "That's a good question, Hande, canım." She took the girl's hand, which was damp and warm. "But don't worry. Someone will help us. After all, whoever comes into power next, they're not going to want a gaggle of interfering harem women in the way, are they? And, anyway, Saskar Kadın, she might be a dragon, but she won't let anyone hurt us, right?" She smiled at her friend, hoping her words would allay some of the younger girl's fears.

Hande turned to the window, a faraway look in her eyes. She seemed to make up her mind about something, and then turned back to Ayşegül with a half smile on her face. "Yes. You're right, Ayşegül. Saskar Kadın. I'm always scared of her, but she is like a dragon mother protecting her dragonlets. I think she will take care of us."

"Good." Ayşegül reached out and placed her arms around Hande. "And Hande?"

"Yes, Ayşegül?"

"Thank you for telling me. It was really brave of you."

Hande blushed.

"Now you can leave me in peace so I can work."

Hande nodded, peeking discreetly at the covered loom across the room.

"And don't forget the tray, *canım.*" Ayşegül tipped her head toward the silver tray, patiently waiting where Hande had placed it after coming into the room earlier. She had not even had a chance to load it up with Ayşegül's dirty dishes. Now she pushed herself slowly to standing, walked over to Ayşegül's little table and began retrieving them. As Ayşegül watched, it seemed to her that her confidante had quietened down and that their tête-à-tête had restored some of her equanimity. That was something, at least.

After Hande had loaded up the serving tray, she balanced it in her hands and made a small bow in Ayşegül's direction.

"Thank you, Ayşegül-*hanım.* I feel better."

"I hope so, Hande. Go now." She paused. "And Hande?"

"Yes, miss?"

Ayşegül put her right index finger up to her lips. "Shhh. Don't tell anyone that you passed on this news to me, okay?"

Hande smiled.

"Of course, not, Ayşegül-*hanım.* I would never do such a thing."

"Good." She jerked her head toward the door in dismissal. "*Görüşürüz.* See you later."

Hande turned and bustled out of the room, closing the door quietly behind her.

Ayşegül was alone again. She walked over to her window, brushing her hand lightly against the open shutter on her left. As her hand lingered against the wooden slats, she thought about all that Hande had just revealed to her.

And she hoped that what she had replied to Hande was true.

That everything would be all right.

∿   ∿   ∿

November 1, 1922 – Constantinople

It was done.

On the first of November The Grand National Assembly of Turkey, masterminded by Gazi Mustafa Kemal, convened. After hours of deliberation, the consortium of members voted. The final outcome was the culmination of Mehmed VI's fears and remonstrances.

Despite the efforts of Suleiman Shafiq Paşa, leader of the "Kuvâ-i İnzibâtiyye, to stave off the successes of the Turkish National Movement, despite the signing of the Treaty of Sèvres in 1920, which handed Britain, France and Italy control of the Empire's financial affairs and some of its territories, but allowed the sultan to keep his position, despite all of Mehmed's battles since he had taken reign, over four years now, the Young Turks, Mustafa Kemal and others in favor of a republic at last had gotten their way.

The Ottoman Sultanate was abolished.

After six hundred twenty-three years of autonomous rule, brutal landgrabbing and cultural inculcation, the illustrious and oft-feared House of Osman had finally succumbed. Sultan Mehmed VI was deposed.

The Supreme Ottoman State would be no more.

Instead, its remaining lands would henceforth be known as The Republic of Turkey.

There was no longer any doubt. Mehmed VI Vahideddin was The Last Sultan.

Under edict of law, he was to be banished from his homeland forever.

∿   ∿   ∿

November 2, 1922 – Constantinople

Demetrius stood on the northern Üsküdar promontory overlooking the Bosphorus. When his people, the Greeks, had founded the area in the seventh century B.C. it was called "Chrysolopolis." Later on, during

249

Byzantine times, it was known as "Skoutarion" in his language. Funny, how names changed according to the peoples who took over a place. From this vantage point he had a clear view northwest toward the municipality of Beşiktaş on the other side of the busy strait, the "European" side of Constantinople, where Byzantium was founded in 667 B.C. That was also a project of the Greeks, specifically Byzas, as legend had it, who chose the spot for its strategic positioning at the confluence of the Golden Horn, the Bosphorus and the Sea of Marmara.

It was the ancient land of heroic deeds, historic battles, culture clashes, religious turmoil. A place where once Greek gods and mortal men vied for supremacy and worship. Where men—and women—of wealth and position competed endlessly and brutally to create one of the most influential and envied power bases in human antiquity.

Now it was called Constantinople, for almost five hundred years the seat of the Ottoman dynasty. But it was soon to change names once more, if the newsreels and the rumors swarming around the metropolis were to be believed. It was going to be called Istanbul. The transition would be easy for the Turks. Denizens of the city had been calling it that, or "Stamboul," for ages, anyway.

Istanbul.

City of spires and ambition, desires and deceit.

Istanbul.

Architect of dreams. And nightmares.

It was a cosmopolis destined for upheaval and change. And it was happening again.

Now, the shoreline of Beşiktaş was dominated by the gleaming white edifices of Dolmabahçe Palace, the modern residence of the Ottoman rulers. He knew of the palace, of course, who did not? It had replaced the old Topkapı Palace, farther south across the Galata Bridge, almost seventy years before for its more contemporary luxuriousness. But as he gazed at its imposing seafacing facade, even from this distance, Demetrius found Dolmabahçe lacked the charm of the former seat of the sultans.

For one, its design was more reminiscent of European Rococo, Baroque and Neoclassical architecture and style than of the oriental assymetry and fancifulness of the previous residence with its medieval turrets and crenellations. Though Dolmabahçe was considered magnificent, to Demetrius it looked much like other modern European estates. To his eyes, it did not measure up as the unique structure it was touted to be. He had heard, too, that instead of the famous İznik tiles that adorned Topkapı,

250

Dolmabahçe's interior boasted an extensive display of gold and crystal. He thought he would prefer the more earthy qualities of the handmade ceramic tiles to the glitz of gold. But it was a palace, after all. And the Ottomans, as most royals, liked to display their wealth. Their symbol of power.

But all that was coming to an end.

Everyone knew now. The sultan had been deposed. Yesterday. At last the long reign of the Osmans was over. Sultan Mehmed VI and his imperial family were to be banished. Exiled.

So, though Demetrius's country did not regain the lands it had hoped to during this godawful power struggle, to which he himself had been called to participate, there was some gratification that the Ottomans were out, too. As soon would be the Allies: the French, British and Italian interlopers who had tried so desperately to carve up the spoils of conflict amongst themselves. No. Instead, the man called Kemal had driven them out with guile, with guts and with guns.

Demetrius nodded. To the victor, the spoils.

It had always been thus, since antiquity. He thought the gods would approve, after all. And the victor, this time, was the Turkish people.

Demetrius pulled his duffle coat closer around him and coughed. The chill of winter was beginning to descend, sweeping down from the Balkans and across the channel. He stood under a stone pine tree, one of many dotted around the shoreline areas and, though it protected him slightly, shaped as it was like a leafy umbrella, he knew he should make his way back to the hostel soon. A fresh brewed cup of tea would ward off the cold. He coughed again.

He had holed up at the hostel for a couple of weeks now. It had been difficult to find, what with the occupation of the city by Allied army forces. Military parades occurred frequently, and the smoke and fumes from French tanks on the Grand Rue de Pera and British guns on aircraft carriers in the harbor added to the general malaise—and even anger—which he encountered in some degree in almost everyone he met.

He had made for the Greek section of Kadıköy, of course, on the Asian side of the city, an hour's walk south of Üsküdar, and had had to ask several fellow Greeks on the street before he finally made his way to the Albergo Miros, twisting and turning along the makeshift alleyways en route. When he finally arrived, the small sign beside the door was faded and barely visible beneath the general filth of the whole place. But at least it was cheap and there was a spare cot in the dormitory, which he shared with other bedgraggled, war-weary men like himself.

No one talked much. The landlady, Kyria Zika, herself was not particularly friendly, but she tolerated his presence as she did the other itinerant hostel dwellers. Her lodgings were not pleasant, like the one in Manisa, but it was relatively safe. It would do. For the time being, anyway.

Whenever possible, he made his way to the water, skirting the makeshift soldiers' encampments and the muddy fields where the Italian army conducted its drills. Sometimes he traveled by ferry across the Bosphorus to Ortaköy village, not far from Beşiktaş, where an attempt at humanitarian aide had been set up in the form of a bakery. Here, he would sometimes nab a small loaf of bread for free. The meals at Albergo Miros were scant and his belly often felt emptier afterwards than before he had eaten, clamoring with growls and gurgles for more. The humble, homebaked bread from the free bakery helped relieve those clamors.

Now he gazed at the imposing allure of Dolmabahçe Palace a few seconds more. Something about the place called him to this site day after day, but he could not say why that would be. The imperial residence was too ornamental for his taste, like a femme-fatale whose outward beauty was a decorative mask, a substitution for real character. But, many a man before him had been lured to abandon his principles in order to explore the thrills of such a sucubus and been willing to sell his soul for the experience. Demetrius smiled at his own metaphor and, plunging his stiff hands deep into his pockets, turned away from the showy mansion. No doubt he would be back soon, wondering what it was that drew him here.

As he made his way down the small hill, his body pushed against the cold wind buffetting across the channel. It was getting colder. The writing was on the wall and it was only a matter of time before Greeks, such as himself, would be even less welcome here than they were now. If anything, what happened in Smyrna should serve as a warning. And not just the fire, which burned for nine days and was so destructive it had razed almost the entire port. That was just the beginning. The rest was more pernicious, if that were possible. For, in addition to the homelessness and destruction forced without warning upon the mostly Greek and Armenian residents of the city, the Turkish army had seized upon the general mayhem and used it as the backdrop for more egregious crimes: rape, massacre, displacement. Or so he had heard from his fellow dorm mates. They also said a few fortunate denizens had escaped, but others who survived the desecration of the city were deported to the interior of Anatolia. Who knew what else was going on? Everything here was chaotic, which made it difficult to sift out truth from conjecture or rumor.

What was certain was that a shift was taking place. And Demetrius knew he did not want to be caught up in it. He had been through enough. Time to make his final preparations to get across the border to Alexandroupolis. Time to get home.

Another three hundred kilometers to go.

But he was stalling, and he did not know why. Demetrius crossed himself. He had been lucky to get out of Dumlupınar when he did. Thanks to his two Turkish friends in the truck. He smiled, thinking about them and their quiet acceptance of his presence. With their help he had been spared the misfortune that so many others had endured. Were enduring. Perhaps it was for a particular reason, one which he had yet to realize.

This thought continued to run through his mind. Perhaps that cup of tea, steaming and restorative, would bring him to his senses.

☙   ☙   ☙

Friday, August 16, 2013, Early Afternoon - Fethiye

"It's him! He's here!"

Paz elbowed me with one arm and began jabbing toward the Silk Road Carpet Shop's open glass door with his other upraised one. The sudden pain of his elbow stabbing my ribs jarred me back to reality. I had been daydreaming about an island boat trip, as we had not even gone to the beach yet. But even in my semi-altered state I had caught sight of the back half of our target stalking across the shop's shadowy threshold.

"Molo, did you see?"

"Yeah, that's him alright." My stomach started to do backflips. And I was rubbing my sore ribcage. Sighting our quarry on top of those two things did not up my happiness quotient as it seemed to have Paz's. Too many emotions. And they were not pleasant ones.

"Damn, I can't believe it," whispered Paz. "He's actually here. You were right."

I nodded in affirmation. "I knew it. Slimy scumbag. Do you think he was following us? I mean, at the airport?"

"How could he? How would he know we were going to be there? I just made the reservations yesterday morning a few hours before we got on the plane."

"Good point. I don't trust him, though. He's got minions all over the place, I'd bet my fortune on it."

253

"Oh, right, your burgeoning millions," Paz countered, facetiously. We high-fived.

"Right," he continued. "Let's hang around a few and see if he comes out. Maybe we can follow *him* for a change."

Again, I tilted my head to one side in agreement. "We'll be like Emma Peel and John Steed. The Avengers in action. I really want to nail that shithead after all he's put us through." I paused. "After what he did to Adrian."

Paz tipped his own head forward in a kind of solemn bow. An homage to our lost friend.

We spent a few moments in silence, each with our own thoughts. I do not know what Paz's were, but mine were about Adrian. Not just about my feelings for him, or our time together, but also about the new information I had gleaned regarding his possible relationship with Ömer. I could not for the life of me think what that might have been. For one, where had they met? Adrian had never been to Turkey, of that I was quite sure, before he talked us all into that first trip in 1998. Maybe Ömer had traveled to the States before. Yes, it was quite possible, now that I knew he dealt in valuable Turkish carpets. The more I thought about it, that had to be the connection. But why? How? When? I shook my head in consternation. And that brought me to my current predicament. I had come back all this way to enact revenge on Ömer for poisoning Adrian because I had thought what he did was a random act of cruelty. But was there more to it than that, after all? Paz, apparently, had known for awhile that the two had been acquainted before the incident.

And where did those two cryptic notes come in? I knew for certain now the two situations were linked: 1) Adrian knowing Ömer and, 2) the deliberate hiding of the carpet sketch and shop name in my book. There was perhaps a third link, as well: Paz's flying to Istanbul at the same time as me (though I would put that one aside for the moment, on the assumption that he was being honest about wanting to help me after he saw Ömer at UC Santa Cruz). They all were related. Had to be.

I drew myself up from my slouch against the wall. Because suddenly, it hit me.

I no longer just wanted to get back at Ömer. To run him off the road in a hit and run or stab him under his porky ribs. Okay, I did want to do both those things—and more—but even my original plan no longer seemed viable. Instead, I wanted to know more. To unravel all these weird secrets and plots and then to weave them back together again into a story that finally made sense. About everything. It would not bring Adrian back—I would have to continue to live with that sad knowledge—but I could maybe put things to right. In my own mind and heart, if nothing else. Instead of hiding behind my own new image.

And where did Paz fit into this whole nonsense?

I turned to my partner in crime where he, too, slouched against the gray stone wall, deep in thought.

"So?" I asked.

"Yeah?"

"I have a question."

"Shoot."

"Where did you meet Barış?"

"What?"

"You heard me. Where did you meet him? I never saw him before the other night and you never mentioned him."

He shrugged. "Dunno. Back in 2005, I guess. When we were staying at the Yeşil Beşik."

"You never said."

"What was there to say? I think I ran into him at a cafe near the hotel one day when I was on my own, and we just started talking."

"I don't get it. If you just talked, how did you end up staying at his house the other night?"

I could swear Paz looked sheepish. But then he (as usual) turned the tables.

"Why are you asking me about Barış all of a sudden?"

I shifted my head away from him, pulling my chin toward my chest, and lifted my eyebrows. I tried to look as innocent as possible.

"Why not? You gotta admit, it was weird the way you sent him to kidnap me like that."

Paz guffawed.

"Kidnap you? I don't think so." He paused, confusion registering on his sweat-glossed face. "Really? That's what you thought?"

"Felt like it. He's not the friendliest guy. I actually thought he was some kind of Turkish thug at first. So it just seems odd that you and he struck up this enduring friendship after a casual chat one night in a cafe."

Paz sighed a deep sigh.

"Look, Mole. We exchanged email addresses, okay? That night. I'd had a couple of *rakıs*, so it seemed like an okay thing to do. And then, awhile after we all went home to the States, he emailed me."

"Really?"

"Yeah, no big deal. I emailed him back and we just kind of stayed in touch."

"That's weird. So you never saw him again 'til the other night."

"Nope."

"Don't you think it's a bit coincidental that he kept in touch and then, suddenly when you're coming back to Istanbul, he puts you up?"

"No. Why not? Plenty of people do that. It's called 'hospitality'." His sarcasm, again, was not lost on me.

I rolled my eyes. Sure. The question was: what was Barış's definition of the word? "Hospitality" as in "I like you and so I give you a place to stay" *or* "hospitality" as in "I have a scheme I want to rope you into, so I pretend I am your friend?" Paz seemed to believe Barış ascribed to the more honorable first approach. I had to admit, the scale I was on tipped more to the side of skepticism, especially in light of all I had come to learn over the last two days. And yet, of the two of us, I would never have taken Paz for the credulous one. That was usually me. I must be changing in more ways than one. I continued my interrogation.

"But, I mean, did he know *why* you were coming back to Turkey?" I asked.

"Not really. I just told him I was coming to meet up with you."

That got my attention. Paz's delivery sounded remarkably naive. I was really beginning to believe he had been on the up and up all along. But I was not convinced about Barış. What if he was in league with Ömer?

"Oh, yeah? And did he, like, say anything about that?"

"He just asked where you were staying."

My eyes widened like the Nile River during Inundation Season. "You told him where I was staying? Dude! What's up with that?"

He put up both his hands, surrendering. "I didn't tell him 'cuz I didn't know, did I? I already told you that. I *thought* you might go to the Beşik."

"And you just happened to mention that to him."

"Yeah? What's the big deal?"

I opened and shut my eyes a couple times and shook my head quickly in exasperation. If Paz noticed my reaction, he did not let on. So I let it go and kept my response as neutral as possible. "Nothing. I'm just seeing a pattern emerge, that's all."

"A pattern of what...?" Paz's question trailed off before he could finish asking it, because I put an index finger to my lips and grabbed onto his shoulder. I saw a questioning look in his eyes, and then he turned toward the direction I was looking.

Ömer was leaving Bulut's shop. *His* shop, as I now knew it to be. He pulled his wire-framed CIA sunglasses down over his eyes and turned right out of the door, heading toward the main street that paralleled the harbor. At that moment, something in the way he moved the glasses sparked a memory. And I realized where I had first seen him. I could not believe it had never occurred to me before. He was the lone man on the Kamil Koç bus who joined the ride after our last rest stop back in 2005. On our first trip to Fethiye.

He was following us even then! I slapped my forehead. *Shit. What is this all about, anyway?*

"C'mon, kid. Let's go," said Paz, grabbing his daypack.

As I stooped over quickly to snatch my bag, as well, a surge of energy zipped through me. I had not felt this galvanized to action since the day Adrian left us eight years before. Even on my arrival in Istanbul the other night, intent on vengeance as I had been, my purpose and my hopefulness were dampened somewhat by the weight on my conscience after all those years in between. For what I might have done to contribute to Adrian's coma—or what I might not have done that could have protected him from it. But now I knew what happened was not my fault. And that the cards had been laid out well before that day. My conscious was clear. The weight was lifted at last.

"Right behind you," I said.

Chapter 19

"Icığını cıcığını çıkarmak." Or... *"Search something with a fine-tooth comb."* - Turkish saying

Wednesday, June 8, 2005, Afternoon - Çalış Beach

I was still mopping up with a spare towel what I could of the mess I had made on the bathroom floor when Paz peeked his head through the doorway.

"What happened?" he asked.

"Guess my lunch didn't agree with me." I smirked at him from below.

His nose turned up in distaste. "Jesus, Mole. That stinks."

"Yeah, tell me about it." I continued my swirling motions with the unfortunate towel. As I mopped, the thought occurred to me that I must do a thorough clean-up or Adrian would be annoyed with me. Then I remembered.

Adrian would never see the mess. I almost wished he would. Because that would mean he was no longer lying insensate in an intensive care unit at some private hospital in a small, backwater harbor town on the southern edge of bumfuck Turkey. It would mean everything was okay. I began to think I might be imagining the whole hospital coma thing, after all. It was such an improbable development in what was meant to be our happy-go-lucky trek to Fethiye, that my brain did not want to acknowledge what it had witnessed. What it had been forced to observe and absorb just an hour or so before. We were definitely in over our heads, Paz and Mallie and me. And most of all, of course, poor Adrian.

I could not think what to make of it all, or how to proceed.

Paz's response disrupted my trance. "Anyway, maybe it was more than just your lunch that didn't agree with you, huh?" He sounded a bit more sympathetic than a moment earlier.

But I did not respond. What was there to say? He was undoubtedly right.

I was just finishing my disgusting task, when he kneeled down a foot away from me, the edge of his shirt pulled over his nose.

"Listen, Mole. I was thinking."

"What?"

"Before Mallie gets here, maybe we should do some research."

"Research on what? Comas? Drinking a cup of death-inducing tea?" I admit, my frustration, my anger, my whatever it was I was feeling, was making me caustic. And it was not fair, I knew that. Not fair on Paz, anyway. None of this was his fault.

But, thankfully, he was too caught up in his latest scheme to heed or respond to my mordancy.

"No. I mean, on..." He let his shirt drop, shifted on his knees and eventually pulled the scrap of paper Doctor Kalabulut had given him out of his front pocket. Then he scrutinized its contents. "...Laburnum. Laburnum Ana-gy-roi-des. That's what..."

"Yes, I know what it is," I interrupted, sulkily. Normally, I would have grinned at his efforts to pronounce an unprounceable Latin plant name, but I could not say I was feeling my most ebullient. My best friend lay, for all intents and purposes, lifeless from some bizarre substance I had never heard of and for no apparent, sensible reason. If that was not enough, I had vomited the entire contents of my stomach—and even, it felt like, my being—onto the tiles of mine and his room. The mess would not have been such an issue normally. If Adrian had been there, he would have feigned annoyance and then laughed. But it would all have been in humor and kindness. He would have turned the whole episode into an uproarious joke.

But that was not going to happen now. The trajectory of his loss was gaining momentum like a train hurtling through a dark tunnel with no discernible light on the other end. The sense of impending thrill and potential danger we had undergone together on the Giant Dipper roller coaster on our first meeting paled by comparison.

I sat back on my heels, the now offensive towel heaped beside me. My hands felt molested with muck. I just wanted to get to the sink and wash the filth off them. The filth of the whole situation. Like Lady MacBeth. But Paz continued and I was too worn out to make a move away from him.

"Molo. Chum. This whole thing sucks. Big time. God, no one knows it more than you and me." He patted my back. "But, hear me out. We don't know what happened. Not really. We only know what the doctor thinks happened. So, I just thought, if we looked up that tree, laburnum whatever, we would at least understand a little bit more about it. Maybe we can even find a cure or something." His shoulders lifted as if in a kind of supplication

259

of hope.

I digested his words and from them seemed to at last harvest a morsel of energy from the depths of my depleted being. I snatched the slimey towel in one hand, holding it as far from me as possible with only my right index finger and thumb, pushed myself off the floor with my left hand, took two steps into the bathroom and chucked the towel into the shower stall. I would deal with it later. Or maybe there was a maid who would take care of it for me. Maybe she could take care of the other, bigger problem for me, too, while she was at it. That would have been a miracle of miracles, Elijah waking the widow's dead son. Not being particularly religious, though, I doubted such a marvel was going to occur. Then I thought:

How would Adrian have responded to Paz if he had been here instead of me? If the roles were reversed and it was my body lying prostrate in that desolate hospital bed instead of his?

He would find a way to be sympathetic. And supportive. That was his nature. And, of course, he would want to help me. He would not wallow in self-pity or sadness. He would take action. In his honor, I decided to follow his example.

"Yeah, Paz. That's a great idea, actually." I was at the sink furiously scrubbing my hands with scalding water and a small bar of cheap hotel soap. As I turned around to dry my hands on a towel that hung behind me, I added with a half smile, "Thanks."

Paz, standing now in the doorway, watching me, beamed. He moved aside as I exited the bathroom and headed toward the small sleeping area.

While I settled onto my rumpled twin bed, looking forlornly across at Adrian's immaculately made one, Paz ran back to his and Mallie's room. I checked my phone. Three o'clock. Mallie should be back soon. She was not one to stay in the water long. And she would get tired of waiting for Paz to join her. Patience was not her number one forte.

Paz re-entered with his Dell laptop. Travel-light. I had been surprised that he had bothered to bring it with him on this trip, but it was proving useful, after all. He plunked down onto Adrian's bed (I winced), opened up the computer scantwise so I could see what he was doing, too, and in the search box at the top typed:

Laburnum Anagyroides

A series of photos popped up on top of the screen. So, this was what the offending killer looked like. Each photo depicted some version of a slender tree burgeoning with lemon-colored flowers that hung down in long trains, like yellow clusters of ripe grapes before being picked. Some of the photos were close-ups of the individual blooms, bound together in trios of tongue-shaped petals, others displayed several whole trees serried on either side of a dirt path to create a copse of golden light, dripping with the bright, happy flowers. Nothing about the pictures were menacing. Nothing betrayed the deadliness lying within the trees' various components.

"Looks pretty harmless to me," Paz said. "What do you think?"

I shrugged. "Doesn't really matter what I think, does it? I'm not exactly a botanist. It's fitting that each of the petals looks like there are tiny trails of blood dripping down them, though. What else is there?"

Paz scrolled down and clicked on the first entry under the images.

LaburnumAnagyroidesBotany.com

We each perused the list of attributes and information: description, uses, et cetera. All seemed pretty normal tree stuff. The laburnum is native to Southern Europe, its flowers are pea-like, with a sweet odor, it blooms from May to June, its nickname is the Golden Chain Tree. All that made sense from what we had just seen in the photos.

"That's it?" Paz said. He sounded disappointed. "Nothing here about poison. I'll click on another site. He scrolled down a bit and clicked on a blue hyperlink farther down on the same page.

I scanned the whole document quickly to see if anything would stand out. Nothing.

"Scroll down some more," I urged. Paz pressed the Page Down button a couple times. He continued until we found what looked more promising for our purposes. It was a site whose entry question echoed ours exactly:

Laburnum: Is it poisonous?

"Eureka," said Paz.

Clicking down, we almost immediately hit on the section titled: "Side Effects."

"Here it is." Paz pointed to the middle of the screen.

I was not sure I wanted to explore the paragraphs behind his thick finger.

"You read it," I said.

"Alrighty. So, according to this, every part of the laburnum is actually poisonous to humans. Wow."

"Great. Let's go harvest some for dinner."

"No, I mean it. That's what it says. The pods, the seeds, the petals, even the bark. It also mentions that after learning how toxic it is, a lot of gardeners and other people dig up their own laburnum trees. I guess safety wins out over beauty."

"Nice."

"And, guess what?" He looked up at me. "It even mentions that the title character of a Daphne du Maurier book might have used laburnum to poison her husband."

That drew my attention. I was a big du Maurier fan. I had read all of her novels. Their psychological mysteries and enigmatic characters intrigued me. Paz was somewhat aware of my fixation as he had often seen me lugging one of her books around.

"Really? Which character? Which book?"

"It says here *My Cousin Rachel*. Rachel being the possible poisoner, though that conclusion is left open-ended. Have you read it?"

"Yeah," I nodded. "But I don't remember anything about laburnum. I guess it was a long time ago."

Paz shrugged. "Anyway, so, there it is. The doctor wasn't making it up. About laburnum being poisonous, I mean."

"Nope, guess not."

"I want to see if I can find anything else."

Paz clicked on a few more sites, most of which repeated in varying ways the information we had just devoured. It seemed that the noxious substance distributed throughout the tree's various components was called "cytisine," an alkaloid that occurs naturally in some plants. Including, of course, laburnum. Cytisine was sometimes used in small doses to help people quit smoking. But obviously, that was not why Adrian had it in his system. Or rather, *might*, if the doctor was right. He was not a smoker.

One site offered more detail about how the alkaloid affected people if ingested: vomiting, diarrhea, drowsiness, irritability and so forth. Children were the most vulnerable, naturally. Most people did not die, however—that news gave me renewed hope. But there were some who developed more dangerous reactions. In a number of recorded cases, the drowsiness caused the pupils to dilate and become insensitive to light. Breathing became difficult and harsh while the pulse sped up. Lips turned blue with cyanosis. And blood pressure lowered. But the worst cases, the ones that, unfortunately, sparked Paz's and my curiosity, were those where the victim exhibited all the above symptoms, but went even further. These people had severer reactions than most, for whatever reason. And because their systems could not cope with the poison's effects, they lapsed into coma. At that point, they became cold and clammy to the touch, their skin turned pale and then, if they could not be revived at that point, the worst occurred. It seemed that the deleterious effects of the cytisine on the poor person's organs became overwhelming. They succumbed to respiratory failure.

And died.

After I recovered somewhat from that bombshell of information, I pulled away from the computer and repositioned myelf on my bed. We had learned a lot in a few minutes about laburnum and cytisine.

But none of the data explained how Adrian had been exposed to the stuff. Neither Paz nor I could figure it out.

The other burning question was...Why? Was it an accident? Had he accidentally chowed on a chunk of laburnum bark? Not likely. Not unless he knew what it was and had tried to off himself.

And I knew that could not be. No one I knew was happier than Adrian. So, what then?

I journeyed back in my mind to the events of that morning, when Adrian had announced his change of plan to abandon our beach outing in order to head out on his own into Fethiye. Though his demeanor was as upbeat as ever, perhaps even hyper, I had sensed even then that something was weird. Besides being hurt that he would renege on me at the last second, I just found it out of character for him to do such a thing. He had always been so reliable—and straight—with me. Furthermore, if ever there was a case against suicide, his cheerfulness when he set off was it. He was excited, no doubt. And that is how I realized at last...

Something—or someone—had intervened.

"Paz," I said, musing out loud.

"Yeah?" He carefully placed the laptop to his side.

"Are you, by any chance, thinking what I'm thinking?"

I watched him squirm on Adrian's bed across from me. Yes, he was.

No doubt, he did not want to broach the subject. The horrible possibility. Neither of us spoke for a moment. But I could not sit quietly for long with the idea that our good friend, our longtime pal and fellow adventurer (and, for me, someone even more than that) had been deliberately tampered with. Poisoned. It was a scenario out of a, well, Daphne du Maurier story.

"Paz? Are you there?"

He twisted his hands in his lap. I could tell he was figuring out how to answer. Then he lifted his head and stared into my eyes.

"Yeah," he answered at last. His voice was quieter than usual, subdued. It seemed at last the seriousness of the situation had sunk in for him, too. "I think I am. I mean, I'm here *and* I think I'm thinking what you're thinking."

"So, what's next? I mean, what do we do?"

"I dunno. Maybe the doctor is wrong. About the laburnum, I mean. Maybe the tests will come out negative." He grimaced.

"Maybe. I'm sure they're doing everything they can. To revive him." But I was not sure at all.

"Yeah, probably. Maybe he's already awake and they just haven't called us yet," he ventured, hopefully.

My intuition told me this was not the case, but I nevertheless appreciated Paz's attempts at positivity and decided to respond again in kind.

"You're probably right. In the meantime, I guess we should figure out what we're gonna tell..."

I did not get to finish my sentence as the very person I was about to mention exploded through the door. From then on, things got a little crazy and Paz and I would not have a chance to finish our discussion until many hours later. During that intervening time, more information would come to light.

And it was not good.

ॐ   ॐ   ॐ

November 4, 1922 – Constantinople

"*Bit-miş!*"

Ayşegül flexed her fingers and flourished her wrists in circles to alleviate the stiffness that had settled into them. The resulting pain was worth it.

Her carpet was done. Finished.

In the morning she had placed her *kirkit* and scissors to the side, tied off the ends of the last row of *atkı ipi* on top of the carpet and reveled at last in severing her wooly painting from its birth place on her wooden loom. Then she had peeled her numb buttocks from her hard, low *halı* stool and pushed off it, struggling to stand. After the hours of weaving and knotting and cutting and tamping, her body had become rigid and tight, her muscles knotted in place like the strands of wool on her creation. But after a small break and a few moments of stretching her limbs and torso, she placed the thick carpet carefully on her work table and spent another hour braiding an intricate fringe onto either end with the remaining strands of warp wool. The final touch. Now she laid her work on her bed and admired it from above.

It was beautiful, she thought. Colorful, vibrant, full of traditional carpet symbols, such as tulips and running water, as Maryam had taught her to weave, and, of course, her personal motto, "*elebelinde*," or "hands on hips." But it was also different, unique. Hers. It spoke of her coming from another land and her subsequent changes, of her strength and power, of possessing something of value. It also contained protection from the evil eye. The dominant crescent moons facing off each other in the center was a striking touch, she decided. A testament to her name and a new future on the way.

Not only was the design itself unusual, her special story, but she had included a secret. Something only she herself knew about. Near the center, but not too near. Part of the design, but not visible unless you knew what to look for. Brilliant. She smiled. The secret embedded into the fabric of the carpet was a kind of token for her other, even more hidden, secret.

Her brainstorm about utilizing the melted wax, after a few frustrating trials and errors, had finally succeeded, too. No one looking at her new carpet would guess what she had done—she had spent at least two hours making sure of that. Now she glanced for a moment toward the spot on the floor where, covered by the small rug she had placed over it, the recent accident with her candle had given her that serendipitous inspiration. The temporary damage to the floor was a small price to pay. Fortunately, no one yet had figured out what she had done, why the rug was there. Why should they?

She would have been surprised if they could. No one here was particularly interested in her. Their curiousity about her life, her background, her motivations, even her actions, was next to nil. But then, many of them had endured similar atrocities and upsets. Were *sürgün,* exiled, like her. In the early years, Ayşegül had hoped their shared circumstances would bind them. But, if anything, it seemed to do the opposite. The other females congregated in small groups, in cliques, and though there were good moments now and then—parties, concerts, ceremonies—the intrigues of the palace, and the never-ceasing competition to win favors, superceded making deep friendships. And so most of the others paid little attention to her presence. Her carpets garnered much appreciation and she was known for them, but that was it. She had a few friends, yes, like her dear confidante Zeliha and the gentle Yasmin. And not to forget naive little Hande. Or Estreya with her wise governances. There was Maryam, too, her beloved weaving teacher. She would miss those people. But the others? Not so much. In fact, if she never saw them again, it would be too soon.

All these years she had struggled to fit into this life, this place, this culture. All this time she had mourned the loss of her family and the home she had been ripped from. And now, equipped with this new carpet and her audacious plan, she had a chance to find her people again. To fly off and be reunited with Mama and Papa and Tevfik and Tagir. She could hardly wait.

She grinned, her pearly teeth glittering slightly in the opalescent light of the nascent night.

She felt vindicated. Liberated. About to be freed of those who had never accepted her. Because she had tricked them all: Saskar Kadın, Tanju, Gülizar and Shahinaz, the gossip-mongers, and most importantly, the sultan himself. She had toiled and slaved and made herself a place here, and against all odds had even worked her way up to *acemi,* a favored one. Well, with the sultan at least. But even that was only because he had desired her at last. And then recent events and realizations had forced her to act. During this time, not one of them had not known what she had up her kaftan sleeves.

They would never know. *İnşallah.* She would not let them. Because if they figured it out, she would suffer serious consequences. And she would never get out. The sultan and his henchmen would see to that.

The world might be in chaos now, but no matter how crazy and unsettled the palace was becoming, some things would never be allowed. Many a girl had perished before her, for crimes less heinous than the one she had perpetrated. And in a lapse of judgement three months earlier, she had committed an unforgivable act of vengeance. The sultan knew it. Or he suspected it. That much was clear when he had sent Tanju to rifle through her belongings and her room. She was surprised Tanju had not come again. No doubt the upset, the bad news, the stark reality of the dynasty's catastrophic undoing, had seen to that.

In a way, she reasoned, the pandemonium plaguing the kingdom might be her saving grace. That, and the moon herself. For the upset in the palace was increasing. The uncertainty about the future of the inhabitants had climaxed. And everyone who lived within these once inviolate walls was scrambling to figure out what to do—how to survive the insanity—now that those walls were crumbling around them.

The person who had the most to lose was, of course, Mehmed, Şahbaba, himself. Now that he had been deposed, his time here was ending. No doubt, with the stress, the uncertainty, the public humiliation, the fear for his family, the stain of history that would undoubtedly dog the entire rest of his life, Sultan Mehmed VI Vahideddin had little space in his mind, in his routine, to think about her. About what he had done. Or, more importantly, about what *she* had done.

That was her blessing.

She was more concerned now about Tanju. He was devoted to the sultan and, despite his imminent departure, might decide to punish Ayşegül, though he had no proof that she had done what the sultan probably accused her of doing. To avenge his idol, it would be one of his last acts of service. She needed to stay vigilant. To keep working toward her goal. To continue praying that the moon and the stars and even her new carpet would rush to her aid when she was ready.

She wiped her brow with her tired knotting hand.

Now she turned to gaze out of her window, closed against the autumn chill. Her hour glass lay dormant on the sill, the white sand now blue in the gloaming. The sun had gracefully relinquished its daytime post, so that his sister, the moon, now took possession of her nighttime stage. She loomed large and amber gold, hovering over the horizon. Ayşegül marveled at the many intricate patterns and shapes, strands and drops of liquid gold, discernible on her surface tonight. It was not always thus. Perhaps, mused Ayşegül, she was in the phase of her perigrinations when she hovered closest to earth. Her "perigee," Ayşegül had heard it called. Being that close, it made sense that the mother moon revealed more details of her epic beauty.

Ayşegül sighed. She took the moon's colossal presence tonight as an augur of possibilites. For her. For her immediate future. Had not Estreya recently portended from the coffee grounds that Ayşegül would soon face difficulties, but that out of those—or in spite of them—her way would open? That all would be well?

She prayed all the signs were lining up for her exactly as she needed them to.

For what she was going to do next was against all propriety, all laws of Islam. Of the court. The law of the land.

She was going to get away. On her own terms. Before they forced her to leave.

And she would need all the help she could muster.

Ayşegül moved back toward her small bed, leaned over toward where her carpet lay slightly arched in its newness, and slowly, slowly, starting at its original beginning point, she began to roll it up. When the tell-tale design was fully hidden inside the coils of the roll, she sighed. Then she picked up the weighty roll and shoved it under her bed.

Tomorrow she would say good-bye to her friends and then she would set her plan in motion.

❧   ❧   ❧

Friday, August 16, 2013, Mid-Afternoon – Fethiye

Paz and I dodged pedestrians and darted along Atatürk Caddesi, the congested road that bissected the harbor front and Paspatur. Taxis honked, women glared, men shouted. The sensation of the Mediterranean's salty spray on my arms briefly made me wish again that I were swimming instead of stalking. But as we skulked behind our target, our sunglasses perched fast over our noses and our hats pulled low over our foreheads, I felt invigorated with a sense of real purpose at last. And that purpose was made more substantial because I was not alone.

Ömer had turned right out of the passageway where his shop was situated. Most of the stores on this main road occupied the real estate to our right, guarded by the austere southern Taurus mountains beyond. They seemed to almost glare down at their subjects on the humble city street. In contrast, the more serene, sympathetic harbor, meanwhile, held vigil only a park's width away to our left. I could feel its breeze waft across my shroud-hot body. In spite of all the distractions, Paz and I kept our watchful eyes on Ömer as he ambled under the green and rust-red awnings on the shady side of the street. Because he was of rather short stature, like many of the local men, we could not let our sightings stray. It would be too easy to lose him in the mayhem. Our man was not wearing any distinguishing clothing—not even a hat—which made keeping him in sight from behind even more tricky. His white, seersucker shirt was identical to the seersucker shirts worn by the other male Turks on the sidewalk. And there were a lot of them.

"Where the hell is he going?" asked Paz, mopping his neck with his ever-ready travel kerchief.

"Who knows?" I answered. My two words sounded breathy, even to me. Ömer himself was not moving very quickly, but keeping up with him proved to be a workout. The afternoon heat added to the challenge.

"Looks like he's heading to the mosque?" Paz queried. He sounded confused.

It did indeed seem possible Ömer had the mosque in mind. We had gone a couple blocks now and were closing in on the chalk blue shrine, the one I had first glimpsed from Cengis's van window on our arrival eight years before. The one whose shabby exterior and unkempt gardens paled by comparison with Hagia Sophia's glorious Byzantine beauty in Istanbul. But perhaps that made sense; Fethiye was small potatoes and far from the imperial domain.

"What's at the mosque? Is it Friday?" I only asked because Friday, called *Cuma*, the "c" in Turkish pronounced like our "j", was Islam's prayer day. I had read once that the word in Arabic meant "congregation." But in my two trips to Fethiye I had never noticed a sudden dirth of punters on the streets or a burgeoning of worshippers streaming out of the mosque's hallowed doors on this important day. It could have been any day. Business as usual.

"I'm not sure. I don't think so," replied Paz. "Maybe."

School kids now flowed out like swarming fish from the open gate of the Fatih Anadolu high school across the road. They chattered, poked at their mobile phones and punched each other in jest, no doubt overjoyed to be freed from their studies, just like my fellow students and I when I was their age. All that was as it should be. Annoyingly, though, they mingled with all the other townspeople in the Fethiye afternoon rush, impeding our progress even more.

"We better hoof it if we're going to keep up with Ömer now," I huffed. "If we lose him, we're back to square one."

"I know. Don't worry, I've got him." Paz indeed quickened his pace and

I, as usual, struggled to stay beside him.

We continued to swerve through the flood of humanity, and I felt more and more like the proverbial salmon swimming upstream: impossible odds, but epic determination. We battled on.

And then, suddenly, Paz stopped. He backed into a tall, dusty shrub that arched toward another, identical, shrub opposite. Together they created a kind of vault over a concrete paving path.

"Whoa!" I said. "Why am I always bumping into you?"

"Sshhh," Paz whispered, holding his index finger up to his sweaty lips. "I was right, after all." He pointed through the opening between the sentinel shrubs. "The mosque."

I stared through the bushes and then scrambled over to the opposite one as quickly as possible in order to take up a post across from Paz. For there was our man, Ömer, positioned next to a shin-high ablution fountain. Its three chrome taps were poised, expectantly, over the marble-lined tub beneath. Two older men bent over the tub, splashing their faces with water spouting from the taps. A couple of younger guys chatted nearby.

But Ömer just stood there.

"He's looking for someone. Or waiting," I said, peering around the opening and then ducking my head back out of view. I felt like Lew Archer in *The Moving Target*, one of the Ross MacDonald 40s mysteries I had once leafed through during my detective fiction stage. In the book, Archer is hired to find a missing oil tycoon and gets embroiled with all kinds of unsavory characters throughout his mission. Substitute gold and carpet magnate for oil tycoon and the parallels were hard to ignore.

"Looks like it," said my fellow flatfoot. "This should be interesting. I think."

We each staked out behind one of the shrubs, hoping our hats would disguise us. We definitely did not want Ömer to know we were on his tail. And there was no doubt he would recognize our faces if he saw us lurking. After all, he had just "happened" to be at the airport at the same time we were. No one could convince me that was a mere coincidence. He knew who we were. So, taking turns peeking out from our stations, getting quizzical looks from passersby, we kept the man in view. I did not think he was meeting up with an ardent fellow worshipper. No, his reason for being here had to be nefarious. Nefarious, as far as I was concerned, anyway.

Observing Ömer close-up after all this time, and being able to study him clandestinely, I noticed a few things:

1) His hair was grayer—and thinner—so he was not impervious to the onslaughts of age, even as he eluded justice,
2) I thought I detected a bit more paunch in his middle section—all that good-living after poisoning a young man and evading punishment,
3) His shoes gleamed with bootblack—an essential detail of the veneer of his successful businessman facade, and,
4) Though he looked calm and in control, he jiggled his keys, or was it *kuruş* coins?, in his front trousers pocket. Was he unnerved about something?

"Who's he waiting for?" Paz called out in a hoarse whisper across the path, his right hand held up as a screen between his mouth and the mosque garden. I turned my attention back to the subject at hand.

"I don't think he can hear you from here, Paz," I returned. "But, to answer your question, I guess we'll just have to wait and see." I thought for a second. "Hopefully whoever it is doesn't come this way. That would be awkward."

"Oh, right. Didn't think about that. Maybe we should move somewhere else?" Paz offered.

"Hmm, maybe. But where?" We both scanned the area.

Paz pointed to a spot further along the row of shrubbery that acted as a fence between Atatürk Caddesi, the street we were staked out on, and the holy grounds. "There?"

I nodded. The fewer words spoken, the better.

We were about to shimmy down the sidewalk to our new lookout point, when Paz, who had to cross the opening in the pathway in clear view of Ömer, gasped.

"What's the matter?" I asked. My partner-in-crime looked ashen-faced.

"Quick, before they see us," he blurted out. He pushed me over to make room for himself at my bush.

"Who?"

"You know who. And someone else. I can't believe it." He slapped his hand on his forehead.

I peeked around Paz and the edge of the bush then immediately ducked back. My heart catapulted into my throat. If I had not recognized him from his rock-hewn face, that colossal carnelian ring on his finger was unmistakable. "Barış?"

Paz nodded vigorously, his eyes bulging behind his shades. I could just about tell through the dark lenses. We had not moved from our spot, and now we both stood rooted. Like the greenery we cowered behind.

"Now what?" I mouthed slowly, exaggerating the motion of my lips so Paz would understand my words. He shrugged, and flicked his hands dejectedly, a gesture of defeat. I understood why. He had befriended Barış eight years before in what seemed a random encounter, and kept genial contact with him all those years between then and now. Even stayed at his house and hired him as a go-between to surprise me in Istanbul the other night. Why in the world would Barış be having an assignation with Ömer in Fethiye? The last we saw of him, he was in the Sultanahmet, presumably with his family. And at his job, whatever that was.

The answer was obvious. Paz surely came to the same conclusion I did.

Ömer and Barış knew each other. They were in cahoots. The thought rang a bell in my brain. Because Paz had just revealed to me earlier that Ömer also knew Adrian. Way back when. The coincidence of both Barış and Adrian knowing Ömer and having a connection to us was too glaring to ignore. Were Ömer and Adrian also in cahoots?

If so, why?

Again, as so many times over the course of these last couple of insane days, the parting warning of Naji echoed in my ears, but it sounded far away, lost in dream fog and, once again, I could not make it out.

Suddenly, as if my head were not jammed up enough already, a horrendous screeching noise rained down on the town from a tannoy loudspeaker. It must have been mounted close by, because both Paz and I jumped with the unexpected aural assault the unmitigated volume of the sing-song call spat forth. He clapped his hands over his ears. It took me a moment to figure out what the clamor was, but then I recognized the familiar male chant:

"*Allahu Akbar! Allahu Akbar! Fawwwwww...*"

Prayer time.

By the time we recovered our equilibrium and glanced back toward the rendezvous site of Ömer and Barış, they had vanished.

"Shit! Fuck!" Paz screamed. "They can't be far. We have to find them. C'mon." I had not seen my friend so galvanized since the days following Adrian's "accident."

I readjusted my bag on my shoulder, shook the prayerful summons out of my ears, and entered through the portal to the mosque grounds side-by-side with Paz.

෨   ෨   ෨

November 5, 1922 – Constantinople

Demetrius donned his shabby red fez, its inside lining scratching at his scalp as always, heaved his duffle bag onto his shoulder and, nodding to the three other roommates in the shabby Albergo Miros dormitory, strode out the doorway. At the end of the hallway he started down the gloomy staircase, descending step by creaky step. At the bottom, he nearly ran into Kyria Zika lurking in the passageway between the parlour and the street door. He tipped his head, unsmiling, and, having already paid for his five weeks' lodgings, exited. Good riddance, he thought.

He stood outside the old building, its rickety sign fading like an unwanted memory, and looked north toward Üsküdar. He would make his way there, then, and board the ferry to cross the fabled Bosphorus one last time, glad that Jason and the Argonauts had long ago defeated the deadly Clashing Rocks, the Symplegades. He wanted to go to Beşiktaş now, not to the free bakery in neighboring Ortaköy this time, but to see the Dolmabahçe palace up close at last. He had to get the place out of his system and he thought that was the only way. Once he had gotten his fill—he chuckled at his own play on words, since "*dolma*" meant "filled" in Turkish—he would somehow make his way along the northern edge of the Sea of Marmara en route toward the border. Another three hundred kilometers or so. Thrace was waiting. Alexandroupolis was waiting. Home.

He had gotten this far, what else could happen?

ॐ   ॐ   ॐ

November 5, 1922 – Constantinople

Thump, thump, thump, thump!

The deafening racket roused Ayşegül from her sleep. She had hardly opened her eyes when Tanju burst into her room, propelling the edge of her door into the wall as he had a few nights earlier. She hurriedly pulled her coverlet across her chest.

"Get up. Sasar Kadın wants you. Now." His eyes fixed on hers with an angry glare.

Ayşegül blinked. "Now? Why?"

Inside, Tanju's booming presence made her tremble, but she tried not to show it. His manner reminded her of that long ago time when two similar domineering brutes rounded her up against her will, tyrannizing her into submission. She hoped Tanju would not linger, now that he had delivered his summons.

"An important meeting," Tanju answered, growling.

"A meeting? Why?"

"Stop asking questions, Ayşegül-*hanım*. You will find out when you get there."

"But where am I supposed to go?"

"To the concert hall. Five minutes."

The loutish man barked out his last words and, without even a bow of respect, turned on his slippered heels and left. He neglected to close her door after himself and the breeze his hurried departure stirred up, sent a whiff of his sour smell across the room. Ayşegül sniffed in distaste.

Ugh. What an insufferable person. I hate him. How dare he barge into my room like that.

Despite her indignation at having her quiet time disrupted, and by the man whom she feared more than any other except the sultan himself, Ayşegül threw her thick covers aside, swiveled around to disentangle her bare feet from the dishevelled bedclothes, and stood on the cold wood floor. She straightened both arms above her head, clasping her fingers together, and then bent to one side and the other to stretch her back. Quickly, before anyone else could come in and disturb her, she dashed to her door and pushed it closed. Then she headed to her water jug on the little stand in the corner of her room and splashed freezing water onto her face, barely taking time to towel it dry. Next, she strode to her clothes chest. She pulled out her cleanest sleeveless chemise, a pair of stockings and garters and her one pair of wide, satin pants with the fur trim and slid them all on, brushing the shiny fabric down her thighs to smoothe out the wrinkles. Though she did not often appear in European-style dress inside the harem, they now somehow made her feel more prepared for the change that was surely coming. The change that would take her out of here and into the world at large. At her nightstand now, she pulled her brush through her thick chestnut hair, wrapped a green silk scarf around her head and stuck her bare feet into her only high-heeled slippers.

Ready.

But why? What was this sudden assembly, unusual enough in itself, all about? And why would Saskar Kadın call one without any warning? Obviously, something had happened. Something probably not good. Even so, Ayşegül breathed a small sigh of relief. If others were summoned, it was nothing to do with her indiscretion. Or with her run-in with Tanju. So, it must be about the sultan. Or the situation in the palace. Certainly, all was in an uproar since the decree that the sultan was on his way out. Since he had been deposed.

She had known right away it really was only a matter of time before a decision about the rest of them would be made. If this was that time, it had come a little sooner than Ayşegül had anticipated. She sighed. Everything had come sooner than she had anticipated. Thank Allah, she had finished her carpet last night. Thank the moon, she already had her plans in place.

Before leaving her room, Ayşegül took one last glance around. The small space was mostly tidy. She had cleaned up all the skeins of unused wool, stored her *kirkit*, scissors and other tools back in her cupboard, and, most importantly, had hidden her new carpet in a place no one would think to look. If anyone was even interested. Of course, they would be if they knew what else was woven into it. But no one knew except her. And she meant to keep it that way.

She took a deep breath and, pulling her door closed behind her, ventured out into the long hallway. Before heading down toward the wide stairwell near the center of the palace, she caught a side view of Tanju at the other end, knocking on another innocent victim's door. It seemed to her that he was much more polite with that girl than he had been with her. She shrugged. Obviously, he had an issue with her. What did she care? By tomorrow morning, she would never have to deal with him again.

Several other young *acemis* dashed down the hall near her, chattering with each other.

"*Günaydın*, Ayşegül," called Zeliha, rushing to catch up. "Where have you been these last two days? I missed you!" She grabbed Ayşegül's hand and squeezed.

Ayşegül squeezed back. "Sorry, Zeliha. I was not feeling very well." She flinched at telling a lie to her best friend. To lessen its negative effects, she added, "And I was working on a carpet. How have you been?"

They were being whisked by the others down the long runners that protected the hallway floor and talked in hurried snatches as they moved along.

"Okay. But, to tell the truth, it has been difficult with all that has been going on." Zeliha leaned closer to her friend and whispered, "You heard about the sultan, right? Allah, what is going to happen to us? I'm worried."

"Yes," Ayşegül replied. "Yes, I heard about *Şahbaba*. It is terrible news. I don't know what to think anymore. But," here Ayşegül murmured, "I will bet you a week's worth of cherry *şerbet* that that is what this meeting with

Saskar Kadın is about. Everything will be okay. You'll see." Ayşegül was not altogether as confident in her prediction as she pretended, but she did not wish to alarm her best friend.

Zeliha turned slightly to look at Ayşegül as they continued their brisk walk. "You're probably right, Ayş. I knew if I talked to you I'd feel better. Look at it on the bright side. We could be free of this place by this afternoon! *'Hiçbir yol iyi bir şirketle uzun değildir.'"*

Zeliha quoted an old proverb: No road is long with good company. Ayşegül realized her friend thought they would stay together when the changes took place. The thought saddened her as she knew this would probably not be the case. But, she chuckled and squeezed Zeliha's hand again. "Come on, Zel. Let's get to this *toplantı* and afterwards we'll go visit Berkan and have pastry and some *kahve*."

Zeliha smiled brightly. "Good plan, *canım*. I could use a piece of Berkan's *revani* cake. Especially since Tanju woke me up and I did not have time for my breakfast!"

The two girls snickered and began to run toward the stairs.

While Ayşegül laughed out loud, she was also thinking: *I will miss Zeliha. What a* nimettir *she has been.*

A godsend.

ﷺ   ﷺ   ﷺ

Chapter 20

"If I had known the real way it was, I would have stopped all the looking around." - Mevlana (aka Rumi)

Wednesday, June 8, 2005, Late Afternoon - Çalış Beach

"What's going on?" shouted Mallie.

"It's Adrian, Mal. Something's happened to Adrian."

After that announcement in Adrian's and my room at the Mavi Dolfin Evi, and Murat's subsequent summoning of us all to the foyer, the three of us, Mallie, Paz and I, harnessed our confusion and frustration, our deep, collective sadness, and followed Murat downstairs. He seemed relieved that Mallie's expostulations and expletives had stopped at last and that the three of us had calmed down. It was as if we had resigned ourselves to our fates. But we did not know what—or who—was waiting for us.

We descended the two flights of stairs, treading dutifully behind our host like bewitched children behind the Pied Piper of Hamelin, and circumnavigated the hotel's three-storied atrium before we arrived at last in its sunny, palm-lined foyer. There, two trim, uniformed men, sporting brown trousers and off-white, short-sleeved shirts with guns tucked warningly into shoulder holsters, stood implacably still in front of the check-in counter. If they had official jackets, they had left them behind. Made sense in this swelter. Patches sewn onto their shirt pockets were stitched in gold lettering with the word "*Jandarma*" onto a curved, blood red background at the bottom. Gendarme. Great. We were going to be interrogated by an arm of the military police. That realization did not brighten my mood.

The men nodded, unsmilingly, at Murat and he slunk off through the door to his proprietor's wing without a word, but with an apologetic parting glance at us. His departure felt like a death knell. At the moment, he seemed our only link to something solid and knowable in this recondite country. I could feel Mallie's body tense up next to me. And I was sure she could feel mine. Paz lingered slightly behind us.

I became accutely aware that no air con or fan was in operation—on holiday, as we were supposed to be. *Oh well, our holiday is over now, anyway. Adrian's accident has seen to that.* The hot air in the foyer clung to my skin like a thousand little limpets. I wanted to scratch it and tear the creatures off, but I willed myself to ignore the discomfort. Mallie pushed her bangs back off her face and wiped her hand on her shorts leg. Paz stood completely still. All I heard was the steady, but shallow, breaths of my friends as we waited for the men to shout. To arrest us. Something. Mallie's nostrils flared. I could see her straining to keep from exploding, and silently implored her to keep her lid on.

Without any introduction, the taller officer approached me. Sweat began to dribble down the back of my neck.

"Follow, please," he said, turning toward the dining room. His voice was sonorous and not unkind, at least. He spoke English with only a trace of accent. And with a more American, rather than British, twang than most of the Turks we had met in this area. So, he was probably not local. And he was obviously making an effort for us. Should I relax then? Or was his congeniality a mere decoy? Perhaps, the two men were employed by a branch of the *jandarma* that dealt specifically with tourists and they intimidated them with a more subtle brand of harrassment in order to gain their trust. Or were they a branch of more insidious, hardened investigators who specialized in unusually heinous crimes?

Suddenly, the seriousness of this encounter seared itself into my consciousness. We were travelers here, we had no particular rights, and something terrible had happened, in which we were somehow implicated. The powers that be had been called in and we were the first point of attack. Or so I figured. It was no time to be glib, or sulk, or act like an idiot. With all this in mind, I jerked my head once, forward, in silent assent. The officer's shorter partner stepped behind his senior in a show of deference, I assumed, to his superior's rank. I solemnly waved Mallie in front of me to let her lead our pack while Paz and I filed behind, side-by-side, as we all steered toward the dining area.

While we walked, Paz turned his face toward me and made an "eek" grimace with his mouth. I responded by lifting my eyebrows and looking askance. Neither of us had a clue what was happening, but did not know what to say, either to each other or to the men that were directing us to follow them. To say the situation was awkward was an understatement.

As all five of us filed into the now unlit, empty dining room, I could not help conjecture over how much a space—and a vacation—could transform. And so quickly. Just a few hours before, I had been hurriedly and innocuously shoveling cucumbers and eggs into my mouth and chatting with the Turkish university student Emre about nothing much—until he mentioned he had seen Mallie and Paz at the dolphin roundabout. That had set my whole mad-scramble Fethiye foray into action. At the time, I had been concerned, yeah, even a little pissed off, about Adrian's reneging on our beach plans, but even so I could never have anticipated the turn of events that would follow both his deception—if, indeed, that was what it was—or my dumb desperation to find him. What had happened since seemed to have usurped all else in my brain.

Except for this unexpected—and thoroughly unwelcome—rendezvous with the local authorities. I tried to stifle my unsavory memories of the infamous 70s movie *Midnight Express*. Surely, I assuaged myself, nothing like what that ill-starred character, Billy Hayes, endured will happen to us. Surely, we are not headed toward a long stint in a sadistic Turkish prison.

We had done nothing wrong, after all. Nothing, but find our friend smack on his back and now on the verge of losing his earthly corporeality after being poisoned by some unknown assailant in a backstreet carpet shop. We had journeyed to this country for some fun and a spot of sightseeing. Well, if the fun was up, it was not our fault. We had not been the ones to bring this hellacious catastrophe to pass.

So, why were *we* being interviewed by the *jandarma*? Shouldn't they be going after whomever had callously slipped a deadly tree part into Adrian's tea? Maybe, right now, marinating in our sweat, like chicken legs waiting to be grilled, for that was what I now assumed was about to occur, the guilty party was celebrating his murderous success somewhere cool and far away, safe from the impending storm of culpability. The thought made me bristle.

I wondered what Philip, the hapless anti-hero, in *My Cousin Rachel* would do in this situation. We had more in common than I would have ever thought.

"Please. Sit." The head guy proffered his open right palm toward the now empty seats at the equally empty table in front of us. Paz, Mallie and I each selected our chairs and, without speaking, slowly sank into them. Mallie placed her hands, clasped and tight, into her lap. Paz crossed his arms over his belt and drummed his fingers against his sides. I just watched. The officer, meanwhile, extracted a similar chair from the adjacent table, scooted it toward us and turned it around. His partner did the same.

Three of us against two of them. In sheer numbers, you would think the odds were in our favor, but I knew they were not.

"My name is Sergeant Demir," our interrogator began. "Please, you must to tell us your names. Officer Güven will write down."

He glanced toward his second-in-command who merely lifted his previously neglected clipboard from his lap. He clicked his ballpoint pen and sat. The silent henchman.

Before Paz or I could speak, Mallie unclasped her hands and crossed them under her breasts in that recalcitrant way that I knew so well. She had been simmering in silence, waiting for the right moment to spew out her attack. I tried not to flinch.

"Can I ask," she snorted, "what is this about?" She flicked her bangs, like an untamed horse.

Sergeant Demir blinked and tilted his head slightly forward. It was a motion I had seen often in Turkish men and usually, I had come to realize, made in a show of conviviality. Not offensiveness. Our man, apparently, had a sense of humor and was nonplussed by Mallie's outburst. No doubt, he had seen many such in his career. I sighed a little in relief. Perhaps this inquisition would not be as hair-raising as I had anticipated. The sergeant flipped open a notebook that he extracted from his shirt pocket and then answered her question with pitying politeness:

"We are here because of the accident in Fethiye. Your friend..." he consulted his booklet, "...Adrian Mick-All-Iss-Tair." His tortured pronunciation of Adrian's last name was, in essence, accurate, but almost comical. Adrian would have gotten a kick out of it. I had to stifle a laugh. Then the sergeant continued. "In point of fact, we do not think it was an accident."

He uttered the last sentence in somber, even tones. And neither Paz nor I flinched at the implication of his words. We had been to the intensive care unit at the hospital, we had done some research on the Internet. We knew about the laburnum. In short, we already understood that Adrian's misfortune was intentional. Had to be.

But Mallie? Alas, we had not filled her in on the salient details yet. Partly, I think, both Paz and I had stalled because we did not quite know how to break the news. Because we ourselves were still stunned by it. But in our defense, we had not known the police would come to our hotel and interrupt our announcement. How could we?

"Not an accident? What do you mean?" Mallie asked, suddenly imploring. She was sitting between Paz and me and now turned to each of us, her mouth open and her small head turning on its axis like a ventriloquist's dummy. When she turned toward me, I sucked my lips in and shrugged, feeling like a heel for not having prepared her for this moment. Yes, Adrian was special to me, but it would be unfair not to acknowledge that he was important to the others, as well. Of course, Mallie would be devastated to discover that, not only was he in critical care, but that his condition had been brought about on purpose. With malice aforethought. But by whom?

Sergeant Demir looked appropriately sympathetic, his intelligent, dark eyes peering at Mallie intently. Then he spoke, more quietly than before. "I have report from doctor at hospital. They make a test of Mister Adrian's blood and they find high levels of cytisine. Cytisine very toxic if too much is ate. In point of fact, we do not believe your friend ate it himself. Doctor Karatepe thinks it was put into his *çay*. Perhaps at the carpet shop where he collapsed. We do not know. Officer Güven and I will investigate this."

Officer Güven nodded solemnly, but his eyes squinted at us, giving the impression that he was not inclined to sympathy like his boss.

I thought Mallie was going to swoon at the word "toxic," but she contained herself, Boadicea that she was, and just stared at the sergeant. For once, she seemed lost for words. So, I helped her out.

"But who would do such a thing? We don't understand. Adrian didn't know anyone here!"

Out of the corner of my eye I noticed Paz sinking into himself, but I did not think anything unusual about it. No doubt, he was just uncomfortable with the *jandarma*. But then, we all were. Justifiably.

Sergeant Demir's neck tweaked to one side and his lips turned downwards—an "I-don't-know" response.

Then he said, "He knew *you*." And here, our interrogater looked pointedly at each of us in turn, starting with me, then Mallie, and finally Paz. We all just gawked back in shock.

Suddenly, the stillness in the room was as thick as Turkish yogurt. And just as sour.

Then Mallie spoke.

"You can't think any of *us* did it." She flapped her hands about in the air. "We're his *friends*!"

As she uttered the last word, panic flashing through her eyes, I recalled our arrival at the main *otogar* a couple weeks earlier and the sign that

Cengis had held up: Adrian and Freinds. And we were—a trio of freewheeling musketeers, devoted to our charismatic newcomer, our D'Artagnan. Adrian. He had become our cherished leader and I could not believe any one of us would have had the desire, the heart or, most importantly, the nerve to trick him into drinking an elixir of doom. It just did not seem possible.

Or was it?

In the flicker of time between Mallie's interjection and my subsequent inner reflections, I realized there *was* one person in our small ensemble who was capable of trickery. He had proven it many times in the past, starting with that time at the Santa Cruz theatrical performance, that night I first met him in 1998. Not only was he a trickster, he had been at the scene of Adrian's demise.

Paz.

Just then, the person in question fidgeted in his seat. A guilty reaction? Or merely discomfiture from being stuck in this god-awful stifling room under the cross-examination of military detectives? I could not say. I did not want to believe my old amigo capable of such treachery, such cruelty. And, more to the point, what would be his motive? There had to be a motive. I struggled with that conundrum for a few seconds, but could not come up with anything that smacked of credibility.

Despite the absence of any satisfying explanation to this perplexing situation, one fact had become very clear to me. Something shady lurked beneath our outwardly bonvivant camaraderie, a dark mystery about which I was obviously completely clueless. Over my head. And I had no idea where to find answers. I did not even know where to start to look. All I knew was that Adrian, my dearest friend, my *optimus amicus*, had been the unfortunate victim of *someone's* anger. And because of it, he now lay helpless, possibly on the verge of death.

And if he died, that would be murder.

The word gave me shivers. I had read about it in novels, watched it on television shows, but now that it loomed for real in my own life, I could not find a place for it.

None of this made sense. None of it had been in the cards.

And yet the cards *had* played a foul hand and all of us were sucked into the nauseating vortex of its consequences. Would another, happier hand, eventually be dealt? Would we find out what happened to Adrian—and why? Could Paz possibly be involved?

As I sat there facing Demir and Güven, immobilized, these questions—

and more—dizzied my head and the more I let them swirl around there, the more they entwined and twisted, creating a kind of overpowering cranial confusion. Frustrated and exhausted, I told myself to stop projecting. To chill out. After forcing myself to take a few deep breaths, I thought I arrived at a temporary resolution.

Let Sergeant Demir and Officer Güven do their job. It was what they were trained for. All would come out in their investigation. Until then, I would have to have faith. That's what I tried to tell myself.

But, instead, I stewed on the problem, letting it simmer and boil in my brainpot until it liquified into a kind of soup of distrust, lingering in the pot long after another suspicion came along and was poured, with remarkable fluidity of speed and justification, into the seething mix.

               ʠ   ʠ   ʠ

Friday, August 16, 2013, Mid-Afternoon - Fethiye

We ran past the men washing up at the fountain while a gaggle of others filed into the front of the mosque for prayers. Paz sliced his arm quickly downwards through the air a few times, signalling for me to check out the paths on the opposite side of us. But I did not see our targets. I shook my head to let him know.

Just as I was making my way back to him, he whooped.

"Got 'em! Look, over there. Let's go." He shot off like a puppy after a pigeon toward the opposite end of the mosque park, toward the busy intersection at the end. I followed, wishing I had brought a daypack instead of the cumbersome bag that kept banging into my sides and sliding off my shoulder.

"Wait up, Paz," I called.

"Can't," he yelled back over his shoulder. "Don't want to lose them."

I kept up as best I could, thinking how I missed the old me that wore suitable clothing for running around and pursuing people. Nowadays, I always seemed to lag behind Paz, though I was taller than him by at least a couple inches. His determination was inspiring, though. At last, we were back on the street behind Barış and Ömer. They did not seem to be in any rush. I put my hands together, prayer-like, in thankfulness.

Paz and I kept a distance now of about twenty feet. It was easier to keep the two in sight than it had when we were just following Ömer. For one thing, Barış towered over Ömer. You could spot his head and shoulders no problem. The crowds had thinned down somewhat now, as well. But there was a third reason we could keep an eye on them. It made me laugh.

"Jesus, Barış is still wearing that leather jacket, the one he had on the other night. How does he do it in this heat?" I said. I was now able to talk without gasping for air.

Paz kept walking. "Yeah, I remember. Weird. Must be his personal uniform or something. I don't get it."

"So, speaking of Barış...just tell me, Paz. You *never* had any idea, through all those years of emailing him and stuff, that he knew Ömer."

"Nope. Not a clue." He suddenly stopped dead on the sidewalk and looked at me, pointedly. "If I had, you think I would've stayed with him when I came back? Or asked him to help me find you? Not a chance."

He began walking again and I stepped in beside him, feeling a huge weight fall off of me. Because at last, after all we had been through the last couple days, and all my questions and doubts, I finally believed him. It was a kind of triumph, like uttering "open sesame," and the impenetrable cave opening to you at last. This renewed faith in my old friend buoyed me on. I felt a renewal in purpose, because I was no longer alone. In fact, this newfound motivation spurred me to ask another question. One of the many that had been dogging me since the other night.

"So, you didn't know about the notes?"

"What notes?" He seemed genuinely baffled by my question.

"The ones that someone left in my book."

"*What* book? What *are* you on about, Molo?"

I was about to tell him, but at that moment our prey crossed the street. We had to dodge a couple of sorry-looking, beater Fiat sedans in order to continue our pursuit. Almost as soon as we managed to arrive alive on the other side, we saw Ömer and Barış duck into a cafe.

"Oops. What should we do now?" I asked. Honestly, I was beginning to wonder why I had ever embarked on this mission in the first place. What was I really thinking? Was I even the kind of person who would have the guts to stick a knife into a creep like Ömer, or even the know-how to sabotage him? Looking back on my years of seething hatred, I realized my fantasies of revenge were just that—fantasies. I wanted Adrian's death to mean something, that he had not died in vain. I wanted revenge, yes. But desiring these things and being able to carry them out were two different animals. I felt my resolve slip away from me again.

I was about to say "Let's go, I'm finished," when Paz made a pronouncement that I would never forget.

"I know exactly what to do. We're going in."

          ~o   ~o   ~o

We threaded between rickety tables strewn about the streetside patio where beige-and-brown-dressed men played "Okey." The players each faced one side of the central board, armed with their allotment of game tiles. They either hunched forward in intense concentration during a play or lounged against the backs of their folding chairs, smoking hand-rolled cigarettes while awaiting their turn. The rapid-fire clickety-clack of plastic tiles against the game boards was inescapable in this part of Turkey, I had noticed in my two tours here, and it was as much a part of the soundscape as the intermittent calls to prayer. But whereas, the prayers were a measure of a man's sense of duty and devotion, the game was a measure of his just-as-powerful penchant for pleasure. Indeed, so popular was Okey, that it reigned as something of a national pastime.

Alongside tiles and an ashtray, each game table was festooned with the ever-present glasses of dark amber *çay* in varying stages of consumption. One might be forgiven for thinking *çay*-drinking was a part of the game. Maybe it was—I never learned to play—but I did not think so. Not technically, anyway. Cengis had informed me back in 2005 that Okey was such an obsession, many a Turkish man had bet—and lost—his family's property over it. Finally, the government stepped in and declared it illegal to serve alcohol at Okey establishments. Thus, the *çay.*

Ömer and Barış each held their own full glasses in front of them when we strode in through the door (I let Paz lead, trying to ignore the battering ram bashing inside my chest cavity). There was no Okey board between them, but the looks they gave us as we entered were worth the price of my plane ticket over. Barış, who was facing the back wall, turned his lined leather face at the ting-ting of the bell over the door, and glared at us with eyes full of dark menace. That colossal carnelian ring seemed to throb and pulse on his finger with warning, and I had to remind myself of the carnelian's courage-promoting properties. The question was, whose courage was this one promoting: mine or Barış's? In any case, his glowering expression convinced me I had not been wrong about him, after all, that first night. The fact that he was here with Ömer at this very moment had to mean he was the dubious blackguard I first feared him to be.

Ömer, though. Well, he was a cool customer. I had to give him that. As

285

cool as the restaurant was not, inspite of the beads of sweat dotting his rotund, jaundiced face—oh, I wanted to smash it! Otherwise his expression was blank. Just as I remembered from 2005. Well, I say blank, but that is not entirely so. I mean to say, there was no scowl, no smirk, no glare, nor even a blink. No immediately evident sign of reaction to our barging in on his clandestine tête-à-tête with Barış. His displeasure showed itself in a more subtle way—and it was infinitely more spine-chilling than Barış's obvious scowl. The subtlety was in his eyes. Ömer's focused on Paz and me, but they did not shine or flash with emotion as most people's did. Instead, they leered, reptilian, colorless slits of vitrious venom, which threatened to discharge at any second. For any reason. And you would not be ready.

That is when I realized. That was exactly what happened to Adrian. Ömer pretended to be his friend, his associate, his accomplice even, but when he had gotten what he wanted out of Adrian, he poisoned him. Whatever his association might have been with Ömer, whatever his history, Adrian would never have been prepared for the kind of foul and unforeseeable retribution a person like Ömer was capable of. I hardly knew Ömer. But I knew he was vile. I always felt it.

I hoped Paz did, too. He was the one with the plan, after all. Or so he let on. Whatever it was, I hoped he understood the potential danger we were in. If Ömer and Barış offered us çay, for instance, I, for one, would not be partaking and I would strongly encourage Paz to follow my example. I did not see any laburnum trees around, but you never knew.

I wished now we had been able to enter the establishment and conceal ourselves in a corner, unseen, before making any move, so that we had a chance for Paz to at least brief me on his scheme, if indeed there was one (or was he pulling one of his stunts again?).

But when we had stepped through the door, the pointlessness of that idea was glaringly evident. For one, the place was a hole-in-the-wall, no wider than my hotel room and, as such, way too tiny to hide in. A case might be made for disappearing in a small place—if it were crowded. But there was no one else here. It was as empty as a church hall on a Saturday night. The believers were all playing Okey outside.

So, we stood there just inside the doorway, Paz and I, two sore thumbs studying the two schmucks who had practiced such deception on us for so long. Who had been so slippery and elusive.

The distinctive odor of grilled meat permeated the room. A razor-thin man, I guessed the proprietor, appeared somewhere from the back, but he must have felt the tense vibe, and scarpered back through his hole to the grill. So, it was back to Paz and me and the two others. The only sound in the room was the whirring of the standing fan in the corner. Waiting, hovering, as we were, I began to feel like we were re-enacting the standoff in *High Noon* between Gary Cooper (Paz and me) and the notorious Miller gang (Ömer and Barış) just before the final showdown. If there was going to be a showdown, I prayed Paz and I would prevail, though I did not see how we would. For one, we carried no weapons.

Or so I thought.

While an invisible clock ticked away somewhere in the existential ether of suspenseful moments, and I waited for something to happen, I noticed the five or six unframed, sepia-brown posters of Turkish landscapes, corners curling outwards, that were taped to the gray walls. There was no other ornamentation in the place. As sparse as a Jesuit monk's cell. This was definitely one of those unadorned, function-before-form venues that did not cater to the expat or tourist community. A locals-only place for locals-only business. Paz and I stuck out like Inuits in the Sahara, intruders, and that realization did not inspire confidence in me any more than Barış's giant carnelian now did.

The staredown continued for a few agonizing, drawn-out seconds more. During the blood-thick silence our adversaries never flinched. But neither did Paz. His fortitude was frightening and I began to wonder, really, what *was* up his sleeve. At times like this he was scary. I thought back to the scene in the makeshift tent in 1998—the first night I met him and Mallie—and his almost spectral transformation on stage. When he had appeared out of nowhere with that gorey goop on his bare chest and wailed like a wounded animal in a leg-hold trap.

He did not wail now. But what he did do would replay, slow-motion, in my head for days afterwards.

"Hello, fellows," he said, calmly, just the slightest sprinkling of sarcasm coating his sugary tone. I looked askance at him, my chin pressing into my neck and my eyebrows raised practically into my hairline. *What's he up to?*

Ömer and Barış both blinked slowly. Otherwise, they exhibited no reaction to Paz's greeting. They were not going to acquiesce to him in any way, that was evident. But now that the banging in my own chest had begun to quieten, I could think more rationally. And it occurred to me that they were probably wondering what was going on as much as I was. Certainly, the last thing they must have been expecting was Paz and me

287

catching them *in flagrante delicto*, as it were, at their secret cave tryst. But they could not allow us to know that. Their glasses of *çay* sat untouched, exhibiting just about the same amount of emotion as they themselves did.

A zing of plus-charged electricity oscillated down my arms and legs. About time we had the upper hand. Or, rather, I hoped we did. I crossed my fingers behind my back, as I did often in this country, and at the same time I sent Paz subliminal "go, go, go" messages. I might not be the quarterback calling the play, but I could cheer him on from the bench.

As I watched expectantly, my old compadre, the consummate con-man, began to stride slowly, deliberately, toward the table where our two nemeses waited, speechless. It only took a few seconds. I watched with curiosity as he plunged his right hand into his front pants pocket. *What's he doing now? Surely, he doesn't have a gun.*

When Paz arrived in front of their table, his hand emerged slowly out of the pocket, curled around an object. An object that was completely hidden in his fist. Not a firearm then, too small. I flashed back to the recent night (was it recent? It seemed an age ago) in the dark room on the back street of Sultanahmet where Barış had led me to my serendipitous reunion with Paz. I remembered that, as we both made ready to exit that room together, he snatched something small off the wooden table and shoved it in his pocket. If I had been more aware, or less exhausted, I might have said he grabbed the object surreptitiously. But at the time, my observation had all the weight of a hummingbird feather on a blustery day. It had barely registered.

Now Paz proffered his brown, hirsute arm, locked at the elbow, straight out from his chest. His fist was clenched, fingers curled ceilingwards. The forelimb hovered over the table between Ömer and Barış like an offering. They stared at it. Barış's right eye twitched almost imperceptibly and Ömer's lizard eyes narrowed. It was the first hint of something akin to curiosity I had marked on them since we had entered their dust-encrusted domain.

Slowly, before any words were uttered, Paz began to uncurl his fingers, starting with his index finger and fanning toward his pinkie. Slowly, a glint of gold, a silvery deep gold, like that on a harvest moon as it lingers near the horizon, began to appear on his thick, sweaty palm. He was milking this moment, taking his time, drawing out the suspense of what his palm held. I shook my head at his audacity. Gool ol' Paz. He was in performance mode and, judging by his triumphant smirk, he was loving it.

A second before his palm was completely exposed, he turned to me and winked. I smiled, though I had no idea what I was smiling about. It just felt like, despite our past together, the subsequent eight-year hiatus I had imposed on Mallie and him, and our last few days of drama and intrigue, distrust and anger, we had finally come home. We were back where we started that day fifteen years before on a balmy Santa Cruz evening at that mesmerizing tent show of magic and mystery. That was when the skeins of our friendship had been spun and we had known that our lives would somehow weave together.

His wink now was definitely worth the price of my flight over. And beyond. Years of dejection and loneliness broke off my encrusted heart. At last. I felt my own true self, start to re-emerge from its cocoon.

Paz and I gazed at each other, knowingly, for a timeless second more, and then he turned back to the two miscreants at the table. They had started to fidget, but had held fast in their seats, not seeming to know how to react to Paz and his theatrics, but curious, it seemed, to find out what the denouement would be.

The cup of Paz's palm was still protected by his fingers unfurling above it and whatever lay within—and I could see Ömer's and Barış's necks crane, ever so slightly, to get a glimpse of it. Then, his fingers flicked apart with a loud pop and the object was finally revealed.

"Is this what you've been looking for?"

Pazs's tone was suprisingly cheerful. As if this whole exploit were one giant joke. But I knew him well enough to realize that his outward flippancy was merely a performance. Underneath that flippancy lurked a steely resolve that, if thwarted, would not bode well for the thwarter.

Okey tiles clackety-clicked outside the otherwise silent room.

Ömer and Barış gasped. Their deadpan posturing had finally been shattered. Paz had scored at last.

I must admit, I gasped, too. For what Paz revealed in his now wide open hand was an object completely unexpected. A ring. But it was not just any ring. Its band was gold, or maybe platinum, I did not possess the expertise to tell. What I could tell was that it was exquisite, stunning, beautiful, and undoubtedly valuable. A man's ring, solid and chunky. And it was old. As we all stared, Paz twisted his wrist this way and that, tauntingly, so that, without touching the ring itself, we could all see it from different angles. The metal parts were intricately etched with filigreed lines and delicate shapes. Not a surface was left undecorated.

But even more astounding was what lay imbedded, bevelled, into its center.

It had to be the largest gem I had ever seen. A ruby. Some talisman, that was for sure. Barış's carnelian ranked a mere bauble in comparison.

The jewel sparkled in the filtered light streaming through the cafe windows. It was shaped into a square, rounded at the corners—what I later learned was called "cushion-cut"—and sliced at all its edges in precision-made geometric shapes that reflected varying shades of deep vermilion.

More remarkable even than these surface characteristics was what laid underneath. For the exterior slices of the stone somehow, inextricably, created an image that gleamed outward from its subsurface. Despite my distrust of the two scoundrels sitting on either side of Paz's outstretched hand, and what they might attempt, I was drawn to look closer at the ring. I leaned in toward it, my peripheral vision on high alert, just in case. As I studied the ruby and its magnificent beauty, the image that stared back at me was even more astounding than the ruby itself.

It was a woman's face.

She sat quietly at the open window, knowing he was observing her, studying her from his spot at his worktable. She fidgeted under his scrutiny. His carving tool in his right hand, he began to cut away at one of his stones, now and then glancing in her direction. She hated that glance. Though he had shown her affection, she knew deep down he was filled with contempt for her, for girls like her. What he did not know, was that she felt more than contempt for him.

She hated him.

November 5, 1922 – Constantinople

Saskar Kadın dismissed everyone. The meeting was over.

During her speech, Ayşegül and Zeliha had sat, straight-backed and attentive on lush floor pillows, along with all the others, and listened to the officious woman. Ayşegül's friends sat near her: Zeliha, of course, and Hande, who waved at her, and...

"Where's Yasmin?" Ayşegül had had to whisper, pulling Zeliha's wild hair away from her ear as she did so. "I don't see her."

Tanju had returned from delivering his summons to all the sultan's female attendants. He and one other eunuch, whose name was Majid, stood guard at the door, but she was sure they would have allowed Yasmin in, even if she had been detained for some reason and was late. Everyone liked Yasmin.

Zeliha had scanned the large room and widened her eyes at her friend. "She's not here," she answered, and tensed her shoulders slightly.

Ayşegül had furrowed her brows in thought. That did not make sense. Yasmin would not have missed an official gathering. She was faithful that way. Reliable. So where was she? Ayşegül kept one eye on the door in case her friend showed up, but she never did.

"And your families have been contacted," Saskar Kadın had continued. The young women sat quietly, their eyes wide in their incredulous faces, as their fates were announced. "It will be difficult for some of them to get here in time, but we cannot help you after 14 *Kasım'dan*. If your family has not come for you by then, you must make your own plans. We will all be gone, including our wonderful *Şahbaba*." She bowed her head slightly, and Ayşegül was surprised to see her wipe her hand under her eye. But even as she watched Saskar Kadın's unexpected display of emotion, she was calculating.

November 14. Only nine days away. How long ago had the palace contacted the girls' families? Had they telephoned? Or written? Ayşegül's lived (or used to live) in a village near Manisa, south of Smyrna, where their family had been forced to emigrate years before. It was at least one day's drive away from Constantinople, but Ayşegül did not know if they even owned an automobile. Or a telephone. Most likely, they did not. It did not seem possible they would be able to get to Constantinople by the fourteenth.

Ayşegül did not even know if her family were still alive. She had not heard from any of them since her arrival ten years before. The palace did not encourage exchange with a resident's relatives once she had been brought here. And now they were all being chucked out. With no assistance whatsoever. It was a good thing Ayşegül had already made her own plans, she realized, sighing. Or at least part of a plan. She had seen this coming. If Mama and Papa did manage to come to the palace, they would not find her here. But eventually, they would go home and she would be waiting for them.

After Saskar Kadın closed the meeting, all the young women pushed themselves off the floor, brushed down their skirts and started for the door. But as Ayşegül and Zeliha were about to pass through, Tanju and Majid blocked Ayşegül's way. Ayşegül pushed against them with her lower arms.

"What are you doing? Let me go out," she insisted. But the two obdurate men, their solid bodies as rigid as the pile poles at Beşiktaş Pier, would not step aside.

Zeliha stood on the other side of the double door calling cheerfully, "Ayşegül. Come on! Berkan is waiting for us."

Ayşegül knew her friend was lying. Berkan did not know about their plans to visit him for *kahve* and cake. Zeliha's lie was meant to disarm the two eunuchs, so that they would think someone else was waiting for them. If they were acting on some hostile impulse, her trick might stop them in their tracks. Ayşegül was impressed with her friend's quick and clever tactic.

"Move over, Tanju-*Bey*. I have to go with Zeliha." Ayşegül did not scream at the infuriating man, but her voice was firm. An order.

Tanju scoffed. "You're not going to Berkan's 'Kitchen Cafe,' Ayşegül-*hanım*." His mocking tone was meant to put Ayşegül in her place—after all, she was merely a servant of the Empire, of the sultan. "You're coming with me."

He seized her upper arm and pulled her to the far corner of the room. As he pulled, he nodded to Majid, who slipped through the door and vanished. Ayşegül struggled against Tanju's grip without success and as he held her fast she wanted to scream at him. Where were they planning to take her? Had he not heard? The Empire was finished. And so was the sultan. Tanju was acting on behalf of entities that no longer existed. Whatever he was planning for her could no longer be condoned. Surely, he realized that. Whatever he realized—or did not—she had to get away from him before he did whatever the eunuchs did to wayward harem girls. But his fingers dug into her flesh and she could not wriggle away.

The rest of the women continued to file out of the door. Some of them looked Ayşegül's way with questioning eyes. But two of them, Gülizar and Shahinaz, loitered by the doorway, like *cadılar*, scheming witches, making lewd gestures. *Boklar,* the shits! Ayşegül knew they were involved in this debacle somehow. Knew they had conspired with Tanju to meddle with her. God, how she had learned to hate those two *sorun çıkaranlar*. As she tried to prise her arm out of Tanju's hand, she gave the two troublemakers the evil eye. They only snickered, before backing toward the door.

Zeliha was still there. Ayşegül watched, suddenly heartened, as Zeliha grabbed Shahinaz's hand when she tried to sneak by, and twisted it at the wrist. She heard Shahinaz shriek in pain. But almost as quickly as Zeliha had caught at her, the shrew fought her way free and ran after her accomplice. Zeliha clenched her fists and glared after them. Now she turned toward Ayşegül and shouted, "I tried. *Ağızla kuş tutmak.*"

Keeping a bird with the mouth. It was a Turkish saying used when someone's actions were not to be tolerated. In this case, Shahinaz. But the saying could also apply to Gülizar, and even Tanju and Majid, by extension. All four or them were part of this charade, Ayşegül knew.

Tanju, during the distraction, had released Ayşegül's arm. She had stopped squirming, hoping her stillness would trick him into letting her go. It worked. As he watched, transfixed, Zeliha wrestling with Shahinaz, Ayşegül snuck past him and ran toward the door.

She did not look back.

෨   ෨   ෨

Zeliha and Ayşegül sprinted down the corridor toward the stairway that led to the upper stories and their rooms.

"What was that all about?" asked Zeliha. Her voice was raspy from her exertion. "Why was Tanju assaulting you?"

"I don't know," answered Ayşegül, gulping air. "He has a problem with me lately. Who knows why?" Again, she hated to lie to Zeliha, especially after she had gone after Shahinez in Ayşegül's defense. But it would not help Zeliha—or her—if she told the truth. The less Zeliha knew, the better. They would both be gone soon and nothing Tanju did could stop that.

She hoped.

As the two friends reached the end of the corridor, they stopped running, catching at their throats while their breath returned. They turned back the way they had come in case Tanju or Majid were following, but the corridor was empty. Ayşegül and Zeliha faced each other, smiling bleakly, and leaned back against one of the crystal and mahogany bannisters of the two-sided Grand Staircase. They had a choice. Go upstairs to their quarters or head down to the lower floors.

"Are we going to the kitchen now?" Zeliha asked.

Ayşegül shook her head slowly. "No, I don't think so. That might be the first place those two," she jerked her head toward the concert room, "will search for us. Maybe Tanju is already on his way there. It's too bad. I could really use some *revani* right now. Couldn't you?"

The girls broke into an unrestrained laughter, which took a moment to run its course.

"God, I'm going to miss you, *arkadaşım*," said Zeliha, still chuckling slightly. "You'll always be my favorite *acemi,* you know."

"I know. I will miss you like crazy, too," said Ayşegül. "You're the best thing about this place." She paused. "Except for the cake, of course." The two laughed again.

"We'd better go, though. Just in case."

"Where to?"

"Our rooms. I'm not going to hide from those bastards."

Zeliha nodded in agreement.

"And I have to pack." Ayşegül rolled her eyes.

Zeliha smirked. "Yes, true. Me, too. Let's go."

Ayşegül and Zeliha mounted the first step of the magnificent stairway, near the Muâyede Salonu, and gazed toward the beautiful crystal chandelier mounted from the giant, domed ceiling high above. It was rumored that the humongous lighting ornament had been a gift to Sultan Abdülmecid I, Mehmed's father, by Queen Victoria.

"Pretty soon this will all be a memory, *canım*," sighed Zeliha. Her thick hair fell across her pretty cheeks. "I wonder if we will ever come back here again."

Ayşegül reached toward her friend, gently drew her hair from her face and then took her by the elbow, drawing her slender body close. "Don't think about it now, *canım*. First, we have to get out of here before it can even be a memory!" She squeezed Zeliha's arm. "And I can't wait."

They chuckled, and Zeliha lightly punched Ayşegül with her free hand. The two friends then ascended slowly, step after step, one side of the wide, carpeted stairs.

Ayşegül's room was closest. Outside the door, she kissed Zeliha's cheeks, one by one. Zeliha kissed Ayşegül's.

"*Görüşürüz*, my friend," she whispered.

Görüşürüz. See you tomorrow."

As Zeliha ambled down the hallway, she turned around and blew a kiss to Ayşegül. Ayşegül waved back. Tears began to form behind her eyes because she knew, as she watched Zeliha get smaller and smaller, her form fading into the half light, that she would never see her friend again.

❧   ❧   ❧

Chapter 21

"And from the Alban Mount we now behold
Our friend of youth, that ocean, which when we
Beheld it last by Calp's rock unfold
Those waves, we follow on till the dark Euxine roll'd
Upon the blue Symplegades..."
- Lord Byron, Childe Harold's Pilgrimmage (1812 – 1818)

Wednesday, June 8, 2005, Late Afternoon - Çalış Beach

"Well, thank God *that's* over," said Mallie. She puffed her cheeks and blew out a huge sigh. "That younger guy, he made me nervous." She looked sideways at Paz and put her hand up to her mouth like a screen and whispered in my direction. "He was pretty hot, though."

Paz shook his head and rolled his eyes. He could never have made a comment like that about another female with Mallie around. Not unless he wanted to have his balls kicked up into his front shirt pocket, anyway. "I'm pretty hot, too, actually," he rebutted, fanning his face with a menu that was sitting on the table nearby. Mallie winced at his use of the double entendre.

It *was* stifling. The air con, for some reason, was still on the blink. But at least the lights were off, giving a vague impression of things having cooled down. A very vague impression.

It was just the three of us now.

Sergeant Demir and his sidekick, Officer Güven, had finally left amid admonitions that we should stay put pending their investigations. Fortunately, Murat had seen to it that no other guests were able to enter the room during our interrogation, or whatever it was, so we were alone and able to air our thoughts out loud without fear of being overheard. I, for one, did not relish the idea of other lodgers in the Mavi Dolfin Evi knowing what was going on, what had happened to Adrian. Especially, those, like

Emre, whom we had met. Adrian's mishap just did not seem an appropriate addendum to a holiday tour. It was bad enough that our group was going through its after effects. And I thought if I heard anyone tell me how sorry they were about Adrian being in a coma, or offering advice on how to handle it, I would punch them. Murat would not like that and might kick us out, a state of affairs that would only add more distress to our already stressful situation. Our two *jandarma* buddies, at least, had kept their disingenuous sympathies to themselves and focused on their questions.

They also promised, in an offhand way, to let us know what they might uncover. But I did not want to wait for them. I did not completely trust them. We were, after all, *yabancı*, here. Strangers. What did they really care if one of us got hurt?

"So, now what do we do?" I asked. "Should we go back to the hospital?" I almost added, "to check on Adrian's status," but I could not bring myself to say the words. I was just about staving off an emotional meltdown. The interactions with Demir and Güven, as well as the doctor and even Murat, helped distract me from my morbid thoughts. Now I needed more distraction.

I could see Mallie and Paz searching for an appropriate response. Sweat ran in rivulets down Paz's forehead.

"I know," said Mallie, holding up her finger, like Merlin ah-ha'ing over a just-invented spell. "You said he—you know, Ade—the accident, I mean, was at a carpet shop in Fethiye, right?"

Paz and I nodded.

"Why don't we go there? Maybe the owners can tell us something. After all, it's their shop, right?" She paused, then I watched a sly smirk spread across her lower face and her eyes light up. "Plus, I really want to check it out. You know, the scene of the crime."

"For fuck's sake, Mal," said Paz, eyeing me sideways and tilting his head in my direction, "this isn't a game, you know."

Despite their closeness, the two sometimes butted heads. Now Mallie riposted to Paz's criticism brusquely. "Don't you think I know that?" Her dark eyes flashed. And then she turned toward me. "I just think we should do a little looking around on our own. I don't totally trust Mutt and Jeff, if you know what I mean." She was angry on the surface, but I could see that underneath that anger was a very sad person wanting to make things right. And I was with her on the distrust thing.

Paz, as usual, recanted his outburst by reaching over and putting his arm around her shoulder. "Okay, Babe, you're right." He turned toward me for affirmation. "What about you, Mole? You think it's worth going back to the carpet place? Maybe we *can* find out something. I kind of agree with Mal that those *jandarma* guys might not care about getting answers as much as we do."

My mind was reeling. My throat constricted. My skin felt like plastic sheeting. I was not sure what was real, what was illusion. All I knew was that Adrian was not here and that someone had done something nasty to him. If I could have dived into the Med, breaststroked out to the edge of time, pretended none of it had happened, I would have been happier.

It was not possible, of course. But, I could not face standing at the side of his bed again, staring at the shell of who he was. Anything would be better than that. Mallie's idea sounded like a good one.

"Yeah." I pursed my lips and nodded slowly. "You're right, Mallie. And Paz. I think it's exactly what we should do. If nothing else, we'll at least be out of this room for a little while, right? I'm suffocating in here."

My friends stared at me for a second, obviously trying to work out whether I was kidding or not. So I smiled at them.

"Then let's go," Paz announced. "But, in the morning. It's getting late and I don't think I can handle another *dolmuş* ride into town and back today."

෯   ෯   ෯

Thursday, June 9, 2005 - Fethiye

"Please, sit."

Bulut hovered behind his desk, but he gestured toward the hand-carved wooden bench pushed against the wall to the right of the desk.

"I will order some tea. Apple or normal?" The shopkeeper was stiff, almost old-fashioned. A fit man in his fifties, I guessed, he thrived on self-discipline and formality. One of an earlier generation. But his eyes shone with kindness and I liked him. Paz, Mallie and I hesitantly obeyed him, perching on the edge of the hard bench with our arms over our daypacks, as we each told him our *çay* preferences. I opted for the cold, refreshing *elma*, or apple, flavor.

We watched, perplexed, as he made a quick call on his outmoded, mustard-colored dial phone. He was ordering the *çay* from elsewhere. After hanging up, and seeing the confusion on our faces, he explained. "When you serve *çay* to customers all day, it is more easy to get from a

298

restaurant." He opened the long drawer in the center of his desk and pulled something out. A small pile of pot metal coins clinked on the desktop. "See?" Bulut continued. "I buy fifty lira of this tokens every month and I give them to the boy who brings the *çay*. A very good system. All the shop owners in Paspatur do this. Much cheaper, also."

We all nodded in agreement. It sounded logical. Saved Bulut from brewing different kinds of *çay* in his back room all day. That would get tiring, I supposed, especially when your real goal was to sell carpets.

But I wondered if Paz and Mallie were thinking what I was thinking. Which was this:

Was the restaurant Bulut got his tea from today the place that brought Adrian's yesterday? If so, perhaps we should politely not drink it when it arrived.

Just as I had come to this conclusion, and was wondering how to pass it on to my friends without announcing it aloud, a teenager, his short, black hair spiked like a hedgehog, rushed in the door carrying a large, round, silver tray suspended precariously from three bent wires. At their apex was a wooden handle, which the kid balanced above his shoulder with incredible dexterity. He had probably been delivering *çay* like this since he was a child. Bulut nodded at us and the boy deftly divvied our tulip glasses to us without a word or a smile. All business. After he handed Bulut his glass, Bulut threw four of the metal tokens onto the tray with a small clank. The kid scooped up the change, pocketed it, bowed curtly and then scarpered off with his empty tray.

I set my glass on top of my daypack and turned to Paz and Mallie. While Bulut was swiping the unused tokens back into his drawer, I nodded at my glass and forced my eyes open as wide as I possibly could. Then I shook my head side to side quickly.

Mallie, who was wedged in between Paz and me, made a silent "What?" face, but Paz nodded. He touched Mallie's hand, the one holding her *çay*. Then he shook his head. She shrugged. If she did not understand what Paz and I were getting at and started to take a sip, I knew he would stop her.

It seemed rude to reject our host's simple hospitality, and we were doing it as subtly as possible, but I figured it would be ruder for all of us to collapse on his floor. Adrian was one thing, but three more casualties on the following day was surely bad for business. Perhaps, while we were engaged in conversation, Bulut would not realize we were not lifting our glasses to our mouths. In any case, this *çay*-serving custom was so pervasive, I was sure many people accepted their *çay* without any intention of drinking it. The gesture was what counted. You could only drink so many glasses of the stuff in a day, after all. This reasoning made me feel less like a cad.

But now we knew that Bulut himself had not served Adrian the day before. I found myself relieved, as I rather liked the man. The question was...who had?

As it happened, Bulut, too, let his glass sit on his desk without taking a sip. But he looked at us pointedly and asked, "How may I help you?"

"Your English is very good," Mallie said. "Where did you learn it?"

Bulut beamed. "I was in Turkish army. I work as a translator for the Canadians." Here, he sat up a little straighter and lifted his chin slightly. "It was many years ago, but most of our customers speak English, so I always have chance to practice."

"Very interesting." Mallie was buttering the guy up, I realized, cajoling him to our side. She continued, "I didn't realize so many Americans bought Turkish carpets here."

"Oh, not so many Americans. Mostly British. But also my German and French customers speak English. It is how we all communicate these days." Our host looked downcast for a moment and then added, "Most Turkish people cannot afford to buy these." He waved his arm in the air. "I hand choose them myself and they are very good quality carpets. So, it is important that we sell to westerners. Otherwise, we will starve." He smiled, wanly.

"That's sad," said Mallie. Her sincerity was genuine, I knew. She was, after all, a mostly sympathetic soul. But she fed off this sincerity to adeptly segue into the matter at hand. Observing her, I was impressed.

"We, my friends and I," here, she dipped her head in Paz's and my directions, "were just wondering about our American friend. The one who was here yesterday?" She paused. "You know, the one who..."

Bulut interjected. "Yes, Mister Adrian, I know. Terrible. How is he?"

Paz interjected. Many Turkish men still adhered to a machismo protocol and I figured Paz thought his remarks would have more weight with Bulut than Mallie's. I was not sure Bulut was like other Turks in this regard, but I did not interrupt. Mallie, for once, did not object either. She was, I was pretty certain, focusing on the end game. That is, getting information about what happened the day before. She and Paz were so in synch sometimes, it was scary. I sat back and let them work on Bulut.

"Well, the last we heard, he was still in a coma. In intensive care," Paz answered.

Bulut bowed his head. "I am very sorry." He regarded all three of us. "I do not know what happened. So..." he gazed around his shop as if the words he was searching for were hidden among his towers of multi-colored carpets. Finally, he seemed to find the right word, though I had not noticed any of the carpets actually speaking to him. "...sudden. A shock. It is too bad because Mister Adrian is a nice man." He shook his head. His eyes glazed over.

"Yes, we are very upset, actually," continued Paz in a subdued tone. "He is our special friend. And that is why we came back here today. We want to find out why he collapsed. It doesn't make sense. We thought you could help us."

Bulut frowned. "I do not know how I can help. We were talking, all of us, and then he fell. Boom." His hand flapped toward the floor as if mimicking Adrian's fall.

"Who was talking?" asked Mallie. "Who else was in the room?"

Bulut's eyes shifted to one side in thought. "It was me, of course. And Gulya, my daughter." His eyes shone for a second at the mention of his offspring. "And you," he turned to Paz. "Mister Paz, correct?"

Paz shifted his body around. He looked uncomfortable. "Me? Not really. I came in just before he fell. I was not really talking."

Bulut nodded, "Yes, that is true, I think. I am not sure." He paused a moment, back in thought. "But there was another person."

"Yes?" asked Mallie, leaning forward. I reached out to steady her *çay* glass, just in case. "Who was that?"

"Ömer. Ömer-*Bey*."

The three of us looked toward each other. Mallie's eyes scrunched up in confusion. Paz shrugged. I felt blank.

"Who's *that,* how do you say, 'Oo-mur?'" Mallie's voice now took on a whispery quality. I could understand. This was a development she had clearly not expected. Nor had I.

I had never heard this name before. I was familiar with "Omar," from Omar Sharif, the famous movie actor. But this pronunciation was slightly different. The "O" sounded like "Oo," as Mallie had pointed out, and instead of "Mar," the second syllable was more of a "Muhr." Must be a Turkish version of the Arabic. Or something. Up to this point, I had kept silent. For one thing, my emotions threatened to erupt at any moment. Secondly, letting my pals carry on with their method of questioning meant I could pretend I was not involved. But now, I could not help butt in. Whoever this other person was, talking to Adrian and present at the time

301

of the accident, I wanted to know.

"Oo-Muhr? Who is this Oo-Muhr?" My voice cracked. As I said the name, my head felt light and I almost toppled my apple drink.

"Mister Ömer," Bulut replied. "He and your friend were chatting."

"They were?" Mallie asked. "Do you know what they were chatting about?"

Bulut shrugged. "I am sorry. I was sitting here," he indicated his desk, "filling out a purchase form. I made a sale just before Mister Adrian and Ömer-*Bey* came in. I did not hear what they were saying."

"Wait," continued Mallie. She almost jumped up. I eyed her tea glass warily. "They came in together?"

"Yes, of course." Famous Turkish last words. The people here used the phrase all the time. "Of course." It could mean almost anything. But in this case, I do not know why, I thought Bulut was telling the truth. Adrian *had* entered Bulut's Turkish carpet shop with this mystery man. Ömer.

"Do they know each other?" I asked.

Bulut nodded. "Yes, I think so. I have seen them together before. In the shop."

"You have?" Now I was really confused.

"Of course." That phrase again. And, again, I believed him. What I mean to say is, I believed he believed they knew each other. But it could not be, or I would have known about it. Who was this Ömer, and how would Adrian know him? Why would Adrian show up at this antique rugs shop with him? I thought Adrian was my best friend. More than my best friend. More, even, than my confidant. Yet, I had never heard him mention anyone named Ömer. I was completely perplexed. It must have been coincidence that they entered the shop at the same time. Otherwise, none of this made sense.

Except.

I thought back to the previous morning. When Adrian stood in our hotel doorway, cagily, as if he were trying to sneak out of our room without me noticing. I had been confused at the time. Why would he act like that? Why would he go back on our beach plans and lie to me about it? What was he up to? I had been curious then, hurt even, thinking he was just blowing me off. But now I wondered.

Was he up to something? Something he definitely did not want the rest of us to know about? Something unscrupulous? I shook my head. Not Adrian. He was an honest guy. Surely, I was jumping to conclusions in my distress and confusion.

I sat lost in my thoughts, trying to piece together the puzzle of the last two days, when a shadow filled the room. Bulut stood up suddenly, knocking over his undrunk tea. He scrambled around for something to clean the spill up with while nervously eyeing the door.

Paz and Mallie and I sat still and waited as a short, slightly portly Turkish man, with gray-tipped hair, entered the small shop. He had the kind of round head, flat at the back, that I had noticed on many local men in this area. I had found out from Cengis that that shape of head was known as the "Anatolian Bump." But I did not know why. The man's mustache was like Hitler's famous upper lip adornment, though less full. More like a fat, fuzzy caterpillar than a toothbrush.

After the man removed his CIA sunglasses from his eyes, I thought, even from ten feet away, that they reminded me of something. And then I realized. They were reptilian. Narrow and colorless and, strangest of all, devoid of expression.

A shudder snaked up my spine.

"Ömer-*Bey*," said Bulut, with a little bow of his head. "*Hoş geldin*."

"*Hoş geldiniz*," the "*hoş*" pronounced in English like "hoesh," meant "welcome," I knew. It was one of the first Turkish phrases I had ever learned back in 1998, that first trip to Turkey. Without the "iz" on the end, I figured Bulut's version was a variant of the phrase I knew, possibly related to pronoun usage. Pronouns in the Turkish language are usually not separate words as they are in English. They are implied in the different endings of whatever root word is being used. In this case, perhaps it was an informal form of welcome. Bulut knew Ömer.

"*Hoş geldin*," the short man replied. He dipped his head toward Bulut. Bulut bowed his head forward. When he spoke, this man Ömer sounded as if his voice had almost never changed. Or not completely. It was rather high and soft and, well, the way I heard it, "flappy." Offhand. Even echoey. I found it disconcerting. But Bulut did not seem to notice. He moved from behind his desk and, passing by Paz and Mallie and me on the bench, approached the man, almost reverently. He shook his hand.

"Let me introduce you to..." he paused, seemingly trying to remember our names. "This is Miss Mallie," he indicated Mal, "and Mister Paz and," then he looked at me with a confused expression.

"Molo," I said. "I'm Molo." I leaned forward and gently placed my *çay* glass on the floor by my feet, then stood up and strode over toward where the two men faced us. As I reached out to shake Ömer's hand, he did not move. In fact, he just stood there, staring at me, hands pressed into his sides, as if I were something offensive. A pile of camel dung, perhaps. His reaction was off-putting, to say the least, but not altogether disappointing. I already did not like the man and I was not really desperate to touch his flesh. I was merely being polite.

So much for that.

Mallie, no doubt observing the brush-off, came to my rescue. She rose from the bench, placing her undrunk *çay* glass in the spot I had myself just vacated, and stood facing the man called Ömer. She did not offer her hand, but instead asked a question. Two, actually.

"Do you know what happened to our friend, Adrian, yesterday? You were here when the ambulance came, right?" Mallie's tone was congenial, but I knew her. Her inner Boadicea lurked between the lines. I was sure she disliked this creature as much as I did. He reeked sinister.

Ömer hardly batted an eye. Perhaps he did not speak English. And yet, I felt that he understood.

Bulut translated, anyway.

Ömer's answer was an icy glare at Mallie. But she was not deterred.

"It's just that he was poisoned, you see. We're trying to find out how." She paused, looking at Ömer pointedly. "And why."

Bulut's eyes widened as he listened to Mallie and then he turned toward Ömer almost apologetically, a slight grimace on his face. Ömer's expression did not waiver. Instead, he waved his right hand a couple of times as if he were shooing a vexing mosquito away. I saw Paz pull his head toward his chin in disbelief. The guy was dissing Mallie! Blood pounded in my skull. I could almost hear it.

Was it my imagination, or was Bulut's voice quieter when he translated this second time? He seemed to shrink into himself as he transmuted what Mallie had just said into its Turkish version. I had to admit, in English her words had the air of accusation. I wondered if Bulut tempered his translation so as not to give offense.

Ömer shook his head quickly. But I did not think it was to say "no." Instead, it was another dismissive gesture, as if Mallie's speaking to him were the height of insolence. He actually sniffed in disdain, jerking his chin toward the ceiling. When he spoke, I did not understand his words, which came out abrupt and curt. But I got the subtext.

Mallie—we—were not worth his time. Bulut filled in the rest.

"Ömer-*Bey*, he say that you," he pointed to each of us in turn, "should not be here. He says what happened is not of your business and that you should go home to America."

Silence filled the room.

Now it was Paz's turn. He had remained remarkably quiet up until this moment. I had even vaguely wondered if he knew something that Mallie and I did not. He jumped off the bench and his *çay* glass flew onto the carpet underneath us, splattering golden liquid onto its woven surface. Normally, he would have apologized to Bulut for his clumsiness. Instead, he stepped right in front of Ömer, his eyes fuming and his face turning a deep brown red. Ömer did not flinch.

"What did he say?" Paz turned to Bulut and I could see his fingers twitching.

Bulut backed away from Paz toward a carpet tower that was almost as tall as he was. I thought for a moment that he was going to fall into it and knock the whole construction over. Like one of the twin towers collapsing. He put his hands out in front of him, too, afraid, I supposed, that Paz, in his anger, might punch him.

But Paz stayed where he was, fuming. Mallie reached out and grabbed his arm. "It's okay, Paz. Let it go. The guy's a jerkwad. He's not worth it." She gently pulled him back toward the bench and Paz let her. But his eyes were locked on Ömer's colorless, cold-blooded orbs.

Bulut, in the meantime, scrambled to the back of the shop. I could see him out of the corner of my eyes searching for something. I hoped he was not searching for a knife.

"Come on, guys. Let's get out of here," I said. "Mallie's right. This asshole," and I glared at Ömer, "is not worth our time. We shouldn't have come here." I thought for a moment, and swiveled to face Ömer. "We should just let the *jandarma* do their investigation. I'm sure Sergeant Demir and Officer Güven will find out who poisoned Adrian."

As I finished my pronouncement, Ömer shuffled his brown, pointy-toed shoes on the carpet and stuck his white, puffy hands into his pockets. His eyes narrowed into slits as he glowered at me. And then I knew. He could understand us. And even more than that, he knew something about Adrian. But he tightened his lips, the fur on his philtrum puffing out slightly, and remained clammed up.

Mallie, still holding onto Paz, began to drag him toward the front door of the shop. I saw Bulut head toward us and wondered if he meant to attack one of us in some way. Then I realized he was holding a dingy, striped handtowel, like one you would use to dry dishes. He was going to sop up Paz's tea.

I nodded to him, rueful, embarrassed. "I'm sorry, Bulut. We didn't mean to cause any trouble in your shop. We're leaving." I started for the door, behind Paz and Mallie.

"And thanks. Thanks for everything."

Mallie, Paz and I, squeezed through the open doorway. As we poured out onto the passageway outside, I felt a warmth wash over me, like liquid sunshine. Mallie scooped me up by the elbow and together the three of us, *socii in armis*, flowed down the pavement toward the busy street beyond.

I had never felt so glad to leave a place.

"What about that?" Mallie asked, pulling us along in her war-happy wake. "Some creep, huh?"

"He did it," Paz said.

"What did you say?" I asked.

"That bastard did it. He's the one who laced Adrian's tea with laburnum."

"You think so?" I asked.

"I know it."

ò   ò   ò

Friday, August 16, 2013, Late Afternoon - Fethiye

As tiny as it was, the face that peered out from beneath the surface of the large ruby ring in Paz's palm reminded me of someone, though I could not think who. It was in her eyes, sharp and intelligent and somehow challenging. Her cheeks were chiselled and her chin curved and soft. Around her oval face, hair fanned like a burning flame into the bevelled edges of the ring. The effect was disquieting. Whoever this visage was modelled after must have been an unusual person. A beauty, but not in the traditional sense.

Or was it only my imagination reading into the ring's surface this stunning image?

The three of us, Ömer, Barış and I continued to stare at the gem. I had no idea if the others saw what I saw beneath its surface. In any case, face or not, the ruby itself—and its setting—were spectacular. Time clicked by. No one spoke.

And then, one of the Okey players opened the door and everything changed.

Barış jumped out of his chair and made to grab the ring out of Paz's hand. But two things happened.

First, Paz was too quick for Leather-face and clasped the precious item within his palm once again, his fingers closing tightly around it. As he did so, he made some weird movements with both his hands around different parts of his body, miming misdirection like an overacting magician.

Second, the hem of Barış's jacket caught on the top rung of his metal chair, causing the chair to fall backwards and pulling the now furious Barış with it.

In the few seconds during which these two actions occurred, I stepped away from the table. Ömer, meanwhile, pushed his chair back and stood up, glaring at Paz. His confederate was on the floor scrambling furiously to unloose his coat from the toppled chair.

Paz smiled mischievously. Then he opened both his palms so Ömer could see.

They were empty. I could have kissed him.

As if on cue, we both turned and skedaddled out of the tiny cafe. The door ting-tinged our exit, and startled Okey players turned their heads as we threaded quickly between their tables on our way to the street beyond. I was fairly sure my oversized bag knocked a couple of Okey tiles onto the concrete floor. I heard them clacking and bouncing. But I did not look back or even attempt to apologize. Instead, Paz and I raced down the length of that block and made several turns onto random *sokaks* off the main drag, scattering ragged bands of cats gathered at overflowing trash bins. I was not sure who was the more desperate to escape trouble at that moment— them, or us.

It was not until we carved a labyrinthian path worthy of the one Daedulus designed for King Minos in ancient Crete that I had a chance to say anything. We stopped at a small park of sparse grass that no doubt served the apartment buildings surrounding it. A couple of small kids were riding fiberglass horses on springs. My long hair clung to my face and I was holding my sides, sucking down air. Paz bent forward at the waist, ragdoll style, almost choking with breathlessness. It took us both a couple minutes, during which Paz returned his torso to vertical, for us both to breathe almost normally. Then, I finally managed to gasp out my question.

"What the hell was all that about?"

My enigmatic friend burst into a paroxysm of laughter. I was too exhausted to do anything but watch him, astounded. When he was finished, he looked at me, winked and shook his head slowly.

"Those assholes. I couldn't stand it anymore. So I just decided to bring it all to a head."

"Bring *what* all to a head? You've lost me, dude."

"The ring, of course." He looked at me as if I had just flown down from Planet Z.

"Yeah, the ring. What's with that? It's stunning, for sure. And it certainly got O and B worked up. Why's that, do you think?"

"I don't think. I know."

He was being cryptic again. True Paz. No matter that he could barely breathe and had come close to getting slaughtered in a bar brawl. Or, rather, a cafe brawl. My *High Noon* comparison awhile earlier had not been so far off the mark, after all.

"Know *what*?" I asked. I could hear the exasperation in my voice. I was so confused about the whole state of affairs, it was as if my brain was trapped in a labyrinth of its own.

Paz twisted side to side a couple times, his arms windmilling in the slight afternoon breeze. When done gyrating, he stared off into space, made that sideways smirk of his and blew out a puff of breath. Then he turned to me. "Mole, I gotta say, for a smart guy, sorry, whatever you are," here, he grimaced and looked at me apologetically before continuing, "you're kind of slow on the uptake." He paused. "Sometimes."

I rolled my eyes. "Come on, Paz. What the hell is going on? What happened back there?"

I pointed my thumb in what I hoped was the direction of the Okey place, though I was probably wrong, just as I had been wrong two days before in Istanbul and Paz had to steer me on the right course back to the Beşik. Direction had never been my strong suit, I had to admit. At least, not since 2005. And, just now, I began to suspect that this defect did not just apply to streets and points on a map. It was as if for years I had been going down when I should go up. Or looking here when I should have been looking there. Even, I thought, glancing down my body at the clothes I was wearing, believing I was *this* when I was really *that*.

As I stood there in the scrappy park with the afternoon clouds beginning to descend on the Fethiye vista, the image of Naji popped into my head unbidden. That irritating *djinn* kept dogging me. He was driving me nuts, but somehow I sensed he was still nagging at me to remember what he had said the other night in the Sultanahmet. I narrowed my eyes in concentration. But it was no use. I still could not quite clutch what it was he had told me. The straws were as elusive as ever. But maybe they were getting a little more tangible. After all, Paz and I had made headway regarding Ömer. I might not be getting my revenge on him the way I had

308

originally planned when I flew over to Istanbul but, with Paz's help, I had gotten down to Fethiye where Ömer *really* lived, and we had made contact. We had even upset that infuriating equanimity of the man I knew had brought about Adrian's demise. Whatever Naji had tried to warn me about, I had a hunch it had to do with that. At least, in part.

My mental perambulations were interrupted when Paz stepped up to me and put his hand on my shoulder. "Let's go back to Can's. I'll buy you a super deluxe *lahmacun* and while we eat I'll tell you everything."

I looked at him, my eyes narrowing in suspicion. Again. "You said you already told me everything."

"I know. I lied." He shrugged. "Sorry."

☙   ☙   ☙

Friday, August 16, 2013, Later That Evening - Çalış Beach

When we were safely ensconced at a streetside table under Can's draping, fruit-laden grapevine, waiting for our Turkish pizzas, I asked the question I had tried to ask when we were chasing our nemeses from the mosque courtyard. The question Paz had never had the chance to answer because they had suddenly crossed the street to the *High Noon* cafe. It was only a few hours hence and yet it seemed like a week ago.

"So, you didn't know about the notes that were left in my book."

"What notes?" Paz took a casual sip of his Efes beer, straight from the blue and gold-labeled bottle. He looked genuinely perplexed. "You asked me that earlier on, but I haven't a clue what you're talking about."

"You're sure? Because you've been a little sketchy on the whole truth thing lately."

"Fair enough. And I'm about to tell you why. But, scout's honor," he raised his right arm, palm facing me, and held up three fingers in the famous salute before continuing. "I don't know anything about notes in books. But I want to. Sounds mysterious." With the saluting hand, he snapped up his beer bottle, downed another mouthful of beer and wiped his mouth on the back of his free hand.

"You can say that again. It was when I was at the Beşik the other night. The first night. After Barış the Bastard 'escorted' me to your hideout and then we went back to catch up at the bar. Remember?"

Paz nodded his head slightly. "Of course. But I wasn't hiding, just so you know."

309

I ignored his interjection. "Anyway, after you left the Beşik and I went back up to my room, I knew immediately that something was not right."

"Really?"

"I checked everything and then I finally figured it out."

"Yeah?"

"It was my book."

"What book?"

"My Daphne du Maurier book. *The House on the Strand.* I brought it with me to read on the plane and I put it on the dresser thingy in my room."

"Wait a minute. Du Maurier, you say? Wasn't that the author of that book with the laburnum poisoner in it? The one we saw on Google when Adrian was in the hospital?"

"Yep, that's her. Good memory. But that was a different novel. Though it is a bizarre coincidence, come to think of it. But, to continue, I realized the book was in the wrong position."

"'Cuz you're anal retentive."

"Haha. And, I knew that it had shifted sometime between when I came back down from my room with lira for the drinks and when I went back up to bed. Because on the earlier trip, everything was normal."

"So, what's the mystery then?"

"The mystery is this." I fumbled at my waist to pull my shirt out from my pants, unzipped my passport pouch and pulled out the two notes I had stuffed in there. I handed the bigger note across the table to Paz. It was the one with the cryptic design on it:

Paz carefully placed his Efes on the table and scrutinized the drawing under the deep amber beam of the sodium lamp that shone down on us from the street a few meters away. He looked perplexed.

"What's this?"

"Good question. You don't know?"

"Noooo, I don't think so."

"I didn't either. Not for awhile. But I figured it out. It was something you said last night." I cocked my chin and scanned the patio. "When we were here, actually."

"I don't have a clue what you're talking about."

"Remember when you were me asking me if I had an old Turkish rug?"

"Vaguely."

"Well, this is it. When you asked me, I had a sudden epiphany about it."

"About what?"

"My carpet, you idiot. Are you listening?"

"What carpet?"

"The one my mother gave me years ago. The one that's in a box in my apartment. The one you were hinting about last night. Now do you get it?"

Paz stared at me for a second, then he studied the note again, turning it this way and that a couple of times. Finally, his eyes lit up.

"Holy shit! It's *the* carpet!"

"Yes, *the* carpet. Bingo."

Paz whistled between his teeth. "That's the one Adrian was telling me about."

"I'm pretty sure. Though I don't know why. Do you?"

My friend swished his mouth side to side a few times, and his eyes flicked back and forth. "Not exactly. The only thing I know is it has something to do with the ring."

Now it was my turn to be surprised. "The ring?"

"Yes, indeedy, the ring."

"I don't get it."

"I'm not sure I do either."

"And yet you have it, right? And you knew that Ömer was looking for it..."

Before Paz could answer, I pulled the other, smaller, note out of my pouch and pushed it across the table at him. "Then there's this."

SILK ROAD CARPET SHOP, SAN FRANCISCO

"What is it?" he asked.

"It's the other note I found in my book."

He looked confused, staring at it, so I elaborated. "It fell out last night. You don't know what it means?"

311

He nodded "no," his eyes fixed on the paper in front of him.

"I didn't either. Except today, when we were at Bulut's, I noticed his shop is basically the same name: 'Silk Road Carpet Shop.'" I wobbled my head back and forth like a bobble doll's. "Obviously, not the one in San Francisco. But, also obviously, they've gotta be connected."

Paz slid the note back to me and immediately cupped his hands around his beer bottle. It was as if he needed something to hang onto. When he began to tilt the bottle back and forth, I could tell from its movement that the bottle was nearly empty. Paz signaled for Can, who was serving a British couple nearby. When Can shuffled over to our table, Paz said,

"*Başka bir bira, lütfen*, Can, my friend. As cold as possible, okay?"

Can nodded and hobbled through the glass sliding doors to the inside dining area of his restaurant. It was also nearly empty. Most of the patrons had opted for al fresco dining.

Paz leaned forward. "I think I need another cold one. My brain is overheating."

I leaned forward, too. Our faces were within inches of each other.

"And, by the way, where did you come by that ring, Paz? What does it have to do with my ratty old carpet? And Ömer? Or, for that matter, Adrian?"

Our eyes were locked in a conunbrum of questions. Around us the gloam of the evening engulfed us in a tug-of-war of chiaroscuro lighting. Shadows from the engulfing night battled with the waning swatches of day sky. The dark seemed to be winning. But at least I felt I was closing in on answers, answers that had lain concealed in a box for eight long years, hiding, waiting for the lid to be removed at last, so they could finally embrace the luminescence they had been seeking.

"I think I can answer that."

And someone snatched the Silk Road Carpet Shop scrap paper out of my fingers.

At the same time, a different shadow, elongated and undefined, loomed diagonally across the table, across Paz's arms and mine where they poised, tense and still. Its sudden appearance made me tremble. More disconcerting than the tenebrous silhouette, however, was the voice that had just perforated the lingering silence. It was a quiet, pleasant voice. Youthful, male. Familiar. And one I had not heard in a long, long time.

I turned my head to my right and glanced behind me. As I did, Paz knocked his just-drunk beer bottle onto the brick floor. A crash of glass shattered the heavy stillness, and Paz swore. The couple at the table behind us immediately called for Can to clean up the mess. I heard their shrill voices yell out, but the sound was muffled. In fact, everything around me slipped into a kind of haziness except for one thing.

"Adrian?"

My voice croaked. I was not even sure whether it had actually spoken. It came from a far off place, a land inhabited by visions and misbegotten memories, smoke-filled thoughts and musty musings. Was I dreaming? Was I so overwrought with tension and stress that I had entered another world beyond the present? A realm of my own imaginings? It was possible. And yet...

The streetlight's beam was real. It cast a golden glow across the figure at my shoulder and the face I had longed for for so long and deemed long gone. When it smiled, its eyes, those peridot apertures I had once known like my own, gazed down at me, both shining and sad. I turned away, afraid of the emotions that swelled inside me.

"Molo," said the voice. "It's been a roller coaster, hasn't it?"

I blinked back tears, gathering in force behind the barricade of my stoic facade. Now, long fingers squeezed into my tingling flesh, and the tension of time melted away.

I heard myself reply, "You can say that again. But not in a good way." I nearly choked on the words as they tumbled out of my mouth.

Adrian spoke once more, releasing his grip from my shoulder. "I'm sorry. I don't know if you'll believe me, but I never meant for all this to happen." He glanced down at the paper in his hands.

Paz had recovered from his own shock by now and blurted out, "Adrian? What? How?" He drooped back in his chair like a wilted leaf, or a deflated balloon.

Adrian, for it could only be him, after all, and not the revenant I feared I had conjured up, reached across the small aisle with his free hand, grabbed a seat from another table, and plonked it down at ours. Slowly, his long legs slipping into place as they had sixteen years ago in our Giant Dipper car the day we met, he sat down. Then he placed both of his tapered hands on the edge of the table. One of them still clutched the Silk Road note. I eyed it there, wondering why Adrian had seized it from me so hastily.

Just then Can strode up, nodded at our old friend, whom he must have remembered from our earlier times dining there, and plunked down a frosty bottle. Paz reached out for it absentmindedly, still staring at the apparition of Adrian. The errant Apollo had returned at last and we, his congregants, could see that he had not expired, as we had supposed, but had merely continued on his inevitable course, the immutable path of his non-earthly orbit.

"Could I have one of those, too?" asked Adrian. His silky, seraphical tone echoed through the twilight encircling us in its now warm embrace.

"Of course," answered Can. "You wish to order a *pide*, Mister Adrian?" Ah, the remarkable recollection of the Turkish businessman. I marveled that he remembered Adrian's name after all this time.

Adrian bestowed a celestial smile on the ever-affable restaurateur. "*Evet*. Just bring me whatever you think I'll like."

Can blinked his sloe-eyes and tipped his head forward sharply, the way the people in this atavistic land do, and limped away. It was like watching Samantha in the 60s television show *Bewitched*, except that Can was larger than Samantha—and not nearly as good looking. But, I was pretty sure he was not casting a spell, unless the spell was in the form of enchantingly delicious dishes he was conjuring up in the kitchen. And, anyway, we were already under a spell—or coming out of one. The spell of Adrian. After Can had gone, our prodigal friend swiveled his head to the left, toward me, and then to the right, toward Paz and said,

"I guess I have a lot of explaining to do."

"You can say that again," said Paz. He picked up his beer and took a long swig.

ॐ   ॐ   ॐ

Chapter 22

*"Lords of Thebes, I and the boy have come together, hand in hand. Two
sees with the eyes of one...so the blind must go, with a guide to lead the
way." - Teiresius, the blind seer, speaking to King Creon in Antigone,
Scene V, by Sophocles*

*O*n a sky-blown, blustery day the youth known as Teiresius, Theban
son of Eures and of Chariklo, wandered through the valleys of
Arcadia and wiped his sweat-damp brow. He came to a copse in
the wood wherein two snakes lay, entwined and writhing in sexual
embrace. The lad was suitably repulsed at the scene before him.
Thereupon, he thrashed the coupling reptiles. In a moment, the serried
scales of the female snake stopped quivering. She lay on the ground before
Teiresius, dead.

Goddess Hera, observing the scene from her throne on Olympus,
jumped up in anger that the brash young man should smite her creatures
thus. In retaliation, she turned upon Teiresius, smote him, and transformed
him into a woman to replace the snake he had slaughtered.

Teiresius thence became one of Hera's virginal female slaves. She
remained thus for seven long years.

But one day, Teiresius the woman chanced upon two snakes copulating
in the woods as before. This time, remembering her earlier fate, she let
them be. As soon as she had done so, Hera made a decision to reverse her
curse at last, and returned Teiresius to her former self.

He became a man again.

       ॐ   ॐ   ॐ

Thursday, June 9, 2005 - Fethiye

We hovered around Adrian's bed, wordless. What was there to say?
Nothing had changed. He was still unconscious. Doctor Karatepe told us

315

there was zero we could do. We left.

At the *jandarma* command office one block off Fethiye Sahil Yolo, the coastal road a few blocks from the hospital, we asked for Sergeant Demir. He could not—or would not—see us, but Officer Güven came out, lips pursed and face as impenetrable as Constantine's eponymous Walls of Constantinople. He had to summon another, even younger, officer to translate. Mallie was not impressed, despite my attempts to mollify her by saying it was not the *jandarma's* obligation to speak English with us.

Güven waved his arm floppily, beckoning, and the three of us, plus the translator, followed him into a small office at the back of the building. Fortunately, the shabby standing fan in the corner was already switched on, its disk-shaped head oscillating reluctantly. Every time it came to a certain spot in its rotations, it clicked four or five times before continuing on its tedious journey. There were only enough chairs for Güven and two others. Mallie and Paz sat in the hard, slat-wood seats. Clearly, the chairs were designed to discourage long visits, so Mallie, who had elected herself spokesperson (with no argument from Paz or me) got to the point quickly.

Güven answered her questions reluctantly.

What we did—or did not—find out was this:

1) Demir and Güven had questioned Bulut at his shop, but they were satisfied he did not know anything about where the laburnum could have come from or how it made its way into Adrian's tea,
2) There was no evidence that the laburnum had been meant for Adrian in particular; therefore,
3) It had probably gotten into his tea by accident and, in conclusion,
4) No indication of foul intent was evident, so
5) No one was to blame for Adrian's coma.

Güven would not budge on this pronouncement. The fan clicked in agreement. From behind the large gunmetal-gray desk, Güven flashed us the document of the inquiry with blue-purple ink squares stamped onto each page. Inside each serrated square was a set of initials scribbled in black ball-point pen. Güven shrugged his shoulders. It was all very official. Nothing more they could—or would—do.

Paz interrupted at one point. "What about that man Ömer? He was there. He was in the room when I came in. Did you question him?"

The translator squirmed. He was standing at the end of the desk near Güven's chair. At the mention of Ömer's name Güven's eyes went blank

316

and his face stony. His head turned toward the photo of Atatürk on the wall to his left as the translator asked Paz's questions. Even I could see he was not interested. But what he said in response—in English, no less—surprised all of us.

"Ömer-*Bey* is good man. We do not need to question him."

Paz and Mallie almost jumped out of their chairs. Mallie shouted, "What do you mean? He's a suspect, isn't he?"

"No one is suspect. Case is closed. Finished." Güven's English was thick, but we understood him well enough. What he really meant was, he was finished with us. As if on some unspoken cue, our translator slunk back toward the wall and slumped there. He stared down at his pointy black shoes.

Officer Güven scooted his chair away from the desk, stood up and eyed each of us in turn. He indicated the door and said, "I tell you everything. Now you must go."

"What about Adrian?" Mallie blurted out. "He's in the hospital."

"Your friend not our problem. Good-bye." Güven reached forward to pick up the remarkably thin pile of papers that made up Adrian's file, tapped the pages' edges so that they all lined up neatly, and shoved them into a blue file folder. He stepped from behind his desk and headed to the door. Then he nodded once and left. The translator immediately followed, though he had the decency to turn his head back and grimace apologetically.

After the two men had gone, Mallie hoisted her hands to her hips. "What the hell was that about? We should try to see Sergeant Demir again. Maybe we can just wait in the foyer for him."

Paz took one of Mallie's arms and pulled on it gently. "Forget about it, Mal. It's over. They're not going to look into it anymore."

"Forget about it? How can I? It's Adrian!"

I had said very little during the entire proceeding; I had not known what to say. But now I spoke, dredging the words up from the depths of my being. "Mal, Paz is right. We're in a foreign country and they have different rules here. We're just visitors. Demir isn't going to do any more for us than this guy. I think we should just get out of here." I smiled wanly. "Before we get arrested for loitering or something."

Mallie stood there for a minute, incandescent with indignation, and Paz and I just watched her, as we had so many times before when her hackles had been raised. In a few moments more, she huffed loudly, dropped her hands and shook Paz free. "Well, it all sucks. I'm going back to the hospital.

At least we can see if Adrian's come around." She glanced at Paz, her eyes still ablaze with anger, then at me. "You guys can come or not. I don't care."

Then she jounced out of the small room, her black ponytail bouncing along with the same ferocity as its owner.

Paz and I eyed each other, then silently followed. The oscillating fan click-clacked behind us, its mechanical version, I supposed, of a salutary send-off. Either that, or its opposite.

When we arrived back at the hospital, our buddy Ferhat at the check-in informed us.

Adrian was gone.

⇛   ⇛   ⇛

Friday, August 16, 2013, Late Evening - Fethiye

I could not help it.

In the dim shadows of the falling night, I could not but think the creature to my right, the one now chewing enthusiastically on a fully-loaded chicken *pide* supreme, might be an illusion, an apparition, after all. Something Paz might have pulled out of his magician's bag. Adrian's profile was the same one I remembered: gently sloping forehead; the nose at its base a slender, truncated isosceles; wide, insouciant nostrils; narrow, dented cheeks; a long mouth with slightly fleshy lips that curved upwards like the ends of a small fishing boat. In the past, I could have sailed away on them and never looked back to shore. But when a wispy forelock fell over his face and I noticed he no longer wore his hair long, the enchantment evaporated and I landed—thump—back in my seat on a brick-paved patio in the heat of an August Ottoman night.

A mosquito buzzed in my ear and I swatted it.

While Paz and Adrian chowed and chatted, oblivious to my mental peregrinations, I checked my palm for insect blood. And it came to me. If anyone had changed in these years of separation, it was not Adrian. It was me. No one ever said much about it. Even Adrian had not mentioned it when he sat down by me, a fact that I now realized was rather odd. For it was pretty evident. To anyone who had known me before June 2005, that is. And that included Adrian.

I wiped my gooey palm on my thigh, the sticky gore reminding me of a dream I had had once, a few months after my return to the States. After the Adrian incident. In the dream, I stripped naked and covered my entire body

318

with red paint. When I had done, I entered a hall with a strangely ornate mirror and, standing in front of it, saw myself transformed into a thing of rapturous beauty, of glowing, iridescent radiance. That was when I had made my decision. It seemed so right. As if my subconscious self had been telling me what I needed to do.

And so...

I had grown my hair, and it often hung in lengthy waves down my back, though in this heat I tied it up and knotted it on top of my head. Surely, Adrian had noticed. There were other changes though. I wore make-up nowadays, even if I only had time to brush on a bit of mascara. I sometimes wore dresses, nothing too elegant, but loose-fitting, flowing, colorful and light. Like tonight. After Paz's and my earlier escapade with Ömer and Barış, I had felt soiled and gross and needed to escape into my current incarnation. Dresses were freeing somehow. I had gotten used to them. Had gotten used to the chilly breezes brushing my now-shaven legs. Had adapted to the strange looks from people on the streets of Santa Cruz. Had learned to ignore my parents' reproachful glances. I had even altered my name. In other words, I had almost completely transformed, both outwards and in.

I had become the other me, prompted by Adrian's disappearance. His death. Or what I had thought was his death. With his death had come my rebirth. Or what I thought was my rebirth.

Now, I sat with my two companions and reflected on what I had done.

And wondered why.

Had I hated myself so much after losing Adrian in Fethiye that I needed to remake myself into the image I thought he might have preferred to the real me?

At the hospital on that desolate June day eight years back when Ferhat announced that Adrian was gone, something in me flipped. Retreated. We, Mallie, Paz and me, had boarded the *dolmuş* back to the Mavi Dolfin Evi, changed our return plane tickets, packed our (and Adrian's) bags and taken the long bus trek back to Istanbul the next day. We had barely spoken the entire trip. Then we flew home. A couple of months later I had had my cathartic dream and stopped returning my friends' calls and emails.

And here I was.

Adrian paused in his chewing and smiled at me. I shook my head and said, "Now what? Are you going to tell us what all this is about?"

Paz added, "Not to mention, where you've been all these years."

Adrian looked sheepish. Then he nodded. "I guess I owe you guys that

319

much."

"I'll say," I said, crossing my legs. "And more."

We ordered more drinks—I decided to break my alcohol ban and asked for a *rakı,* Paz eyeing me in surprise—and leaned back in our chairs.

ॐ　　　ॐ　　　ॐ

Adrian's Story

"I worked in a carpet shop, believe it or not, in San Francisco. Silk Road Carpet Shop it was called. The store's address was a small street in Pacific Heights, not too far from the Presidio. Funny thing, too, the building was about ten blocks from Turk Street. I thought that pretty hilarious, considering what happened later on.

"I'd been there maybe a year or so, you know, making a few extra bucks for school, trying to talk people into buying crazy-priced carpets or some of the collectable furniture that our backroom staff reupholstered with hand-woven *kilim* and stuff.

"One day, this man comes in. Turkish. A real Turk, from somewhere on the south coast. He's this short guy with a square head and he's wearing Ray-Bans, pointy shoes and a giant gold ring on one hand. When he took his sunglasses off, I noticed right away that his eyes were strange. Like, soulless. He never smiled.

"He wanted to talk to Halki; that was the owner. He told me this in very simple English and by making gestures with these thick, mealy hands. So, I led him to our office and before I turned away to go back onto the floor, I heard Halki call the man 'Ömer-*Bey.*' Well, I didn't really quite catch the name at the time; it wasn't one I was familiar with. But I got a sense of it, anyway. I also got the impression that my boss and this Ömer person knew each other from the old country. I left them to their reunion.

"About an hour later, Halki comes out of the office with Ömer. He's agitated, excited, he's got this weird smile on his face and I know something is up. After introducing me to Ömer, so that I now know how to pronounce the name, he asks me if I'd like to make some extra money. I wasn't sure at first, but Halki assures me how great it would for me and also that it was for a really good cause. I wondered how good a cause it could be if it had to do with antique rugs, but after Halki patting me on the back and telling me I was his best worker and all that crap, I thought, 'Sure, why not? I could use the bucks.' Halki was only paying me minimum wage. I really had no idea what I was getting myself into. I have no doubt now that Halki was counting on a hefty commission from this scheme.

"Anyway, they take me back to the office and close the door. This Ömer dude stands in the corner the whole time, watching me with those creepy eyes, while Halki explains my 'assignment.' And this is where it gets strange.

"Once upon a time, in Constantinople, the capital of the Ottoman Empire, as you guys know, there ruled a sultan called Mehmed VI Vahideddin. The Empire was in a shambles after World War I. In 1922, Mehmed was deposed by a committee led by Mustafa Kemal, you know, Atatürk, who wanted the country to go in a new direction. So Mehmed and his entire family were exiled. Most of them moved to Malta in November 1922. Not long after, Constantinople became known as Istanbul, the capital of the new Turkish Republic.

"But Mehmed, like his forebears, kept a harem in his palace. Dolmabahçe Palace. We never saw it during our trips, because it's farther up the Bosphorus even than Galata, and we never went that far when we were there. But to continue the story, even though he was married a few times, Mehmed also slept with his favorite concubines. One of them, according to Halki, was a young carpet weaver. There was a rumor around the palace that this carpet-making girl stole something from Mehmed, from his chambers. Something very valuable. He sent his men to get it back from her, but the palace was in turmoil with the new political pronouncement. Before they could get the item back, the girl had disappeared. They think she hid the item in a carpet she had woven. There was a hand-drawn template of its design on some paper they found on the floor stuck under her loom. But the carpet itself was nowhere to be found. Just like the girl.

"If times had been different then, apparently, the harem miscreant would have been flushed out and punished. But Mehmed left suddenly, and the palace was taken over by Kemal, who was soon to be elected Turkey's new president. No one cared about the ex-sultan's missing object.

"Halki continued to explain to me that the girl's family traveled to the palace in order to take her back to their home in Manisa. Her parents had sold her into the sultan's service when she was ten, but now that the sultan had been deported from Turkey, she was free. They didn't find her.

"Her given name was Nexdaxe Dcchen. She was Ubyhk, a tribe from the Caucasus region. But by the time Nexdaxe was born, 30,000 Ubykhs had migrated to Anatolia to escape Russian insurgences. A lot of the 30,000 ended up in Balıkesir Province, north of Manisa, and that's where Nexdaxe was taken from. Once she entered the sultan's retinue, she was given a different name. All the harem women received new names when they arrived at the palace. No one knows what Nexdaxe's original was replaced with. That, of course, made her difficult to trace.

"However, Halki told me, the carpet she wove, the one they believe she took with her when she vanished from Dolmabahçe, reappeared. And guess where it turned up?"

Paz and I had been listening to this extraordinary tale with rapt attention. I had hardly noticed the mozzies nipping at my bare arms. But Adrian's question yanked us back to the present. By then, our plates lay coagulated with the remnants of our meals and the sodium streetlight held us all within its amber embrace. I felt like we were actors under a spotlight on a stage with no audience beyond. Paz and I raised our shoulders and splayed our palms upwards. Adrian's question had to be rhetorical because it was clear we would have no clue as to its answer.

Adrian grinned.

"Hang on, guys, this is where the weird scenario gets even weirder, believe it or not," he went on.

Paz and I leaned back in our chairs. The moon was glimmering above us now, not full, though not a sliver either. But she was very close. I thought there was a word for the part of her cycle when she is closest to Earth. But I could not recall what that word was. I stared at her glowing visage while I recrossed my legs and waited for Adrian to go on with his story.

"It turned up in a 1920s Craftsman bungalow in Santa Cruz." His eyes burrowed into mine as he mentioned the bungalow. I sat up, uncrossing my legs, and bracing my hands on the table's edge. My brain was buzzing louder than the mosquitos.

"It turns out, the owners wanted this rug looked at, to see if it was authentic or had any value. They contacted the Silk Road Carpet Shop in San Francisco for advice. Halki's father drove down to Santa Cruz one day to valuate the thing. He took a few photos of it, as well. But he told the couple who had asked for help that even though it was, indeed, a vintage weave, it was not particularly valuable. He also noted the blemish on its backside where wax had gotten into the weft and become cracked and discolored. That damage lowered the value of the rug. And he went away. The woman was disappointed—the carpet had passed to her from her grandmother—and she put it in a box to give to her son. Or so the story goes."

322

What was he saying? I shook my head. Adrian's last few sentences reminded me of something. And then I realized. He was talking about...

"Shit! My carpet!"

"Hold on. Before you say anything more, Molo," said Adrian, holding his right hand up. "I'm not done."

I slumped back in my chair.

"The thing is," Adrian continued, "Halki's father, after he took the photos, eventually had them developed—this was in the good old days before digital, you know—but he just stuffed them in a file folder. They stayed there for a few years. But one day, Halki was organizing and came upon the pictures. He was intrigued. Something about the design of the rug shown in the photos sparked a memory. He remembered a rumor going around in the Turkish carpet circuit about this unusual carpet that came from Mehmed VI's reign and that had disappeared with the harem girl who had taken something of value from the sultan. So, Halki photocopied the photos and sent those copies to a carpet shop owner in this place called Fethiye. And you both know what *that* is, right? Their shops even had the same name! They knew each other from conferences and meetings back home.

"It turns out, the Fethiye carpet shop guy was named—you guessed it—Ömer. Our pal. He didn't run the shop, but he owned it. Well, Ömer had inside information. He'd been in the business for a long time and, I have to add, I've found out since that he's got his mitts into all kinds of stuff."

"Yeah," I interjected. "We found out."

Adrian nodded and smiled at me. My throat tightened. Then he continued his monologue.

"So, Ömer recognizes the carpet in Halki's photocopies as the one that matches that hand-drawn paper design that the girl weaver had left behind back in 1922. He had been looking for this carpet for years, but no one in the business could tell him where it had gone to. It had simply vanished.

"The thing is, he wanted the carpet because it was valuable in its own right—for being from the palace of the last sultan of the Ottoman empire, yes. But also because, and this is where it gets really crazy, he was absolutely convinced it was the key to the sultan's missing item. The item supposedly stolen by Nexdaxe."

"Let me guess," blurted out Paz. "A ring. *The* ring." He proferred his fist and opened up his palm for us all to gaze at the precious jeweled band in question.

"Exactly," said Adrian, snapping his fingers.

"But where do you come in?" I asked. "I still don't understand."

"Hold on, Molo, I'm getting to that." He plucked the ring out of Paz's hand and held it reverently, turning it this way and that, its deep, ruby-ness glinting under the streetlight's cast. I even thought the woman inside it winked at me. But I knew that could not be true. Then Adrian handed the jewel back to Paz. "Be careful with that thing, brother."

Paz dutifully shoved the ring back into his pocket. I watched, perplexed. Why was he putting it in his pocket again when, actually...?

Adrian broke my chain of thought with his next words.

"So, this Ömer character explains to Halki that he wants me to make friends with the son of the people who have the carpet. That way, I can finagle my way into getting close to the carpet itself. He instructed me what to look for when I got access."

My head was swimming, the world started to recede again, and I could feel myself turning red, almost as deep a shade as the ruby.

"You mean, that day at the pier...you weren't there by accident?"

Adrian shook his head. His lips turned into each other in a line, a scar across his lower face. And though his eyes held a kind of sadness in them, I suddenly felt an explosion welling up inside me, like a volcano about to blow.

"You asshole! You scheming, cheating bastard. I trusted you, I believed you were my friend. All these years I felt like shit that I had let you down. That I'd betrayed you. And all along, from the very fucking start, it was you who betrayed me. You used me!"

As I screamed, I burst out of my chair so quickly that it overturned, taking my bag with it as it banged onto the brick flooring. The chair was plastic, so there was no damage, but the vehemence of my movements and my anger crashed through the still night. My hands had flown to my hips during my tirade.

The restaurant was nearly empty now, but Can dragged himself over to the double-wide sliding door and gawked at us with his huge, round eyes. "Okay?" he asked, nodding.

"It's okay," said Adrian, pressing his palms downwards into the still air a few times. "No worries." Can nodded and disappeared into the recesses of his lair.

I was still standing there by my upturned chair, fuming, but I lowered my voice into a harsh whisper. "What's wrong with you, Adrian? Do you know what you've done? How frickin' devastated I was," I tipped my head toward Paz, who had grabbed the armrests on his chair, ready to leap up if

324

needed, "how devastated all of us were? When you, well, when we 'thought' you'd died. Jesus! I can't believe all this."

I felt like crying. But I would not allow myself. Instead, I leaned over, quietly picked up the upturned chair and sat down.

Throughout my harangue, Adrian sat silently. His face looked ashen. Distraught. "I'm sorry, Mole. Truly, truly sorry. Sit down, buddy. Let me finish, okay? I want to tell you the rest of this thing before Can kicks us out."

I wanted to shake his neck, thump his face into the table and kick him. But, as always, his voice had that effect on me, that calmed me and seduced me into caving to his wishes. I could not ever seem to help it. So I sat, unmoving. I was still shaking, though. My hair knot had come loose and now my long mane hung about my face. I brushed it aside. When I had settled a bit, Adrian smiled at me, a rueful smile, those boat lips turning up ever so slightly, and then he continued.

"So, I did as I was asked. I thought I'd meet you, see the carpet, extract the thing for Ömer, get my money, and be done. Easy peasy."

I smirked. "Nice."

"But, listen, Molo. When I met you, I liked you straight off. I'm not lying. How you were reading that stupid pier sign out loud, and so obsessed with roller coasters and shit. I'd never met anyone like you."

"Hmmph."

"I mean it! Believe it or not. But still, it's true, I did what Ömer requested. I asked you if you had any cool memorabilia around, and you pulled out that cardboard box. I never mentioned the carpet. But I sent you into the kitchen to get some snacks, remember?, and while you were gone, I fished out the carpet and scrambled around trying to find the ring. I didn't think I would, especially after all these years. But, there it was, buried in the depths of the wool and covered with dried up wax. I had a Swiss Army knife on me and, sorry, but I had to cut some of the woof and weft away in order to get the ring. Nexdaxe had actually woven the band deep into the pile. And I guessed she had used the wax for double protection, keeping it in place. Clever. She already knew she was going to take it out of the palace. Though I'm not sure why.

"Anyway, just before you got back from the kitchen, I thrust the ring into my pocket, pretended I had barely noticed the carpet, and, well, that was that."

Paz and I stared at each other. I could see he was just as dumbfounded as I was hearing this absurd explanation. The whole spiel was almost as unbelievable as some of Paz's own tricks. So much for all my misgivings about him. Adrian, it turned out, was an even bigger trickster than he was.

"So what was the whole charade about, the four of us vacationing in Turkey?" I asked. "You said we'd all have an amazing adventure."

"We did, didn't we? It was really true that I wanted us all to travel there and have fun together. By then, I'd really come glued to you guys. All of you. Especially you, Mole. I'm not lying about that. But, the reason I convinced you to go to Istanbul instead of Italy or France was that Ömer's visa had run out and he went back home. I was supposed to meet him in Fethiye to hand over the ring. I guess he wasn't as interested in the carpet, anymore. The plan was, when I handed over the ring, he'd pay me. I'd never see him again, and no one would be any the wiser."

"So, what happened?" This, from Paz.

"What happened is, I couldn't do it. I couldn't betray you. Even for the money (which was a lot, by the way. It would've paid for my trip and quite a lot more besides)."

"What did you do?"

"I lied. I told Ömer I couldn't find the ring. That it wasn't there. That I'd have to try again. I don't know, I told him a bunch of stuff just to stall him off. That it wasn't even worth me going to Fethiye, after all."

"But then we all went to Fethiye," I said. "Seven years later. Why did you wait so long to go back to Turkey?"

Adrian sighed. "Because I told Ömer that you and I had a falling out and also that you had moved away, that I couldn't find out where you lived. But there was another problem—and this turned out to be a real lifesaver. Ömer got really ill. Cancer or something. He wasn't very healthy looking back then, and he was going through treatments at the local hospital."

"Wait, not *the* hospital? Your hospital?" Paz looked confused.

"Strangely, yes."

"Wow, that's too oo-ah-ee-oo, even for me." Paz wiped his forehead with a napkin.

"Tell me about it. And then, one day out of the blue, I got a message from Halki. Obviously, I was not working at Silk Road Carpet Shop by then, but he had my cell phone number. He told me that 'Mister Ömer-*Bey*' was well and waiting for me to complete our 'agreement'." Adrian made air quotes around the word. "I had held onto the ring all that time 'cuz I really didn't know what to do with it. I mean, really, it's your ring, Molo. But how could I tell you that? How could I give it to back to you without you wondering how I had gotten it in the first place? I thought that if I told you how I had come by it, it would ruin our friendship. But also, I had gotten to know a bit more about our friend, Ömer, by then. He's got mafia ties. Everyone in Fethiye—and some even in Istanbul—is in his pocket. A real shitbag. I was afraid if I didn't make the effort to see him, I'd be..." Here, Adrian sliced his fingers across his throat. "You know. Or maybe he'd do something to one of you guys. I couldn't stand that possibility."

I listened to Adrian's expanding tale, but the more he talked, the more I could feel my blood coursing in my temples. My feet and legs were twitching. But my curiosity about what else he had to divulge kept me quiet and in my seat.

He went on.

"So, I came up with a plan. A sort of plan. I wasn't sure it would work. I thought, what if I get you all to go back to Turkey again, and I could convince you to go to Fethiye? We'd have fun, but I'd also meet up with Ömer at some point. I'd tell him that I never found the ring even though you and I had settled our differences and become friends again. That I'd checked the rug several times more and still not found his prize. I didn't realize until we were on that Kamil Koç bus trip from Istanbul to Çalış Beach that he was actually on the bus, too. Keeping an eye on me. I was really freaked out, but I tried not to show it. So, that's when he figured out who you guys were, what you looked like and all that. I had to pretend I didn't know him. He did the same. I hoped that, now that he'd seen you, he'd realize you were just some regular young guy and that he'd have a change of heart about stealing from you. Cancel our arrangement. Ha. Even with everything I'd learned, I didn't know who I was dealing with. Obviously."

"But how did Ömer know we were going to be on that bus? That's too weird," Paz interrupted. He had read my mind, which was good, as I could not trust myself to speak.

"That was Barış, I'm pretty sure. One of Ömer's lackeys in Istanbul," Adrian explained.

"Yeah, we know Barış, don't we, Paz?" Paz rolled his eyes at me.

Adrian went on.

"I met up with him in secret a couple times when you guys were swimming or shopping or whatever. I tried to convince him I didn't have the ring. He didn't believe me. So, he ordered me to meet him at his carpet shop in Paspatur and we'd discuss the arrangement we had. I agreed. What could I do? I wanted to persuade him once and for all that I did not have

327

what he was looking for, that it was not in your carpet anymore, and that our agreement was null and void. I wouldn't even take any of his money."

He paused, stared at his feet for a second, and then looked back up. "You see how that went."

We were all silent for a moment, remembering the day of Adrian's accident, the day Mallie, Paz and I believed we had lost our guiding light for good. It was me who broke the uncomfortable silence.

"Where was the ring all this time? And how did Paz end up with it?" I jerked my head towards the opposite side of the table where Paz sat, transfixed. Was that guilt on his face?

Adrian brushed his forelock away from his eye and rallied back to the moment at hand. "Good question. In 2005, before we took that second trip, I fabricated a rather outlandish story, I admit, about how I had bought this item that some freaky asshole in Turkey was trying to steal from me and could Paz hang onto it for safekeeping until we returned from our trip. Paz agreed. Reluctantly. I made him swear not to tell you about it, Molo. I told him it was going to be a gift for you."

I turned to Paz for confirmation. He shook his head, affirming Adrian's account.

"But, wait," I added. "How did Paz end up knowing about Ömer? You didn't tell him who he was, did you?"

"I don't know. Ask him."

Before I could, Paz interjected. "I just figured it out, with what happened to Adrian in 2005 and all that crap about the *jandarma* blowing us off and protecting the O man, you know. And then you flying back here after all these years to do whatever you thought you were going to do to him. It just fell into place. But I wasn't really sure about it until this afternoon. At that Okey palace."

"Really?" I could not keep the scepticism out of my voice.

"Just a hunch, believe it or not."

Did I believe him? I clasped my hands on top of my head and exhaled deeply. "I don't know. This is all too bizarre. I can't wrap my head around it."

"I know." Adrian's expression was rueful. "I don't even know how to express my regret to you, Mole. If it weren't for me, none of this insanity would have happened. To you. To any of us."

"Yeah, but you were the only one who was poisoned into a coma."

"True." He nodded, thoughtfully.

"Which brings us to that. We were sure you had, you know," how could

I say it?, "moved to the other side. We were pretty devastated. It changed me." I pointed to myself. "As you can see."

Adrian nodded, lips pursed, then said, "Yeah, I know. It's cool, though. I mean, it's an interesting look."

Paz spewed out his latest sip of beer in a paroxysm of mirth, while I twisted a few strands of my loose locks in my hand, feeling suddenly self-conscious. I did not see the humor in the situation, as Paz clearly did.

Then he spoke.

"So, what did happen? Where did you go? Where have you been all this time?" Paz asked, wiping his mouth.

Adrian crooked his index finger over his lips and his thumb under his chin and shook his head. His eyes glazed over. Then, removing his hand from his face, he answered.

"I knew we'd come around to that. I've dreaded it."

"Why is that?"

"'Cuz I felt like a shit for dragging you all into the mess, for one thing. So, after I came out of the coma and found out you'd all gone home thinking I was dead, I made a decision."

"Yeah, what was that?"

Adrian took a deep breath and let it out slowly. Paz and I waited, our chins in our hands. Our almost empty plates were pushed to the far edge of the table now as Can had yet to clear them. Several *rakı* glasses and a few beer empties circled the table. Somehow, the detritus of dirty dishes suited our discussion, the unpleasantness of the past dredged up at long last.

Adrian finally answered. "I decided it was better to leave things as they were. Disappear. For one, if Ömer thought I was dead, too, he'd stop hounding me. We'd all be off the hook. Paz had the ring, so it was safe. Maybe he'd end up giving it to you when he realized I wasn't coming back."

"Oh, that's a good point. Why didn't you, Paz?" I grinned, mischievously.

Paz pulled his head out of his hands, glancing quickly from left to right and back. "Wait, what? Me? I don't know. I just...you know, we lost touch. I didn't know what to do. I guess I was waiting for something to happen." He smirked. "And it did."

I shot him a look as if to say...Right, eight years on...

"Seriously. Mole, I wasn't gonna keep it. Even Mal knew it was yours. She kept bugging me to find you so I could give it back. Because Adrian had said it was a gift for you." He cast his eyes toward the table for a moment. "Especially because it was from Adrian. We knew it would mean something to you."

"Right." I screwed up my face. "'Cuz you can be a bit flimflammy sometimes. That was a pretty good trick back at the cafe this afternoon, by the way. You really had O and B in a state."

Paz did his sideways mouth thing. "That's true. One of my better moments, I must admit." He told Adrian briefly what had transpired at the Okey cafe. Then he rubbed his shirt front with his knuckles and looked heavenwards.

Adrian chuckled. And even in the purple blue ether surrounding us, I could see the gleam in his eyes, stars twinkling around their home satellites.

Adrian, my Adrian, was back. It was a miracle. After all the years of emptiness and anger, the transformation of my outward appearance, the distancing from everyone I knew, the realization that Adrian was alive and okay and sitting next to me should have settled a kind of peace over me.

And yet, it did not.

"My next question, though, is this," said Paz. "What do we do now? I mean, our pals back at the Okey Buffet are not going to just let go of all this. Especially now that they know the ring does, indeed, exist, after all."

"Don't worry about them." Adrian's grin was so wide, even his teeth looked like they were grinning. "I've got it all taken care of."

"What do you mean?"

He beamed even more. "Oh, let's just say, those guys won't be bugging us again."

"I don't get it. What did you do?"

"Alright, if you want to know...I haven't just been lying around all these years."

"Oh, and where have you been? You didn't actually tell us."

"Here and there. I stayed around Fethiye for awhile, while I recuperated from the laburnum debacle. Until my visa ran out. I kept pretty incognito, but I also kept an eye on Ömer. I mean, he is the asshole who poisoned me in the first place. I wanted to get back at him somehow. Then, eventually, I headed back to the States. Monterey, mostly. So, I'd be near you guys, but not too near. I didn't want to bump into you accidentally and freak you out. I had to work and stuff, but I spent a lot of my free time doing research. On the carpet-selling business. On Ömer. He really is a piece of work. Has his fingers in a lot of nefarious pies."

As Adrian began to explain his whereabouts during his "missing years," I felt puzzled. He had been in Monterey, a mere few miles from Santa Cruz, and never even attempted to let me know. Why? Part of me wanted to believe his intentions were noble, that he wanted to wait until he had sorted out his beef with Ömer, but another part of me began to see things from another angle. If Ömer was such a bigwig in Fethiye, wouldn't he have found out that Adrian hadn't died? I continued listening.

"So, after a few years of all this, I had gathered quite a bit of Intel on him. For one thing, it used to be illegal to take antique carpets out of Turkey. But Ömer got around all that with his backhanders and his contacts. He made a small fortune selling valuable carpets overseas to wealthy clients. I managed to track down a few of these carpets and interview the people in the U.S. he sold to. But I found out other things, as well. I went to the Turkish Embassy and told them what I knew. They were surprisingly helpful and interested. They said to leave all my data with them and they would look into it. That kind of surprised me."

"And that's why you're really here, isn't it?" I suddenly realized what had brought my Lazarian confederate back to this perplexing place. It was not about his friends; it was about revenge.

Adrian bowed. "It is. I got a message from someone I had become chummy with at the embassy. It said they were moving in on Ömer. I wanted to be here when they got him. It's pure coincidence that you headed here at the same time."

I thought about this for a second. Was it coincidence? What about my years of fretting over Ömer and the vile act he had committed against Adrian? What about my own changes, my transformations these past years? Could that be coincidence? Or my strange dreams of *djinn*s and flying fezzes and unearthly lights twirling and twisting into the sky? No, it did not seem to me at all that these occurrences, this periapsis of actions regarding Adrian and Ömer simultaneously, was mere happenstance. Especially at this moment of convergence: us finding Adrian again, or rather, him finding us; Ömer about to be arrested; my discovery about my family's carpet and the ring; my newfound realizations about myself.

I looked up toward the sky. There, the moon continued to bend her glowing face down at us, that silver-gold visage smiling almost mischievously, or so it seemed to me. Her celestial substance hovered so close now, I felt I could reach out and touch it. But that might have been the *raki*.

Paz's voice interrupted my reflections.

"So, when is this phenomenon supposed to take place? The seizing of the serial offender Ömer, I mean." Paz posed his questions while peeling the silver and blue labels off his beer bottle.

I was a little surprised he had not moved onto *rakı* in the excitement of Adrian's re-appearance. Maybe he was changing, too. Was he seeing this situation the same way I was beginning to, or had he known all along?

"Tomorrow," said Adrian. "Fingers crossed." He actually raised both his hands over the table and crossed both his hands in front of us.

"Can we go? I'd love to see that bastard get his come-uppance after all the damage he's caused." Paz set down his beer, but held onto it like a weapon.

"No." Adrian shook his head, his hair swashing back and forth with the movement. "It's not allowed. I already asked. A hush-hush affair, you know. Probably won't even hit the news. But believe me, nothing would have been more gratifying for me than to see that guy pilloried in public."

Paz and Adrian clinked their nearly empty drinks together with aplomb. I watched them, uncertainty, and a feeling I was not sure I could name, beginning to take hold of me. I began to drum my fingers on the table.

"Hallelujah," Paz called out. "There is a God, after all. Or, rather, Allah. I guess." He opened his eyes wide and made a weird grimace with his mouth.

I turned toward the moon again. "Maybe, maybe not, but there is something."

I thought about that for a moment. I thought about all my turmoil, sadness, change, groping for truth, desire for revenge, everything that had happened in the last years. None of it really made sense. An otherwordly tale from another time. Like Ali Baba. Taking one last sip of my milky *rakı*, the image of Naji poured into my whirling thoughts. Naji and my crazy dream the other night. And then, I remembered what had been dogging me so much throughout my last few days running around the highways and byways of Turkey. The words of wisdom that Naji had squawked at me, before he starting swirling and blinking and transforming in the hazy atmosphere of my post-traumatic, transatlantic flight. Now I understood what it was he wanted me to know.

Ah, yes. How it all made sense. At last.

All the desires, the deceits. The dreams and nightmares. What began all those years ago in a funky beach town in California with a bizarre art performance and a roller coaster ride had all come down to five simple words. That crazy, black-toothed *djinn* was wiser than he looked (or

332

smelled). He knew more than one would have ever believed and deserved more credit than I had given him when he had traveled all the way from ancient wherever to enlighten me. But I believed now. I had seen the light at last.

I turned to Adrian and then to Paz, watching them chat and drink again, the creases of worry and fatigue smoothed away from their careworn faces. I shook my head. Then I drained the last sip of aniseed liquor from my little glass of Turkish ambrosia, set the glass quietly on the table and stood up. This time I did not knock my chair over.

The other two stopped talking, their brows furrowed in question.

"What's up?" said Paz, holding onto his bottle.

"What's up, you ask? Hmm. Oh, I don't know. Maybe what's up is that I've finally come to my senses after all these years." My voice trembled. This was not going to be easy.

Adrian stared at me, confusion darting around in his beautiful eyes. "What are you talking about?" he asked.

"Yeah, what are you on about, Mole?" Paz echoed.

I glared at Paz. "And stop calling me that. I'm not a mole. Or a Molo either, for that matter. You guys have been calling me those names for so many years, I almost forgot who the real me was. I thought it was cool. That you really cared about me and that's why you came up with that name."

"It was because of your tee-shirt..." Paz interjected.

"Bullshit. You know and I know, it had little or nothing to do with my shirt. It was because you all saw me as easy-going, easily manipulated. And I was too stupid and gullible to realize it."

"That's not true!" Adrian shouted. He started to push away from the table.

My heart was thudding in my chest now, but I knew the moment had come for me to face myself and acknowledge the truth. Or what seemed like the truth.

"Don't, Adrian. You know, I really, really cared about you. But you knew that. And you took advantage of me."

Adrian's head was shaking back and forth, while his mouth was forming a silent "noooo."

"Okay, maybe you didn't mean to hurt me. Maybe you did. I don't really know. But it's time to end this charade now. You guys have taught me a lesson that's taken a long time to learn."

"What do you mean?" said Paz, twirling his beer bottle, nervously.

"The truth is I believed you guys were my friends. I believed it to the core of my being." I let my gaze dart between both of them, as disbelief began to lodge on their faces. "And now I see I was mistaken."

They looked confused, so I explained a little further. "The truth is, *nothing is as it seems*. You've both taught me that."

As Adrian and Paz faced each other and lifted their shoulders in question, I turned away. Then I turned back, remembering something.

"And, Paz, you can give me my ring now."

ॐ   ॐ   ॐ

Epilogue

"Out beyond ideas of wrongdoing and rightdoing, there is a field. I'll meet you there." - Mevlana (aka Rumi)

November 6, 1922 - Constantinople

*T*he mist from the nearby Bosphorus descended on the palace grounds. A young woman wrapped in a patterned paşmina, and with a dark green scarf covering her head, snuck out the servants' entrance at the back of the palace, surveying the deserted grounds. It was just before dawn, and the first call to prayers began to reverberate from the palace minarets.

Cradling a bundle in her arms, she hurriedly exited the gardens. They were renowned for their colorful and varied beauty. But now, in autumn's harsh grip, the walnut trees had shaken off their leaves, the magnolia's proud white blooms hung in brown clumps of papery desolation and the flower beds' usual gay welcome lay heavy and mired in wet mud. Only a few trees, such as the Lebanon cedars, held onto their green and leafy adornment.

Just before she disappeared through the Treasury Gate to the world beyond, the fleeing girl glanced over her shoulder. There, a white lion statue, its giant front paw crushing a snake, crouched among concentric rings of withering tulips, monitoring her passage. She passed the tiered clock tower next, its four stories rivaling in height that of the Dolmabahçe minarets nearby. Now she nodded good-bye to the clock, whose stalwart, stony face had kept a watchful eye on her for ten long years.

She knew she would never be back.

What she did not know was that she was also being observed by someone outside the gate. A young man in a crumpled fez stood on the boulevard outside. He had arrived not a half hour before, just as the moon was beginning to relinquish her nighttime post. The man had not known why he had come except that he had been inexplicably drawn to the palace for weeks and wanted to have one last look at its decadent beauty, take one last gaze at the place that had beckoned to him despite his urgency to leave the city.

He watched the young woman hesitate outside the gate. As she turned and caught him staring in her direction, a bluster of wind blew his fez off his head and it bounced across the wide road toward her. He raced after the offending hat, embarrassed and flustered at its betrayal. To make matters worse, it stopped at the girl's feet.

The man almost knocked into her in his flurry to retrieve his ratty fez. He felt his face go as red as the felt lining on the outer surface of the cylindrical headpiece. But after he had bent forward and snatched the thing from the leaf-strewn walkway where it lay, he brought himself to standing again. And there he came face to face with the girl. The look she gave him was one of great amusement. But what caught his attention was something else.

She had the most remarkable face he had ever seen. Yes, she had clear, smooth skin, wide, almond-shaped eyes, and her eyebrows were arched and thick. Her lips were a shade of deep red and turned up at the corners. Even so, he could not have described exactly what it was that captivated him. Perhaps it was her knowing smile. He had to catch his breath. Then he placed the fez on his head. Slowly, after introducing himself, the young man asked in simple Turkish where she was going.

"Home," she said, responding also in Turkish. Her voice, though, was unlike any he had ever heard, clear and bright and with an almost echoey quality in its chiming cadence. He waited for the echo to fade before he spoke again.

"What a coincidence," he finally had the courage to respond. "That's where I am headed, too. It's been a long time." He paused, thinking, gathering up his courage. Then he added, daringly, "Perhaps we can go there together."

The young lady fixed her eyes on him. They were an extraordinary shade of steely blue, speckled with tiny flecks of gold. They reminded him of the Mediterranean Sea with the afternoon sun sparkling on its endless ripples. He felt their intensity burn through him like an unquenched fire. Suddenly, she nodded.

"But, we must go now," she whispered. "They will be coming for me soon."

"May I take your bundle?" the man asked. He did not ask her who was coming for her.

His new companion glanced at the roll in her arms. The man waited patiently as she seemed to ponder whether she could trust him or not with whatever it was she was carrying. It must be very precious, he decided.

At last, the girl thrust the roll into his unexpecting arms—he almost dropped it. The expression on her face, as he struggled to adjust the roll, was decisive. She had made her choice and she would stick with it. She would trust him.

His heart beat faster now, and he knew it was not from chasing his hat.

The man in the fez and the woman with the scarf began to walk. Instead of hurrying, they took their time. Slowly, slowly, they made their way down the wide boulevard.

The sun was just beginning to glow.

The girl looked up. Just in time, she saw the moon, her guardian, fade into the morning clouds. But before she disappeared altogether, the moon winked. The girl was sure of it. Then she recalled the prophecy of a reading just days before. That she would go through a difficult journey, but she would not be alone. Someone, a friend, would come along to help her through it.

She did not know exactly what was before her, but all at once a calm filled her being. A calm she had never felt before. It was as if she stood at the brink of a new beginning.

This is true, she thought. She pulled her paşmina *around her, to protect her from the biting autumn wind. But also, she felt, as a gesture, a promise, to the other bundle she carried. And this bundle, she knew was something far more precious than what she had just handed to the stranger, her new friend, at her side.*

She turned to look at him. The situation was absurd, but...

It would do.

It would have to do.

ã€€ã€€ã€€ã€€ã€€ðŸª¶ã€€ã€€ã€€ã€€ðŸª¶ã€€ã€€ã€€ã€€ðŸª¶

"Three apples have fallen from the sky. One belongs to the storyteller, the second to the listeners and the third to me."
- Turkish Fairytale Ending

About the Author

Marcia Kellam currently resides in Santa Fe, New Mexico with her husband and two cats. She is a graduate of the University of California, Los Angeles (UCLA). This is her first novel.